The RUNAWAY BRIDE

Books by Jody Hedlund

The Preacher's Bride
The Doctor's Lady
Unending Devotion
A Noble Groom
Rebellious Heart
Captured by Love

BEACONS OF HOPE

Out of the Storm: A BEACONS OF HOPE Novella
Love Unexpected
Hearts Made Whole
Undaunted Hope

ORPHAN TRAIN

An Awakened Heart: An ORPHAN TRAIN Novella
With You Always
Together Forever
Searching for You

THE BRIDE SHIPS

A Reluctant Bride
The Runaway Bride

THE BRIDE SHIPS ⚓ BOOK TWO

The
RUNAWAY
BRIDE

JODY HEDLUND

BETHANYHOUSE

a division of Baker Publishing Group
Minneapolis, Minnesota

Published by Bethany House Publishers
11400 Hampshire Avenue South
Bloomington, Minnesota 55438
www.bethanyhouse.com

Bethany House Publishers is a division of
Baker Publishing Group, Grand Rapids, Michigan

Printed in the United States of America

Library of Congress Cataloging-in-Publication Data
Names: Hedlund, Jody, author.
Title: The runaway bride / Jody Hedlund.
Description: Bloomington, Minnesota : Bethany House Publishers, [2020] | Series: The bride ships; 2
Identifiers: LCCN 2019040930 | ISBN 9780764232961 (trade paperback) | ISBN 9780764235535 (cloth) | ISBN 9781493422845 (ebook)
Subjects: GSAFD: Historical fiction.
Classification: LCC PS3608.E333 R86 2020 | DDC 813/.6—dc23
LC record available at https://lccn.loc.gov/2019040930

Scripture quotations are from the King James Version of the Bible.

Cover design by Jennifer Parker
Cover photography by Mike Habermann Photography, LLC

Author is represented by Natasha Kern Literary Agency, Inc.

20   21   22   23   24   25   26   7   6   5   4   3   2   1

Be strong and of
a good courage, fear not,
nor be afraid of them: for the
LORD thy God, he it is that
doth go with thee; he will not
fail thee, nor forsake thee.

Deuteronomy 31:6

one

VANCOUVER ISLAND
SEPTEMBER 18, 1862

*T*oday she might meet the man she'd marry.

On the ship's main deck, Arabella Lawrence stood absolutely still as a lady ought to do, even though the prospect of seeing her husband-to-be flustered her to a near faint. Like the others around her, she peered at the top rung of the ladder waiting for a glimpse of the men, her breath choppy, her cheeks flushed.

After one hundred days aboard the *Tynemouth* bride ship, she thought she'd be ready for this moment. She'd had plenty of time to prepare during the long days at sea with little to do. But now that she and the rest of the brides had reached Vancouver Island, all her uncertainties had decided to pay her a visit.

She opened her fan and pumped several gusts across her face. The sea air was balmy for September, drenched with the odor of the salmon the natives had bartered the previous evening after the ship had dropped anchor off Esquimalt Lagoon.

In the dusk, the sight of the long dugout canoes gliding across the glassy water had been terrifying, especially with so many dark-haired and dark-skinned bodies in each vessel. Some of her companions had whispered frightened epithets of doom, fearing the natives would attack the *Tynemouth*, afraid their group had come halfway around the world only to fall prey to beheading and cannibalism.

The sailors had assured the brides that the natives meant no harm, that if they'd wanted war, the canoes would have been full of well-armed men with their faces painted black. As it was, the dugouts had contained a mixture of half-naked men, women, and children hoisting fish, not weapons.

Now with the light of day, the natives were gone and the visitors readying to board had arrived in longboats, attired in suits and top hats.

"You must all be at your best for the welcoming committee," said their chaperone, Mrs. Robb, as she walked past. She'd spoken the same thing earlier when she instructed them to don clean outfits in preparation for mingling with the first group of distinguished gentlemen, who would be coming over from Victoria to greet the women and bring fresh provisions.

Over the port side of the ship, the saltwater lagoon gleamed like a mirror, reflecting the coniferous forest and rocky outcroppings. On the opposite side, the distant snowcapped peaks of the Olympic Mountains across the Straits of Juan de Fuca rose up in a magnificent display so unlike anything Arabella had ever witnessed, a sight she wouldn't mind waking up to every morning.

At a shout from starboard and the *clank* of the ladder, she drew in a shaky breath.

"Shall we form a more orderly line?" Mrs. Robb clapped her hands at the women. The tall, severe-looking matron had been thin at the beginning of their journey, but she was positively skeletal now, her cheeks sunken and her hair listless.

Arabella supposed they were all rather decimated. She fingered a strand of her long auburn hair. She'd done her best to stay true to her grooming regimen during the voyage, brushing her hair one hundred strokes every night before bedtime. Yet after going the past three months with only sponge bathing and the most basic of hair washing, her thick locks hadn't cooperated today. Likewise, no amount of rice powder could hide her freckles, which had only grown more numerous on her nose and cheeks in spite of her efforts to avoid the sun's rays.

Not only were her hair and freckles troublesome, so were her gowns. Perpetual seasickness had taken its toll, and the beautiful creations of organdie, silk, and grenadine that had once fit her snugly now hung from her bony frame. While all the ladies had discarded their cumbersome crinolines shortly after boarding, today they'd donned the steel-hooped underskirts that made their gowns fuller.

Joining the other gentlewomen in shifting into a presentable receiving line, Arabella knew she should be smiling and chattering too. After all, marriage was something she'd always longed for but never expected—at least not with a husband of her own choosing. But she could no more tame her unruly nerves than she could tame the changeable sea.

The midshipman leaned over the railing and grasped at the first man coming up the ladder. At the emerging form, silence fell over the deck, and Arabella gawked at the newcomer along with everyone else, even though such behavior was extremely unbecoming of a lady.

As the man's top boots landed against the deck, he straightened and grabbed his tall black hat to keep it from toppling off. The tilt of his head revealed distinguished features set amidst a white mustache and long, white sideburns, a decidedly older man than she'd expected of the prospective husbands.

The vision of another older face pushed to the forefront of her mind. One fleshier with bristly sideburns. One with hard, demanding eyes. One with lips firmly creased in displeasure.

The skin on Arabella's back prickled, the bruises there having healed but the scars still lingering. She closed her eyes against the memory of the beating, but couldn't block the pain that haunted her.

'Tis in the past. 'Twill not happen again. She silently recited the words of assurance as she had often since boarding the bride ship. In London society at the old age of twenty-five, the only man who'd wanted a spinster like her had been over twice her age. But here . . . in this new land where men reportedly outnumbered women ten to one . . .

She pried open her eyes in time to see Captain Hellyer approach the elderly gentleman and shake his hand. At the same time, the midshipman hefted another man onto the deck, then another. The visiting gentlemen soon swarmed the deck, some in civilian clothing, others wearing the blue uniforms that belonged to those in the Queen's Royal Navy.

They took turns shaking hands with the captain and several other illustrious passengers, including Lord Colville, the ship's surgeon, and Reverend Scott, the second chaperone the Columbia Mission Society had assigned to the brides.

The women around Arabella found their voices again and resumed their excited conversations, especially as the men began to mill about. When the last of the visitors boarded the ship, Captain Hellyer finally addressed the gathering.

The older gentleman who'd been the first to arrive spoke next, introducing himself as Victoria's mayor, Mr. Edward Harris. He issued kind words of welcome before pointing out the most prominent men of the committee—the chief immigration officer, the president of the Chamber of Commerce, the local Anglican minister of Christ Church Cathedral, and a blur of others whose names Arabella couldn't remember.

All the while the mayor spoke, some of the men boldly perused the women. At the attention, the younger orphan girls tittered and whispered among themselves. Mercy Wilkins, one of the poor women from London's slums, tried to shush them. Hardly older than the girls herself, Mercy had been like a mother to them on the trip, and she'd been more than kind to Arabella, tending her whenever she'd been ill.

The lower-class women like Mercy would find their future husbands on the morrow after going ashore and meeting the laborers, tradesmen, and miners who dominated the community. If the rumors were true, then hundreds of such men were waiting in Victoria for their arrival. On the other hand, Arabella and the other middle-class ladies would draw husbands from the upper echelons of Victoria's society, from among elite and important men like those who'd come aboard.

Whatever the case, their chaperones had assured them that every woman, both poor and wealthy, would have the opportunity to find a good and kind husband.

As brandy and sherry were passed among the gentlemen, they began to mingle more freely, approaching the women and making introductions. Arabella's stepmother would have been appalled at the brazenness of well-born men making their own introductions without proper protocol. Yet under the circumstances, Arabella didn't see any other option.

She swallowed past the nerves constricting her airway. For the millionth time since running away, doubts crowded her mind. Had she done the right thing in leaving? While she'd never wanted to hurt her family, her disappearance was certain to have caused them untold problems.

Smoothing the overlapping layers of her skirt, she fought against her guilt. The elegant gown with its emerald muslin trimmed in ebony velvet reminded her not only of her family but also of the standard of living she'd left behind. Though the sponsors of the trip had assured the gentlewomen that Victoria contained high society and followed Paris trends, Arabella had feared along with the others that she'd be subjected to backwoods fashions and customs.

Mentally she chastised herself. She couldn't give way to her misgivings. Instead, she needed to focus on being as composed

11

and refined as possible so at least one gentleman present would notice her. After so many days at sea in cramped quarters, she wasn't at her best. But surely she had some chance of attracting a suitor in a place where so many men sought wives.

Several naval officers meandered toward the receiving line. Attired in spotless white trousers and crisp blue coats, the men carried an air of authority. From the stripes of gold rounding their cuffs and the epaulettes decorating their shoulders, Arabella guessed they were officers of some important rank.

"Ladies," said the tallest of the three as he stopped near Arabella and her cabin mates. He inclined his head and body in a slight bow. "Would you be so gracious as to allow us to introduce ourselves?"

For several moments, the men stated their names in a dignified manner. "Lieutenant Drummond of the HMS *Foxtail*," the tall officer said, his attention flitting first to Arabella, then to the other women.

Beneath his flat-brimmed naval cap, his raven hair was wavy but combed into submission. Dark sideburns along with a trimmed mustache lent him a debonair aura, as did the arch of his dark brows above deep-set eyes.

As the other women made introductions, Lieutenant Drummond gave the appropriate responses, but all the while his attention kept shifting back to Arabella, so noticeably that a flush crept into her cheeks.

She waved her fan to cool her face, at the same time willing herself to remain calm.

"This is Miss Arabella Lawrence." Miss Spencer filled the silence that had descended. Having lost weight during the voyage, the young woman's frame was still rounded but more gently so. Rather than the looped braids she normally wore, Miss Spencer had asked Arabella to primp her hair so that the overall effect was to make her pleasantly becoming. Now, beaming with a delighted smile, Miss Spencer was positively pretty.

"Miss Lawrence," the lieutenant said with another bow, "it is a pleasure to meet your acquaintance. I pray you have found Vancouver Island to your liking thus far."

With the focus upon her, Arabella responded with the controlled decorum her stepmother had drilled into her. "Yes, thank you. Vancouver Island is truly lovely."

His lips rose into a slight smile, one that told her she'd answered exactly the way he'd expected of a lady.

"Once you're settled into Victoria, I do hope you ladies will allow us to show you more of the area." The lieutenant's invitation was directed at everyone, but his gaze never left Arabella.

She should have been flattered. This was what she wanted, wasn't it? But instead of feeling a thrill, a shiver raced up her backbone reminding her of the hurt men were capable of inflicting. Her mind returned to four months ago, to the day her father had called her into his office to tell her he'd made a match for her.

Half hidden behind mounds of papers on his desk, he'd delivered the news without looking up from the document in front of him.

She'd stared at the rounded bald spot at the top of his head as questions thundered through her. *Who? When? Why?*

After going years without suitors, and then finally watching her younger sister, Florence, get married and later have a babe, Arabella had privately grieved the loss of the lifelong dream of marrying and starting a family. And she'd resigned herself to spinsterhood, joining so many other women of her station who were in the same predicament. 'Twas no secret in London circles that there weren't enough eligible men, not when so many had migrated during recent years.

Arabella stood in her father's office and waited demurely for him to give her more information, even as her stomach churned.

After several moments of silence, he sighed heavily, returned his pen to the inkpot, and sat back in his chair. Even then he refused to meet her gaze. "Arabella, this is the best for every-one," he began, then stopped, running a hand down his trim beard, something he always did when nervous.

Again, Arabella waited for him to continue, attempting to remain composed on the outside while her insides swirled faster.

"Your stepmother thinks you will be satisfied," he said, as though Elizabeth's declaration was all that mattered.

Arabella wished she could rely upon her stepmother's judgment, but she'd learned the hard way over the years that Elizabeth cared about only two people—herself and her son. Whatever Elizabeth did, including all of the training and mothering she'd extended to Arabella and Florence, was designed to improve her own status.

"He'll be able to provide well for you," her father added.

"Who, Father?" She squeezed out the question, though she wasn't sure she wanted to know the answer.

Father fumbled for his pen, dipping it in and out of the ink. "Mr. Major."

Arabella wasn't able to prevent the quick intake of breath.

"He insists upon you, Arabella." Her father's voice contained a rare note of apology. "I could say nothing to dissuade him."

"He's older than you are, Father." The complaint was as rare as her father's apology. Arabella knew ladies ought to keep their negative thoughts to themselves, that one should speak only agreeable and pleasant words.

"There are other matters of more importance than age." Father stared at the sheet of numbers in front of him. "As your stepmother says, you will finally be able to run your own home, bear children, and will never want for anything your entire life. Surely that will make up for any deficits?"

Not only was Mr. Major old enough to be her grandfather, but he was a difficult man. As president of the bank where her father worked, Mr. Major had been the source of much discontent in her father's life. Perhaps this union would put her father into a better position and make his life easier at the bank.

And perhaps her father was right, that the benefits of marriage would make up for Mr. Major's disagreeable qualities. She'd have a place of her own and wouldn't need to burden her father any longer or impose upon Elizabeth. She'd be able to have a babe and ease the ache that only grew every time she saw Florence with her infant. And Mr. Major would certainly be able to provide all the luxuries she was accustomed to and more.

"Well?" her father asked, meeting her gaze for the first time. The tired crinkles at the corners of his eyes and the droop of his brows told her she could give only one answer.

"Certainly, Father."

"He wants the wedding to take place at the church in four weeks."

"So soon?"

"He says he's too old to waste time on courtship."

Of course. A man of Mr. Major's age wouldn't want to put off anything for fear of landing in the grave first.

Arabella bit back her rude comment. "Very well, Father. I shall begin the wedding preparations immediately."

A measure of kindness filled his eyes. "You are a good girl, Arabella."

The praise only strengthened her resolve to make the marriage arrangement work. She'd given up her dream of having a family of her own. Now God was graciously offering her a chance. Maybe she and Mr. Major would never share an abiding love, but she could try to develop some affection for him, couldn't she?

"The welcoming committee is planning a regatta this week," Lieutenant Drummond was saying. "We would be honored to share your company during the race."

Arabella pulled herself back to the present moment and shook off the foreboding she felt. Were these men trustworthy?

Her gaze darted from one gentleman to the next. Dressed in their best attire, they carried themselves with honorable bearing. They all appeared to be the sort of men who would make suitable husbands.

Yet how could one really know what was underneath, especially when etiquette demanded politeness and gentility above all else, glossing over true feelings and true expression in favor of rigid composure?

How had she ever believed herself capable of starting over here? What if she'd run away from one awful predicament only to find herself in another just as dreadful?

Her breathing turned suddenly rapid and shallow. Her hands fluttered, and she clasped them tightly to keep from calling attention to herself. She glanced around for a way of escape, needing to compose herself before she made a bad first impression on these men. "Will you please excuse me for a moment?" she said to no one in particular.

Lieutenant Drummond reached out as though to steady her. "Is there anything I might do to be of service?"

She inclined her head in gratitude. "I thank you, sir. But I shall be gone only a moment."

Before anyone could inhibit her departure, she slipped into the passageway that led away from the main deck back to the staterooms. All she needed was a few seconds to gather her thoughts and remember all the reasons she'd joined the bride ship.

She sped away from the gathering much too quickly, but even as she attempted to slow her gait into one that was more ladylike, the slap of footsteps behind her urged her to go faster.

At the sight of the half-open door of the ship's dining parlor, she slipped inside and quietly closed the door behind her. With her hand on the knob, she leaned close and tensed as the hard footfalls drew nearer. When they passed rapidly by, she sagged and braced her forehead against the smooth oak door.

She expelled a loud breath. "Gracious heavens, Arabella. What are you doing?" Her whispered chastisement echoed against the door and into the unlit chamber. "You cannot run away every time something frightens you. Where is your courage?"

Though she tried to remain brave over the past months, all too often she let her fears dictate her actions. She took several deep breaths and then lifted her chin. "You must go back out there, mingle, and accomplish what you came here to do."

A throat cleared in the room behind her.

She gasped and spun, pressing her hands to her chest. There, across the long dining table, stood a man holding round loaves of bread in each hand. He was poised above a platter, which contained additional loaves as well as smaller buns. From the nearly empty basket that sat on the table, she guessed he'd been in the process of unloading the fresh bread.

The several portholes on the wall behind him provided scant lighting but enough to reveal handsome features shadowed by a layer of stubble that matched the dark brown strands of hair that curled at his forehead. Even in the dim lighting, there was no disguising the blue of his eyes or the humor dancing in them.

"Mayhap I can help you with what you came here to do," he said in a warm tone while offering her a grin that brought out a dimple low on his chin.

For several seconds, Arabella was speechless, trying to make sense of her predicament. Apparently, while running from one uncomfortable meeting, she'd thrown herself headlong into one even more so.

He lowered the loaves to the platter, positioned them next to the others, then wiped his hands on an apron in much need of laundering. "Arabella?" He stretched his hand across the table toward her. "I'm Peter Kelly. Pete. Your humble servant."

Arabella could only stare in mortification at this man's audacity to address her by her first name and to presume to shake her hand. Both were completely unacceptable ways to interact with ladies. Rules of etiquette demanded she turn away from this man and pretend not to notice him. But since they were the only two in the room, she wasn't sure what to do. Her step-mother's training hadn't prepared her for a situation like this.

"Miss Lawrence," she said, needing to put them both on proper ground.

Should she exit immediately? After all, she was breaking another rule by being alone with him. And he was a complete stranger. She couldn't predict what he was capable of doing to her, even with the table separating them.

As if sensing her mounting worry, he dropped his hand and grinned again—a slightly crooked grin that lent him a boyish quality. "Well, *Arabella*," he said with an emphasis on her given name, "is it too much to hope that you rushed in here to meet me, the handsomest fella on the island?"

"I didn't know you were here." She said the first thing that came to mind and then wished she hadn't.

"Mayhap God arranged it." His bright blue eyes teased her and contained a kindness that disarmed her.

"I was visiting with the welcoming committee." Her tongue seemed to have a mind of its own, tripping and stumbling over itself again. "And I needed a breath of fresh air. That's all."

"Aye." He waved a hand at the dim interior of the room. "I suppose the air in this room is as sweet as it comes?"

"As a matter of fact, 'tis very refreshing." She wanted to palm her forehead at the stupidity of her comment.

"In that case, don't let me stop you from enjoying your breath of fresh air. In fact, mayhap I'll join you."

As he audibly inhaled and then loudly exhaled, she could only watch him with a mixture of embarrassment and fascination. The movement caused his shirt to stretch tight at his shoulders, highlighting the broadness and thickness of his muscles.

He repeated the process, this time blowing out an even deeper breath. "It is sweet," he said, his gaze touching on her features. "Very sweet."

Was this man flirting with her? She wasn't accustomed to interacting with men, much less handsome young men. Should she feel flattered or offended?

She gave her head a shake and squared her shoulders. What did it matter how she felt? This man wasn't her concern, not like Lieutenant Drummond and the other gentlemen on the welcoming committee. Very fine men who were hopefully still waiting for her.

"I must return to the gathering." She started to turn the knob.

"Aren't you forgetting something?" he asked, his blue eyes turning serious.

Her hand stalled. "Pardon me?"

Before she could decide whether he was truly safe or not, he was rounding the table. As he approached, she opened the door wide, her heart thudding harder. She started to exit into the passageway, but before she could make an escape, he caught her hand and pressed something into it.

"Your courage." He closed her fingers around an X-shaped object and then took a backward step toward the table.

"My courage?"

"Aye, wasn't that what you were seeking when you came in here?"

She opened her hand and stared down at a silver cross. It was plain, without any fancy engravings, worn smooth and yet solid and sturdy.

"He'll give you courage like no other can." His words were sincere this time, without any hint of flirtation.

She hesitated. She couldn't accept such a gift . . .

"Keep it," he said.

Her fingers glided along the smooth beams. *Courage.* She'd been in short supply of it for a long time. "I shouldn't—"

"I won't be taking it back," he said firmly as he skirted the table, moving farther away from her. When he reached the basket, he resumed his task of emptying it.

She let her fingers fold around the cross. "Thank you."

He paused, roll in hand. "You're welcome."

Somehow, the warmth in his eyes and in his words sent a flutter to her stomach, a flutter that was both foreign and frightening. She dropped her gaze, tilted her head at him in a slight nod, then made her escape.

two

*P*ete Kelly kneeled next to the old Haidas native lying on a tattered blanket. He held out a hunk of bread, and the man took it with a shaking hand covered with open sores and scabs.

"I must pay you," the native said in Chinook, which was a combination of English, French, and the local native language. Pete's friend Sque-is had taught him Chinook in exchange for English lessons. The jargon wasn't always adequate to express everything Pete wanted to say and sometimes left him frustrated that he couldn't communicate better.

Like today. And every week when he rowed up to the Northerner's Encampment to deliver bread leftovers.

"When you're well again," Pete said, "then you can trade salmon."

The old man nodded and then tore off a mouthful of bread.

Pete could only pray the native would live to repay the debt. Not that he cared about the compensation. He never expected it, but he understood the need to retain a measure of pride.

With the large baskets now empty, Pete stood, his head brushing against the cedar planks of the hut, one of two roughly built hospitals Mr. Garrett had constructed back in May when the smallpox epidemic had been in its early stages.

Though the huts were still filled with suffering patients, the plague had thankfully begun to slow its course, mainly because missionaries like Mr. Garrett were getting their hands on the vaccination and were working hard to inoculate the survivors.

Pete ducked through the low opening and pulled in a lungful of fresh air, a welcome relief after the foulness inside. He straightened into the sunshine of the early afternoon. The position of the sun told him he didn't have much time—if the rumors were true regarding the bride-ship women coming ashore midday.

Wafts of smoke rose from the scant campfires burning among the remaining lodges. Charred piles of cedar dotted the barren area where other dwellings had recently stood, having been destroyed in a futile effort to stop the smallpox from spreading.

The camp just north of Victoria had once boasted of over one hundred huts and two thousand natives consisting of Tsimshian, Haida, Stikine Tlingit, and Heiltsuk. The groups had assembled on Small Bay to form a trading center, a place where they could bring their goods to barter with each other and, more important, trade with businesses in Victoria.

Now the bustling village was nothing more than a dozen dwellings where only the sickest and weakest languished.

The steady tapping of a hammer drew Pete to the hut on the opposite side of the Indian Smallpox Hospital. Squatting next to a half-constructed coffin, Rupert added another nail before glancing up. Even in the shade, the pocked scars on the old sailor's face were plainly visible.

Pete tipped the brim of his hat. "Tell Mr. Garrett I'll be back next week."

"Aye, will do." Rupert squinted ahead at the stretch of beach dotted with clusters of blue mussel shells and rusty seaweed, his tanned, leathery face solemn. Was he seeing the bloated bodies left untended upon the shore during those first days when the natives had died so rapidly that no one had been able to keep up with building coffins or digging graves?

Pete's dreams were still haunted by those visions, along with all he'd experienced while trying to fight the scourge. He guessed that such sights stayed with a person forever, especially a man like Rupert who'd been among the few willing to live at the camp these past months with Mr. Garrett. Hired on as a carpenter and cook, Rupert had done much more than he'd likely ever bargained for.

"Heading back to get my bride." Pete hefted the straps of his empty breadbaskets onto each shoulder.

"Bride?" Rupert's normally somber tone contained a hint of interest.

"Aye. By this time next week, you might just be looking at a married man." Pete didn't expect to be married so quickly, but he'd say just about anything to draw Rupert out of his personal grave.

Rupert hefted himself onto his makeshift bench and leaned back against the hut, his hammer lying idle across his dusty corduroys. "And who might the lucky gal be?"

Pete warmed up to the rare conversation. "Set my sights on a pretty little lady who arrived on the *Tynemouth*."

For long seconds, only the calls of the migrating kestrels and ospreys carried over the still waters of the bay. "You deserve a nice lass," Rupert said at last as he gripped his hammer and twisted it in his marked hands.

As much as Pete boasted, he knew he'd be the lucky one if any woman would have him. Even so, he kept his tone light. "Right you are, Rupert. Now, let's just pray the good Lord feels I'm as deserving too." After the past year of turning his life around, surely God was smiling down on him.

With a final farewell, he made his way across the beach to his canoe, dropped the baskets inside, and made quick work of pushing off and starting back to Victoria. Only when he was well out of sight of Rupert and the camp did he let his shoulders sag under the weight of dejection that fell upon him every time he rowed away.

If only he'd been able to do more to stop the smallpox from gaining ground so much earlier . . .

A gold prospector from San Francisco had come ashore with the highly contagious illness. As soon as city officials learned of it, they had worked quickly to quarantine those who were affected and start vaccinations.

Pete along with others had called for vaccinations among the natives too, since in the past they'd been particularly susceptible to diseases the colonists brought to the New World. He'd been relieved when Governor Douglas had enlisted Dr. Helmcken for that purpose. First, the kind doctor had reached out to the Songhee Indians, whose main village was across the inlet from Victoria. He started the process there, but it was too little too late. The disease had already spread.

When the Anglican missionary Mr. Garrett reported the outbreak of smallpox at the Northerner's Encampment, Pete had canoed up to Small Bay and found that the camp was in a panic. Dozens of natives were already infected and quarantined in huts or tents by themselves, mostly left to die.

To help Mr. Garrett take care of the suffering and bury the dead, Pete had temporarily closed his bakehouse and stayed on at the camp. With so few hands to help the sick and dying, he'd worked himself to the point of exhaustion.

Finally, Mr. Garrett had encouraged Pete to take a break, and he'd returned to Victoria for supplies and sleep. While he was away, the Royal Navy had ordered the natives to evacuate the Northerner's Encampment and return to their homes. The presence of naval gunboats had ensured the compliance. The various tribes had packed up their canoes and rowed away. And they'd taken the disease with them.

Upon returning to the nearly deserted camp, Pete had been outraged, and he'd gone over to the naval base in Esquimalt to voice his complaint. There for the first time, he'd come face-to-face with Lieutenant Drummond, who'd been one of the officers in charge of the gunboats that had forced the natives to leave.

The order had been devastating. Within weeks, reports had trickled back into Victoria of the thousands upon thousands of natives succumbing to the disease, that their dead bodies were strewn all over the coast and in abandoned villages.

Every trip to the Northerner's Encampment since then only made Pete wish there was more he could be doing. While he'd continued to probe into the navy's involvement in the poor decision to disperse the natives, all he could do at this point was comfort and feed the afflicted.

Upon reaching the outskirts of Victoria, Pete beached his canoe and jogged toward James Bay. Though his spirit was troubled, he cast off his concerns and joined the throngs of people making their way to the waterfront.

As he wove through the crowds, he was relieved he hadn't missed seeing the women coming ashore. He nodded and called out greetings in passing.

"Better close your mouth, Hank!" He grinned and waved to one of his customers. "Or soon you'll have us all standing around in your drool."

His comment brought guffaws and good-natured jesting in return.

The excitement throbbing among the crowd began to pulse through Pete as he came upon the wharf and took in the scene. Men lined every possible spot along the water's edge, perched on fences and masts, with some wading waist-deep in the water.

"Whoo-hee," he whistled under his breath. Every male who lived within a hundred-mile vicinity of Victoria had to be present. Now joining them, he felt as foolish as he was sure he looked, and yet he hadn't been able to stay away.

"How much longer before they arrive?" he asked, stopping alongside Dodge, who stood on his toes in an attempt to see the bay. At only five-foot-two and skinnier than a sapling, Dodge was still too young and too short to see anything other than the backs of the men's heads.

"Just heard the first batch of 'em be stepping onto the wharf."

Pete rose to see above the men in front of him—men who'd camped out along the harbor last night so they'd be able to get front-row viewing.

"You see 'er?"

Pete scanned the women, searching for just one. Arabella Lawrence. The woman he intended to marry.

"She there?" Dodge grabbed Pete's arm in an attempt to boost himself higher. "Which one is she?"

Some of the surrounding men tossed them quizzical glances. And for an instant, Pete wondered if he should have kept his big mouth closed yesterday when he'd returned to the bakehouse. Instead, in his eagerness he'd rushed in and blurted, "I met my wife."

Dodge and Blind Billy had been setting sponge. At his bold words, Dodge had spilled flour onto the floor, and Blind Billy had nearly fallen into the trough of fermenting pre-dough.

Pete had laughed heartily at their reaction, and then while he'd helped his two assistants finish the midday task, he'd regaled them with his trip out to the *Tynemouth* and his meeting with Arabella Lawrence.

"Mayhap it was ordained," he'd jested. "Mayhap God brought her right to me."

"More like you brought yerself right to her," Blind Billy said in his usual low monotone, his back hunched and his shoulder blades protruding as he hand-mixed the flour into the sponge.

"I may have finagled my way onto the ship, but God practically threw that beauty right into my arms."

"More like you threw yerself at her feet," Blind Billy added.

The men on the welcoming committee had been more than willing to allow Pete to go aboard the *Tynemouth* when he'd offered to deliver the fresh-baked items without cost.

From the moment Arabella had burst into the dining parlor and started talking to herself, he'd been smitten. Who could resist a woman who talked to herself? Especially when she had the most irresistible red hair he'd ever seen.

"Of course, she had no idea I was standing there listening in, and I wondered if mayhap I should duck under the table and hide until she left."

Dodge's thin face was wreathed in expectation, his eyes telling Pete he was hanging on every word of the tale just as he always did.

"But then she turned around, and I was a goner. About dropped dead."

"Too bad you didn't," Blind Billy mumbled under his breath.

"Then she was a looker?" Dodge asked, his smile spreading.

"Aye. The most beautiful woman on the ship."

Blind Billy shook his head in obvious disgust at the same moment that Dodge sighed in satisfaction.

"I should have asked her to marry me right then and there to keep her away from Drummond." Pete's gut hardened at the remembrance of how attentive Lieutenant Drummond had been to Arabella during the rest of the visit. The snake had hardly left her side, making clear to everyone he'd staked his claim upon the redheaded beauty.

"That lieutenant, he's sure a fine dandy," Dodge said, only adding to Pete's dismay.

"Drummond can go jump from a cliff—" Pete cut himself off abruptly at the sight of Dodge's admiring eyes upon him.

"More like you'll have to jump first," Blind Billy muttered.

"I won't let Drummond get his way. Not this time."

All night long, as Pete had mixed and kneaded, weighed and shaped, baked and cooled the many loaves his customers would expect fresh in the morning, he'd thought of little else but Arabella Lawrence and how he could win her heart before Drummond or any of other hundreds of men who wanted a wife.

"You see 'er yet?" Dodge asked again, tugging on Pete's coat sleeve. The boy's face was smudged with coal and flour. After their morning deliveries, they both ought to have been getting some sleep like Blind Billy was doing. But here they were with the rest of the population of the colony, ogling over a shipload of women.

Pete stretched up, searching the women as they made their way cautiously out of the longboat and down the wharf toward land. From what he could tell, none had Arabella's red hair. His sights turned toward the HMS *Forward* at anchor in the harbor. The smaller Royal Navy gunboat had transported the women from the *Tynemouth* anchored in Esquimalt over to James Bay, since Victoria's harbor wasn't deep enough for large sailing vessels.

He scanned the deck of the *Forward* for any sight of Arabella. But he didn't see her among those milling about at the railing. He didn't see Drummond either, which was a relief. Hopefully, he wasn't one of the naval officers accompanying the women today.

The lieutenant could have any woman he wanted when he finished his duty on Vancouver Island and returned to England. He didn't need Arabella or any of the other women who'd just arrived. But of course, gentlemen like Lieutenant Drummond believed the whole world belonged to them, and they took what they wanted without thought to anyone else.

Pete's sights snagged upon a woman at the bow, away from the rest of the group still waiting to be rowed to shore. Although most of her hair was covered with a fancy hat, the wind had teased loose some decidedly red strands.

"I've found her," he said to Dodge. "At the bow, in the blue gown."

Using the shoulders of two men in front of them, Dodge hoisted himself and peered at the gunboat, searching eagerly for Arabella. When the men grumbled and shrugged off Dodge's hold, he returned to his soles. "I don't think that was 'er."

"Sure it was." Pete's gaze locked onto her again. She was fanning herself, the sign she was nervous. He'd watched her do it yesterday on the *Tynemouth*. After he finished unloading the bread and rolls, he'd mingled with the sailors, and from a distance he'd been able to catch glimpses of her.

On another day and at another time, he wouldn't have hesitated to cross over and speak with her again. He wasn't afraid of confrontation or breaking the unspoken rules that prohibited a laborer like him from socializing with those of a higher rank. But he hadn't wanted to cause a scene and be ordered back to the longboat. Instead, he'd waited and hoped she'd run away from the party again. But she hadn't. Had his impetuous gift— his dad's cross—given her courage?

"The pretty lady with the red hair?" Dodge asked.

"Aye. That's her." Pete grinned. "Told you she was pretty."

Dodge didn't reward him with a return smile. Instead, the boy's eyebrows puckered. "You can't marry 'er."

"'Course I can."

"No, you can't." Dodge's tone was matter-of-fact. "She's a right proper lady. And you're—well, you."

"Only the most charming fella in these parts." He rubbed his hand over Dodge's head, ruffling his already messy straw-colored hair.

His jesting and his affectionate mussing finally earned him a smile from the lad. But even with the smile, Dodge shook his head. "You're mad if you think she'll have you."

"Oh, she'll have me alright. In fact, once I'm done wooing her, she'll be asking me to marry her and not the other way around."

Dodge snorted a laugh.

For all Pete's bluster, a strange disquiet crept in. Had he set his sights too high with Arabella Lawrence? Was Dodge right that she'd never consider a man like him? Deep inside, old insecurities rose up to taunt him, insecurities that told him his class wasn't good enough, that he was nothing but a poor tradesman.

For just a moment, his gaze shifted to the women who'd already landed and were beginning to make their way up the shore. Mayhap he needed to search among the poor women of the group, the ones who didn't have any high-and-mighty ways, who'd be happy enough to have a common laborer like him for a husband. After all, he didn't want to miss out on his chance to finally take a wife, not after he'd been struggling so much lately with his wayward desires.

The truth was, over the past year, his yearning to have a woman—a wife—had grown to such proportions, he'd almost been tempted a time or two to revert to old habits—habits of the flesh he wasn't proud of, habits he'd developed during the years of running away from his faith and everything his dad had taught him.

Although he'd repented of his rebelliousness and experienced God's forgiveness in a powerful way, he'd figured out soon enough that the temptations were still there. Every time he passed a tavern, he had to fight off the craving to satisfy the desires of his flesh. Mayhap he always would . . .

Even so, his mentor, Pastor Abe, had encouraged him to get married, had said that God hadn't made man to live alone, that his desires were natural but needed to be fulfilled within the bounds of marriage. They were the same words Pete suspected his dad would have spoken had he been there, if they hadn't been separated by an ocean, a continent, and a whole lot of hurt.

The problem with Pastor Abe's advice was that there weren't any marriageable women in Victoria, at least none he knew.

The few respectable single ladies were the daughters of English colonial officials or Hudson's Bay Company magnates. As landed gentry, the women moved in closed social circles, and only officers in the Royal Navy or gentlemen of means were granted access to them.

When Pastor Abe had informed him the Columbia Mission Committee had answered his colleague's request for brides, Pete had been just as excited as everyone else. Reverend Lundin Brown, another of the missionaries sent by the Church of England, ministered to the miners in Lillooet and had written to England, asking the mission-sending board to deliver women to the colony so the men could marry Christian wives.

Earlier in the month, Pete had been among those waiting for the arrival of the first bride ship, *Seaman's Bride*, from Australia, only to be bitterly disappointed that the thirty or so brides had jumped ship in San Francisco and been snatched up by waiting Yankees.

When word had reached Victoria last week that the *Tynemouth* would arrive before the month's end, Pete had determined that this time, with this new ship, he'd be among the lucky ones to get a bride. And when Peter Kelly set his mind to something, he'd do it.

He zeroed in on the beautiful woman with the red hair. Of all the brides he'd watched yesterday—and he'd studied each one carefully—she'd drawn his attention again and again. Not only was she the prettiest, but he'd liked her humble and gentle spirit, the kind way she'd interacted with the other women, and how she'd fought to remain composed even though she was obviously nervous.

More than any of that, she'd won him over fully when one of the poorer of the young women had tripped and fallen, embarrassing herself in front of everyone. When others had been too stunned to assist the woman, Arabella had rushed to her side and helped her back to her feet.

He'd known in that moment that he wanted her. And only her.

The odds might be stacked high against his winning a proper lady like Arabella Lawrence. But the odds had always been stacked against him, and he'd never let that stop him before. Somehow he'd figure out a way to win her heart.

First he needed to find a way to see her again. And he had an idea of just how he might be able to do that.

three

Arabella opened the door on the stove, stood back, and stared at the darkness inside. 'Twas no wonder the water in the pot she'd placed on the front burner was still tepid. The fire was out.

Maybe she ought to head back upstairs and attempt to sleep a little longer.

She rolled her head to ease the kink in her neck and shoulders. Though she was still tired, she knew she wouldn't be able to fall asleep now any more than she had an hour ago when all-too-common frightening dreams had plagued her. She'd prayed for a while, and then with dawn making its appearance, she'd decided to make a cup of coffee only to find the kitchen a disaster.

She braced a hand on her hip and studied the remnants of supper still strewn about—crusted plates and utensils, greasy pans, and even some of the leftover food that hadn't been properly stored.

Last evening, she'd been too exhausted to consider the ramifications of walking away from the dirty dishes. Like the other wealthy ladies of the group, she'd always had servants to take care of the cooking and cleaning, had never needed to consider the work that went into preparing and clearing off a meal.

Of course, they'd had to make do on the ship without the aid of any servants for tasks like preparing simple meals, laundering their clothing, and grooming themselves. But now that they were in Victoria, Arabella hadn't realized they would have to continue to fend for themselves. She'd hoped the welcoming committee would assign them a servant to handle the kitchen duties, or that the poorer women of the group would take over the task of serving.

Alas, neither had happened, at least thus far. Most likely the remaining brides would need to come up with a system of sharing the kitchen duties just as Mrs. Moresby from the welcoming committee had instructed them yesterday after she'd brought them to their temporary home in the Marine Barracks.

Mrs. Moresby was an intimidating woman, somewhat coarse, not as well mannered as a lady ought to be. Arabella couldn't help but wonder if that was what would become of all the ladies in the group. After living for a while in the wilderness away from civilization, would they lose their gentility?

Arabella had decided she wouldn't allow herself to fall into such a base predicament, that she'd remain a lady and do her best to retain the manners she'd been taught. According to the men on the welcoming committee, that was one of the reasons why the brides had been brought over, to maintain the same sense of culture and propriety that existed in the motherland and have a positive influence on the colony.

Now in the morning, faced with an unkempt kitchen and a rumbling stomach, she realized she'd have to make some contribution to the well-being of their group. She could surely do so for a short while longer, at least until she was married and had servants again. Besides, she'd spent countless days in the kitchen when she was younger before her father had remarried, during those years when Hayward had mothered her.

Early in her father's banking career, they'd been able to afford only one servant. So Hayward had been a maid of all trades, doing the cooking, cleaning, mending, and even the care-taking of Arabella and her sister, especially when their mother began to spend more and more time in her bedchamber with her bottle of laudanum.

Of course, at the time Arabella had been too young to understand her mother's problems, had only felt the sting of rejection of a mother who'd abandoned her long before she'd gone into the grave.

Hayward's love and attention had filled the void. The dear woman had taken Arabella into her arms and heart during those years. She'd taught her how to love and be loved. She'd taught her what it meant to truly trust in the Savior, not just in word but in deed. And she'd also taught her how to bake . . .

Or at least Arabella had helped Hayward from her position sitting atop the tall stool at the worktable. Occasionally, Hayward had given her small tasks to complete—like chopping nuts or grating cheese. After such experiences and after watching Hayward, she could surely manage a few simple tasks now.

Arabella surveyed the smattering of supplies the welcoming committee had provided, then crossed to the cupboard. The interior of the hutch revealed basics like salt, flour, coffee beans, and sugar. But other than a few more serving bowls and mismatched dishes, the kitchen boasted little to work with.

Maybe later she'd request more items from Mrs. Moresby. For the moment, the least she could do was heat water for coffee and for washing the dishes. With only scant light coming through the window, she searched the hutch drawers until she found matches. Though she'd never lit a stove before, she didn't suppose it could be that complicated.

A quarter of an hour later, an empty matchbox and a roomful of smoke was all she had to show for her efforts. Coughing, she waved her hand in front of her face and wished she had her fan.

Instead, she crossed to the standing sink basin and tugged

at the window above it. The frame didn't budge. She dragged her fingers along the sash, searching for a lock, but couldn't find anything.

"Arabella, admit it. You can't do anything right." She stared at the stubborn window, her eyes watering—from both frustration and smoke. *"You can't do anything right."* Her stepmother's sharp words reverberated through her head.

Florence had been the one to excel at everything their stepmother had taught them—embroidery, painting, dancing, piano, and even French. Arabella's efforts had always fallen short of her sister's. She'd never been quite good enough at anything. She had no talents or skills to speak of.

That was why, after disembarking yesterday, she hadn't been among the middle-class ladies who'd been given immediate employment as governesses, those more intelligent women with better educations who would be able to live with Victoria's elite families and continue to socialize with Victoria's elite men. Their lives would be pleasant, without the pressure of having to find a secure arrangement. And they'd be able to take more time in choosing a suitable husband.

Even if there were other middle-class ladies who hadn't been able to secure governess work either, she couldn't help but feel as though she'd fallen short again. She let her shoulders slump, something a lady should never do.

A throat cleared behind her.

Gasping, she spun around and clasped the basin behind her.

There, leaning against the doorframe, was the same man who'd startled her two days ago in the dining salon on the *Tynemouth*.

With a racing heart, she slid her hand through the slit in her skirt to her pocket, to the smooth silver cross she'd kept with her since he'd given it to her. She'd only had one fit of hysteria yesterday. Thankfully, the ship's surgeon, Lord Colville, had been close at hand and had tended her, attributing her faint to the anxiety and stress of all that awaited her.

After that first spell, every time worry had swelled, she'd stuck her hand into her pocket and made sure to cling to the cross. While landing upon the shore that overflowed with hundreds of men and then walking through the cheering and whistling crowd to reach the government building, she'd clung to the cross so tightly it had left imprints in her palm.

His courage. Somehow that small reminder of God's strength had soothed her soul enough that she'd made it through the rest of the day without any more bouts of hysteria.

At night when she'd taken the cross out of her pocket, she'd briefly considered how she might find a way to thank the man who'd given it to her. But she'd tossed aside the notion, counting it as impossible. There was no way she'd ever be able to locate him among a city teeming with so many men, especially when she couldn't remember his name.

And yet here he was . . .

He leaned against the doorframe casually, his blue eyes sparkling with mirth, and his lips curved into a crooked grin—one that showed the dimple in his chin beneath a layer of scruff.

How long had he been standing there? Obviously long enough to find humor in her predicament.

"You can do it the right way," he said, "if someone shows you how."

And obviously long enough to hear her talking to herself again. She lifted her shoulders and chin in an attempt to regain her dignity. "You really shouldn't make such a habit of surprising people, Mr. . . . ."

"You'll find I'm full of surprises, Arabella." He stretched out her name.

"I prefer not to be taken by surprise."

His grin only widened, charming and irritating her at the

same time. He pushed away from the door and strode directly toward her.

Part of her warned her to flee from the kitchen—that once again she was alone with a man she didn't know. But the other part of her sensed he was safe. How could a man who'd so kindly given her his silver cross keepsake be anything but safe?

Besides, she was mesmerized by him. He was so unlike anyone she'd ever met. The playful quirk of one of his brows and the tilt of his head dared her not to run away. When he stopped in front of her, his off-kilter smile baited her, as if he didn't believe she'd be able to stay.

Her grip on the basin tightened in her effort to prove him wrong and keep from fleeing. When he leaned in and stretched both arms around her, she sucked in a breath. He was so close that she had to bend slightly backward over the sink to put some distance between them.

For an instant, the memory of other arms closing about her, of another body pressing in sent a jolt of panic through her. She squeezed her eyes shut. What was she doing? Why wasn't she using more caution?

"Someone hurt you?" His whisper was more of a statement than question.

At the gentleness of his tone, her eyes flew open, and she tugged at the high collar of her bodice. Had he seen the mark? She didn't think so since she made sure her collar covered it at all times.

He took a step back, the mirth gone from his expression. Instead, he studied her face as though trying to see into her head and into her memories.

She wasn't exactly sure how to respond and somehow suspected her silence would be answer enough.

"May I?" he asked with a nod behind her.

She didn't quite know what he was asking, but she moved away from the washbasin.

He tugged at the window. At the rasp of the sliding casement, she realized belatedly that he'd walked over to help her efforts to air the smoke out of the kitchen.

He shoved the window halfway up before releasing it. "Pete."

Cool air blew in. For a second, her mind couldn't register the name, still stuck on the fact that he'd asked if she'd been hurt.

"I'm Pete," he said again as he turned away from her and strode to the stove. "I'll be bringing fresh bread to you ladies every morning."

Pete. She let the name tumble around in her mind. She wasn't accustomed to thinking of men by their given names. But somehow *Pete* had a solid ring to it and seemed to fit him.

"Looks like you had trouble getting the stove going. If you'd like, I can show you how to light this little beast." He crouched before the open stove door. "And once I'm done, you'll be the best coal lighter here in Victoria."

Like the last time she'd seen him, she couldn't keep from noticing his good looks—his strong square jaw, broad forehead, and well-defined cheeks.

"Second best after me, that is." He tossed her a smile, a cocky one that made her pulse hop an extra beat.

As she crossed to stand beside him, he rummaged through the matches she'd discarded until he found one he could salvage.

"First, you'll need a starter—something that will burn easily. Round here we use dried leaves, twigs, and bits of bark." He nodded to a large oval-shaped tin pail against the wall next to the stove. "Go ahead. Grab a handful or two."

Patiently he guided her step by step through the process of arranging the starter material and then the best place to insert the match. As the flames spluttered to life, he showed her how to add a few thicker logs. After the fire was burning high, she arranged shovels of coal on the flames, spreading the black lumps around. Finally, when the coals had absorbed the heat and were blazing on their own, she closed the door.

"You did it," he said from where he kneeled next to her.

She sat back on her heels, a waft of satisfaction settling over her. "I'm not sure I can replicate the process again on my own."

"Sure you can." He bumped her shoulder amiably with his.

The gesture took her by surprise. It was something one close friend might do to another. And she'd never had a close friend. "'Tis easy for you to say so. But I should not be surprised if the next time I burn the place down altogether."

His grin widened, bringing the sparkle back into his eyes.

Had she really just jested with this man? She, Arabella Lawrence, never jested with anyone, especially not with men. A flush climbed into her neck and cheeks. She folded her hands in her lap and focused her attention there.

"So I'm guessing you didn't want to start the stove just so you could sit here and admire the heat." His voice contained a note of teasing. "Then again, mayhap you're looking for an excuse to sit with me a while longer."

With all the grace of a cow, she scrambled to her feet, quite sure her cheeks were flaming as red as the fire. This man was too brazen.

"I have no intention of sitting with you now or anytime," she said, shaking out her skirt, thankful she hadn't put on her crinoline yet. "I am grateful for your assistance, and now I must busy myself with the chores at hand."

She began to gather the dirty plates, searching for a place to scrape off the food remains.

Behind her, she could hear Pete rise. She paused, expecting the door to open as he took his leave. But she was startled at the *clank* of a fork against one of the tin plates.

A glance over her shoulder revealed him at the center table, using a knife to swipe the contents of the plate into a greasy pan. He made quick work of emptying the plate before reaching for another, doing the same.

Plate in hand, she pivoted and stared at him, not only amazed at his proficiency but confused by why he was helping her.

"It's a big job for one woman," he said, as though sensing her need for an explanation. "Especially for a woman who's never been in a kitchen before this morn."

His statement was softened by one of his grins. Even so, she had a need to prove herself to this capable man. "If you must know, I've been in a kitchen quite often. I watched our servant, Hayward, do many kitchen tasks."

She waited for Pete to point out that watching and doing were two entirely different things. Instead, he continued scraping plates as though he relished the job. "What was your favorite thing to watch Hayward do?"

His question was unexpected. "What makes you think I had favorites?"

"Your tone. It contains fondness."

It did? She let her mind wander back to the big kitchen, to the sweetness of confection hanging thick in the air, to Hayward's deft strokes as she smoothed the buttercream frosting over a cake, to the rich almond flavor of the batter she licked off the spoon.

"Well?" Pete paused, plate suspended above the pan.

"Hayward loved to bake cakes and puddings and custards." Arabella gathered several more plates. "Even though she had more than her fair share of responsibilities, she always had time to make something sweet for my sister and me."

She carried the plates to Pete, who scraped them clean and then showed her how to wash the dishes, all the while asking her about the various creations Hayward had made, the necessary ingredients, and what she'd liked best.

"So your favorite was caraway cake?" he asked after they'd finished drying the dishes and stowing them in the cabinet. She spread the damp towel over the edge of the sink while he swiftly wiped the top of the worktable.

"Yes, I haven't had it in years, not since my stepmother hired her own cook and Hayward was banned from the kitchen, just as I was."

"Caraway cake is easy to make."

"Not for me. As you can see," she said, waving her hand around the kitchen at the smoke that still lingered, "I'm quite helpless when it comes to domestic tasks."

"With a little training, you can do anything you want."

She couldn't contain a soft scoffing laugh. "Though my father made sure I could read and write, I've actually never been skilled or smart, which is why I'm living here rather than being assigned to one of the governess positions."

He swiped the crumbs off the tabletop into his palm before pausing and studying her. "What have you always dreamed about doing?"

She hesitated. The question was quite personal coming from a man she'd just met. Yet the kindness in his eyes beckoned her to answer. "Naturally, I've always wanted to get married and have a family."

"Naturally." His tone imitated hers. "But beyond that. If you could do anything, what would it be?"

If she could do anything? He was asking the impossible. A woman like her was raised to become a wife and have children. If that didn't happen, then a governess position was the only respectable employment. The last option, as she knew all too well, was living with family and being a burden as a spinster.

He held out a hand to halt her rising protest. "God's given us each a gift—a talent—to use for His purposes. Mayhap that's why you're here in this place. To discover what that is."

A talent? She almost scoffed again. But his expression was sincere, and she swallowed her retort. "You seem to be very talented in the kitchen. How is it you know so much?"

"I'm a baker. Have my own bakehouse." He nodded toward the door, to the basket on the floor. The forms of round loaves and buns were visible beneath a cloth. "My father and grand-father and his father before him were all bakers. Vowed I'd never be a baker, that I'd choose my own way. And for a time, I ran away from God."

So he'd run away. Perhaps not for the same reason she had. But he had nonetheless. She examined his face more closely, noting the shadows lengthening upon his countenance in spite of the bright sunlight now streaming into the kitchen.

"God chased after me. And even though I sailed halfway around the world, He never let me go."

She wanted to hear more than just a vague few sentences about his past but guessed his running-away story was much too complicated to explain to a stranger. Besides, her stepmother had always said, *"Polite gentlewomen don't pry for more information. They wait for it to be offered freely."*

Even so, he had an easy way about him that made their conversation seem natural. The only other person with whom she'd ever been able to talk to so effortlessly had been Hayward.

"Spent six months up in the mining camps," he continued. "Didn't strike it rich, but panned enough gold that I put a down payment on the bakehouse and equipment when the previous owner got sick and decided to move back to San Francisco."

"So even though you didn't want to be a baker, you decided upon it after all?"

"For now. Someday I plan to buy my own land. Got a fine piece of property already picked out. But this is a start, especially with the high demand for fresh bread and the income about as good as gold."

Was it possible here in this new land that people had choices, that they weren't bound by a trade, that they could do or become whatever they aspired to? Was it possible for her to do that too?

For the tiniest of moments, a thrill whispered through her. But just as quickly as it came, she let it float away. Women of her class were nothing without a husband. She'd been a spinster long enough to learn that lesson well. She needed to stick with her plan to find a good and kind husband. That was why she'd come to this place.

Pete tossed the dishrag so that it landed in the sink behind her with a splat. Then he leaned back against the worktable and crossed his arms. "Besides, if not for being a baker, I wouldn't have had an excuse to come into the government complex this morning. And sure as the sunrise I wouldn't be standing here looking at your pretty face."

Something in the way his blue eyes swept over her, from the top of her head down to the hem of her gown, made her insides flutter the same way the breeze coming in the window gently rustled the curtains.

She tucked a stray loose curl behind her ear, wishing she'd taken more time with her toiletry. As it was, she'd finally had the opportunity last evening after the months of travel to take a warm bath and wash her hair. She was gloriously clean again. Even so, her gown wasn't properly ironed, and her hair wasn't fashionably styled. No doubt she looked frightful.

"Saved this delivery for the last and was hoping you ladies would be sitting down to breakfast when I came so I could see you."

Had he come this morning with the intention of seeing her? She shook her head. Certainly not *just* her. "On any other morning, you may have had the opportunity to see all the women. But our baths last night took longer than we antici-pated. Everyone retired to bed much later than usual."

Baths? Bed? How could she have mentioned something so personal in the presence of a man? Where was her fan when she needed it?

"You're the only one I wanted to see, Arabella." The delib-erate way he spoke her name made her insides flutter again.

Overhead, the creak of the ceiling and the pad of footsteps

told her the other women were finally beginning to awaken. Today the welcoming committee had a full day planned for them, starting with the regatta, then ending with a luncheon and watching a cricket match at Beacon's Hill cricket grounds.

She'd hoped some of the gentlemen who'd visited the *Tyne-mouth* would be present at the gatherings, especially Lieutenant Drummond. He was the type of man who would excel at being polite and refined and gentlemanly. He wouldn't say and do things that would embarrass her and make her blush. Not like this man.

"Tomorrow morning I'll make my delivery earlier so we can be alone again." Pete pushed away from the worktable and crossed to his basket of bread.

Alone again? She shouldn't have allowed their time together this morning to go on so long without a chaperone. Actually, she shouldn't have allowed any time at all. "'Tisn't proper for us to be alone—"

"I'll bring a companion."

"Even so, we really shouldn't—"

"And I'll show you how to make caraway cake." He began to take bread and rolls from the basket.

Her rebuttal stalled. He was willing to teach her how to make caraway cake?

She ought to turn down his offer. Ladies of her status didn't bother themselves with baking cakes or any other items. Once she was married, she'd have servants again to do the cooking and baking. There was no reason to learn to do it for herself.

Except that she'd always loved watching Hayward bake, had always been fascinated by the process. Except that at the possibility of trying it, the tiny thrill whispered through her again. Except that she had a strange longing to accomplish something, and maybe creating a cake was a task she might actually be able to do.

Pete finished placing the last loaf onto the table and then

moved to the door and opened it. "I'll see you tomorrow right after dawn." With a wink, he was out and had closed the door before she could decide what to do.

His offer of instruction was like his offer of the cross—she couldn't turn him down, even though she sensed she should.

four

$\mathcal{P}$ete trudged up the shore away from the bay and his canoe. He'd spent the morning and well into the afternoon taking measurements of the land he planned to purchase. On his way back, he'd paid a visit to the six-hundred-acre Bowker farm to discuss the possibility of sharing their waterfront warehouses and docks.

If he was going to get serious about marriage, then he needed to get serious about his future plans. Once he bought his land, the Bowkers would be his closest neighbors, and he needed their permission for loading and unloading goods onto their docks. It didn't make sense to waste the time and money building his own when they could share.

Thankfully, Mr. Bowker was a kind enough man and had seen the reasoning. Yet even with one obstacle out of the way, Pete hadn't found a way around the biggest obstacle of them all—saving enough for the purchase.

Jennie nudged his hand as though to sympathize, and Pete scratched the English springer spaniel's snout in appreciation of her sensitivity to his moods.

"If only I had another baker join me," he mused. "I could make double the quantity." With Victoria the stepping-off point for miners heading to the mountain camps, the demand far outweighed what he was capable of producing in a single night, likely because he refused to gouge his customers as some of the other bakers did.

He was grateful for the steady work, even if most days he spent eighteen hours at his duties. The previous baker had given him a good deal on the land, house, and equipment. Yet in spite of a fair loan and steady income, he had several months before he'd be able to pay the last of his debts and could begin to save for land.

And not just any land. His place was east of Victoria near the coastline along McNeil Bay, a gently sloping area with a glorious view of the Olympic Mountains, plenty of wildlife, and room enough not only for fruit orchards but also for a house, barn, and outbuildings.

He'd gone there enough over the past year that it already felt like his own. He'd also visited the surveyor general's office on numerous occasions regarding the prospect of purchasing it, so much so that the surveyor's assistant had promised to do his best to steer other potential buyers away from the spot.

The problem was, ever since Governor Douglas had opened up for settlement the fur trade reserve land the Hudson's Bay Company had owned for decades, the wealthier families were buying up the acreage. By the time laboring men like him saved enough to make purchases, the best land would no longer be available.

Pete just hoped no one would show interest in his little spot. It wasn't particularly suited for cash-crop farming since it was hilly and mostly uncleared. But eventually it would be the perfect place for the fruit trees—apple and plum—he wanted to grow. Mayhap he'd even eventually have sheep and cows.

Back in Birmingham, he wouldn't have had the opportunity to think about doing anything else other than baking bread. With over three hundred bakeries in the city, he'd have struggled to make ends meet, just as his father had. Baking would have been his lot until he died, which made him all the more thankful that here in the colony he could do and be whatever he wanted without the constraints of society holding him back.

Ahead, the Beacon's Hill cricket grounds were filled with both men and women milling about. Seeing the players standing idle on either side of the field, Pete guessed the game had just ended.

With so many women in attendance, that could mean only one thing—the bride-ship women were out of the government complex and were socializing.

Was Arabella among the crowd?

His pulse picked up pace, sputtering with the need to see her and protesting the possibility that she might be talking with other men.

"I've got my sights set on her," he whispered to Jennie, "and I don't want any of those fancy blokes thinking they can win her."

His early morning visit to the Marine Barracks had gone much better than he could have anticipated. Of course, on the way out, the constable at the gate had questioned why he'd taken so long with his delivery of the donated bread. But he'd talked his way out of the confrontation by promising to bring the constable his own special batch of rolls next time.

He scanned the faces—and hair—of the women until he landed upon long red curls. Arabella's hair was half hidden underneath the wide brim of her beribboned hat. But there was no hiding her loveliness, from her dainty nose all the way to her trim waist and every womanly feature in between.

She was surrounded by men vying for her attention. With a jolt of possessive energy taking hold of him, he veered in her direction. As he closed the distance, one of the cricket players intercepted Arabella, bowing in the fashion of a gentleman and then straightening to reveal the distinguished-but-arrogant Lieutenant Drummond.

Pete's gut kicked against his ribs. "No you don't." He picked up his pace. "You're not about to get the chance to impress her. Not today."

Drummond lifted Arabella's gloved hand and pressed a kiss against her knuckles.

An irrational growl formed deep in Pete's chest. He knew he shouldn't feel so jealous. But if he couldn't have her, the last person he wanted her to be with was Drummond, not after the callousness the man had shown since the smallpox epidemic.

Sensing his tension, Jennie yipped, her warm molasses eyes peering up at him quizzically.

"Aye," Pete said to Jennie. "Go on now and introduce yourself to the lady. And make sure the lieutenant knows he shouldn't be touching her."

Pete gave a pointed nod at Arabella and then affectionately slapped Jennie's hindquarters. The brown-and-white-spotted dog bolted forward. With flapping ears and lolling tongue, she scampered toward Arabella ready to flush the lady away from Drummond the same way she'd flush a grouse from underbrush.

Though not big, Jennie was lean and powerfully built. Would the sight of the creature frighten Arabella?

Realizing the possibility too late, Pete slipped his fingers into his mouth against his tongue and whistled at Jennie to stop. But she was almost upon Arabella, nearly jumping up on her with her front paws.

At the sight of the dog, Arabella reached out a gloved hand. Pete cringed, waiting for a scream or shout or some kind of frightened reaction. Instead, Arabella rubbed at Jennie's head. And laughed.

The laughter wasn't nervous or strained, but tinkled with delight. "And who are you, my lovely?" she asked with the affectionate tone only animal lovers used.

"Bad dog!" Drummond grabbed a fistful of the loose skin at the back of Jennie's neck and yanked her away. "Down!"

Jennie released a piercing yelp of pain at the twist of her skin and hair.

"Oh, Lieutenant, you're hurting the poor creature." Arabella's voice rose with alarm. "Do let him go."

"Her," Pete said as he approached.

Arabella's sights shifted to him. Framed by long lashes, her green eyes had taken on the hue of the grass that grew lush and thick on the island.

"Lie down, Jennie," Pete ordered. The dog lowered herself to the ground, giving Drummond no choice but to let go or look like a brute.

As Jennie spread out docilely, Drummond straightened to his full height and brushed his hands together as if to rid himself of dog hair or fleas or perhaps both. "She needs to be on a leash."

"There aren't any laws that say she has to be," Pete retorted.

"Maybe there should be."

"We both know that law or no law, you'll do whatever you want and try to get away with it." This was neither the time nor place to lob caustic remarks at Drummond, but seeing the man with Arabella, somehow Pete couldn't help it.

Drummond's dark brows furrowed. They both knew exactly what Pete was referring to—the English laws set in place to protect the natives and Drummond's disregard of those laws, especially in light of the raging smallpox epidemic.

Pete hadn't stopped petitioning the naval office in his efforts to understand why they'd ordered the natives to leave instead of quarantining them and completing vaccinations. The men responsible for sending so many natives to their death needed to be held accountable for their actions. Otherwise, what was to prevent something like that from happening again?

On his last visit to the naval base, Drummond had sent him away with a warning to drop the matter. The lieutenant's order had contained a note of threat, one that told Pete he'd stir up trouble for himself if he persisted. The threat had only strengthened Pete's resolve to find out what had really happened.

"She's adorable." Arabella bent and began to stroke between Jennie's ears. She'd changed her earlier gown and now wore one with a wide hooped skirt that made petting the dog difficult. "How old is she?"

"Two."

"Then she's still a puppy."

"She acts like one alright. Gets in her fair share of trouble."

"I'm sure 'tis not overly much trouble, is it, girl?" In spite of the bulky skirt, Arabella scratched further down Jennie's body. "Likely just a bit of playfulness and energy."

"Hardly," Pete scoffed, even as his affection for the dog swelled. Jennie had been a good companion these past two lonely years. "She's been a handful since the day I got her."

As the dog's back leg began to pump in rhythm to the head scratching, Arabella smiled. "Pete's exaggerating, isn't he?"

At the mention of Pete's name, Drummond's shoulders straightened even more. "Miss Lawrence, I did not realize you'd already met Mr. Kelly."

Arabella pulled her hand away from Jennie and took a rapid step back. Pete supposed that in her world, ladies didn't interact with men like him on a first-name basis.

Before she could answer the lieutenant, Pete spoke first. "We've already met a couple of times. Haven't we, Arabella?" He made sure to purposefully use her first name.

She hesitated, then nodded. "I have met Mr. Kelly briefly, in passing."

"I wouldn't call washing the dishes together *brief* or *passing*."

"Washing dishes?" Drummond asked, his brow creasing into deep grooves. "Miss Lawrence, surely you have a servant for such things?"

"'Tis no trouble really. Those of us staying in the Marine Barracks must take turns with the daily chores for the short duration we live there."

"The women from London's slums ought to be doing the domestic work," the lieutenant said indignantly. "Not you."

"I don't mind, truly."

Pete watched the interaction between the two with growing understanding. Arabella hadn't been hesitant to do the work earlier in the privacy of the kitchen. She'd been an eager learner and participant. But she was obviously embarrassed to have the lieutenant know about the manual labor. And about her interaction with him.

Jennie bumped against Arabella and whined softly. Arabella seemed almost relieved to have some place else to focus, and she rubbed the dog between the ears again.

"I shall speak to the welcoming committee about hiring a servant." The lieutenant held out a gloved hand and beckoned her to take his assistance. "Until they do, I insist that you allow the domestics to do what they're intended to do."

Pete had the urge to shove the lieutenant aside so Arabella could continue to pet Jennie to her heart's content. But he sensed he'd only embarrass her further if he threw Drummond to the ground and pounded his fist into the man's face. And it wasn't exactly the kind of conduct that would please his Heavenly Father—or his earthly father, especially now that he'd recommitted his life to following the Lord's ways.

Arabella held out her hand to Drummond in return, and he settled it in the crook of his arm. She stood demurely by his side, the smile and the delight over Jennie gone.

"Shall I accompany you to the Marine Barracks, Miss Lawrence?" He nodded at the other women from the bride ship, most already strolling away from the town green.

Arabella glanced after them. "Why, yes, Lieutenant. I would appreciate your kindness very much . . ." Her words trailed off, and her eyes widened, focusing on someone in the crowd.

For an instant, Pete glimpsed the same fear and wariness he'd seen in her eyes when he'd gotten too close to her while opening the window in the kitchen. He guessed from the way she'd flinched and the rigidness of her body that someone had hurt her.

But who? And why?

She surely didn't have anything to fear here in Victoria, did she?

He followed her gaze and attempted to discover what was causing her anxiety, but amidst the dispersing crowd, he couldn't find anyone or anything that stood out.

She started to release her hold on Drummond's arm, almost as if she planned to run. But the lieutenant clamped his strong hand over hers, keeping her securely by his side. As he maneuvered her forward, she ducked her head in an obvious attempt to shield her face with the brim of her hat.

Pete couldn't tear his focus from her and wasn't sure what bothered him more—that she seemed to accept Drummond's control so easily or that she was in some kind of trouble.

He watched her walk off, waiting for her to look over her shoulder at him, to give him some indication she remembered he was still there. But the farther away she got, the more he realized she'd forgotten all about him.

Drummond cast him a glance, however, one that said he hadn't forgotten about Pete. From the arrogant tilt of his head, the lieutenant was clearly declaring himself victor in the contest for Arabella—a woman beyond Pete's reach, a woman he didn't deserve, a woman he shouldn't pursue.

Again as yesterday, doubts rushed in. Arabella was used to a life of comfort and ease. One involving activities like embroidery, painting, receiving callers, and other things he didn't even know. One wearing gowns with layers of silk and lace such as he'd never even touched. One in which she wasn't used to doing anything for herself, not even getting up in the morning without a maid.

What did he have to offer a woman like her? Perhaps she'd be happier with a man who could provide her everything she'd been accustomed to.

He retreated a step, ready to relinquish her to Drummond. But then he remembered how easily they'd talked that morning, how much he'd enjoyed her company, and the eagerness in her eyes when he'd mentioned teaching her to bake a cake.

Pete lifted his chin a notch and hoped his expression gave Drummond his answer—he wouldn't give up so easily. He planned to pursue Arabella, and there was nothing Drummond could do to stop him.

Wagging her tail, Jennie trotted after Arabella.

Pete called her back and she came, but only reluctantly.

"Don't worry, girl." Pete bent and combed his fingers through the dog's thick coat. "We'll win her over so much that she won't be able to get us out of her mind."

He just had to increase his efforts. And without delay.

five

M r. Major took Arabella's hand into his. "You were
the most beautiful woman there tonight, my dear."
"You're much too kind." Arabella allowed herself to relax
against the velvet carriage seat, the darkness of the late night
providing a quiet calm after the hours of glittering lights and
endless dancing.

As the carriage bumped along the rutted London street, Mr.
Major's shoulder brushed against hers, but he made no move to
put any distance between them on the seat as he'd so carefully
done on other outings.

With their wedding only one week away, she supposed the
hand-holding and shoulder brushing was to be expected. Mr.
Major would surely know more about such things since he
was so much older and had been married several times before.

With his bulbous nose and overly round face, he wasn't a
handsome man anymore, especially with his thinning silver
hair and the speckled, raised moles on his face.

So far during their short courtship, he'd been attentive and
at times even extravagant—like earlier in the evening when he'd
arrived to pick her up and had given her a diamond bracelet.

Though she'd protested, he insisted she wear it, telling her that as his wife, she'd have new diamonds to wear every day.

Underneath her glove, the jewels now sat uncomfortably against her wrist, chafing her skin, and she was anxious to take off the bracelet once she was home.

With a peek out the window, she could see they were drawing near to her father's townhouse.

"Arabella," Mr. Major said, his voice low and very near her cheek. The warmth and the sourness of alcohol on his breath made her want to draw back. But she knew to do so would be rude, so she held herself motionless and waited for him to continue.

He released his hold on her hand, and she almost expelled a breath of relief, but then jumped when his hand slid to her thigh.

"Mr. Major," she chastised softly as she attempted to scoot away.

At the same time, he clamped her bosom. She barely had time to release a startled and horrified breath when his mouth covered hers.

She shoved at his chest, attempting to push him away. She freed her mouth only to find that he angled in and began kissing her neck.

"Mr. Major, please stop this instant," she said, her voice trembling and breathless. "This is entirely inappropriate."

Before she could speak again and urge him to wait until after they were married to indulge in such intimacies, a sharp pain in her neck made her scream. He'd bitten her. The surprise of such an action was too much to comprehend.

He gripped her with bruising strength, and she feared he'd only hurt her more if she struggled any further. For a long moment, he remained motionless, his labored breathing filling the air between them.

The carriage rolled to a stop, and she wanted nothing more

than to scramble out and get as far from him as possible. But his clasp was too tight.

Finally, he pushed her away and released an almost disgusted sigh. "This is your fault, Arabella. You should know better than to lead a man on, only to act the part of a prim maiden at the last moment."

She was fumbling for the door handle when his hand shot out and encircled her wrist, holding her back. "Before you go, you need to apologize for your coyness."

"My coyness?" Had she somehow led him to believe she'd welcome his touch?

His fingers tightened, digging the diamond bracelet into her flesh. "Yes. You need to take better care not to entice me." His tone was like that of a parent chastising a wayward child.

Perhaps she was to blame. Perhaps she'd been careless.

"Do you understand?" His voice turned more demanding, his grip harder.

She winced. "Yes, and I do apologize for my carelessness this eve."

He released her and sat back. "Very well, I forgive you. Just make sure it doesn't happen again."

"I shall do my best."

"Good. Now go."

She reached for the handle again. As if on cue, the driver opened the door. She couldn't escape the confines of the carriage fast enough. All she wanted to do was run, and run, and run.

Arabella sat up in her bunk, her breath coming in gasps. For a moment, she peered through the darkness and tried to gain her bearings.

In the faint light of dawn coming in from the window, she could make out the wooden frames of the other bunk beds crammed into the room. At the heavy breathing of Miss Spencer on the bed across from hers, the tension eased from Arabella's muscles.

She touched her neck and felt the sting of the bite mark even though it had healed weeks ago. The scars on her back rippled with a wave of phantom pain.

With trembling legs, she pushed out of bed. She was safe in Victoria. Wasn't she? Certainly Mr. Major wouldn't send someone to hunt her down. He wasn't so desperate to have her that he'd go to such lengths.

But even as she tried to still her rapid pulse, her mind filled with the image of the diminutive man with the red bow tie and bowler hat whom she'd seen after the cricket game yesterday. Although she'd only glimpsed the figure from a distance, the clothing along with the round face and fleshy double chin reminded her of Mr. Major's most trusted servant, Pym Nevins, who'd been like a jailer during her last days in London.

She gave herself a mental shake. She was allowing her fear to grow into something bigger than necessary. The man yesterday was probably a complete stranger, and next time she saw him, she'd realize how foolish and unfounded her worry was.

As with the previous morning, Arabella dressed in the dark before creeping down to the kitchen. She would change into something fancier and take more time with her appearance later so that she was presentable for church . . . and for socializing with the men of the community again.

Though she'd been nervous, she'd mingled with a number of different gentlemen at the regatta. Lieutenant Drummond had been especially attentive and provided pleasant company as they'd watched the boat races. He'd also been kind to escort her back to the barracks after the cricket match. From what she'd learned, he was exactly the kind of man she'd hoped to find. He came from a wealthy family, his manners were impeccable, and he was a gentleman in every way.

Even so, her fingers shook as she opened the stove door. Mr. Major had been kind to her at first too and look what had happened.

"Not everyone is like him," she whispered to herself. Then just as quickly as the words were out, she glanced to the door expecting to see Pete standing there, listening to her babbling to herself.

But light from the lone lantern revealed an empty spot and deserted kitchen. Since dawn had yet to break, it was too early for his arrival. Besides, even if he'd claimed he would come to teach her how to make caraway cake, surely he had more important things to do.

At the very least, she could try boiling water for coffee. She'd watched one of the other women do so last eve. She would replicate the process on her own now that Pete had shown her how to light the stove.

The lieutenant's words from after the cricket match came back to rebuke her: *"From now on you must allow the domestics to do what they're intended to do."* And from now on she must also behave appropriately as women of her class should.

Lieutenant Drummond hadn't said as much, yet he'd implied it. A lady of means didn't lower herself to doing the work of servants. Such behavior was considered almost scandalous.

Still, a few days spent in the kitchen wouldn't harm her, especially if she kept it private. After all, what other choice did any of the ladies have but to continue their shipboard arrangement of fending for themselves?

After several attempts and at least half an hour later, she finally had a fire glowing and turning out decent heat. She pulled the pot onto the front burner only to discover it was empty. Though she knew where the pump was outside the house, she'd never gathered water before and wasn't sure she'd be able to work the handle. Nevertheless, with a pail in one hand and a lantern in the other, she slipped out the back door of the barracks and made her way to the pump that stood at the center of the yard between several of the government buildings.

At a clanking from the side of the barracks, she slowed her

steps. Ought she to be out by herself? What if some of the men were lingering around the perimeter as they had been the past two days, waiting to see the bride-ship women? What if one of them was even now creeping up on her?

A movement near the large garbage bin at the rear of the property brought her to a halt. Maybe the intruder wasn't human but rather one of the wild creatures the lieutenant and other officers had so vividly described.

She held herself motionless and watched the bin, ready to race back inside the barracks at the first sign of danger. After a moment of silence, a head poked upward through the garbage. Hands gripped the edge of the container. One leg and then two slipped over, and a lithe form jumped to the ground, dark braids bouncing against shoulders.

'Twas no animal. Rather 'twas a girl.

What was she doing in the garbage bin?

Arabella took several hesitant steps toward the child. At the movement, the girl spun, revealing the dark hair and brown skin of an Indian. Through the faint lantern light and the first glimmer of dawn, Arabella caught sight of the fear on the girl's face—her pockmarked face.

It took a moment for Arabella to understand what was hanging out of the girl's mouth. A chicken bone and a chunk of a roll.

Revulsion swelled in her throat. The child was eating garbage.

Arabella swallowed her disgust and instead gave way to pity. If this Indian girl was hungry, she needn't rummage through a trash bin for food. Remnants from last evening's meal remained in the kitchen. Surely none of the women would take offense if Arabella gave what was left to this child.

"Good morning," Arabella said gently.

The child backed up several rapid steps until she reached the fence.

"I mean you no harm." Arabella didn't move except to reach out a hand, as if by doing so she could stop the girl. "I'd like to give you food."

The words had the desired effect—the child froze.

Arabella pointed in the direction of the Marine Barracks. "If you'll wait a moment, I shall bring some food out to you."

The child stared back with wide, frightened eyes.

"Wait right there," she instructed, praying the girl could understand her. "I shall return shortly."

She raced to the kitchen faster than was becoming of a lady. Finding a clean towel, she grabbed the food that was left—a wedge of cheese, half a loaf of bread, and two apples. She wrapped them in a clean towel, tied the ends together, and rushed back outside.

Half expecting the girl to be gone, she was relieved to see her still standing by the fence, gnawing at the chicken bone, picking it clean of every morsel. She tossed the bone to the ground and warily watched Arabella approach.

Only feet away, Arabella halted and held out the bundle. With the growing light of dawn, she could see the girl's features more clearly and guessed her to be in the range of eight to ten years of age. She was dainty and would have been pretty—if not for the circular indentations that dotted her face and arms. She had no shoes, wore only rags, and carried the stench of someone who'd gone far too long without washing.

What had happened to reduce the child to such circumstances? "Please." Arabella thrust the food closer. "Take it."

The girl hesitated. Then without a word, she yanked the bag from Arabella, spun toward the fence, climbed over it, and disappeared from sight before Arabella could draw in a full breath.

For long seconds, she watched the spot, waiting for what, she didn't know. Finally, she released the tension in her shoulders. The girl was gone, and there was likely nothing more she could do to help her.

Something wet touched her hand, and she jumped. Glancing down, she found a friendly spaniel peering up at her.

"Jennie?"

The dog sat and began to swish her tail back and forth, her big warm eyes begging Arabella for attention.

Arabella couldn't resist. She bent and scratched Jennie on the long part of her nose, up between her eyes. Toby had always liked when she scratched his nose. A familiar ache formed in her chest at the thought of the little dog she'd left behind. Hayward had promised to take care of Toby, her bichon frise, but that hadn't stopped Arabella from missing her faithful companion.

"What are you doing here, you sweet thing?" she asked, scratching underneath Jennie's chin now.

The dog's tail moved faster.

"Does your master know you're here?"

"Aye, he does." At the sound of Pete's voice near the kitchen door, Arabella's heart did a tiny flip. She told herself such a reaction was only because she was eager to bake and not because she was eager to see the baker.

six

$\mathcal{P}$ete stepped away from the shadows of the Marine Barracks where he'd been watching Arabella since she'd approached the child and held out a bundle of what appeared to be food.

He'd been surprised to see her interacting with the girl since most people around Victoria and on Vancouver Island disliked the natives, believed they were filthy, lazy thieves and murderers. The negative attitudes had worsened since the smallpox outbreak, and people shunned the natives even more out of fear they carried the disease.

"You were kind to give that girl food," he said, noticing she hadn't yet styled her hair and that she wore it down in long, loose waves, which softened her features.

"She needs much more than I gave her." Arabella scratched behind Jennie's ears.

"Aye. That she does."

Arabella glanced at the fence again, her forehead wrinkling. "What was wrong with her?"

"My guess is that she survived the smallpox epidemic but her family perished, leaving her an orphan."

"Does she not have other relatives who can take care of her? Friends in her tribe?"

"Mayhap not." A familiar sadness settled over Pete. "The epidemic devastated natives all throughout the island. She might have been the only one in her tribe to live through it."

He showed her how to fill her pail with water from the pump. Then he followed her inside, carrying the two baskets he'd brought along. He unpacked the bread as she set about making coffee. All the while, he answered her questions about the spread of the disease.

"Sounds like you care about the Indians and want to help them." Her hand rested on the handle of the coffee grinder, her expression full of compassion.

He appreciated her interest. There weren't many in Victoria who wanted to talk about what had happened. Most simply ignored the injustice. Some even came out to support the decline of the native population, saying fewer Indians made the island cleaner as well as safer for settlement.

The more people Pete talked to, the more he was beginning to believe the whole purpose of sending the natives away was to destroy the threat they posed to the growing colony.

After all, if the natives were immobilized from illness, the Royal Navy's job of patrolling the waterways and keeping the peace would be much easier, especially because so many tribes congregated around the city for trading purposes. Mayhap the navy had decided that spreading the disease would be less costly and more effective than using guns and cannons.

But how could Pete prove there had been ulterior motives in sending the disease-ridden natives away from Victoria?

"I owe my life to the natives," he admitted. He wasn't proud of his past rebellion. He'd made mistakes and sinned in ways he was ashamed to admit. Yet, as far as he'd fallen, God had held on tight. When he'd been at his worst, God's grace had been at its best.

Arabella watched him, obviously waiting for him to continue but too polite to pry.

"When I left home, I decided to leave my faith behind." He could still remember the last day he'd worked in the bakehouse, when his father had refused to add the chalk dust to their bread to cheapen the cost and bring in a greater profit.

"Why can't you just be normal?" Pete had shouted at his dad. "Why can't you do what everyone else is doing?"

"Lying and cheating?" his dad asked sadly.

"Our customers want white bread. The whiter the better. They don't care if it has additives."

"I care. Even if no one else lives with integrity, I will."

"Why does it matter? Especially since you'll run yourself out of business?"

"The world around us will always shift their definitions of what's right and wrong. But God's Word never changes. His truth is steadfast. Why build my life on sinking sand when I have something much more solid I can live upon?"

Pete had kicked the twenty-stone bag of flour, letting his frustration loose at his dad's stubbornness to adjust with the times and do what was necessary to help the bakehouse survive. As if the hard manual labor of mixing and kneading the bread wasn't enough, the struggle to pay the rent and bills had been growing. They'd had to work longer hours and survive on less sleep.

He'd decided his dad's faith was the cause of their problems, that if his dad hadn't been so dogmatic about his beliefs, had been willing to change his practices like everyone else, then mayhap they could have made the business thrive. But they'd been slowly killing themselves and their bakery. With each step further into demise, Pete wanted out, had for a long time.

At the break of dawn, after he'd helped his father with the last of the fresh rolls for their middling-class customers, he'd packed his bag and left. When he walked out the door, he'd told his dad he didn't plan to step foot into a bakery or a church for as long as he lived, that he didn't want to be a part of a faith that made life such a drudgery.

He'd tried to brush off the pain in his dad's eyes as he said goodbye, but he knew it would haunt him for the rest of his life.

Even now, he couldn't forget his dad's expression. It hadn't contained disappointment or anger or even frustration. No, his dad's eyes had held terrible heartache, as if he'd already known all the trials and trouble Pete would experience and wanted to stop him from having to go through it.

"Rejected everything my dad ever taught me," Pete said, meeting Arabella's gaze directly. "Committed just about every sin a man is capable of and lived for my own pleasure."

Her eyes widened at his admission, and yet she still didn't probe.

"When I moved here in sixty, I headed up into the mountains like most men coming through. Believed all the stories about miners getting rich off gold and thought I could too. Panned for gold, but mostly drank and gambled and caroused."

At his bold declaration of his sins, she quickly glanced down and fidgeted with the still-empty coffee grinder. "Everyone I've spoken with claims the mining camps are heathen."

"Worse than heathen," he replied. "One night, I drank so much I couldn't find my way back to my tent. Got lost in the woods, tripped, and nearly fell down a ravine. Found myself tangled in the roots of a tree and hung head-down for hours. In the freezing cold."

Arabella's hands stilled. The soft glow of the lantern turned her hair the color of roasted almonds, making her face seem even paler and her sprinkling of freckles stand out. Her green eyes were luminous, taking him in so thoroughly that he wanted to pause his story so he could cross the kitchen and sweep her into his arms. He'd tangle his fingers in her hair and kiss every freckle on her face and then some.

The urge was strong and swift, and he had to swallow it down. The man he was a year ago would have acted upon the desire, would have charmed her until she was like dough in his hands. But he wasn't that man anymore. He was living a new life, walking the narrow path, taking the hard road. Things were going well. God was blessing him. And he couldn't mess up now.

He bent and removed the flour from his basket. While he might not be that old man anymore, he couldn't shed all of his mischievousness. Since she'd been hanging on to his every word, he'd make her ask him for the rest of the story.

She tapped her fingers.

Smothering a smile, he retrieved several more items and made a point of arranging them neatly next to the flour.

"Well?" she finally asked somewhat breathlessly.

He added the eggs and sugar to the ingredients before pausing and shooting her an innocent look. "Well what?"

She released an exasperated sigh. "Aren't you going to tell me how you were rescued? I'm assuming by the natives?"

"Do you want me to tell you?"

"Of course. You cannot share half the story without finishing it."

"I can't?"

"No." Her tone was turning sassy, and he liked it.

"Mayhap I should wait and tell you the rest tomorrow morning when I come."

She fisted her hands on her hips. "And why must you wait?"

"Because then you'll look forward to seeing me even more than you already do."

"You're making quite grand assumptions about your importance, Mr. Kelly." She ducked her head and focused on the coffee grinder, but not before he caught sight of the pretty pink rising in her cheeks.

He let his smile have free rein as he finished unloading the last of the supplies for the caraway cake. "A lot of thoughts go through a person's mind when they're hanging upside down in a ravine by the roots of a tree."

"I imagine so." Her gaze was riveted to him again, and he found he liked that too. Immensely.

"If God wanted to get my attention, well, He sure got it. While I was hanging there, I had nothing else to do but think about how meaningless my life had become. I'd thought doing whatever I wanted and following my own ways would fulfill me. But there I was, completely empty. And dying. Alone."

Whenever he thought back on that day, to the near delirious state he'd been in, having lost all feeling in his feet and legs, he couldn't keep from whispering a prayer of gratitude he'd come out of the ordeal intact. Even if he hadn't lost his life, he very well could have lost his feet or his legs.

"Guess God decided He wasn't ready to bring a bullheaded man like me into paradise quite then. Either that or He figured there were too many things He still wanted me to do. Whatever the case, He sent Sque-is."

"A native?"

"Aye. Sque-is was out hunting and came across me. Don't know why he didn't just pass me by and leave me to my misery. After the way the miners treated the natives, it would have served me right."

From the tilt of her head, he sensed she wanted to know more details. But the skirmishes had been too bloody and brutal. Rehashing them would only make her needlessly fear the natives, as so many others did.

"Turned out Sque-is became one of my closest friends. And now after the smallpox outbreak, I don't know if he's dead or alive. I keep putting out word, hoping I'll find out what happened to him and his tribe." Including his wife and unborn child.

Sque-is's people, the Haida, were a northern tribe from the Queen Charlotte Islands. From everything Pete had heard, the

Queen Charlotte Islands had been hit as hard with the smallpox as every other area.

As summer had turned into autumn, the sickening sensation in the pit of Pete's stomach had only deepened. He'd canoed out into the straits on several occasions to see if he could discover any news regarding the tribes from the Queen Charlotte Islands, but an unusual quiet had met him everywhere he'd gone.

"You fear the worst?" she asked.

"Aye."

"I'm sorry." Her expression held compassion, something he wasn't accustomed to. It brought a strange tightening to his throat, along with the need to lighten the mood and change the subject.

"So are you ready for your cake lesson?"

"You said you were bringing a companion." She finally dumped a spoonful of coffee beans into the grinder.

"I did. Jennie." He nodded toward the dog that had followed him inside and was now lying in front of the door. Head on her paws, her ears perked at hearing her name.

"We should have a real chaperone."

"Then you really do like me." He couldn't keep from teasing her. Flirting had always been easy for him. But now, with Arabella, he sensed flirting wouldn't be enough, that perhaps *he* wouldn't be enough. Even so, he had to try.

"How could I like you?" she asked indignantly, even though she kept her attention on her task. "I hardly know you."

"If you didn't find me attractive and if you weren't worried about falling in my arms, we wouldn't have need for a chaperone, would we?"

Finally her eyes swung up to meet his. The mortification there was laughable. "That's not true. Absolutely not true. I'm not worried about falling into your arms." Her gaze shifted to first one arm, then the other. Was she thinking about his arms surrounding her? Mayhap she was more attracted to him than she let on.

"If you're not worried," he said, dropping his tone to a low challenge, "then walk over to me and prove it."

She pressed her pretty lips together and lifted her dainty chin as if preparing for battle.

He wanted to grin, but decided against it. In the art of flirtation, there was a fine line between persuading and irritating. And now was most definitely the time for persuasion.

Schooling his expression into one of casual neutrality, he leaned a hip against the worktable and crossed his arms. And dared her again with his eyes.

Worry flashed for just an instant before she squared her shoulders and stalked rapidly toward him.

"There," she said and stopped two feet away. "I proved it."

He shook his head and let his lips curve into a lazy smile, one he'd been repeatedly told was irresistible. "A little closer."

She took a baby step.

"Closer."

Her chin notched higher, and she drew several more inches toward him. Standing only a foot away, she was vibrant and beautiful, and his muscles tensed with the need to hold her. Mayhap his teasing had been a bad idea. Mayhap being alone and near her was like playing with fire. Mayhap they needed a chaperone after all.

He was tempted to reach for her, but then stopped himself and instead touched one of the long strands on her cheek.

At the contact, she froze.

He hoped it wasn't from fear but sensed as he had yesterday that someone had hurt her and now she would have to learn to trust men again—at least trust him. With feathery gentleness, he slowly tucked the strand behind her ear.

Her chest rose with an inhale she didn't release, and her pupils darkened with an emotion he couldn't name but hoped was attraction, because he liked her more every moment he was with her . . . which was why he had to be careful.

He dropped his hand. "Close your eyes."

"What?" she said on an exhale as her brow quirked.

"I have a gift for you. Close your eyes."

She studied him a moment as though testing his trustworthiness. Finally, he must have passed her silent trial because she lowered her lashes.

He reached into the basket and removed the last item.

She started to open her eyes, and he quickly straightened and covered them with his hand. "No peeking."

"What is it?" she asked.

"Be patient," he teased as he propelled her around so that she was facing the worktable in front of him. He kept his hand as a shield over her eyes, which put him directly behind her, close enough that her hair tickled his chin and her feminine, flowery scent teased his senses.

With his other hand, he placed the gift onto the table next to the ingredients.

"Are you ready?" Her voice lilted with anticipation.

He chuckled and released her eyes. Immediately she reached for the gift. As she lightly fingered the copper cake pan, he stepped around her so he could gauge her reaction. She was smiling, and the delight in her expression made the cost of the pan worth it.

"It's beautiful." She traced the raised pattern that resembled something like a tulip—although he wasn't a flower expert and couldn't be sure.

"It's the best cake pan I could find in Victoria. Also the only one."

"I love it."

Those three simple words went straight to his heart and warmed his chest with a fullness he'd never experienced before with any other woman. "You'll need it not only for the caraway cake but for the other cakes."

"Other cakes?"

"This morning's lesson is just the start."

She took in the ingredients spread over the table, ran her hand over the cake pan again, then shook her head. "I cannot take all this. 'Twouldn't be right."

"I thought you might say that. Which is why I'm prepared to offer you a deal."

"What kind of deal?"

While arm-deep in dough last night, he'd plotted and planned how to spend more time with her. Teaching her how to bake seemed like the best way. But she hadn't seemed like the kind of woman who'd indefinitely accept something she considered charity.

"I'll teach you how to bake—anything you want. And in exchange, you can teach me how to read."

"You don't know how to read?" Once the question was out, she had the grace to look chagrinned. "I'm sorry."

He wasn't offended and shrugged off her apology. "Since the time I could walk, I helped my dad in the bakehouse. Didn't have the time or need for schooling."

She tilted her head and waited for him to say more.

"I can read and write a few basic words to get by," he offered. "But I'd like to be able to read everything—the newspaper, the bills, and letters from home." Especially a letter from home when it finally came—if it ever came.

More important, reading lessons would give him another excuse to spend time with her and more opportunities to win her heart.

"Perhaps you'll want someone more qualified than me," she said hesitantly. "I've never been very smart or learned—not like some of the other ladies."

"I thought you said you knew how to read."

Her gaze flew up to meet his. "Of course I do—"

"That's all that matters."

She returned her attention to the shiny copper cake pan. "Even with our deal, I cannot possibly keep this."

"It's a gift."

"You already gave me a gift." She delved into her pocket and pulled out the silver cross, the one his dad had worn on a chain for as long as he could remember. Somehow his dad had slipped the cross into his knapsack the day he'd left home. He hadn't found it right away or he might have tossed it into the sea. Eventually he'd discovered the necklace at the bottom of his bag. Though he'd tried to ignore it, the token had beckoned him until he'd begun to wear it just as his dad had.

He'd almost lost it the day he'd hung by his feet above the steep ravine. The chain had become hopelessly tangled in twigs and roots. When he'd finally been freed, he lost the chain. But at least he'd saved the silver cross.

Ever since then, he carried the cross in his pocket as a constant reminder that he aspired to be like the man he'd once despised. Impulsively, he'd given it to Arabella the day he met her, and he hadn't once regretted the decision. He'd sensed she needed it more than he did.

"I haven't had the opportunity to thank you for the kindness in giving this to me," she said, rolling the cross around in her palm. "I'd forgotten my need to turn to God in my direst moments. And the cross is reminding me to do that."

Her words contained a vulnerability he suspected was rare for her. "You're welcome."

When she lifted her eyes to his and smiled, he sensed they'd moved from being acquaintances to friends.

For the next hour, as he walked her step by step through the process of preparing the cake batter, he relished every moment of being together and getting to know her better. He observed her reluctance in sharing about her family, a deep sadness and even regret where they were concerned.

Rather than push her, he talked about his family, his mum and dad and two sisters, about growing up in a small village in the West Midlands, how several bad years for crops had sent the price of wheat soaring, and how people couldn't afford bread, not even the less expensive dark barley and rye. His dad had resorted to making baker's cram—lard mixed with bran and anything else on hand. It had earned the name "cram" because it was so awful, not even the chickens liked the mixture, and it had to be *crammed* down their throats.

After so many people were forced to move to the cities to find work, his dad lost too many customers and had to close the bakehouse—the one that had been in the family for generations. They'd packed up and moved to Birmingham, where his dad was able to rent a place and start baking again. But after relocating to the city, life had never been the same.

"You sound as though you miss your family very much." she said, crouching next to him as he placed the cake pan into the hot oven.

"Aye, I haven't heard from them since I left."

Pastor Abe had helped him write a letter to his parents over a year ago, a letter asking them for forgiveness for his rebellion and for all the cruel words he'd spoken before he ran away. He'd been waiting to hear back. Though his parents couldn't read, they surely could have found someone to read his letter to them and then write a response.

The more months that passed, the more he feared he'd hurt them too much so that reconciliation would be impossible. It was also likely something had happened to them and they hadn't received his letter. Without his help, mayhap they'd had to give up the bakehouse and move once again.

"Well that does it." He closed the door and latched it. As they straightened, she wiped her hands on a towel, and he did likewise.

Dawn had come and gone. Daylight poured through the kitchen window, along with a cool morning breeze that stirred the aroma of the coffee she'd set to brewing. He was tempted to ask for a cup and draw out their time together but was distracted by the batter above her lip, remnants of one of her tasting trials.

Without thinking, he lifted a hand and touched the spot, intending to wipe it off.

At the contact, she sucked in a breath, and her eyes flew to his.

"You have a little batter," he explained, not wanting to scare her away.

When she didn't back up, he took that as the sign to proceed, and he gently wiped her upper lip. The delicate dip of her Cupid's bow made his thoughts stall. All he could think about was the feel of her, the smoothness of her skin and the fullness of her lips. With her mouth slightly parted, her lips all but begged to be kissed, the kind of lips that should be kissed often and thoroughly.

Entranced, he couldn't make himself look or back away.

She drew in another shorter breath and was staring at his mouth with both curiosity and fascination. Was she thinking of what it might be like to kiss him?

Footfalls sounded on the stairway that led from the kitchen to the bedrooms above.

Arabella spun away from him, hurrying to the dirty dishes on the work counter. Seconds later, another of the bride-ship women entered the kitchen, stifling a yawn behind her hand.

When she caught sight of Pete standing near the stove, she stopped short. Her attention shifted to Arabella, who was focused on the dishes, clanking spoons and knives and bowls.

"Everything all right, Miss Lawrence?" asked the newcomer, the fair-haired, blue-eyed woman Pete had heard many of the men around Victoria talking about.

"Of course, Mercy," Arabella remarked brusquely as she began to place the remaining cake ingredients back into his basket. "I made a caraway cake and have just put it into the oven to bake."

"You, miss?" Mercy's brows lifted in an expression that said she didn't believe Arabella capable of making anything, much less a cake.

"With assistance from Mr. Kelly, the baker," Arabella added.

Mercy's mouth opened as though she might say something but then just as quickly clamped shut. From the style of her garments, Pete guessed Mercy was among the poor women in the group, the kind of woman he should have set his sights upon. But even with so fair a woman among the group, his attention homed in on Arabella, who was working swiftly to repack his basket.

"I've never had caraway cake," Mercy said, not moving from her place in the doorway. "But it smells right good."

"Let's hope it tastes as good as it smells." Arabella tucked the last ingredient away and picked up the basket.

"It's my granddad's recipe," Pete said, "so I guarantee it'll be mighty fine."

"I'll look forward to trying it," Mercy replied.

"Here you are, Mr. Kelly." Arabella held out the basket without meeting his gaze. She'd set aside the camaraderie they'd shared while baking the cake and put in its place the stiff formality of her class. Clearly she was in a hurry to bring their time together to a close.

It was the same attitude she'd displayed at Beacon's Hill yesterday when she was with Drummond, almost as if she was embarrassed for anyone to know she'd been doing *domestic work*. She wasn't also embarrassed to be seen talking with him, was she?

He approached and took the basket. "Tomorrow I'll bring ingredients for another cake." He paused and tried to look into her eyes, needing to see the sincerity and friendliness from earlier.

But she turned away and returned to the worktable. He watched her a moment longer before giving a short whistle that drew Jennie up from the rug in front of the door. As he exited, he felt Arabella's gaze trailing after him, but he refrained from looking at her again.

Once the door closed, he blew out a breath, not sure whether to be pleased with how things had gone or frustrated. All he knew was that he had his work cut out for him if he hoped to win her heart.

seven

"*Your face should always wear a smile. You must always have a graceful bearing and light step.*" As Arabella used her mallet to hit the hard red ball across the lawn, she could hear her stepmother's instructions as clearly as if she were present.

"Very nicely done, Miss Lawrence," Lieutenant Drummond said from behind her, even though her ball was as far from the wicket as it could possibly get.

Arabella forced another smile just as she'd done all through the croquet game.

"You are catching on rather quickly." The lieutenant fell into step next to her.

"Thank you, Lieutenant Drummond." Her heavy hooped skirts swishing, she attempted to move gracefully across the grassy yard of the government complex, where the lieutenant and several other officers had set up the croquet game and invited some of the bride-ship ladies to join them.

While the game was becoming all the rage across England, none of the ladies had played it before, and their gentlemen visitors had been patiently instructing each of them on how

81

to hit the croquet balls through a succession of wickets while deterring their opponents' balls at the same time.

The Sunday afternoon was as pleasant as the previous day had been for the regatta. The sunshine was warm, and the feel of the grass beneath Arabella's feet was welcome after the months aboard the ship. As the wind teased the lace tucker of her bodice, her fingers fluttered up to make sure her neck remained covered.

"Perhaps a little more to the right with your next hit," the lieutenant suggested, swinging his mallet nonchalantly. In his naval uniform, he made a dashing picture. From the trim of his dark mustache and the neatness of his sideburns, she could tell he'd taken special effort with his appearance for the visit.

She too had made extra efforts for the church service earlier and was still wearing the light blue silk gown with the short sleeves and cape of Valenciennes lace, although she'd put aside the headdress wreath made of blue velvet and silver cord and had donned a large-brimmed straw hat with dainty blue flowers.

Even with so elegant a company and with so entertaining a game, her attention kept wandering to the garbage can at the rear of the yard and thoughts of the native child she'd seen there that morning. Invariably, images of the little girl brought to mind Pete and the caraway cake they'd baked together. That, in turn, brought a measure of shame that she'd behaved so ungratefully at the end of their time together.

Truthfully, her shame had lingered with her all day, even earlier through the church service and the dinner afterward. Even though she'd already vowed on the morrow to show Pete greater appreciation for his kindness, just the prospect of his coming again sent her thoughts into a dozen different directions.

On the one hand, she knew she shouldn't repeat the clandestine activity. Manual labor of any kind—including cake making—would cast serious doubt upon her eligibility for gentlemen suitors, as well as for polite society.

Yet another part of her couldn't wait for the chance to bake again. The women had complimented her caraway cake, raving between mouthfuls, and their praise had filled her with a satisfaction heretofore unknown . . . a satisfaction she wanted to feel again.

While she'd savored not only the cake but also their praise, she'd tried to push aside the guilt that she hadn't been completely honest with the women about Pete's help, having led them to believe he'd done nothing more than give her the instructions before leaving.

The guilt, however, had only increased as the afternoon wore on. Even now in the middle of the croquet game, the weight upon her chest had more to do with the fact that she'd asked the ladies not to mention her cake-making efforts to any of their callers, particularly to Lieutenant Drummond.

Of course, the women understood. They were all embarrassed by the domestic work they were still having to do at the Marine Barracks. And they'd all looked on enviously as two more of the gentlewomen, Louisa and Charlotte Townsend, had left earlier that afternoon to go live with the Pringles, old family friends who'd come over from New Westminster for them. The two sisters would settle into a comfortable life they'd been accustomed to in England, no longer needing to worry about where they would go or who would take care of them.

"I admit," Lieutenant Drummond said, "I am rather surprised you did not have the opportunity to play croquet in England."

Arabella was tempted to ask the lieutenant how it was he believed she should have had occasion for the game, not when she'd been a reclusive spinster living in her father's home, but she swallowed her words. Again, her stepmother's instructions directed her etiquette: *"Never introduce your own affairs for the amusement of the company; such discussions cannot be interesting to others."*

"I see that you are quite good," she said, directing the conversation away from herself and back to him. "Are you naturally inclined toward it?"

"Perhaps I am," he replied with a slight smile. He stopped next to his ball, positioned himself perfectly, then tapped the mallet so that the ball rolled through first one wicket and then the next.

"Well done, Lieutenant Drummond."

"If you enjoy watching me at croquet, then you'll most certainly enjoy watching me at horse racing."

"Perhaps I shall." While she'd never been to a horse race, she didn't dare admit it lest he question her again and learn exactly how dull a life she'd led in recent years.

When he launched into a description of the recently formed Jockey Club and his participation in the organization, she tried to respond appropriately, hoping she didn't seem too ignorant. By the end of the afternoon, she wasn't sure what kind of impression she'd left on Lieutenant Drummond, but when he took his leave, he seemed pleased enough.

"Do they like us?" Miss Spencer whispered once the officers had closed the complex gate.

Trying to tame her tangled nerves, Arabella pressed her palms together, feeling the dampness beneath her gloves. "Of course they like us, Miss Spencer." But even as Arabella reassured the young woman, a litany of inadequacies assaulted her. She was too old, unskilled, and uninteresting. And she had red hair.

Though she'd done her best to behave as a proper lady should, why would Lieutenant Drummond want to see her again? He was too polite to ever say anything negative, but surely he and the other officers had discussed the possibility that bride-ship ladies were the outcasts of England, the unwanted women, the ones who hadn't been able to attract men yet.

After coming so far, would these men reject them too?

The very prospect tightened Arabella's throat. At the silence of her companions standing alongside her, she guessed they were thinking the same thing.

eight

*A*rabella paced the length of the kitchen and paused by the window. Morning light was chasing away the shadows of the previous night. The others would soon be awake, which meant her opportunity to bake was slipping away.

"Where are you, Pete?" she asked, parting the curtains to peer out.

After the caraway cake on Sunday morning, Pete had arrived both Monday and Tuesday before dawn with a basket of freshly baked bread, as well as another basket of cake ingredients. They'd made a pound cake one morning and a queen's cake the next. The recipes had been similar, requiring a great deal of whisking, so much that her arms ached today.

Though guilt for the early meetings still nagged her, she couldn't make herself say no to his visits—didn't want to say no, not when she found such satisfaction in the process of creating something so tasty and beautiful out of ordinary ingredients.

She peered past the curtains to the deserted courtyard and trash bins. She'd searched for the Indian child every morning, having set aside a portion of the evening meal hoping to give the girl something more filling than bread and cheese. But Arabella hadn't seen anyone since the morning she'd baked her first cake.

Pete said the child likely wouldn't show up again, was probably afraid of being caught snooping around Victoria when the smallpox was still raging among the tribes. The realization only made Arabella wish she'd done more when she'd had the opportunity.

She turned away from the window and resumed her pacing. Yesterday, when Pete had departed, he'd winked and said, "Don't miss me too much."

She'd only shaken her head and informed him she wouldn't, but once he'd exited, she hadn't been able to contain her smile. Even if the man was impossibly arrogant, she was growing accustomed to his teasing comments and was learning that, underneath his playfulness, he was genuinely kind.

After all, she didn't know many men—if any—who would take the time to show a simpleton like her how to bake. Already after three cakes, she was doing more of the steps independently. Perhaps soon she'd feel confident enough to try one all on her own. And even if baking cakes was beneath her, she didn't want to stop.

In fact, her desire to continue was only growing . . .

Which was why she still hadn't told Lieutenant Drummond about her cake-making activities. He'd gained permission to come calling last evening, and they'd sat together in the parlor for close to an hour, until one of the other women had needed the room to meet with a caller. The barracks had been busy with a stream of visitors, particularly with local tradesmen and laborers seeking brides from among the poor women.

As the lieutenant took his leave, he'd asked if she'd save him several dances at the upcoming wedding festivities of the first bride-ship woman to be married. To celebrate the momentous occasion, everyone in town had been invited to the wedding.

The arrangements had been made rather hastily. Then again,

the proposal had been hasty as well. From what Arabella had heard, a miner by the name of Pioneer had proposed to Sophia, one of the poor women, as she'd walked ashore, promising her two thousand pounds on the spot if she'd marry him.

Arabella and the other middle-class women had been shocked when they heard the news of Pioneer's proposal, not having disembarked yet when the event took place. When they'd discovered Sophia had agreed to marry the stranger, they were positively scandalized.

Even now, after a couple of days of letting the news settle in, Arabella couldn't imagine accepting a proposal so quickly, not without truly knowing the person. Unlike Sophia, she didn't want to rush into a relationship. She wanted—no, needed—to take her time. But even after deliberating, was it possible to ever be certain?

She paused by the door and considered throwing it open. "Peter Kelly," she murmured, "you're late."

She couldn't blame him. Over the course of the past few mornings, she'd learned he was up at night working in his bakehouse, that he and his assistants spent the greater part of the dark hours making bread and rolls so the baked goods would be warm and ready for delivery first thing every morning.

By the time he finished his work and arrived to meet with her, he was likely exhausted. Yet he never complained, nor had he yet asked her about the reading lessons. She decided he was too busy, that he'd bring it up when he was ready. But with each passing day, she knew she had to return the favor soon.

At the distant echo of the opening and closing of the front door to the Marine Barracks, Arabella's pulse hopped. It had to be Pete. As footsteps sounded in the hallway drawing toward the kitchen, she smoothed her hair back even though there wasn't a strand out of place, ran her hands down the front of her skirt, one of the plainer garments she'd worn aboard the ship that she needn't worry about soiling.

She shaped her expression into one she hoped displayed consternation. After all, he didn't need to know she'd been eager for his arrival. If he discovered any hint of anticipation, he'd misconstrue it and think she was looking forward to seeing him. And she wasn't. She merely wanted to bake another cake.

In fact, perhaps she needed to act as if she'd been busy and unconcerned about his arrival. Quickly, she spun and grabbed the dishrag from the washbasin and began wiping the closest thing her hand landed upon, a jar of pickles.

As the footsteps clomped into the kitchen, she pretended she didn't notice the tiny flutter in her stomach. "So you decided to finally make an appearance?" She tossed the words as indifferently as possible over her shoulder at the same time that she glanced at Pete, only to find it wasn't him.

Mrs. Moresby, from the welcoming committee, stood in the doorway holding several large baskets, her heavyset frame heaving up and down from the exertion of carrying them. At Arabella's greeting, the older woman's brows arched high enough to touch the brim of a gaudy hat filled with the colorful feathers of at least a dozen different birds.

Heat rushed into Arabella's face. "I beg your pardon, Mrs. Moresby. I was expecting someone else entirely."

"Apparently so." She continued toward the worktable with the baskets, and Arabella rushed to assist her, praying the woman wouldn't pry into the matter.

Mrs. Moresby set down her burdens and flexed her arms. "And just who were you expecting at such an early hour, Miss Lawrence?"

Arabella fumbled to come up with an answer. She should have known better than to hope for good manners from Mrs. Moresby.

"Clearly a man," Mrs. Moresby persisted, pulling a handkerchief out of her reticule. "Who has captured your attention so much that you're already having clandestine meetings?"

"I'm not having secret meetings," Arabella insisted, a fresh wave of mortification rushing through her. She peeled back the clean towel to find round bread loaves underneath. She pulled one out, still warm to the touch. Why was Mrs. Moresby delivering the bread this morning instead of Pete?

In the process of removing the contents of another basket, Mrs. Moresby paused. "Although you've had a number of interested men, I do recall Lieutenant Drummond paying you particular attention."

"Yes, he's been very solicitous thus far."

"I don't take the lieutenant as the kind of man who'd meet with you alone here in the kitchen before everyone else awakens." There wasn't censure in the woman's voice, only curiosity.

"Of course not. He's a gentleman in every way."

Mrs. Moresby resumed unpacking, revealing a host of staple items, including eggs, butter, fresh milk, and more. Thankfully, she was a talkative woman and launched into the details of Sophia's wedding, particularly the bridal bouquet Mrs. Moresby herself had designed.

Arabella only half listened as she assisted in emptying the basket of bread and rolls. With each one she placed on the counter, the question of Pete's whereabouts resounded louder until she could think of nothing else. When Mrs. Moresby finally took a breath, Arabella's question flew out before she could stop it. "Why didn't Mr. Kelly deliver the bread himself this morning?"

In the middle of folding a towel, Mrs. Moresby's movements came to a standstill. Her keen gaze sharpened upon Arabella. "You've been meeting with Peter."

Arabella wanted to deny it, but she guessed it wouldn't do any good, that Mrs. Moresby was too insightful. "He's been teaching me how to bake. Nothing more."

"How to bake?"

"Cakes."

Mrs. Moresby set down the half-folded towel, her brows once again arching into her hat.

Arabella deserved a scolding. She'd known from the start that meeting with Pete alone was improper, that his dog wasn't enough of a companion. But she'd made one excuse after another—telling herself the lessons were only temporary, that with a houseful of women they weren't truly alone, that Pete was only a baker and nothing inappropriate would happen between them.

Whatever the case, Arabella let her head droop with the contrition. She just prayed she hadn't overstepped the bounds so completely that Mrs. Moresby would cast her out of the Marine Barracks and make her fend for herself. Whatever would she do then?

"Is there any cake left?" Mrs. Moresby asked. "I'd like to try a piece."

Arabella's head shot up. "You would?"

"I love cake, and there's no one here in Victoria who makes a decent cake—except for Peter. But that young man can hardly keep up with his bread orders, much less provide confectionaries."

"His recipes are very tasty," Arabella admitted as she crossed to the cupboard and located the tin where she'd stored the leftover slices. She took down a plate and fork, laid out a piece, and delivered it to Mrs. Moresby.

"This is queen's cake." Arabella hesitated, not wanting to disappoint Mrs. Moresby with her creation.

"Yes, I can see the currants." Mrs. Moresby made a show of examining the cake on the plate, sniffing it, then pressing her thumb into it as if testing the softness or moisture or both. Finally, she picked up her fork, used the edge to cut a bite-sized piece, then placed the morsel into her mouth.

Arabella's muscles tensed as she watched Mrs. Moresby chew. When the woman swallowed, Arabella held her breath, waiting for the verdict. But instead of saying anything, Mrs. Morseby broke off another forkful and filled her mouth with more cake.

"Well?" After the third bite, Arabella's patience had reached its limit. "What do you think?"

Mrs. Moresby slipped another piece onto the fork. "I'd say you need to go into business with Peter making cakes."

"I do?" For the span of a heartbeat, Arabella let herself run away with the idea of baking and selling cakes. But just as rapidly, she tossed the notion aside. Her cake making was a hobby, a way to pass the time while residing at the Marine Barracks. "I couldn't," she said more adamantly.

"Sure you could," Mrs. Moresby said between bites rather than waiting to speak until her mouth was empty. The woman was uncouth. And yet there was something about her Arabella liked.

Once more, Arabella's mind spun with the possibilities. What if she took orders? What if she developed a base of paying customers? What if she could earn money? The very idea was so unimaginable that she shook her head. "I came here to get married, Mrs. Moresby, not run a confectionary."

"If it's something you love doing, then who says you can't do both?"

Could she do both? Arabella watched Mrs. Moresby finish off her last bite. Who'd ever heard of a woman running her own business? Especially a woman of her class? Once she was married, a true gentleman wouldn't want a wife who baked cakes. He'd want a graceful wife who focused on the home and raising children and was available for social gatherings and hosting parties.

After all, she'd longed for marriage and a family of her own more than anything else, especially after watching her sister get married and have a baby. Seeing the joy and contentment on Florence's face had only made Arabella want that kind of life all the more.

She supposed, in some ways, that desperation had driven her to accept Mr. Major's proposal without more of a fight.

Her thoughts returned to the day after Mr. Major's indecencies in the carriage. After a sleepless night, she'd hurried down to the dining room to speak with her father before he left for the bank.

"I'm sorry, Father," she'd said once she was situated across from him at the long dining room table.

"About what, my dear?" he replied without looking up from his newspaper as he sipped his tea.

She hesitated but then spoke the words that had been formulating all night. "I've decided I cannot go through with the plans."

Her father didn't respond, still intent upon his paper.

She waited for the servant to pour her a cup of tea and place a warm bun slathered in jam in front of her. When the servant exited the room, she forced herself to continue even though she hated the thought of disappointing her father. "I cannot marry Mr. Major."

"Whatever do you mean?" asked her father, finally glancing up. "The wedding is in less than a week."

"I realize that. But I have changed my mind."

"The decision is already made." Her father lowered the newspaper. "We've given him our commitment, and we cannot cancel the plans on your whim."

"'Tis no whim, Father. I've thought about it most thoroughly."

"Every bride and groom has second thoughts before the wedding. That is normal. The doubts will soon pass."

"Please don't make me marry him, Papa." The pet name she'd used when she was a little girl slipped out. She hadn't called him that since her stepmother had insisted on the proper address of *Father*.

"Arabella," he replied, "the marriage is the right thing for all of us."

He didn't have to tell her that Elizabeth was eager for the marriage and the connection it would bring. He didn't have to mention that this might be Arabella's last chance at finding a husband. And he most certainly didn't have to bring up the fact that their house had grown very full in recent years after her older brother had returned to live there with his wife and children.

"I understand the marriage is advantageous in many ways," she said, choosing her words carefully. "But I've realized that I cannot abide Mr. Major. He is a cruel man."

Her father sighed. "He may have a temper at times, but he will provide well for you. And that will have to be good enough."

Arabella shook her head. The previous evening with Mr. Major was all too vivid, and the bite mark on her neck she'd covered with her high collar was still painful.

Father drained the last of his tea, placed the cup on the saucer, and pushed away from the table.

"He hurt me last night." She blurted the words before she lost the courage to do so.

In the process of laying his linen napkin on the table, he halted.

She stood and pushed up her bell-shaped sleeves, revealing the blue welts on her arm where Mr. Major had squeezed her.

Her father glanced at them but then finished setting his napkin aside. "Perhaps you bumped yourself."

"And he bit me here." She hadn't planned to show her father the spot on her neck, but with trembling fingers she tugged the high collar down so the teeth marks and surrounding purple bruise were visible.

As her father shifted his gaze to her neck, she focused on the decanter and crystal goblets positioned on a silver platter on the sideboard. She couldn't bear to look at her father's face. The predicament was simply far too humiliating. Here she was a woman of twenty-five, and the only man who wanted her was not only old but also frightening.

"You're sure Mr. Major did that to you?" her father asked in a sad voice.

She nodded, smoothing the collar back up before any of the servants entered and saw the mark.

Her father was silent, and a flurry of chirping came in through the open window. The May morning was alive with the finches that made their homes among the shrubs surrounding the house.

"Very well, Arabella," he finally said, scrubbing at his beard. "I shall speak with Mr. Major and let him know we shall not proceed with the wedding."

Arabella sat back in her chair, her body sagging with relief. "Thank you, Father."

If only the relief had lasted . . . If only her father had been successful . . .

Arabella dragged her attention back to the present and tried to ignore the pain, heartache, and guilt that had plagued her for so much of the journey to Victoria. She couldn't dwell on the past. What was done was done. And now she had to move forward just as Hayward would want her to do.

She had the chance to choose from many fine men, men like Lieutenant Drummond who would hopefully cherish her and give her everything she'd ever dreamed of having. Besides, if she made a happy and successful match, then perhaps she could justify the choices she'd had to make—choices that had hurt her family.

"I think you should definitely consider your options," Mrs. Moresby said, dabbing several crumbs from her plate and licking them off her fingers. "The baking would give you a means of supporting yourself until you're married and settled in."

Supporting herself? A gentlewoman like her? Again, the notion was unthinkable. "Are we not allowed to reside here at the Marine Barracks until we're wedded?"

"We're doing the best we can to support you women, but our resources will only stretch so far. And with another bride ship coming in the near future, we'll need to make room for the new arrivals."

"I understand." Mrs. Moresby was right. The brides couldn't live off the charity and good graces of Victoria's ruling class forever. Most of the gentry had already provided for the ladies, bringing as many into their homes as they could support. Surely no one expected the remaining ladies like Arabella to take up domestic work with the poor bride-ship women, who were finding positions as housemaids and scullery maids. And yet if she couldn't stay at the Marine Barracks indefinitely, where would she go and what would she do?

"If I were you, I'd talk to Peter about partnering up to make cakes." Mrs. Moresby handed Arabella the empty cake plate. "He's a good boy, even if he did land himself in jail again."

Arabella fumbled with the plate. "Jail? Again?" Even as she kept from dropping the dish, her heart dropped to the bottom of her chest, and the delicate trust she'd begun to have in the kind baker shattered into pieces. He'd claimed to have given up his wild living and that he was now a changed man. But apparently he wasn't quite so changed as he'd led her to believe.

She swallowed the rising disappointment.

Mrs. Moresby waved a hand as if to dismiss the matter. "Don't worry. He'll be out in a day or two, and you can broach your ideas and plans to him then."

Arabella pressed her lips together to keep from saying something unpleasant, namely that if she hadn't already been opposed to forming a cake-making business with Mr. Kelly, she certainly had even less motivation now. Why would she want to partner with a criminal?

Part of her wanted to press Mrs. Moresby for more information, to discover the truth about why Pete was in jail. But did the reason even matter? Whether he was a thief, thug, or drunk, she needed to put an end to the cake lessons.

As much as she longed to continue learning how to bake, she'd known all along that she oughtn't to be doing it. Now with Pete not showing up and being thrown in jail, she had no choice but to stop.

nine

$\mathcal{P}$ete leaned his head against the iron bars and attempted to hear the conversation coming from the front room of the police headquarters. Made of brick and stone, the building was bigger and nicer than the other structures around it, most of which were hastily erected during the height of the gold rush two years ago.

The place might be fancy on the outside, but the inside was worse than a city gutter. After a long night and even longer day in the dark, unheated cell, he was beyond ready for release. His joints ached from the cold, but more than that his heart thudded anxiously.

He'd paced the length of the cell for most of the past hour since Pastor Abe had arrived. Surely if anyone could get him out, Pastor Abe would be the one.

"What's taking so long?" he grumbled under his breath, even as his stomach growled its own complaint. After going the day without food or water, he was hungry to be sure. But more than that, he needed to see Arabella and explain why he hadn't shown up that morning. She had to be wondering. At least he hoped so.

With the way all the men around town were still talking about the newly arrived women, he had to continue to act fast or he'd lose out, especially with a fine woman like Arabella. Just yesterday, Richard Henry, one of the longshoremen who worked on Griffith's Hudson's Bay Company wharf, had proposed to one of the brides and the young woman accepted.

With mounting worry, Pete had sent word for Dodge to deliver the bread and give Arabella the news of his absence, but apparently the constable at the gate hadn't allowed the boy inside the complex. Dodge had come to the lockup later and told him a lady with a fancy feather hat had taken the bread inside for him.

"They'll probably hold you till morning," said the old man, who was lying on the cell's only cot. Grizzly and jaundiced, he'd been sprawled out there since Constable Green had tossed him into jail that morning after charging him with urinating on a public street. When he'd been shoved in the cell, he was so drunk he didn't even know where he was and had promptly passed out and slept the day away.

"Pastor Abe's bailing my friends and me out," Pete said, praying it was true.

The three natives sat unmoving on the dirt floor behind him—silent and sullen. They weren't really his friends. He'd never met them before last night and guessed they'd slit his throat just as fast as anyone else's. But that hadn't stopped him from barging out of the bakehouse and defending them when a group of drunken miners had started taunting the trio, throwing stones and insisting they weren't allowed in town.

Pete had only meant to stand up for the natives and help them get away. But when several of the miners pulled out knives and lead pipes, the fight turned dangerous. Thankfully, bluejackets had arrived quickly. But it hadn't mattered that the natives had unsheathed their knives only in self-defense. And it hadn't mattered that one of the Indians had been wounded and none of the miners had.

Regardless of Pete's protest, the constables had rounded up the natives and thrown them in jail. And with six miners accusing Pete of starting the riot with the natives, the constables had locked him up too.

The door at the end of the corridor squealed on hinges that had rusted as a result of the cold, damp air in the windowless cell. Officer Green in his crisp uniform stepped through, carrying a lantern in one hand and jangling a set of keys in the other.

Pete halted in front of the cell door and gripped the bars, the incoming light revealing the filth of the jail, the rancid corner where they'd relieved themselves, the dirt floor with a few ragged blankets, and the trails of black mildew crawling up the stone walls.

"Alright, Mr. Kelly," Officer Green said brusquely. "You're being released."

"What about the natives?"

Pete didn't think the three spoke any English. During the brief times they'd talked among themselves, Pete had detected a Tsimshian dialect. The Tsimshian tribes lived on the northern part of Vancouver Island and were considered the most war-like of the coastal tribes. While it was true that the Royal Navy patrolled Beaver Harbor, where large numbers of Tsimshian lived, Pete wasn't entirely convinced that the Tsimshian were plotting hostilities as much as was reported.

He suspected the navy was looking for excuses to drive the natives away and stirring up anxiety among the people so they'd aid in the expulsion. If only he could give his friends and neighbors a glimpse of what he'd learned about the natives from Sque-is—that they weren't so different from each other in their love of family and zest for life.

Pete had tried to communicate with his prison mates in Chinook, hoping they might have information about the other northern tribes, including Sque-is's people. But they hadn't made any attempt to converse in return.

"The Indians will be escorted out of Victoria on the morrow," Officer Green said, twisting a key into the lock. "We've got a gunboat lined up to take them well away from town so that we don't have any more problems."

"They weren't the ones who started the fight," Pete explained as he already had a dozen times since the constables had arrived swinging their bats the previous night.

"Maybe so," the constable said.

His easy acquiescence silenced Pete's next words of protest. Apparently, the police officers had time to investigate and learn the truth about what had occurred. More likely Pastor Abe had rounded up unbiased witnesses and brought them down to the police headquarters.

As a missionary of the Church of England in the Fraser River Valley mining camps, Pastor Abe had earned a reputation as a man of his word. Everywhere he went, he was respected by both miners and natives alike. But no one respected Pastor Abe more than Pete, and now he owed the man again.

Officer Green finished unlocking the cell door, slid it open, then jerked Pete through before slamming the door and turning the key all in one motion, as though he expected the natives to attempt an uprising right then and there.

Before following the constable, Pete relayed the news of their release status using Chinook. He wasn't sure the men understood him until the oldest one gave a curt nod.

When Pete stepped into the office area a moment later, a glance out the front windows revealed that dusk was already settling. That meant he didn't have much time before he'd need to join Dodge and Blind Billy at the bakehouse. Although Dodge had assured him they'd managed fine without him the previous night, Pete guessed they hadn't completed all the work needing to be done.

"Pete," Pastor Abe said, moving away from a cluster of officers lounging at their desks. Abraham Merivale was a head higher than most men and had the strength of two. His muscles and body were built as solid as the lodgepole pines that covered the Canadian Rocky Mountains.

Pastor Abe offered Pete a smile, one that lit his blue eyes and reminded Pete of the clear skies that spread out above the grand peaks of the mainland. "You're looking as handsome and charming as usual." Pastor Abe extended his hand.

"Aye, at my best." Pete grinned as he shook his friend's hand, appreciating the firm, warm grip.

"As always, God's timing is perfect." Pastor Abe combed back an errant lock of his fair hair. He was in need of a haircut and shave, like the miners who came down out of the mountains and into town. But today he'd exchanged his usual wool trousers and flannel shirt for his clerical collar and suit.

Unlike some of the other Anglican missionaries, Pastor Abe looked like the men he ministered to. But that was where the similarities ended. The gentle leader stood out among the men like a candle in the dark. Though Pastor Abe couldn't have been much older than Pete's twenty-six years, the reverend had the wisdom of a man who'd lived a hundred lives—or at least that was the way it seemed to Pete.

"I wasn't planning on coming over to Victoria until later in the month," Pastor Abe continued. "I'm glad God timed it so I was here today and could help you."

"I'm obliged." Pete's previous stay in jail had lasted several days, another incident where he'd gotten caught up in trying to mediate a brawl. This time, he didn't have that kind of time to waste, not with the race to win a bride in full swing.

As they stepped out of the headquarters onto the plank sidewalk, the last light of the evening brushed the tips of the pine on the western edge of the bay, turning the evergreen a shade of gold. Did he still have time to pay Arabella a visit this eve?

Pastor Abe glanced around as though to gauge who might

be listening. "I see the citizens of Victoria are still evicting the natives."

The street was strangely empty at the hour of night when men were finishing their work and heading in and out of the taverns. Pete caught the strains of music in the air. Was an orchestra playing?

"Most folks are afraid the natives will bring the smallpox back to Victoria," Pete said, bringing his focus back to his friend. "The fear is valid, but rather than offering vaccinations to those who come to town, they kick them out again."

"Kick them out to their deaths," Pastor Abe whispered sadly, his eyes haunted.

The last time Pete had seen Pastor Abe during the summer, the reverend had described the devastation he'd witnessed in camp after deserted native camp—doors left open, belongings scattered on the floors of the lodges, rotting bodies left unburied. Those who weren't immediately infected were leaving their homes behind in an attempt to escape death but were unknowingly taking the disease with them and spreading it further.

"I'm meeting with the commissioner and police superintendent tomorrow," Pastor Abe confided. "I've spoken with Reverend Garrett, and he wants to allow the natives to return to the Northerner's Encampment. If he can get more smallpox vaccine, perhaps they can make the vaccination mandatory for those who want to resume trading in Victoria."

Pete nodded in appreciation of Pastor Abe's initiative. He was already a busy man with his ministry to the miners—a much-needed ministry that had certainly changed the course of Pete's life. But since the smallpox outbreak, Pastor Abe, along with other missionaries, had been doing whatever they could to alleviate the spread of the disease.

Like Arabella, Pastor Abe was one of the few Pete could speak to about the natives. They conversed for several more minutes before Pastor Abe started to take his leave. "Pioneer asked me to officiate his wedding today. It was a beautiful ceremony, and now I need to make an appearance at the dance before heading out."

The wedding and dance? That was today? Pete's pulse sputtered. No wonder the street was so deserted. Everyone in town was at the dance—including Arabella and a hundred other men attempting to win her.

"I'm surprised Pioneer beat you to the altar," Pastor Abe said, his eyes twinkling. "I thought for sure you'd be the first to snatch up a bride."

"I'm working on it." Pete scratched his head and prayed he didn't have lice after a night in jail. "You can count on me to be the second to marry."

"Is that so?" Pastor Abe's smile matched the merriment in his eyes. "Does that mean one of the brides has already captured your attention?"

"Aye," Pete replied with a grin. "Only the prettiest of them all."

"Of course."

"Had her about ready to drag me to the altar before I landed in there." He nodded at the police headquarters building.

"But now? Are you worried she won't have you?"

"Oh, she'll have me," Pete said, wishing his jests were true. "I just need to do a little more convincing. That's all."

Pastor Abe laughed. Then he clamped Pete on the shoulder. "God sure did give you a good dose of confidence, Pete."

"If you need some, I can lend you a little. Then mayhap you can do some dragging to the altar yourself."

Pastor Abe shook his head, a little too adamantly. "Not here, and not with the kind of life I lead."

"Someone wise once told me that God said it wasn't good for man to live alone." He quirked a brow at the reverend.

Pastor Abe chuckled again. "I wouldn't want to subject a

woman to the harshness of life up in the mountains. I'll wait until I return to England."

Pete knew all about the harshness. And the depravity. Pastor Abe was right. Life in the mining camps was no place for a godly woman.

With another handclasp and a good-bye, Pete hurried to his apartment above the bakehouse for a change of clothing— his only suit—then went directly to the bathhouse. After a thorough scrub to erase the grime of jail, he opted to forgo a shave. The growing darkness meant he'd need to begin his night's work soon. But he aimed to have at least one dance with Arabella.

He practically sprinted to the Swan Hotel to find it was so full that people were dancing outside on the sidewalk and street to the strains of music coming from the open windows—the orchestra music he'd heard earlier.

Unable to calm the anxious thud of his heart, he forced his way inside and pushed to the line of onlookers who were waiting for the chance to join in the quadrilles and minuets on the crowded floor. The air was stale with a mixture of perfume and brandy and body odor. Yet the atmosphere was merry, the town certainly appreciating the chance to come together to celebrate the success of the bride-ship endeavor.

Every woman had at least a dozen men competing for her attention. But among the flurry of dancers, he saw none with Arabella's stunning red hair. And among the officers present, he didn't see Drummond.

Pete's chest tightened with the need to find her and make sure she wasn't with the lieutenant. He couldn't allow her to spend time with the man and develop feelings for him. If she did, Pete's job of winning her would be more complicated. Not impossible, but certainly more difficult.

With a new urgency prodding him, he wound through crowds until he was back outside. He searched among the couples until finally one young marine informed him that he'd seen Lieutenant Drummond leave the dance with a young woman a short while ago.

From the direction the marine had seen the couple walking, Pete guessed they'd decided to return to the Marine Barracks. He'd just turned the corner and started down the path leading to the government complex when he caught sight of them entering through the front gate. He sprinted and started to call Arabella's name but stopped short when the constable closed the gate.

Pete veered away from the main entrance, knowing the constable wouldn't allow him inside the complex, not at the late hour and not without an excuse—namely the bread delivery. Instead, he rounded to the west end, where the native girl had climbed over the fence. It was the darkest spot, the best place to sneak in without his being seen.

By the time he slipped to the ground, his admiration of the native girl had grown tenfold. The climb hadn't been easy. A glance around told him he was alone, that the government complex was as deserted as the rest of Victoria. Even so, he kept to the shadows, crept to the kitchen door, and entered without a sound.

Voices came from the front hallway, and he guessed the lieutenant was trying to convince Arabella to allow him to visit with her for a while. The image of Drummond sitting with her alone in the parlor brought back the desperation and helplessness he'd experienced in the lockup earlier. He had to stop the lieutenant and do it now.

Combing his damp hair into place with his fingers, he made his way through the darkened kitchen, pushed open the door, and entered the hallway. "There you are," he said, locking in on Arabella. She was magnificent, wearing a fancy gown that was worthy of the queen. Suddenly he felt like a lowly servant in the presence of royalty.

He pushed aside his hesitation. "I've been waiting for you." He said the first thing that came to mind. "So that we could start our next cake lesson."

The lieutenant and Arabella spun to stare at him, their expressions confused, clearly not knowing what to make of his unexpected appearance. In a sharp naval uniform, the lieutenant looked as though he belonged next to Arabella, and Pete's best suit seemed shabby by comparison.

Even so, he continued down the hallway, intending to pick her up and carry her away from Drummond if need be. "Thank you for escorting her back to the house for me. I appreciate it."

The lieutenant's surprise rapidly faded into irritation. "Cake lesson?"

"Aye," Pete said, ignoring the quick shake of Arabella's head and the flash in her eyes that warned him she didn't want him to say anything about their early morning meetings. Mayhap she didn't want anyone to know about their cake-making lessons. But he'd never intended for their time together to be a secret. In fact, he most definitely wanted Drummond to know every detail.

"I've been coming every morning to teach Arabella how to bake. Very early. Before everyone is awake." Pete lobbed the words like cannonballs at the lieutenant and waited for his reaction, watching his face expectantly, hoping the man would explode. "If you haven't yet tried one of her cakes, you really need to."

For a moment, Drummond didn't speak. The only sign he'd been impacted by the intended bombardment was the darkening of his eyes and the twitch of his mustache.

"'Tis a way to pass the time," Arabella rushed to say, filling the awkward silence. "I'm certainly not very good at it."

"Don't say that," Pete responded. "You're a natural."

She shook her head in protest, her eyes pleading with him to stop speaking.

"You're learning very quickly," he continued, fighting against a feeling that he wasn't good enough, that his past sins and lifestyle made him unworthy, that she was simply out of his reach. "How could you expect anything less since you have such an excellent teacher?" His grin followed his jest in an attempt to lighten the tension of the moment, but somehow his words fell flat as he noticed the embarrassment in the stiff way she held herself.

Was she embarrassed about the cake making or about anyone knowing she was spending time with him? Or both?

He assumed she'd begun to put aside her reticence. The past couple of mornings she'd seemed eager—almost excited—to bake. The coolness and rebuff from the end of their first lesson had been gone, the friendliness back in place. He'd believed she had enjoyed their time together and their conversations as much as he had.

"Mr. Kelly," Drummond interjected in a voice edged with steel. "Such meetings with Miss Lawrence are highly inappropriate. I insist you cease imposing upon her, or I shall take measures to ensure you do."

Did Arabella feel he was *imposing*? He hadn't gotten that impression when they'd been together. He tried to catch her gaze again, hoping she'd defend him and explain to the lieutenant she welcomed the instruction. But she stared at the rug that ran the length of the hallway and refused to look at him.

Aye, she was ashamed of him. And even though he'd known from the moment he met her that they were of different classes, he hadn't taken her for a proud, shallow woman, the kind who'd see herself as better and look down on him as a result. Underneath all the layers of social niceties she used as a defense, he'd sensed her to be a strong and capable woman who wasn't easily swayed by her peers.

Apparently he'd been wrong.

Would she have danced with him tonight if he'd approached her? Or would she have turned away and refused to acknowledge him just as she was doing now?

"Don't fret, Lieutenant," Pete said, hurt twisting inside and giving way to the need to expose their relationship. "Arabella's agreed to teach me to read in exchange for the baking lessons."

He watched her, and this time when she glanced at him, her eyes flickered with guilt.

"You leave me no choice but to speak with the welcoming committee." Drummond's voice contained a sharp edge, which told Pete his words had the desired effect of rankling the officer. "I'm sure they'll agree with me that your visits are highly inappropriate and will henceforth take steps to ban you from the premises."

At the lieutenant's threat, Arabella's gaze jumped up. "Lieutenant Drummond, such measures are surely not necessary—"

"Do not worry yourself over the matter, my dear Miss Lawrence." Drummond took her hand and held it as if she were a breakable piece of porcelain. "As Mr. Kelly has already proven himself to be a troublemaker, we shall simply ensure he's not able to cause any more nuisance here than is necessary."

The lieutenant's words fired rapidly at Pete, and he scrambled to find a way to deflect the artillery round. The lieutenant certainly knew how to wage a battle. Pete could give him credit for that.

Even so, Pete wasn't about to let the man outsmart him. "Sometimes stirring up a little trouble is a good thing, Lieutenant, especially when the pot is full of cra—" At Arabella's widening eyes, Pete forced out more polite terminology—"full of garbage and in need of a cleaning."

The lieutenant stiffened, clearly taking Pete's words as the insult he'd intended. "Perhaps one night in jail wasn't long enough to tame your rebellious nature, Mr. Kelly."

"Aye, you're finally right about something. I'm not tamable. Except, of course, by the good Lord himself."

Pete wasn't afraid to meet Drummond's gaze directly. He'd never been the type of man who doffed his hat and bowed to gentlemen, and he didn't plan to start now.

"I'm sure Miss Lawrence is quite relieved to learn of your untamable and criminal nature before you're able to do damage to her reputation. Isn't that right, Miss Lawrence?"

With the attention fixed upon her, Arabella kept her sights on the floor. "If you will both excuse me, I must retire for the evening."

Pete knew he should protest her going, but her rejection and easy dismissal stung too much. Did she think he was a criminal? Had she already judged him without letting him say his piece? After getting to know him this past week, surely she had some faith in him and wouldn't dismiss him so easily.

She lifted her dainty chin and stepped away, emphasizing her desire for them to take their leave.

"Time for you to exit the premises, Mr. Kelly." Drummond pointed toward the door.

Pete waved a hand at the door in return. "Only after you."

Drummond glanced at Arabella and hesitated. "Very well." He started to move away from her, but then reached for her hand, lifted it to his lips, and pressed an impassioned kiss against her knuckles.

Though she quickly pulled her hand away, Pete couldn't contain the frustration mingling with his hurt. Drummond was the kind of man Arabella had come to Victoria intending to marry—the son of English aristocrats or a wealthy merchant family sent to the colony to do his duty to queen and country. She hadn't come seeking a lowly baker like him, especially a baker who ended up in jail.

Pete set his shoulders, knowing he needed to walk away and never come back.

Drummond straightened his hat and started toward the door, and Pete followed, but not before her gaze flicked to him and he glimpsed remorse within the beautiful green depths.

At the sight, sadness filled him too—sadness for what might have been but now would likely never be.

ten

"I hope you understand," her father said. "Arabella is still such a young woman and isn't ready for the match." From outside her father's study, Arabella remained motionless, leaning near the slightly open door. The waft of cigar smoke tickled her nose, making her want to sneeze, but she held in her breath to keep from uttering a sound.

Mr. Major hadn't yet responded to Father's suggestion to put off the wedding indefinitely, and his eerie calm made her heart race faster.

From the moment Mr. Major had arrived to the small dinner party Arabella had arranged, he'd been pleasant, bestowing upon her another gift of exquisite jewelry. Never once had he hinted at the carriage ride home earlier in the week and what had transpired between them. His every behavior toward her was respectable, his smiles genuinely gracious, and his manners impeccable.

If she didn't have the vicious red teeth marks on her neck or the bruises on her arms, she might have begun to wonder if she'd only imagined the unpleasant incident. Whatever the case, her father had agreed to speak with Mr. Major after the other guests departed.

And now that Father had explained her wish to call off the wedding, she couldn't keep from second-guessing herself. Was she losing her chance at marriage over a misunderstanding? What if Mr. Major had been right, that she'd enticed him and led him to believe she'd welcome his affection?

"Am I to assume that Arabella spoke to you of our quarrel?" Mr. Major finally said, his voice low and tight.

Her father cleared his throat. "She made brief mention of it."

"After having two wives yourself, I'm sure you are well aware that quarrels are bound to happen from time to time. You wouldn't suggest separation from your wife at the first quarrel, would you?"

"Of course not—"

"Then how can you support your daughter's whim to do likewise?"

"I had not thought of the situation like that."

"You apparently had not thought at all, otherwise we wouldn't be having this conversation." Mr. Major's voice rose with irritation. "I must say I'm rather surprised you would allow your daughter to have so much sway over you. I took you for a much stronger and wiser father and employee."

"I'm sorry, sir—"

"I most certainly cannot have weak and ignorant employees running my bank, Mr. Lawrence. That simply would not make for good business practice."

"Of course not, sir." At the desperation in her father's voice, a sickening lump formed in Arabella's stomach. Was Mr. Major threatening to fire Father from his job?

"And I certainly wouldn't be able to recommend such an employee to any other company in and around London," Mr. Major continued. "In fact, I would need to make sure everyone knew that to hire such an employee would most certainly be bad for their business as well."

Arabella pressed her hand against her stomach to ward off

the rising nausea. Mr. Major would not only fire Father but would turn everyone against him.

"I think it's in your best interest to take control of your daughter, don't you, Mr. Lawrence?" Mr. Major's tone now sounded like a kind father chastising a wayward child.

"You may be right. I shall talk some sense into her." With her father's employment at stake and subsequently her family's well-being, she had no choice but to move forward with the wedding. If she had to risk her own happiness and comfort for the sake of her family, she'd do it.

Nevertheless, her father's easy acquiescence sliced into Arabella. Surely he would defend her honor, would at the very least make some effort to confront Mr. Major regarding the bruises.

Quietness settled over the study, and more cigar smoke wafted out the door into the dark hallway.

"Very well, Mr. Lawrence," Mr. Major finally said. "I trust you will exert your influence over your daughter so that the wedding may proceed according to schedule."

"Yes, rest assured, I shall do so."

With a strangled cry, Arabella sat up. Her heart pounding and breath coming in gasps, she struggled to see past the darkness that surrounded her. Where was she?

She pressed a hand into the flimsy mattress beneath her. Her bunk. At the Marine Barracks. She drew in a gulp of air and wiped at the tears on her cheeks.

She'd had another nightmare. That was all. Except it was the third night in a row. Like all the other times, the dream was much too vivid, the pain so fresh, the heartache desperately real.

Sitting on the edge of her bed, she linked her shaking fingers together. When would she finally be able to forget her past?

If only she hadn't gone to the wedding celebration . . .

Her thoughts returned to the dance earlier in the week at the hotel following Sophia and Pioneer's wedding. She'd been enjoying herself, had danced with at least half a dozen men, including Lieutenant Drummond. In fact, she'd been dancing for a second time with the lieutenant when she'd seen him—Mr. Major's most trusted servant, his butler Pym Nevins.

At least she thought she'd glimpsed his short rotund form through the crowd, along with his ever-present red bow tie. Just like the afternoon of the croquet game, she'd known her fears were irrational, that Pym Nevins wouldn't come for her again. Nevertheless, she'd been filled with such dread that she'd raced to a corner to hide. When Lieutenant Drummond followed her, she hadn't been able to come up with any other explanation for her strange behavior other than that she was tired and ready to return to the Marine Barracks.

"You're worrying again over nothing," she whispered into the quiet of the bedroom. Through the darkness she let her fingers skim under her pillow until she found the cross. As she closed her hand around the simple artifact, she whispered a prayer for courage. Would she always be haunted by the choice she'd made to run away? Not only haunted by all that had happened with Mr. Major but also by the devastation she'd brought upon her family?

The cross and her prayers usually brought her comfort, but as she touched each smooth beam, her thoughts strayed back to the encounter with Pete in the hallway after the dance and the hurt in his eyes when she'd dismissed him.

Over the past few days, she'd learned more details from Mrs. Moresby regarding his arrest—that he'd been thrown in jail for defending several natives in a brawl. Some part of her was relieved to know he hadn't fallen back into the rebellious ways of his past. And that same small part suspected he was still trustworthy.

Whatever the case, she hadn't seen him since the night in the hallway with the lieutenant. The last few mornings, his assistant, a boy named Dodge, had delivered the donations of bread. He'd informed her that some hoity-toity lieutenant had gotten Pete banned from coming inside the government complex. She suspected that even if Pete had still been allowed to visit, he wouldn't have come. Not after the way she'd behaved.

She expelled a sigh. She'd seen the hurt in his eyes when she made light of their cake making and time together, as if it hadn't meant anything to her.

The truth was, it had meant a great deal. She missed his coming, missed his instructions, missed the easy way they could talk and interact. Whenever she was with him, her stepmother's voice in her head was silent. She wasn't worrying about whether she was speaking and acting appropriately. She could simply be herself, the same way she'd been able to around Hayward.

In spite of shunning him, he'd still sent an extra basket of ingredients each morning so that she could continue to practice making cakes. But making the cakes hadn't been the same without him. Or perhaps the weight of her guilt had taken the joy from the process. Regardless, her desire to apologize only grew with each passing day.

She caressed the cross one last time before tucking it back under her pillow for safekeeping until it was time to arise and start the day. A glance to the window and the low bright moon told her there were still several hours until dawn. She ought to try to slumber a little longer, except she didn't feel in the least bit sleepy—not after her nightmare.

She arose from her bed on the bottom bunk and tiptoed to the window, careful to remain soundless so she wouldn't awaken the other ladies. On a clear night, she could see the bay to the west. Pressing her forehead against the cold pane, she peered over the other government buildings to the harbor where the moon poured down soft amber light over the many small boats at rest.

As one of the northernmost and remotest parts of the British Empire, she'd known the land would be rugged and dangerous and wild. But the beauty of her new home had far exceeded her expectations—the distant mountain peaks, the thick evergreens and jagged rock formations along the coasts, the variety of birds that flew over the bay. It was all breathtaking.

A movement in the yard drew her attention—a movement near the garbage bins at the west end of the complex. She squinted through the darkness. Had the native girl returned? Perhaps the child had been coming well before dawn to search the trash, hoping to avoid Arabella and any other early risers. Was that why Arabella hadn't seen her again?

The shadows mostly concealed the remote area, but at another movement and the outline of a girlish form, Arabella stepped away from the window. Even if the girl was afraid of her, compassion welled within Arabella along with the need to do something, especially because she understood the pain of losing everyone she loved, of being alone in the world, of having to make her own way.

She tugged one of her everyday dresses over her nightgown, slipped into her shoes, and hurried down to the kitchen. After rapidly gathering the leftover food items, she exited through the back kitchen door as silently as possible and made her way across the dark yard.

Her footfalls must have been stealthy because she crossed most of the yard before the girl looked her direction from where she was kneeling on the ground.

Arabella halted and held out the bundle to show she meant no harm. "I have food for you again."

The child trembled but otherwise remained motionless.

Arabella dared to take another step. Then another.

With a whispered word Arabella didn't understand, the girl rose, backed away, but then swayed and would have crumpled if she hadn't grabbed on to the side of the garbage bin.

Was she weak with hunger?

"I want to help you." In the darkness, Arabella couldn't see the girl's face clearly, but her body shook so that her spindly legs finally buckled, forcing her to the ground.

Arabella used the moment of weakness to span the distance. At her approach, the girl curled into a ball and cowered as though she expected a beating.

"I won't hurt you." Arabella placed the food next to the child and then crouched low. She waited, hoping the girl would trust her or at the very least stop fearing her.

Then, before she lost courage, she touched the girl who was hardly more than a pile of rags and bones. The child started to scramble away, but not before Arabella felt the heat radiating from her body.

The child was on fire with a fever.

"Wait," Arabella said softly, but the child was clawing at the fence, attempting to hoist herself up. Within seconds, she fell to the ground and lay unmoving, clearly too weak and sick to master the feat.

Arabella hesitated. What should she do? She didn't want to chance frightening the girl again, yet the child was in need of more than just food. Ought she to fetch the doctor?

She glanced to the dark night sky, to the endless array of stars that signaled morning was still hours away. It was too early to disturb the doctor. Besides, with the current attitude of unfriendliness toward the natives, would the town physician even agree to treat this child? What if he turned her away, deciding she wasn't worth the time or effort?

Of course, Lord Colville, the ship's surgeon from the *Tynemouth*, was still in Victoria, and he'd proven himself kind to those less fortunate than himself. Nevertheless, Arabella didn't know where he was living.

Arabella touched the girl's back again. This time the child didn't move except for the rise and fall of her chest. Apparently, she'd lost consciousness.

Indecision warred within Arabella. Did she dare move her

inside the Marine Barracks? But what if she had smallpox and spread it to the women?

There must be someplace she could take the girl for help.

The kind face and empathetic eyes of Peter Kelly took up residence in her mind. If anyone would aid this poor sick child, Pete surely would. And if he couldn't assist, he would know of someone who could.

eleven

With a burst of determination, Arabella scooped the child into her arms, expecting to struggle under the weight, and was surprised instead at how light she was. The girl didn't protest, not even when her eyes fluttered open for a moment. Instead, she lay listlessly, having no fight left in her frail body.

Arabella carried the child out of the complex, grateful a guard wasn't posted at night. She was horrified to feel each curve of the child's spine and ribs through her thin leather tunic. And she was equally horrified by the filth and stench. She'd never beheld an animal as neglected, much less a child.

In the dark, she made her way down the deserted streets and only had to duck out of sight into an alley once as several men exited a tavern. Thankfully, they went the opposite direction, and she was soon on her way, trying to remember how to get to the bakery, which hadn't been far from the grand hotel used for Sophia and Pioneer's wedding.

Finally turning onto Humboldt Street, she aimed for the light glowing from the ground-level windows of a simple two-story structure. It was halfway down the block amidst other businesses that were dark for the night.

Arms aching and chest heaving, she paused in front of the bakehouse door, the roasted malty aroma of bread heavy in the air and assuring her she'd reached the right place. From what Pete had told her about baking bread, he and his assistants were still hard at work, and she'd likely be interrupting their routine. Should she turn away and seek the doctor instead?

The native girl gave a low moan and started to stir. What if she awoke and attempted to get away again?

Feeling a new sense of urgency, Arabella hefted the child higher on her hip. With the girl's head situated against her shoulder, Arabella managed to let go and knock.

Seconds passed with no answer, except for a flurry of barking. Was that Jennie?

At a strange bellow down the street, Arabella stepped closer to the door and this time pounded her fist against it.

The door swung open, revealing the boy who'd delivered bread to the Marine Barracks the past few mornings. His hat was absent from his head, revealing messy locks of blond hair tied back with a leather strip. His thin face had a smudge of flour across one cheek, and his hands were coated in a sticky layer of dough. As he took her in, his mouth dropped open.

Jennie stood next to the boy, her nose lifted high, her ears perked, and her tail wagging in a friendly greeting.

"Who is it?" came an older, rusty voice from inside.

Arabella was suddenly conscious of how frightful she must look. She'd been in such a hurry that she neglected her appearance entirely. Her gown was only half buttoned, and she hadn't bothered to brush, much less style, her hair.

"Probably the constable," the rusty voice grumbled. "Again."

As the native child moved restlessly, Arabella decided this wasn't the time to worry about niceties and proper conduct. She had to do something for the child, now, before it was too late. "May I speak with Pete—Mr. Kelly—please?"

The boy nodded but made no effort to go after his master.

"A woman?" said the older voice with a note of derision. "Don't tell me the master's got one of those brides chasing after him. If so, give me the gun so I can shoot myself now."

Arabella didn't know quite how to respond to so brash a statement. On the one hand, she wanted to insist she wasn't interested in Pete—at least in the way the man had assumed. But on the other hand, his vulgar comment didn't deserve a dignified answer. She'd do best to ignore it and get straight to the point of her visit.

"Where is Pete?" She stepped around the boy into the bakehouse. The heat from several brick ovens set into the wall radiated in the workroom, which was much smaller than she'd imagined. The place was crowded with a worktable, two troughs, baskets filled with freshly baked quartern loaves, and an assortment of utensils she couldn't begin to name.

What would Pete think of her coming to him for help after the way she'd treated him the other night? Maybe he wouldn't want to see her. Yet she could think of no one else who would care the way he did. "I need his assistance with this poor sick child."

Before the words were out of her mouth, a rear door opened and Pete ducked through carrying a sack of flour that was almost as thick and tall as his own body. His eyes snagged on her and he stopped short, dropping the flour to the wood floor with a thump that reverberated between the walls.

"Arabella?" His voice rang with a note of worry that warmed her heart. As his gaze swept over her and the native girl, his brow furrowed.

He reached for a garment on a peg next to the door and began to tug it over his head. Only then did Arabella realize he was donning a shirt. He was partially concealed by the dark shadows of the room, but even so, she glimpsed his bare chest.

The sight was so shocking, Arabella couldn't look away. Only when he finished yanking the material down did she rapidly jerk her attention to Jennie. "I found the child by the garbage containers. She's feverish and weak."

Removing his apron, Pete wound through the maze of baking equipment toward her, passing by a trough and stoop-shouldered man with a headful of thick white hair that rose in wavy puffs. The older man was elbow-deep in the trough and appeared to be mixing the sticky dough with his hands.

"She was frightened and tried to get away," Arabella continued, trying to make her burning muscles cooperate with holding the girl. "But then she fell to the ground unconscious."

Pete had every right to turn up his nose at her and tell her he couldn't be bothered. But upon reaching her, he lifted the little girl from her arms and relieved her of the burden.

"She's very hot," he said, cradling her gently.

By the light of the oil lantern hanging above the work area, Arabella was able to see the girl's face clearly for the first time. While covered in pockmarks and emaciated, her features were delicate and her skin a beautiful brown. "Do you have any idea what might be wrong with her?"

Pete examined the child. "From her scars, it looks like she's already had smallpox. But just in case she's still contagious, I want you to get vaccinated first thing in the morning."

"I've already been vaccinated. My stepmother's first husband died of smallpox, and she was deathly afraid of it as a result and so insisted that everyone in our household get the vaccination."

The furrow in Pete's brow relaxed. "Good. Then we need to attempt to get her fever down."

Pete retreated the way he'd come in, and Arabella followed him, relieved he'd used the word *we* and that she wasn't alone anymore in trying to figure out what to do.

Once outside, she hastened after Pete to a set of wooden stairs that led to the second floor of the building. Upon reaching the top, he hardly paused at the small landing before throwing open the door and barging inside with Jennie on his heels.

Arabella paused at the door, uncertain whether to continue.

Pete's footsteps thudded across a wood floor. After a thump and clatter and then the distinct strike of a match, the glow of lantern light illuminated the room.

"Pardon the mess," he said as he stepped over a pair of shoes before kicking trousers and underdrawers to a more obscure place along the wall.

Arabella tried not to be mortified at the sight of the unmentionables.

"I wasn't expecting such a lovely visitor tonight." His voice, as usual, held a hint of teasing.

She hesitated. He was being much too gracious to her. She didn't deserve his kindness or his jesting, not after the way she'd spurned him the other night.

While waiting in the doorway, she took in the table only big enough for two chairs, a cookstove along one wall, and a sideboard against the other. The other half of the room contained a sofa, rocking chair, a worn wing-back chair, and a pedestal table holding the glowing lantern. Jennie trotted to a worn rug in front of the chairs, walked in a circle, then lay down and stared at Arabella with her head resting on her outstretched front legs.

Aside from the garments discarded on the floor, the place was tidy and cozy. Though the walls lacked paper, they'd been painted a cheerful yellow and decorated with a framed painting of a mountainous landscape.

This was obviously Pete's private residence. If she feared she would taint her reputation by socializing with him alone in the kitchen of the Marine Barracks, she'd bring herself to utter ruin if anyone discovered she was in his home.

He'd entered into a second room—which she assumed was his bedroom—and her pulse lurched with the need to stop him. "Is there anywhere else we can take her?" she called after him.

"No," came his muffled reply. "Other than the storage building that Blind Billy and Dodge call home."

Arabella couldn't make herself move. She was being too cautious and prudent, and this was most certainly not the time for it, not when someone's life was in danger. "You'll be just fine, Arabella," she whispered to herself while forcing her feet forward. No one would discover she'd been in Pete's apartment, and if anyone did, she'd have a very good excuse for being here.

Even so, she halted at the bedroom doorway. A double bed in a metal frame took up the majority of the space, along with a chest of drawers.

Pete had placed the girl upon the bed, which was unmade, the sheets and coverlet a tangled mess at the footboard. For an instant she pictured Pete sprawled across the mattress in slumber, the sheets shoved aside. The moment the image flashed in her mind, a strange heat pooled in her belly, heat that spread rapidly to her face.

Why was she thinking such indecent thoughts?

Pete brushed a hand across the child's forehead tenderly, and Arabella made herself focus instead on his kindness and gentleness toward the ailing girl. Even though she was so frail and sick, an outcast, and unwanted by everyone else, Pete handled her as if she were a rare gemstone.

The guilt from the past few days swelled. How mistaken she'd been to put so much emphasis on titles and trades. No matter his status or background, Pete was an honorable man. Maybe she'd thought he wasn't good enough for her, but she'd been wrong. She didn't deserve a friend like him.

As he straightened, urgency emanated from his tense posture. "There's water in the pot on the stove. Heat it for willow-bark tea while I go fetch more water."

By the time the tea was ready, Pete was already at work bathing the girl's face with cool cloths. She'd awoken, and thanks to Pete's steady assurances in a language Arabella couldn't understand, the girl didn't move, except to widen her eyes upon Arabella, revealing fear in their depths.

"Her name is Haiel-Wat," Pete said from the opposite side of the bed. "Means thunder."

The frail child was more like a faint rattle of a breeze than thunder. It took some time, but thankfully Pete coaxed her into drinking the tea. When finished, she fell against the pillow and lapsed into sleep or unconsciousness, Arabella couldn't determine which.

"Should we fetch the doctor?" she whispered.

Pete hesitated. "Perhaps the ship's surgeon, Lord Colville? He's assisting at the hospital, and I've heard he's kind to the natives and doesn't turn them away."

"He was very kind to me whenever I was ill during our journey." At one point, she'd been so seasick she'd become faint and weak. Lord Colville and the captain had given her a room amidships, where the motion of the ship was gentler. Their thoughtfulness had likely saved her life. She'd spent several weeks there, adjusting to the ship's rocking back and forth while Mercy Wilkins nursed her back to health.

Although their chaperones for the voyage had forbidden the women from interacting with any of the men, including Lord Colville, somehow Mercy had ended up earning the wealthy aristocrat's affection.

None of the women, Arabella included, had expected the blossoming feelings to go anywhere. Even if Mercy was a beautiful and compassionate woman, she was unskilled and uneducated, from London's poorest slums, and had absolutely no hope of fitting into Lord Colville's life.

They'd all been shocked to hear the news earlier in the week that Lord Colville and Mercy were engaged to be married. Arabella was still trying to grasp how such a marriage arrangement would work, especially since the two were from such starkly different worlds.

Whatever the case, Lord Colville was still in Victoria. Would he help this child?

"I'll seek him out this morning." Pete glanced at the lightening sky out the window that overlooked the backyard of the bakehouse. "In the meantime, we'll do what we can for her."

"I shall cool her," Arabella offered. "I know you need to return to your duties."

He didn't disagree, even though she'd half expected him to make some excuse to linger. Instead, he stood and plunged his fingers through his dark brown hair, leaving it unruly and sticking up in some places. He stared down at the child's unmoving form, his brow creased, his eyes more serious than she'd ever seen them.

"We'll keep her here for the time being," he said. "But it would be best if no one else knows of her presence, especially since she's sick."

Arabella nodded and dipped the cloth into the basin of cold water. "Rest assured I shall make no mention of it to anyone. I should not like to see her sent away like the men you tried to help earlier in the week."

One of his brows quirked.

She rose from her perch on the edge of the bed. Now was as good a time as any to make her amends, wasn't it? "I owe you an apology."

He didn't refute her or tell her not to trouble herself as a more polite man might have done. Instead, he watched her as though waiting for her to continue.

"You have been nothing but kind to me since my arrival. Yet the night of the dance, I repaid you with rudeness. I regret now that I did not defend you to the lieutenant as I should have." The words tumbled out in an honest confession. She'd expected that such forthrightness would be embarrassing, but instead her heart felt lighter, as if a burden had been lifted. "I am heartily sorry," she continued, the words coming easier now. "Will you forgive me?"

His gaze softened upon her. "Aye. That I will."

"Thank you."

He nodded, and she couldn't keep from noticing how in the soft lamplight the blue of his eyes resembled the evening sky at sunset. The color was mesmerizing, even beautiful. Devoid of humor, his expression took on a rugged edge, one that hinted of a toughness and danger that still lingered from his past, one that made him attractive. Had there not been a shortage of women in the colony, he surely would have had his pick of the best.

Flustered at the runaway direction of her thoughts, she sat back down on the bed and busied herself with wringing excess water from the rag.

He moved to leave.

"Thank you also for the cake supplies every morning," she added, her words bringing him to a halt once more near the door.

"You're welcome."

"You were generous to me when you had no reason to be."

Again he didn't rebut her or try to make her feel better about her transgressions.

She focused on the rag and squeezed it even though she'd already drained it nearly dry. "And thank you for being willing to help with Haiel-Wat. I didn't know who else to turn to."

He didn't say anything for a moment, and she sensed him watching her as she pressed the cool rag to Haiel-Wat's forehead.

"Arabella," he finally said, softly.

The tenderness in the way he spoke her name drew her attention. When he offered her a smile, it was guileless and full of genuine warmth. "I'm glad you brought her here. You did the right thing."

His words were like a soothing balm covering over the voices inside always taunting she'd never be good enough. He'd accepted her in spite of her mistakes. He approved of what she'd done. And he believed she was capable.

If he believed in her, was it time to start believing in herself? Somehow his confidence in her made her want to do more and be better. But how?

"You need to go," she said, removing the cloth from Haiel-Wat and plunging it into the basin.

"You'll need to be getting back soon too," he replied, "before anyone realizes you've been away."

She paused, leaving the cloth in the cold water. She hadn't considered the repercussions of her actions. What would the other ladies think if they discovered she'd been gone, particularly if she returned to the complex looking so disheveled? How could she explain what she'd been doing? If word of her nighttime exploit reached the welcoming committee, she'd most definitely ruin her good name.

Even so, she hesitated at the edge of the bed. If she was to start believing in herself, didn't she first have to stop worrying so much about what other people thought of her? "I want to keep working on bringing Haiel-Wat's fever down."

"I'll check on her as often as I can."

"What if she awakens and attempts to run away?"

"If she gets out of bed, I'll be in the room right below and will hear her moving around."

Arabella examined the child's face, now restful but still filthy and scarred. She wanted to give Haiel-Wat a bath, and if she could find new clothing for her, she'd throw away the rags the girl was wearing.

"Mayhap you can make an excuse to leave the barracks later," he suggested. "And you can return then to take care of her for a little while this morning."

"I didn't bring her here to burden you. You already have enough to do."

"She's not a burden."

Arabella wrung out the cloth again and laid it gently across Haiel-Wat's forehead. Then with a sigh, she rose. "I shall return just as soon as I'm able."

"I know you will. And she'll be here waiting."

She gathered her hair and lifted it away from her face and neck, the thick strands heavy and most definitely in need of a brush.

"What happened to your neck?" he asked, returning to the bed in two easy strides. "Looks like someone bit you."

She dropped her hair and let it settle around her like a protective curtain. She'd forgotten her shirt wasn't buttoned all the way to the top so that the ruffled collar could conceal the mark that filled her with such shame. "'Tis nothing. Just an old scar. That's all."

"That's not old."

"Old enough." She tugged at the lacy collar and attempted to pull it up, but the layers of her nightdress underneath made the effort difficult. Giving up on the collar, she fumbled at the buttons on her bodice that in her haste earlier she'd neglected to fasten.

"Who bit you?" he asked quietly, his voice tight.

Was he angry? Did he think someone here in Victoria had harmed her? "Please don't concern yourself. The incident happened before I left London. And now that I'm here, I have nothing to worry about."

"Then you *are* running away from someone." His words were a statement, leaving no room for argument.

"The past is behind me, and I'm perfectly safe now." At least she hoped so.

His furrowed brow told her he'd like to ask her more. But then he glanced out the window again. "You really need to return to the barracks."

She nodded, suddenly eager to put distance between them, away from his probing gaze and pointed questions. Yes, she

131

had run away. When she'd left, no one had known she was leaving—except for Hayward. And no one besides her faithful old servant knew where she'd gone.

She had to make sure it stayed that way.

Arabella crept around the Marine Barracks toward the back door, hoping she could sneak through the kitchen and upstairs without anyone noticing her.

The other ladies would be awake by now, some of them likely even sitting down to breakfast. She still hadn't figured out what she would say if anyone caught her coming inside and looking so disheveled. What excuse could she possibly give?

She couldn't tell them the truth about Haiel-Wat. She'd only put the girl in further danger. And she couldn't say anything about going to Pete's bakehouse. The ladies would assume the worst, no matter what she might say to the contrary.

With a glance at the bright morning sky, she inwardly chastised herself as she had all the way back for getting herself into this predicament. Though she'd meant to leave before daybreak, Haiel-Wat had started thrashing with fever, and so Arabella had stayed and continued to sponge bathe her with cool cloths. By the time the child had settled back down, dawn had already broken.

Ducking low so no one would see her from the windows, Arabella hurried the last few steps and turned the corner to the back of the house. Once there, she paused and allowed herself the first full breath since entering the government complex.

At a movement by the kitchen door, her breath stalled.

"Miss Lawrence?" Mercy rose rapidly from where she'd been sitting on the step.

Arabella froze. She'd been caught.

"Just came out for a breath of air, that I did," Mercy said, swiping her cheeks. "Just a little breath is all."

At the tremble in Mercy's voice, Arabella studied the young woman more closely, noting that her eyes were red-rimmed and her cheeks streaked with tears. Had Mercy, the strongest woman she'd ever met, been crying?

Arabella took a tentative step closer. "Mercy, is everything all right?"

Mercy turned her head away so that Arabella couldn't see her face. "I'm fine, miss. Right as I've ever been."

Never once had Mercy displayed anything but courage and kindness during the entire voyage over, even in the midst of the bleakest circumstances. What could have happened to shake this sweet woman's spirit now?

"Is it your sister in the workhouse?" Arabella asked, thinking back to the little bit that Mercy had shared with her on the ship. "Have you received news of her?"

"No, miss. Not yet."

"I'm sorry. I shall continue to pray for her."

"Thank you, miss." Mercy hugged her arms and rubbed her shirtsleeves.

"'Tis too cold to be outside without a coat this morn." A breeze laden with the chill of the autumn day and dampness of the sea rustled Arabella's skirt and coat, sending shivers over her skin.

"You should go on in, miss. Get out of the cold and join the other ladies for breakfast."

Arabella didn't move. The sadness in Mercy's tone wasn't normal, and Arabella couldn't pass by without offering some word of comfort, although she didn't know for what and wouldn't pry. "I shall pray not only for your sister but for you too."

Mercy didn't respond or move for a long moment. "Then you believe like the others that I'm carrying Joseph's babe?"

At the bluntness of Mercy's statement, Arabella drew back. She wanted to pretend she didn't know what Mercy was talking about, but ever since Mercy had announced her engagement to

Lord Colville, the ladies had been gossiping. Just last evening, Miss Spencer had remarked that she wouldn't be surprised if Mercy had trapped the wealthy lord into marriage by getting pregnant.

Arabella hadn't dignified the rumor with a response. She'd hoped Mercy wouldn't hear the tale. But it was clear she had. "I'm sorry the women are speaking so ill of you, Mercy. I know you had no designs for Lord Colville."

Mercy brushed at her cheek again. "He's been honorable toward me, and I don't want to see his name tainted."

Arabella suspected this wouldn't be the last time Mercy and Lord Colville would face such gossip. "He is honorable. And so are you. Eventually everyone will see that."

Mercy nodded. "Aye. You're right. I have to stop worrying about what everyone is saying and believing. If we're living rightly before God and pleasing Him, then that's all that matters."

Mercy's statement echoed Arabella's thoughts from earlier. Was it possible God was trying to give her the message again? Arabella suspected she too often cared more about pleasing people than living rightly before God. At least she had where Pete and the baking lessons were concerned.

"I know you're likely not approving of my engagement with Joseph any more than the rest of the ladies, but you're kind anyway."

"'Tis not disapproval, Mercy. Just surprise."

Arabella had never expected the shipboard romance to blossom, had even attempted to caution Mercy with the hope of preventing heartache. But who was she to dictate the course of love?

"I wake up every morning surprised too," Mercy admitted, a glow lighting her eyes and chasing away the sadness.

Arabella gently squeezed Mercy's arm. "I shall endeavor to support you and Lord Colville better."

"Thank you, miss." Mercy stood straighter, drew in a breath, and then, as though seeing Arabella's unkempt condition for the first time, raised her brows. "You've been gone, miss? In your nightdress?"

Arabella's fingers fluttered to her dress and the buttons still open, revealing her nightdress beneath.

"Were you with Pete again?" Mercy's eyes contained a hundred questions. As an early riser, Mercy was more aware than any of the other women of Arabella's time spent with Pete during the baking lessons. But what must Mercy think now? Seeing her like this?

Should she make something up? Brush Mercy off? Push past her and run up to her room? As the options tumbled around in her mind, Arabella let her fingers slide away from the errant buttons. She had no choice but to trust Mercy with the truth.

Arabella glanced to the kitchen door and window to ensure their privacy before lowering her voice. "I discovered a very ill native child here in the yard last night. I knew no other place to take her than to Pete's bakehouse from where I have just returned. Now I must slip inside and get dressed without anyone else being the wiser for my duplicity."

Mercy studied Arabella's face, her eyes widening. Then she too shot a look at the door and window before taking hold of Arabella's arm and dragging her toward a nearby shed. "You go on and hide while I fetch everything you need."

Sudden tears stung Arabella's eyes. She halted, then impulsively wrapped her arms around Mercy and squeezed her tight. "Thank you."

twelve

*D*on't say it," Blind Billy grumbled from where he mixed froth with flour. "I don't want to hear it."

"Hear what?" Pete tossed the last of the rolls into a basket and then wiped his arm across his perspiring forehead.

"Yer confounded plans."

"What plans?"

"You know what plans."

Pete grinned. How was it that Blind Billy could see so much even though his eyesight was nearly gone? "Since you already know, I guess I don't need to tell you."

His faithful assistant harrumphed and scraped more froth from the bucket of dregs. The brewer's yeast was an expensive but necessary ingredient for starting the sponge. Thankfully, Blind Billy had perfected the process of separating the yeasty froth from both the top and bottom of the beer.

"Any woman in her right mind will tell you no," Blind Billy muttered, his thick tufts of white hair standing on end.

"Any woman with half a mind would tell me yes." Pete lifted his face and let the cold morning breeze blowing through the open windows and doors soothe his overheated skin and drive away the lingering heat from the ovens.

Ever since he'd escorted Arabella back to the government

137

complex, his mind hadn't stopped working to come up with a plan—any plan that would allow her to spend her days above the bakehouse, nursing Haiel-Wat back to health.

But as far as he could see, she couldn't visit him at the bakehouse for hours on end every day, not without arousing suspicion and drawing attention to Haiel-Wat.

His conversation with Mrs. Moresby from several days ago had returned to him and now formed the basis of his plan. She'd breezed into the bakehouse and informed him that Drummond had convinced the welcoming committee to ban Pete from visiting the women at the government complex.

She'd tilted her large hat up and pinned him with her steady gaze. "Now that doesn't mean you can't find other ways to meet with the women. Or should I say woman?"

"Aye, you could say that." Even after he'd told himself he wouldn't seek out Arabella again, he hadn't been able to stop thinking about her.

"Miss Lawrence seems to like making cakes," Mrs. Moresby continued. "And the piece I tasted the other morning was delicious. With more training, I suspect she'd be able to garner enough customers to start a business."

"What kind of business?"

"A confectionary, of course."

A confectionary? For cakes? Pete liked the idea. In fact, he could envision her learning how to make tarts and scones and other baked goods to sell in addition to cakes—sweet items that would surely attract many customers.

"You'll need to help her." Mrs. Moresby pulled her handkerchief out of her reticule and blotted the perspiration on her temples and then her upper lip, the leftover heat from the ovens making the shop all too warm as usual.

"I'm not so sure she's keen on my help."

"I don't think she knows yet what she needs or wants. And you're just the man to help her figure it out."

"She's made it clear I'm not up to her high standards."

"Nonsense. Miss Lawrence doesn't strike me as a conceited woman. If so, she wouldn't have joined you in the kitchen at all."

Mrs. Moresby was right. Arabella could have refused to meet with him that first time or any of the mornings. But she hadn't. She'd been waiting for him every day.

"However, you need to do things properly with a gentlewoman like Miss Lawrence or not do them at all."

"I'm not a 'proper' kind of man."

Mrs. Moresby had narrowed her eyes upon him, her feathery hat slipping low. "You'd best make an effort to shape up your behavior or you'll never have a chance with her. You'll lose her to a man like Lieutenant Drummond."

"I refuse to lose her to anyone, especially a dandy like Drummond."

"Then you need to start thinking more with your head than your heart."

He wanted to protest that all he'd done was plot how to win her, but he realized he was prone to let his passions drive him first and handle the consequences later.

Mrs. Moresby started to leave with the dozen sweet rolls she'd purchased but then stopped. "Offer to rent out the bakehouse to her during the day for her business. I doubt anyone will be able to find fault with such an arrangement."

"Except for mayhap her."

Mrs. Moresby smiled, a challenging gleam in her eyes. "You have the charm of a dozen men, Peter. If anyone can convince Miss Lawrence, I trust you'll figure out a way."

He'd been mulling over Mrs. Moresby's suggestion ever since and attempting to come up with a way to show Arabella she needed to open a confectionary in his bakehouse.

Now a way had just dropped into his lap. Mayhap it was heaven-sent. Or mayhap it was only a temporary solution.

Either way, he planned to take full advantage of the predicament.

He stepped into the doorway and surveyed the street. His next-door neighbor, a barber, had turned his sign to *Open*. A public bathhouse a few doors down was already busy. Across the wide dirt street was the laundry shop where Pete took his garments, and next to that a store selling men's clothing.

His business wasn't in the liveliest part of town near the taverns and hotels. But he never wanted for bread orders, baking upwards of ninety quartern loaves in a night. Surely Arabella would soon find herself just as busy.

Back in Birmingham, he wouldn't have been able to consider going into business with a woman like Arabella, and he most certainly wouldn't have been able to entertain thoughts of marrying her. Thank the Lord for this new land and for the opportunities it offered. With his life turned around, God was surely giving him a second chance to do things right and would bless him for his efforts.

With a final glance down the street and with no sign of Arabella's return, he stepped back inside.

"If I was a betting man, I'd bet she'll tell you no," Blind Billy said as he finished scraping off the last of the froth.

"Then it's a good thing you're not betting." Pete paused and listened for any noises coming from his residence above. All was silent.

Haiel-Wat had woken when Lord Colville arrived last hour. Thankfully, Dodge had tracked the young doctor down easily enough at one of the hotels they supplied with bread.

Pete had been surprised at how quickly Lord Colville had arrived and at how kind he'd been, not only to Pete but also to Haiel-Wat. Pete had acted as translator during the doctor's assessment of the girl's condition. Since she belonged to the coastal Salish people, another tribe of Indians who made southern Vancouver Island their home, Pete had communicated through Chinook—although she hadn't been willing to divulge much.

Pete was considering canoeing along the eastern shore to see if he could find her family. But last time he'd gone there, the Salish camps were deserted and the longhouses left empty. He had the feeling nothing had changed over the ensuing months. Instead, he'd decided to canoe to the Northerner's Encampment and see if Mr. Garrett knew anything about Haiel-Wat.

"All you young curmudgeons are in too much of a hurry to get married," Blind Billy said, disgust lacing his tone.

Pete swiped his hand across the worktable and gathered crumbs to throw into the backyard for the birds. "What's wrong with being in a hurry?"

"What's wrong? Everything's wrong, that's what."

Pete crossed the kitchen to the rear door where Jennie rested, her expectant eyes watching his every move as though she knew his plans and didn't want to miss out on the canoe ride. He tossed the crumbs outside and reached down to pat Jennie's head.

Aye, he was in a hurry to get married just like most of the other men in the area. After going so long without any prospects or hopes of marriage, now the idea was even more appealing.

"Just 'cause you're an old curmudgeon who doesn't want to get married doesn't mean the rest of us have to hold back."

Blind Billy fumbled with a flour sack, finally got it open, grabbed a handful of the flour and tossed it into the dregs. "I'll have you know I was happily married for over forty years."

"Forty years?" Pete rose and studied the assistant he'd inherited when he bought the bakehouse. Blind Billy had come from San Francisco with the previous owner and apparently had decided that moving back was too much trouble. Since Pete had needed the help, he was all too willing to keep on someone who already knew what he was doing.

"I suppose yer surprised anyone could put up with me for that long," the old man said as he stirred the flour into the fermented mixture, staring straight ahead, his hands guiding him through the familiar work.

"Surprised anyone could put up with you at all," Pete teased.

Blind Billy harrumphed, the closest he ever came to laughing. "I didn't deserve her. That's for sure."

At the hint of affection, Pete grinned. "She must have been a saint."

"She was." Blind Billy dug his hands into the froth and flour, turning it over and blending it together. He was silent a moment before speaking in a low voice. "She was the best thing that ever happened to me."

Pete didn't know quite how to respond to this gentler side of Blind Billy. He watched the man work, the steady thump of his mixing the only sound in the room.

"You ain't ever gonna find a perfect woman," Blind Billy finally said. "But you better do yer best to make sure she's the right fit."

"Right fit?"

Blind Billy released a sigh that was laced with his usual exasperation. "Don't just look at the outward trimmings. Go deeper."

Before Pete could make sense of Blind Billy's advice, a hesitant knock sounded against the open door. He spun to find Arabella standing just inside and casting a glance over her shoulder as though she didn't want to be seen entering his shop.

Even as he remembered the sincerity of her apology from earlier, he couldn't keep from wondering if her secretiveness was because of Haiel-Wat or him. What if he wasn't the *right fit* for a woman of her upbringing?

"How's Haiel-Wat?" Arabella swung the door closed behind her.

"She's asleep and doing just fine."

In a fresh gown covered by a cloak, she was much more put together than she had been earlier. Her hair had been brushed into submission, pinned into a knot, and covered with a fancy hat.

Even though she was elegant and as stunning as always, he missed the wild beauty he'd witnessed earlier when her long hair had hung in abandoned waves and her gown had been thrown on in haste, revealing a side to her that showed she cared more about people than her appearance.

"What about the doctor? Should I call upon Lord Colville?" she asked as she tugged her bodice higher.

He realized now why she always wore a collar. To hide the bite mark. Anger swirled in his gut, just as it had every time he thought about that mark on her neck. He wanted to punch his fist into the face of the person who had dared to injure her that way. What kind of animal would do such a thing?

"I checked with Mercy, Lord Colville's intended," Arabella continued, "and she gave me the address of the hotel where he's staying."

"The doctor came by an hour ago."

"Oh. And what did he say?"

"She's malnourished and likely suffering from dysentery."

Arabella's shoulders visibly relaxed, and the worry lines in her forehead smoothed away. "Then she'll live?"

"Aye. With some good care, the doctor thinks she'll recover."

"Then I should go see to her care." Arabella started across the room, intending to use the rear door. He settled himself in her way so that she had no choice but to stop and wait.

He waited too, enjoying the proximity that allowed him to fall into the vast green forest of her eyes.

She propped her hands on her hips and started to frown.

"Before you go up," he said, "I have a proposal to make."

"Here we go" came Blind Billy's grumble from where he was still mixing up the sponge. "Hand me the dregs and let me drown myself first."

143

Arabella turned scandalized eyes upon Blind Billy.

"Don't mind that old weasel," Pete said.

"More like don't listen to that young weasel," Blind Billy muttered.

"He thinks it's too early in our relationship for me to do what I'm about to," Pete said, relishing every second of the teasing. "But personally I think the timing is perfect."

Arabella's eyes widened. "Timing for what?"

"For this." He lowered himself on one knee before her.

She sucked in a sharp breath.

Although Pete doubted Blind Billy could see exactly what he was doing, he had no doubt the older man knew he was on his knee before Arabella, especially when he grumbled again under his breath.

He reached for Arabella's gloved hand. "Arabella, will you do me the honor—" he paused, wanting to enjoy the moment for as long as possible—"of becoming my business partner?"

She blinked once, then twice, clearly not having expected his proposal to end the way it did.

Blind Billy stopped mumbling and then harrumphed his acceptance at having been bamboozled.

Pete kept his hold on Arabella's hand and peered up at her as innocently as possible, trying to stifle a grin that desperately needed to break free.

"Business partner?" she managed.

"Aye. I'll rent you the bakehouse during the day for making your cakes."

"Why would I do that when I can use the kitchen in the Marine Barracks for free?"

"One simple reason."

She cocked her head in that adorable way she did when trying to figure him out. "And what is this simple reason?"

"Me."

"You?"

"You'll get to see me every day."

She stared at him, clearly still not sure what to make of his bold statement.

He could no longer contain his smile and set it free.

Her lips quirked in the beginning of her own smile. "Peter Kelly, you're the most arrogant man I've ever met."

"Thank you."

Her lips finally curled into the smile he'd been hoping to see. The beauty of it lit her eyes. "You're impossible."

He released her hand and stood, feeling mighty proud of himself for making her smile. "So, what do you say? If you bake here, then I can continue to give you lessons. In no time you'll be making your own cakes and can sell them for a profit."

Her expression brightened as if the idea pleased her immensely. But then, just as quickly, a cloud settled over her countenance. "'Tis a grand plan and I thank you for the offer. But I cannot accept it."

"It's the perfect arrangement. I can continue to give you baking lessons. And you can sell the cakes for a profit."

"No." Her tone was firm. "It wouldn't work."

He'd known she'd resist. He just hadn't expected her to do so quite as readily. His charm-of-a-dozen-men wasn't working on Arabella, and now he had to lay down his most important card before she dismissed his idea altogether. "Opening the confectionary is the best solution to allow you to be here at the bakehouse with Haiel-Wat without drawing any suspicion."

Her rebuttal died upon her lips.

"I'll rent you the living space above. Then you can stay with her all the time, and we won't have to worry about anyone suspecting she's here."

"I cannot take your home from you—"

"I'll move into the storage house with Blind Billy and Dodge."

"That wouldn't be fair to any of you," she said with a glance at his assistant, who was still stirring the sponge. "I cannot consider it."

"Let's try it temporarily, at least until Haiel-Wat is stronger." While Pete liked his cozy apartment, especially since it had come furnished, he wouldn't mind giving it up if it meant he'd be able to see Arabella every day whenever he wanted.

Again she studied Pete's face as though testing the sincerity of his plan. "I don't know," she said slowly. "It's not proper for ladies to do domestic work."

"You'll be baking cakes. What's not proper about that?"

She hesitated.

"You enjoy baking, right?"

"Yes," she admitted softly.

"Then why not spend your life doing what you enjoy?"

Indecision warred across her features, yet a light glowed in her eyes, one that told him she was seriously considering the offer.

He waited and silently prayed for patience.

"What if people make assumptions?" she asked. "About us?"

Let them, he wanted to say. *What difference would it make?* But Mrs. Moresby's advice from earlier in the week kept him from speaking his mind. Instead, he attempted to view the situation the way a proper gentleman would. The problem was, he didn't know all the rules that proper gentlemen lived by.

"What can we do to make the living arrangement better?" he asked. "To prove to everyone that by living and working here, you're not doing anything indecent?"

She pursed her pretty lips and tapped her finger against them.

"Another woman companion," Blind Billy said, his tone exasperated. "Have her bring a companion with her."

Arabella's gaze connected with Pete's. And as Blind Billy murmured something about the solution having been as obvious as a wart on a toad, Arabella smiled at the same time as Pete.

"I think I might know just who," she said. The relief in her eyes brought a strange lightness to Pete's chest. She'd agreed to the plan, and mayhap now he'd have the chance to finally win her heart.

Arabella folded another gown into her trunk, her motions growing slower with each gown she packed.

"Joseph thinks taking an apartment over the bakery will be a good change," Mercy was saying from where she kneeled next to the trunk, helping Arabella stow away the last of her belongings.

Arabella paused and absently fingered the velvet trim on the gown. As she'd guessed, Mercy had been more than agreeable to the living arrangement, eager to get away from the other women and their gossip.

But with the coming of eve and the reality of the move, Arabella's brave resolve from earlier in the day had faltered by degrees until now she wasn't sure if she should go. Ever since she'd told the other ladies of her plans to move above the bakehouse and temporarily open a confectionary, they'd been whispering about her so that she couldn't keep from second-guessing her decision more with each passing moment.

A knock against the doorframe drew their attention to the flushed face of one of the other poorer women, one whose name Arabella couldn't remember. "Miss Lawrence," she said, "ye've got a gent here to see you. One of them fancy officers."

Arabella's nerves tightened. "Lieutenant Drummond?" Had he heard about her decision to move? Was he here to oppose her?

"Nah, it ain't Lieutenant Drummond. Not as fine-looking, that's for sure."

Arabella could feel her shoulders relax. "Would you please tell whoever it is that I'm currently indisposed?"

The woman started to back away but then paused. "Ye don't want to see him then?"

"I'm busy this evening."

"Aye then."

Once they were alone again, Mercy slid a sideways glance at her. "So does that mean you've narrowed down your choice of a husband?"

The shadows of the evening darkened the quarters. As crowded as the room had been only a week ago, with trunks, clothing, and all their earthly possessions, it was clearing out as more of the women found homes. Earlier, another of the ladies had taken a position as a music teacher for a wealthy family.

Across the hall in the other large room, one of the poor women had been hired as a maid, and a second had accepted a position in a dry-goods store, taking a room with the couple who owned the shop. Soon all the women would find places to go or husbands to marry, and Arabella didn't want to be the last one.

Still, she wasn't yet ready to say yes to marriage. Of all the men who'd called upon her, Lieutenant Drummond had seemed the most suitable candidate. But certainly it was too early to know, wasn't it?

The best thing for her to do was accept the apartment above Pete's bakehouse, she reassured herself as she started folding her gown again. She couldn't forgo the opportunity to nurse Haiel-Wat. And perhaps she'd do more baking. Perhaps.

At the very least, she'd buy herself more time before having to settle upon a husband. Even if several of the ladies had already become serious with their suitors, Arabella didn't want to rush the process.

"You've had all kinds of nice fellas paying you attention," Mercy persisted. "Guess it must be hard to figure out which one you like best."

"Yes, 'tis difficult to be sure." Had she expected the choosing to be easier? That with so many men she'd be able to find the right one without any trouble? If anything, having so many choices seemed to make the decision harder.

Arabella's hands stilled again on her trunk. All the more reason why she needed the time and space away from all the attention from the men as well as the other women constantly talking about suitors.

Two ladies passed by in the hallway outside the room, pausing in their conversation at the sight of Arabella. Only after their footsteps moved on to the stairway did they resume their animated discussion—likely about her. Were they questioning her association with Pete and assuming she was having an illicit relationship with him?

"Is living above the bakehouse the right thing, Mercy?" Arabella's question tumbled out. "Perhaps we should find another place?"

"If you think so, miss." At the hesitation in Mercy's tone, Arabella knew the pretty young woman was thinking of Haiel-Wat and the difficulty they would have in taking care of the little girl somewhere else.

Mercy peered out the open door and then lowered her voice. "We've got to be real careful, miss. I get the feeling not many around here like the natives. The women were talking earlier about how some families are even casting out their native servants in favor of hiring some of us as domestics in their place. Said they don't like the Indians, and the whole island would be better off without the undesirables."

Arabella sat back on her heels and met Mercy's gaze, seeing in the young woman's eyes the hurt of rejection she'd suffered in being an undesirable herself at one time in London's slums. Though Arabella's situation couldn't compare to Mercy's, as a spinster, she too understood to a degree the rejection of being considered undesirable and unwanted.

Her heart swelled with the ache of wishing for something

better, for a world where no one had to be undesirable. Could she, in her small way, be a part of making that happen?

"None of us is undesirable any longer," Arabella replied, letting her new resolve stiffen her backbone. "We're not going to allow anyone to make us or Haiel-Wat feel that way ever again."

With that, she closed the lid on her trunk and stood. She might not be able to eradicate every prejudice around her, but she had to start somewhere to make a difference. And the best place for that was with herself.

thirteen

Arabella lifted the spoon to Haiel-Wat's lips and fed her the last sip of broth. "Good girl," she said.

Haiel-Wat reclined against the pillow and closed her eyes, her dainty features taut with wariness. From the first moment Haiel-Wat had awoken, Arabella expected her to jump out of bed and run away and was surprised that after three days she was still here.

Arabella suspected the endless supply of food enticed the girl to remain—as did the warmth and comfortable bed. Though Pete attempted to speak with the child whenever he came around, he hadn't been able to learn how long Haiel-Wat had been homeless. They could only speculate she'd gone months without a full meal and a safe place to lay her head.

Arabella set the bowl aside and brushed a strand of the girl's silky black hair off her forehead.

Haiel-Wat opened her eyes and shrank back, fear flickering in her face.

Immediately, Arabella pulled away. "It's okay, little one. I won't hurt you."

Arabella wanted to sigh, but she refrained and instead straightened the covers. After all she'd done—the feeding, washing, and tending—she'd hoped the girl would begin to like her. She'd even spent hours cutting up an old gown and remaking it to fit the child. Haiel-Wat's eyes had rounded at the sight of the simple but pretty dress. But instead of letting Arabella help her into the garment, she'd kicked the gift away and refused to look at it.

At the clicking of paws on the hardwood floor, Haiel-Wat sat back up. Jennie trotted across the room directly toward Arabella, her tail wagging in enthusiasm, having realized from the start that Arabella would always take the time to pet her.

Haiel-Wat spoke a soft word, and the dog shifted toward the girl, her tail moving at double the speed, which shook her entire body. When she reached the side of the bed closest to Haiel-Wat, she stood on her hind legs and rested her front paws on the mattress, sticking her nose up and begging Haiel-Wat for attention.

The girl obliged, scratching Jennie's head and earning a lick on the arm.

Haiel-Wat smiled and spoke again to the dog.

From her chair positioned next to the bed, Arabella couldn't keep from smiling at the tender picture the two made . . . one that stirred desires she'd tried to bury but that had always throbbed whenever she was around children, especially around her sister's babe.

Now, watching Haiel-Wat interact with Jennie, the longing swelled so that her insides hurt and her arms ached with the need to hold and nurture and give her love away.

"Jennie was whining to come up here," Pete said from the doorway. "And now I know why."

The morning light streaming through the window cascaded over Pete's face and drew attention to the shadows under his eyes, as well as the dark layer of unshaven stubble. His grin was half cocked as usual, and yet behind the smile and teasing she could sense his tiredness.

He'd spent the past few days canoeing to different places and making inquiries about Haiel-Wat's family and tribe but hadn't discovered anything about the child or her family. All he had to show for his efforts was exhaustion.

As he joined Jennie at the edge of the bed, he rubbed the dog's head and said something to the girl that widened her shy smile and darkened her eyes with admiration.

How had Pete won the child with so little effort, but Arabella couldn't gain any ground with her?

Arabella picked up the bowl and spoon from the bedside table and slipped out of the room into the other half of the apartment that served as both a kitchen and living area. She supposed she had to accept that she wasn't good at forming friendships, not even with a child like Haiel-Wat. She didn't have Pete's natural ability to make people feel comfortable. And she'd never been talkative and able to banter, certainly not the way Pete could.

"Maybe you need to learn her language," she quietly admonished herself. But even as she spoke, she let her shoulders fall. The truth was, even if she could speak to Haiel-Wat in her own tongue, she'd never have Pete's charm and friendliness or even Mercy's compassion.

With a sigh, she placed the bowl and spoon into the basin of water that remained from her earlier attempt at washing dishes.

"We need to resume the cake lessons this morning." Pete spoke from directly behind her, startling her so that she bumped the basin, causing it to wobble and slosh water onto the floor.

He reached past her and steadied it, his arm brushing against her.

She froze, mesmerized by the solidness of his arm, of the warm pressure where his flesh connected against hers, of his presence so close she could almost feel him breathing.

Ever since she'd moved into the apartment earlier in the week, she hadn't once been alone with Pete. He'd been gone or too busy with his baking. Or Mercy had been present.

His absence had been perfectly fine, especially because Arabella had resolved to remain above reproach while living at the bakehouse so that no one would have any reason to censure her or accuse her of indecencies. Which meant Pete shouldn't be in the apartment. But how could she kick him out of his own home?

"You shouldn't sneak up on me," she chided as she stepped away from him, grabbed a towel from the peg on the wall, and bent to wipe away the spilled water.

"And miss out on overhearing you talking to yourself? Not a chance."

"'Tis entirely rude to eavesdrop on private conversations."

"Even private conversations you have with yourself?" The humor in his tone never failed to lighten the moment.

"Especially those." She straightened. Pete seemed to take up half the small kitchen. Less than a foot away, she was conscious of him again, especially of the way his gaze lingered upon her hair, almost as if he was imagining combing his fingers through it as he often did to his own.

She'd hastily plaited her hair when she'd arisen, anxious to attend to Haiel-Wat. Now the long wavy strands had loosened, and she self-consciously tried to tuck them back.

He immediately untucked it. "It's pretty when it's down."

"This," she said, tugging a red strand, "is never pretty."

"This"—he caressed one of the loose pieces—"is finer than anything I've ever seen in my life."

"But it's red."

"It's the most magnificent color on God's earth."

His words and his gentleness were like a low breeze, making something deep inside her rustle with pleasure. "I really must get back to tending to Haiel-Wat," she said, fumbling with the damp towel and breaking contact with him.

What was wrong with her that she so quickly lost track of herself and all her training whenever she was around Pete? Why did he have this kind of effect on her?

"You can't keep putting off our baking lessons, Arabella."

The way he said her name made her stomach flip, and again she silently chastised herself for her reaction to him.

"I don't want to leave Haiel-Wat alone."

"Mercy can watch her."

"Mercy's still at the hospital helping Lord Colville."

"She's just returned. I had her purchase some items for me, and now she's storing them in the springhouse."

Although Arabella longed to make another cake and had even planned how she might add different spices for variation, she hesitated.

"You have to make some effort at baking cakes," he continued. "Otherwise people will begin to question your motive for moving here. And we don't want anyone to discover Haiel-Wat, do we?"

She shook her head, suddenly flustered at the prospect of spending the morning with Pete. Was that why she'd been avoiding the cake making? Because Pete flustered her? Made her feel things she didn't understand? Caused her to question everything she'd always known?

Besides being with Pete, once she made her first cake, everyone in Victoria would know she was doing domestic work. She wouldn't be able to turn back. Was she really ready to take that step?

Even if she was ready, the truth was she didn't know if she really could make a confectionary work. There was the possibility she wouldn't be good enough at baking cakes, that she'd fail at earning enough money to pay Pete for the rent.

"You're tired and haven't slept much all week," she said, offering another excuse. "Surely you'd much rather slumber than make cakes."

He shrugged. "I'll gladly give up sleep if it means I get to be with you."

She twisted the towel until it was as taut as her muscles. Even if he said such things in jest and likely wasn't serious half the time, she took too much pleasure in his compliments. She supposed it was only natural for a spinster like her to finally enjoy the attention and flattery of a young man—even if he was the wrong man for her.

"We shall need a chaperone." She threw out the last excuse she could find.

"Have no fear." He walked to the door and held it open, waving her to precede him. "I've already asked Dodge to stay in the kitchen this morning with us."

"Haiel-Wat? I should tell her—"

"Already did."

She stared at him, the anticipation inside swirling faster.

His answering grin was crooked, showing off the dimple in his chin and making him look altogether handsome. And arrogant.

Fisting her hands on her hips, she tried to glare at him. "You're much too confident in your powers of persuasion, Mr. Kelly."

"Can't help that God's made me irresistible."

She tossed the towel at him.

With a laugh, he caught it.

She tried to maintain her glare but her lips betrayed her with the need to smile at his easy bantering. "Very well. One cake."

"Two."

She hesitated, knowing full well she'd never be able to stop after one. "Okay. Two."

Again, he waved her through, and this time she finally gave way to her longings not only to keep baking but to spend time with him—although she sensed both would only lead to trouble.

As she entered the bakehouse, she paused. Dodge was there just as Pete had assured her, but the boy was curled up and asleep near the back door, his head resting on a bag of flour.

For a moment, Arabella was tempted to flee. But at the sight of fresh butter, cream, and eggs already laid out on the worktable, she pushed aside her worries and decided she would simply enjoy the morning.

The chocolate cake came together easily, as did the miniature queen's cakes filled with currants. While glazing the last small creation with a mixture of egg whites and finely ground sugar, she released a breath of satisfaction and stood back to admire the dozen pretty queen's cakes waiting to go into the oven.

"They'll be so delicious, I don't know if I can bear to sell them."

Pete wiped his hands on his already-crusty apron. "We'll put a sign in the window this afternoon once everything is finished baking. You'll be surprised at how much money you'll make."

Already the delectable scent of the baking chocolate cake had drawn men from surrounding businesses, and they'd stopped to inquire about buying a piece.

Pete stifled a yawn and glanced to where Dodge still slept upon the bag of flour.

"Leave the cleaning to me," she said, gathering several bowls and utensils, "and go to bed."

"Now that you're becoming the expert, I suppose you think you can order me around." He smiled and tugged at her apron strings. It was one of his aprons and much too big, but it had helped shield her silky skirt from batter.

She tried to resist, but he used the strings like a fishing line to reel her in. Even without him pulling, his grin was magnetic, beckoning her and breaking down her resistance all at once. Somehow with him, every task was a pleasure and every moment filled with the unanticipated.

"Someone needs to order you around once in a while, Mr. Kelly," she said. "Especially since it's become quite clear you're accustomed to getting your own way."

"I like getting my way."

Now, only a foot from him, she held herself back, forcing him to release the apron string. "If we're to be business partners, then you'll have to eventually learn to trust me to do something as simple as cleaning up on my own."

"I already trust you."

She held up her fingers coated with a sticky sweet sugar. "Then sleep and let me finish in here by myself."

He circled his fingers around one of her wrists and studied her hand. "What if I *want* to help?"

"You haven't slept in days." She was tempted to touch the dark circles and weary lines around his eyes.

He lifted her hand until it brushed his lips. Before she realized what he was doing, he licked at the sugar mixture.

She froze, her breath catching.

"I'd give up a month's worth of sleep to do this cleanup," he whispered. His lashes fell—long, thick lashes that were a rich brown like his hair. His tongue grazed the granules on the next finger. When he looked up again, his pupils had widened, turning his eyes dark with desire.

She couldn't breathe, couldn't move, couldn't think. She could only watch and let heat spread into the far reaches of her body.

"Miss Lawrence?" At a sharp voice from the main doorway of the bakehouse, she gasped and jerked her hand free.

Pete's large frame blocked her view of the newcomer, but she didn't have to see to know who'd entered. It was Lieutenant Drummond.

Blood rushed to her head, making her suddenly dizzy. What was she doing? How had things with Pete taken a turn so quickly from friendly teasing to . . . something else? And what if the lieutenant had witnessed it?

Mortified, she hastily wiped her hands on her apron and stepped around Pete, avoiding his gaze and leaving him behind as she attempted a welcoming smile. "Lieutenant Drummond, what a pleasant surprise."

His attention dropped to the apron, and his eyes flashed with disapproval.

Her fingers fumbled with the long ties, unwinding them until the apron fell away. She tossed the offending object onto the worktable.

"When the ladies at the Marine Barracks told me I could find you here, I prayed they were wrong." The lieutenant glared at Pete with unflinching coldness. "But sadly it seems they were correct."

"This isn't what it appears, sir," she started.

Pete crossed his arms and smiled smugly, almost as if he relished the lieutenant walking in and finding them in such an intimate situation.

"Lieutenant Drummond," she said, scrambling to find the right words to ease the discomfort of the predicament. "I am only baking here temporarily—"

"If you were so desperate to find employment, you should have informed me," he said, gentling his tone. "I could have inquired among my acquaintances whether any of them had need of a governess."

"I'm afraid the governess positions have all been filled by other women from the bride ship."

"Surely I could have persuaded a family to hire you temporarily as a language or music or even an art instructor."

She wasn't proficient in languages or music or art, although her stepmother had tried to make her so. But she certainly couldn't admit such shortcomings to Lieutenant Drummond.

"She likes baking," Pete cut in. "If she wants to bake, then why not support her in it?"

"Mr. Kelly, you know nothing about what's suitable for a lady of Miss Lawrence's status. Please kindly refrain from inserting your unwanted remarks."

At the sharp anger etched into the lieutenant's countenance and the animosity simmering beneath the smirk on Pete's face, tension radiated between the two as it had every time they'd been together. And she guessed some of it had to do with her.

Though she'd been flattered by Pete's compliments and enjoyed his attention, he had to know she couldn't consider him as a serious suitor. By accepting his proposal to move upstairs, had she misled him, given him false hope?

She would need to clarify with him the boundaries of their relationship just as soon as she could. They were business partners and nothing more.

"Miss Lawrence," the lieutenant said with a bow, "I do hope you'll accept my invitation to attend a dinner party at the Pembertons' this evening. I believe Governor Douglas and his wife will be there."

A part of her resisted leaving Haiel-Wat. But she knew she couldn't turn down so favorable an opportunity and that Mercy could watch the child for a few hours. "I'd be honored to attend such a gathering."

"Very well." The lieutenant tipped up his chin and slanted a look at Pete as if to dare him to find something more impressive than dinner with the governor.

Pete's cocked grin didn't waver.

Lieutenant Drummond sniffed at him dismissively before holding out a hand toward her. "I shall look forward to this evening."

"And I shall look forward to it as well." She walked with him to the door and made the final arrangements for the dinner. When he left the shop a few moments later, she spun expecting to fend off a disparaging remark from Pete. But he was gone.

And as she took in the kitchen with the remnants of their morning baking session strewn about and the delicious aromas in the air, she realized the happiness and contentment she'd found earlier as she'd been baking with him was gone now too.

fourteen

Pete took a swig of coffee and stared at the glowing light coming from the window of the apartment above the bakehouse where Mercy was tending to Haiel-Wat.

Perched on an empty barrel, he leaned against the outbuilding that had now become home and tried unsuccessfully not to think about Arabella being with Drummond.

Ever since she'd ridden away with him in the chaise he'd hired from the livery stable, Pete had done little else but think about her and the fact that Drummond was working hard to win her.

Pete's gut twisted at the prospect of Drummond sitting next to her at a fancy dinner party and conversing with her the entire evening, watching her laugh, making her smile.

Pete lowered his mug, rested it against his thigh, and shifted his attention to the black night sky, too frustrated to pray—though he knew he should.

He didn't want Arabella to favor Drummond over him. Yet she'd made no effort earlier to disguise the fact that she coveted Drummond's attention more than his. Aye, the lieutenant was a wealthy and important gentleman, but what else about the man did she find even the slightest bit attractive?

And what was Pete doing wrong that he couldn't woo her?

He supposed he could take some comfort that Drummond was more than a little angry about the new arrangements with Arabella. The dandy had attempted to keep him from Arabella by getting him banned from the government building. But Pete had outwitted Drummond, and now she was practically living in his pocket.

Drummond's sharp glare earlier had been a warning that he would make Pete pay for the insolence. Aye, Pete didn't deny the man was dangerous to have as an enemy. Not only was he powerful in the naval forces, he was also well liked among Victoria's ruling class. Still, Pete wasn't about to let that kind of man intimidate him—not in any way, especially not where Arabella was concerned.

At the scuff of footsteps on the dirt-packed path leading past the bakehouse to the back entry, Pete held himself motionless. A deeper, aristocratic voice was answered by a womanly one, one that sounded like Arabella's.

She was home. Finally.

Part of him wanted to jump up and greet them. But he forced himself to stay in his unobtrusive spot in the shadows. If he could watch them interact for just a moment without their realizing it, perhaps he could figure out what he needed to do differently to win her heart.

As they stepped through the gate and moved to the base of the stairs that led to the apartment, Drummond said, "I had a very nice time this evening, Miss Lawrence. Thank you for gracing me with your company."

Gracing me with your company? Pete almost snorted. Why were aristocrats like Drummond always so formal? Didn't they ever tire of putting on airs?

"'Twas a lovely evening, sir" came Arabella's reply as she stopped at the steps. With her hand on the rail, she seemed to be sending the silent message that she wanted to end their evening at the bottom of the stairway rather than the top.

Pete was fine with that. More than fine. In fact, he wouldn't be able to stay in the shadows if Drummond went any farther.

"You will consider everything I said about the scandalous undertaking?" Drummond asked.

"Of course."

What had the dandy said? Pete guessed Drummond had tried again to convince her to take a position with a wealthy family. Had Arabella told him how profitable her baking had been today? About the line of men out the door, all those who'd been waiting to purchase cake? When Pete had insisted on five shillings per slice, some of the men had offered even more.

They'd sold out within minutes of opening and had earned almost as much as what he made in a day of baking bread and rolls.

"May I call on you again on Sunday afternoon?" Drummond asked. "If the weather remains fair, the Pembertons are hosting a picnic with boating and games. I'd be honored to have your company."

"That sounds delightful."

It sounded terrible, but Pete clenched his jaw and forced himself to stay silent. Blind Billy's words from earlier taunted him: *"You ain't ever gonna find a perfect woman. But you better do your best to make sure she's the right fit."*

Arabella was sure enough the right fit for him. But what if he couldn't make her see that *he* was the right fit for *her*? How could he? Not when he couldn't invite her to mingle among Victoria's oldest and most important families. Not when he couldn't offer her lovely picnics with boating and games. Not when he couldn't come close to providing the lifestyle she was used to.

"Then I shall take my leave," Drummond said.

"Good night, Lieutenant." Arabella moved to the first step, clearly eager to go to her apartment. Pete had no doubt she was anxious to check on Haiel-Wat after being gone from the little girl for so many hours.

"I know we have only recently just met," he said. "But under the hasty circumstances, would you call me Richard?"

All the men were racing to win the brides, especially since some women had already paired off. If Pete and the other hopefuls wanted to succeed with those who were left—like Arabella—they couldn't abide by the normal courtship rituals. Apparently Drummond knew it the same as the rest of them.

She hesitated. "Very well. If you like."

"I would." He sounded too pleased with himself, as if her agreeing to use his given name was the same as her accepting a proposal of marriage.

"And may I call you Arabella?" he persisted.

"Yes, Lieutenant."

Pete rolled his eyes while inwardly his muscles tensed. He didn't like how the evening was ending. If Arabella wasn't more careful, she'd lead Drummond into thinking he could steal a kiss from her.

No sooner had the thought entered his mind than Drummond leaned forward and pressed a kiss against her lips. On the step, she was nearly at his level and an easy target.

In an instant, Pete was off the barrel, his coffee splashing over the rim of his cup. Before he could make his presence known, Drummond broke the connection and took a step back.

"Good night, Arabella," he said in a husky voice before spinning and striding away.

Pete could only stare, his heart thudding a painfully anxious rhythm. How had he allowed that dandy to kiss Arabella? Wasn't that why he'd been watching and waiting for her return? To make sure Drummond didn't do something like that?

Arabella stood unmoving. With only the glow of light from the upstairs window, Pete couldn't make out her expression. But he sensed she was as stunned as he was by Drummond's boldness.

Maybe he should expose Drummond's hostility toward the

natives not only in the smallpox outbreak but in the continued push to keep them off the island. With how much Arabella cared about Haiel-Wat, such a revelation would surely dampen her feelings toward the lieutenant. But even as he searched for the right words, he hesitated at using such a tactic.

Before Pete could figure out how to salvage any chance he might still have with her, she lifted a hand and wiped the back of her glove across her mouth. Not once, but twice.

He allowed himself a slow smile, one that eased the tension from his body and calmed his racing pulse. Then he pushed away from the barrel. "Guess you thoroughly enjoyed every moment with Drummond."

At his words, she gasped and hiked up another step.

He ambled farther into the light so she could see him. Taking a long slurp of his coffee, he tried to act like he hadn't been anxiously waiting for her return—even though he had.

"You're awake," she said, her voice tinged with embarrassment. "I thought you'd be asleep for a couple more hours at least."

She'd obviously learned his baking schedule, likely having heard them entering and starting their work in the quiet of the night, usually around eleven. He'd have to warn Dodge and Blind Billy they all needed to take care not to make any loud noises that might disturb the women unnecessarily.

"Haven't been up long," he said before he took another sip.

She glanced at the apartment window. "How's Haiel-Wat?"

"When I last checked, she was sleeping."

"Good." The stiffness in Arabella's posture loosened just a little.

"Mercy takes care of her almost as well as you do."

"Almost?" Arabella's tone contained a smile.

"You're right. Mayhap she's a little better. After all, she's marrying a doctor."

Arabella huffed, but the sound was playful.

Pete grinned, the insecurities from moments ago fading. He could do this. He could win her. All he had to do was convince her he was a better man than Drummond.

"I'm guessing after your passionate kiss with Drummond, you're too excited to think about sleeping."

"Peter Kelly, were you spying on me?"

"It was just extremely difficult not to notice a kiss like that."

She fidgeted with her reticule and started up the next step.

He couldn't let her get away. Not now. Not when he needed to make her fall in love with him. "Since you're wide awake, mayhap you can give me a reading lesson."

"You're right. I agreed to teach you to read if you taught me to bake, and I haven't carried through with my end of the bargain."

He hadn't brought up the reading because he didn't want her to feel obligated. But how else was he supposed to spend more time with her? "Then you're willing to start tonight?"

She hesitated. "Very well. I shall go check on Haiel-Wat and gather a few supplies."

After her return and debating an appropriate place for the lesson, Arabella finally convinced him to sit on the top step of the landing, leaving the door open enough so Mercy could keep an eye on them from her spot at the kitchen table where she was mending. Although Pete would have preferred the privacy of the bakehouse, he settled onto the step and, for a little while at least, made himself focus on the reading lesson.

She'd wrapped a blanket around her shoulders in addition to her cloak to ward off the chill of the autumn night. It wasn't a particularly cold night for late September or he would have insisted on going inside. Even so, he could tell she was grow-ing chilled, especially when she tucked the blanket around her hands more securely.

"Here," he said, taking one of her hands.

She started to tug away, but he quickly blew warmth against

her fingertips before rubbing them between both his hands. He couldn't keep his thoughts from straying to earlier when he'd intended to playfully nibble the sugar off her fingers and had licked her instead.

As usual, he hadn't thought before acting and realized his mistake too late. Especially after his body had reacted so strongly to the mere touch of her. In some ways, the interruption from Drummond had been a godsend. No telling how carried away he could have gotten before he'd listened to the still, small voice of reason.

"I'm waiting for a letter from my dad," he said, trying to take his mind off her dainty hand pressed between his. "And when I get it, I want to be able to read it."

"You're already able to recognize some words," she said in the same encouraging tone she'd used so far during the lesson. "I have a feeling you'll learn quickly."

He reached for her other hand, blew warmth against it, and rubbed it the same as the first. "It's been months since I posted my letter. Guess I expected to hear back from him by now."

"It surely must be on the way."

"I don't know. After the bitterness of my parting, I wanted my mum and dad to know how sorry I was, how much I respected their faith, and how much I loved them."

She squeezed his hand in a gesture that told him she was listening.

"But what if after all the terrible things I said, my dad decided to put me out of his life for good? Mayhap he'll never be able to forgive me for leaving him and the family business."

"Maybe in time he'll learn to forgive you," she whispered, her voice wistful.

Was she waiting on forgiveness from someone too? If she was, then mayhap she could truly understand his dilemma. "He had no way to afford to hire someone to replace me," he explained. "And since the business was already floundering, I don't know how he could have lasted. What if he had to close up shop? What if he and mum had to move to the workhouse? What if my letter never reached them?"

He'd considered writing to one of his sisters, all of whom were married with families of their own, and asking them how Mum and Dad were faring. But of his sisters, only Teresa knew how to read—and only a little. What if his sisters hated him after abandoning their parents and causing their ruin? Mayhap they wanted nothing to do with him.

Arabella squeezed his hand again and didn't release her hold. "I'm sorry, Pete."

He nodded. "What about you? Who do you hope learns to forgive you?"

The lantern glow emanating from the opening in the apartment door turned her pale skin into a creamy butter color and highlighted the smattering of freckles on her nose. With her hair styled into a fashionable twist, the elegant lines of her chin and cheekbones were visible. Her neck would have been too, except that her high collar rose nearly to her chin.

He wanted her to share what had happened, but just because he could spill his thoughts and feelings easily didn't mean she could.

Arabella expelled a breath, one laced with regret. "Just like you, I have no doubt my leaving led to my father's and my family's utter ruin. I have worried about him—about them—every day since I left, praying they have found a way to recover from the disaster I caused them."

"You don't think they'll forgive you?"

She was silent, staring straight ahead through the dark, more likely seeing into the past than seeing anything in the present. "No, I don't think they will ever be able to understand why I had to leave."

Her tone contained pain so deep it stabbed his heart.

"Sometimes I believe I made the right choice in coming here.

Other times, when I think of the distress they are surely experiencing, I wonder what kind of selfish person I am to have hurt them so much."

He scooped up her other hand and pressed it between his own, hoping she'd feel his warmth but also his willingness to share her burden.

"Pastor Abe was there for me, willing to help bear my burdens," he said. "I'll be here for you, Arabella. Whenever you're ready, you can tell me what happened. I promise I won't cast judgment upon you."

From the rounding of her lips to the slight pucker in her brow, he sensed she wanted to share more, wanted him to know the truth.

He hoped she'd trust him tonight. Instead, she began to tug away as though readying to stand and put an end to their lesson. Since it was nearly time to begin making bread, and Blind Billy and Dodge would be emerging from the storage building soon, he needed to let her go.

But rather than loosening his hold, he pressed his palm against hers. Then he slowly slid his fingers through hers like the tines of a comb, letting her long delicate fingers caress his work-roughened skin. The softness was intoxicating, and he lifted his hand away so he could slip their fingers together again.

Her lips were slightly parted. After Drummond's kiss, she deserved to have a real and passionate kiss, one that would make her forget all the reasons she'd run away and remind her of all the reasons she should stay—with him.

He leaned in, wanting—no, needing—to breathe her in. His shoulder brushed against hers, and she didn't move except for a quick intake.

With a final plunge that captured her fingers, he tightened his grasp, hoping it revealed the power of his attraction. At the same moment, he grazed her ear with his nose and mouth, as soft and light as glaze, there for a heartbeat and then gone.

Even so, she exhaled a shaky breath, one that made his blood pump faster, one that told him she wasn't unaffected, one that told him he might be able to steal a kiss from her the same way Drummond had.

The problem was, he didn't want to steal a kiss. He wanted her to give him one—willingly. In fact, he wouldn't mind if she ended up asking him for a kiss.

He half smiled at the image of her not just welcoming his kisses but pleading for them. He might be delusional in thinking she'd ever do that, but he'd sure have fun trying.

Releasing his intimate hold on her hand, he rose and stretched, attempting a nonchalance to mask his need to pull her up into his arms and never let her go.

"Thank you for the lesson tonight." He held out a hand to assist her to her feet.

"You're welcome." She complied and let him pull her up. "I should have given the lesson sooner."

Once standing side by side on the landing, he didn't immediately release her hand. Instead, he slid his thumb across her knuckles. "Mayhap we can meet again Sunday evening after you get back from your *delightful* outing with Drummond—or should I call him Richard?"

"Yes," she replied, her attention dropping to his caress.

"Yes to our meeting Sunday, or yes to calling him Richard?"

She looked up, tilting her head as though trying to figure him out.

He grinned.

"You're teasing me."

"Aye. But count yourself lucky, since I only tease pretty ladies."

Before she could respond, he tugged her close so that only a hair's distance remained between them. He ignored the fact they were in plain view of Mercy, who glanced up but then made a show of focusing intently upon her needle and thread.

"I guarantee," he said softly, letting his breath brush Arabella's temple, "when I kiss you, you won't wipe my kiss away afterward. You'll be asking for more."

He wanted to test his theory, but he forced himself to let go of her and saunter down the steps. Even though he could feel her gaze following him, he didn't look back until he was at the bottom. Then he winked up at her before entering the bakehouse.

fifteen

Arabella reached for the brush and held it up to Haiel-Wat. She ran it through her own hair, then pointed to Haiel-Wat's. "Will you let me brush your hair?"

Tucked in the bed next to Arabella, the girl hesitated, her eyes wide. The sores from smallpox had ravaged her forehead and one of her cheeks but had left only a dusting on the rest of her face and body.

"Brush?" Arabella again combed the bristles through her loose hair before gesturing to Haiel-Wat's.

The darkness of night was broken only by the low flame in the lantern on the bedside table. Mercy was already slumbering in the other room. But Arabella never felt entirely comfortable shutting her eyes until Haiel-Wat was sound asleep.

After lying abed for five days, the child had finally climbed out yesterday and taken her first shaky steps. She'd been weak and had tired easily but would be fully recovered soon. And then what would happen to her?

Arabella's chest pinched every time she thought about the child's future. She wanted Haiel-Wat to stay at the bakehouse until Pete could find her family or tribe so she didn't have to resort to living on her own and eating out of garbage bins again.

But why would she stay when she could hardly tolerate being around Arabella? Mercy hadn't fared much better and received the same cold and sullen treatment. Pete was the only one who'd been able to draw the girl out—making her talk, smile, and even laugh. Haiel-Wat liked Jennie even more, spending hours every day cuddling with the dog.

Nevertheless, Arabella was afraid one morning she'd awaken to find the child gone.

Haiel-Wat stared at the outstretched brush, then turned her head away to look out the dark window.

Arabella stifled a sigh and returned to her nightly ritual of brushing her hair one hundred strokes. The thick strands fell in soft waves over her shoulders, the red-brown a rich mahogany in the dim light.

She'd always hated the color, had blamed the red—in addition to her other shortcomings—for the reason she'd never had any suitors. But after Pete's compliment—"*It's the most magnificent color on God's earth*"—she'd started to think that maybe the color wasn't so awful.

Was it possible she was prettier and more capable than she'd believed? After all, Lieutenant Drummond had invited her to another outing and had even dared to kiss her. While he wasn't as flattering as Pete, he'd been very attentive during the recent dinner party and had indicated that she was as graceful, poised, and genteel as he'd hoped to find in a lady.

He'd also expressed his displeasure with her cake making. And her living arrangements. It hadn't helped that several other bride-ship ladies were also present at the Pemberton dinner and had asked about her confectionary in front of everyone. Thankfully, the awkward moment passed quickly, but Arabella had noticed a decided change in the atmosphere toward her the rest of the evening. The lieutenant had spoken of little else during the ride back to the bakery, urging her to abandon the "scandalous undertaking."

"You can't do anything right." Her stepmother's voice echoed through her head. Though Arabella had found immense pleasure baking each morning, guilt always plagued her afterward along with a dozen questions. What if she was making a mistake? What if she ruined her reputation? What if Lieutenant Drummond decided not to pursue her as a result?

Were things moving too fast with the lieutenant anyway? While he was nothing like Mr. Major, she still had to be cautious.

A touch to Arabella's shoulder halted her runaway thoughts. She twisted to find Haiel-Wat kneeling on the bed beside her. Before she could protest, the girl skimmed Arabella's scars, showing above the scalloped neckline of her nightgown.

Arabella stiffened with the need to pull away and hide the marks. They were ugly and a daily reminder not only of all she'd suffered but all the pain she'd caused her family. But she forced herself not to move, especially as Haiel-Wat traced the scars for a second time and murmured gentle words in her own language.

Haiel-Wat's fingers moved to Arabella's hair, and she whispered a word that sounded like "fire." When the child reached for the brush, Arabella relinquished it. At the pressure of the bristles, she remained motionless, afraid any reaction would scare the child.

Haiel-Wat moved the brush carefully, drawing it through Arabella's thick strands. "Brush?" the girl finally asked.

"Yes. Brush."

Haiel-Wat said something soft, almost reverent, and continued to stroke Arabella's hair.

With each gentle motion, happiness rose inside Arabella like soft, tender dough in the kneading trough.

Finally, Haiel-Wat pushed the brush back into Arabella's hand. Her ebony eyes were sad and filled with an understanding that brought an ache to Arabella's throat.

"Brush?" the girl asked, touching her own hair.

Arabella nodded and shifted on the bed so that she was behind the child. Then with the same reverence Haiel-Wat had used, Arabella stroked the girl's hair, knowing she'd never forget this night.

A short while later, as Arabella drew the covers, Haiel-Wat didn't flinch or pull away as she usually did. Instead, she cupped Arabella's cheek, her eyes radiating trust.

Swift tears formed at the back of Arabella's eyes, and she smoothed her hand over the girl's cheek in response, ignoring the scars and seeing only the beautiful girl she would someday become.

"Good night, little one," Arabella whispered.

As Haiel-Wat's lashes drooped, Arabella's heart swelled with the motherly love it had been denied for so long. What if she could become Haiel-Wat's mother?

Just as quickly as the thought came, Arabella thrust it aside. Even if the child had lost her family, she belonged with her people and needed to return just as soon as Pete could find them.

For now, Arabella would have to content herself with the brief taste of motherhood and pray that someday she'd finally have a family of her own.

Jolted from sleep, Arabella sat upright in bed. For long seconds, she stared through the darkness and tried to silence her racing heart. She listened to Haiel-Wat's even breathing and attempted to figure out what had awoken her. After a moment with nothing more than the usual thuds and thumps coming from the bakehouse below, she settled herself against her pillow.

When a shout resounded from the room below, Arabella pushed herself up again. At a clatter and crash followed by more shouting, she shifted to the edge of the bed. Had someone fallen and gotten hurt? Perhaps Blind Billy? Or what if something had happened to Pete? He never got enough sleep, and in his exhaustion maybe he'd injured himself.

With her pulse picking up speed, Arabella slipped from the bed and rapidly donned her gown, surprised that Haiel-Wat could sleep so soundly through all the commotion. As Arabella stepped into the main room, Mercy rose to her elbows on the sofa. "What do you think is going on down there?"

"I'm not certain. But I shall feel better if I investigate."

"Would you like me to go, miss?"

"No. There's no sense in both of us getting up, and as I'm already properly attired, I may as well check on the situation."

"Right then, miss." Mercy lay back and situated her blanket over her arms. "Holler if you need me."

"I shall. Thank you, Mercy." As Arabella crossed the room and exited, she was struck by the strange relationship she'd ended up having with Mercy. Of everyone on the bride ship, she hadn't expected a poor woman from London's slums to be her closest friend. But somehow over time, their relationship had shifted—or perhaps her view of Mercy had shifted so that she no longer saw the pretty young woman as a servant to do her bidding, but a person with the same hopes and dreams as herself.

With hurried steps, she made her way to the rear entry of the bakehouse. The door was ajar, with Jennie resting on the inside mat. As Arabella entered, the spaniel peered up at her, not daring to lift her head, as though she was afraid she might get blamed for whatever had happened.

At the center of the room, Dodge was kneeling on the floor and retching, his head bent over a bucket. A half-empty bag of flour stood open near him. And at the largest trough, Blind Billy and Pete both stood, up to their arms in dough.

"Get off the floor and pour the flour," Blind Billy yelled. "It ain't gonna pour itself."

Dodge attempted to pull himself up, grabbing on to the

corner of a nearby table. But his hand connected with a pan only to send it toppling to the floor where it landed with a clatter.

Arabella didn't have to study the scene for long to grasp that Dodge was sick—much too sick to work. She crossed to him and placed a hand on his back. "What ails you?"

At the sound of her voice, Pete and Blind Billy ceased their mixing, and Pete craned his neck to see her.

Dodge wiped a sleeve across his mouth and attempted to straighten. "I'm well enough, Miss Lawrence. Don't mind me a mite."

When he swayed, she caught his arm to keep him from crashing to the ground. In spite of his brave façade, his skin was ashen, his eyes glassy, and his limbs trembling. "You're sick, Dodge. You need to be abed."

"Ain't nothing.'" He offered her a weak smile but an instant later bent over and heaved into the bucket.

"He's too sick to be here." Arabella leveled a glare at Pete and for the first time noticed he was bare-chested and that his trousers hung low on his waist. The perspiration coating his flesh glistened in the lantern light, and his thickly corded muscles gleamed.

Heat spilled into her cheeks.

His half-clad attire was entirely inappropriate, and she forced herself to look anywhere but at his bare torso—at Blind Billy, at the mounds of sticky dough, the worktable, and then at Dodge.

But somehow her attention snapped back to Pete's beautiful body, to the ridges of exposed flesh. Thankfully, he was watching Dodge, his brow furrowed, and hadn't realized she was ogling him.

"If you're too sick to work," Pete called, "then head on out to bed."

"You can't do this without me," Dodge replied weakly.

"We'll get along."

"I shall stay and help," Arabella offered.

Both Pete and Dodge started to protest, but Arabella shook her head. "If you need someone to pour flour, certainly I'm capable of the task."

"You need to sleep," Pete insisted.

"If you can get by on so little sleep, then I can as well." She lifted her chin and dared him to deny her.

He was quiet for a moment, his expression reflecting his inner debate.

Grumbling under his breath, Blind Billy started stirring again.

"All right," Pete conceded. "But only until the mixing is done. Then Blind Billy and I can finish up on our own."

"I'll tend to Dodge" came Mercy's voice at the rear door. The young woman didn't wait for anyone to agree with her plan, but instead strode to Dodge, wrapped her arm around the boy's waist, and led him out of the bakehouse.

Once they were gone, Arabella moved to the bag of flour, attempted to heft it, and quickly discovered it was much heavier than it appeared.

"You gonna stand there all night?" Blind Billy said, "or you gonna help?"

"I'll take care of it." Pete lifted his sticky arms out of the trough.

"No," she said firmly and then picked up one of the tin mixing bowls that had fallen to the floor, dipped it into the sack, and held it above the trough.

Pete nodded, beads of sweat drawing lines down his temple. "Add a little at a time."

As she tipped the flour and let it flow into the sticky mixture, Pete began stirring the dough more vigorously, his muscles straining against the effort. Every beautiful muscle in his arms and upper body.

She tore her sights from him, forcing herself to concentrate on the flour and the dough, the heat in her cheeks pouring down into her abdomen. Inwardly, she chastised herself and considered asking him to don a shirt, as he'd done the first time she'd come into the bakehouse while he was working.

But if Pete was aware of his nakedness this time, he didn't seem bothered by it. Either that, or with his sticky arms he'd deemed it impractical to stop and attempt the feat. Whatever the case, he'd tease her mercilessly if he discovered her reaction to him. Or throw out another challenge like he'd done the night of their reading lesson when he'd taunted her about the kiss with the lieutenant.

Of course, she hadn't been expecting the lieutenant to kiss her. It had been rather forward on his part. Even if courtships were destined to move faster than normal in this untamed land, she'd believed a gentleman like Lieutenant Drummond would still maintain proper boundaries—unlike Pete who'd practically stated that it wasn't a matter of *if* he kissed her, but *when*.

The warmth in her stomach flared at the remembrance of his low taunt, his breath caressing her skin, and his nearness making her body tense with awareness.

Not that she wanted Pete to kiss her. She most certainly did not. And not that she'd allow it when he got around to trying. Because she would not. He was his usual arrogant self to think she'd even consider kissing him.

It didn't matter that the merest whisper of kissing had sent her stomach tumbling and her heart racing. It didn't matter that his fingers against hers had done the same thing. And it didn't matter that the lieutenant's affection hadn't elicited a similar response. His would have if he'd taken the time to work up to it the way Pete had.

Whatever the case, she wasn't planning to do any more kissing. And she needed to maintain her composure in all situations, even when Pete surprised her.

With fresh determination to establish appropriate boundaries with Pete, she focused on pouring the flour, having to return to the bag several more times before the dough began to thicken.

By then Pete and Blind Billy were kneading—folding and then pummeling. Sweat dripped from both of their faces into the trough and onto the enormous mass of dough, but they didn't notice or care.

Blind Billy's shirt was drenched with perspiration and stuck to his back. She could understand now why Pete hadn't bothered wearing the garment since it would only end up wet and useless.

Was this how hard they had to work every night?

Arabella could only watch with a growing sense of awe. Like most people, she ate bread each day—it was a staple item at every table. But she'd never imagined how much work went into the process—was ashamed to admit she'd taken the loaves for granted.

When Pete gave the word, they finally ceased the kneading. He carefully covered the dough with a towel, and Blind Billy skirted along the trough and table to a corner where he sank down, leaned his head back, and closed his eyes.

"It's proving," Pete explained as he wiped his hands and arms on another towel.

"Proving?" She rolled the top of the flour bag down to close it.

"The dough has to rise for a couple of hours. And while it's rising we catch a few winks."

She glanced to where Blind Billy sat, his legs stretched out in front of him. "You sleep here, on the floor?"

"Most nights. For an hour or two. Then once the dough is ready, we get up and start weighing it into two-pound loaves."

Two pounds was the standard size, and bakers who tried to cheat customers by going below the weight could be fined a hefty amount.

"Blind Billy shapes the dough into the quartern loaves, and then I take care of getting them into the ovens as quickly as possible before they lose their shape."

The glow from the ovens told her Pete and his assistants had already set the bricks to heating hours ago in order to bring the ovens to the right temperature for bread baking. "How many loaves can you bake at a time?"

"A dozen per oven."

"If I were to guess, I'd say they take about an hour to bake before the crusts turn hard and golden."

"You'd guess right."

She smiled, allowing herself a small measure of satisfaction. She'd worked hard over the past few days to determine the baking times of the cakes, as well as the necessary heat of the ovens. If not for Pete's patient instruction, she surely would have burned more than one cake.

"We bake the common household bread first." He pointed to another trough that was already covered with a towel. "Then we do the wheaten last so that it's still warm when we deliver it to customers."

He didn't have to tell her the wheaten bread—which was made with a better quality, finely ground flour—was for his wealthier customers who could pay extra for a tastier loaf. 'Twas the kind she'd eaten all her life.

As she finished tidying up the supplies she'd used, she straightened to find Pete at one of the washbasins. She couldn't keep from watching him, even though an inner voice nagged her not to. With hands cupping the water, he tossed it against his cheeks and forehead, swiping it back into his hair until the strands were wet. When he finished, he dashed the water against his bare chest, letting it run down in rivulets so that his flesh glistened.

She had the strange urge to let her hands glide down his contours the same as the water. Just the notion of trailing her fingers over his flesh sent warmth pouring into her belly like a stream of melted honey. What kind of brazen woman was she becoming? But even as she silently berated herself, she couldn't look away from the well-defined muscles.

Pete's motions ceased.

She tore her sights from his chest and lifted her eyes to find that he was watching her. She knew she ought to be mortified he'd caught her admiring him. He was already too boastful and didn't need her or any other woman adding to his self-pride.

Yet his expression didn't contain a hint of the teasing or humor she'd expected. Rather, his eyes were dark and serious and laden with bold desire.

Her breath hitched in her chest, and a flurry, like that of a bird beating its wings, unleashed in her middle, filling her with a wanting, almost like an aching need.

His sights dipped to the rise and fall of her chest, which she realized was heavy and unsteady. She lifted a hand and pressed it against her bosom to calm her breathing, only to realize her fingers were trembling.

When his gaze collided with hers again, the heat smoldered into her, searing a trail through her blood, making her want to be with him, near him, against him—without anything holding them back.

"Young man, I'm still awake" came Blind Billy's crusty voice from the corner. "So don't think you can get away with any hanky-panky."

As though waking from a dream, Arabella first cupped her hands against her flaming cheeks. Then she spun and reached for the nearest item—heedless of the fact that it was one of the iron cylinders used in weighing the bread.

"Sorry to disappoint you," Pete retorted calmly, "but there's no hanky-panky going on here."

The older man snorted. "Could have fooled me. There's more heat in this room now than when the ovens are a-blazing."

The room *was* hot. Arabella shifted the iron weight from one hand to the next. Then she set it down and grabbed a spatula, flapping it in front of her face like a fan. She shouldn't have been staring at Pete so openly or with such interest. What was wrong with her? Hadn't she chastised herself a short while ago about maintaining high standards and behaving as a lady?

"Can't help it if I set hearts ablaze," Pete said, his voice finally taking on the teasing tone she was used to.

"More like you set yerself on fire," Blind Billy muttered.

Arabella couldn't bear to face either man. Her behavior and now the conversation both were entirely inappropriate.

Everything about Peter Kelly was unsettling. He had a way about him of turning her carefully ordered world inside out and upside down.

"I should go check on Dodge." She ducked her head and hurried to the door, not daring to look at Pete again. She tripped over Jennie in her haste and stumbled outside. Even though the place wasn't on fire, she couldn't have gotten out faster if it were.

sixteen

"And that is everything there is to know about my family," Lieutenant Drummond said from his spot on the blanket beside her.

"Your mother and father sound lovely." Arabella pulled her attention away from the breathtaking view that spread out before her—the changing leaves in their array of gold, ruby, and sienna. With the blue of the bay and the sky as a backdrop, the colors were even more vibrant.

The Sunday afternoon sunshine provided warmth against the cool breeze blowing off Esquimalt Harbor. The grassy bank along the shore was secluded and quiet and peaceful, the perfect place for a picnic.

Around the bay to the west stood Esquimalt Village, where the Royal Navy had its headquarters. The lieutenant had explained that the village was comprised of ship chandleries, a dockyard complex, munitions depots, barracks, and dwellings for officers.

He was stretched out on his side, his head propped on his elbow, peering up at her as she attempted to remain demure and ladylike. Several other bride-ship ladies were present again, mingling with mostly the same group of Victoria's upper class who had been present at the Pembertons' dinner the previous week.

The ladies had been full of the latest news, particularly regarding all their gentlemen callers. They also gossiped about one of the poor women who'd left the barracks and was frequenting the dance halls around town.

Arabella had no doubt the ladies continued to gossip about her too, but thankfully no one made mention of her cake-making business this time. In fact, from the civility of the afternoon, she could almost believe they'd begun to accept her endeavors.

"I cannot complain," the lieutenant remarked. "My parents did everything possible to ensure my brother and I had every advantage. And they continue to support my work here in the colony."

He'd already explained to her that one of the reasons the navy had such a strong presence was to offset the possibility of American squatters forming settlements. The navy provided security in the newly developing colony, especially since the gold rush had attracted so many Americans from California.

"Will you not tell me about your family?" he asked. "I should like to know everything about you."

Laughter from other couples wafted their way. Some were out in rowboats, others at a nearby archery target, with one pair hiking along the shore. The day was perfect in every way, and yet the mention of her family cast a shadow as if a cloud had appeared and darkened the sun overhead.

She plucked a long strand of grass and twisted it. Surely at some point she needed to be honest with the lieutenant about all that had happened in the days before she'd run away from home.

"My father works for the London and Westminster Bank," she said, although she doubted he worked there any longer. Had his circumstances been so reduced that he was in the workhouse now? Ever since Pete had mentioned the possibility of his parents living in one, she'd been envisioning her father there as well.

"You sound as though you miss him," the lieutenant said.

She swallowed the lump in her throat, her regrets pushing up all too swiftly. She had no wish to speak on the matter. Besides, her stepmother had always said, *"It is better to say too little than too much in company."*

He reached out and covered her hand. She'd long past discarded her gloves, so the gentle contact should have comforted her. Instead, her mind filled with the image of Pete sitting next to her on the landing, their fingers intertwining, his touch sending shivers of pleasure through her.

He didn't need to touch her to make her swoon. All he had to do was look at her. Last night during the bread making was proof of that.

The lieutenant shifted so he was lying closer. "If I have any say in the matter—and I hope I do—then you shall get to see your family again someday."

She wasn't sure she wanted to see them again. And she doubted her family wanted to see her. They likely hoped she was dead or at least living in misery.

"Thank you, Lieutenant." She said the words expected of her. 'Twas not polite to share such negative and private feelings so openly. "You're too kind."

"Will you not call me Richard as I've requested?" he asked, securing his hold on her hand more firmly. "I should like it a great deal."

"I shall try. It's just so soon . . . and I'm not accustomed to such informality." Except with Pete.

The lines in the lieutenant's thinly handsome face had softened, as had the steel in his eyes. Without his hat, the sun made his dark hair shimmer and his long sideburns and trim mustache a blue-black. "I fear you may think I am too forward or hasty in making my intentions known to you."

Was he referring to his kiss?

When his attention darted to her mouth and then away, she knew she'd guessed correctly. He cleared his throat as though he could just as easily clear away his thoughts. "While I do not wish to presume anything, I feel the nature and purpose of your arrival here in the colony makes some haste necessary."

"Nature and purpose?"

"Surely it's no secret you came here to find a husband." He focused on the blanket and swiped at crumbs left from their picnic.

"Of course." But that didn't mean she and the other ladies had to marry the first man who showed interest. Maybe Sophia had accepted an immediate proposal, but Arabella had no intention of being so unwise—not after she'd already made such a terrible mistake in her past. She could never go back to being that naïve girl.

The lieutenant continued to brush at the crumbs. "As you are intent upon having a husband, I feel I must make my availability and interest in that role quite clear before anyone else does."

His declaration should have pleased her. It was everything she'd wanted and hoped for. He was the perfect gentleman, from a prominent family and with a promising future. He'd been kind and considerate to her every time they'd met. She'd had none of the same misgivings she'd experienced with Mr. Major. Even so, she needed more time. With her past still haunting her, she wasn't sure she was ready to trust again or that she would make him a good wife.

"I cannot deny what you say is true," she said, choosing her words carefully. "It's just that I should like to use caution since I was in a difficult situation in my past."

He pushed himself so that he was sitting next to her, careful to avoid the fullness of her skirt she'd arranged neatly around her. "Since you'd like to use caution and avoid difficult situations, then I must ask you once more to consider your current living arrangements."

Holding in a sigh, Arabella shifted her attention to the beauty of the changing leaves again. Interspersed with the varying evergreen hues of the Douglas fir, spruce, hemlock, and cedar, the forests were lush. They beckoned to her to come away and lose herself amidst them, especially because she didn't want to repeat this conversation with the lieutenant.

"Please, Arabella," the lieutenant pleaded gently, "tell me you'll move back to the Marine Barracks this week. You'll make me a very happy man if you do."

Were his feelings all that mattered? What about her own happiness? The impolite question pushed for release, but she held it back. "I don't understand your insistence, Lieutenant. Why does it matter where I live, so long as the situation is above reproach?"

"My point exactly. It's not above reproach. People continue to talk. Like me, they simply do not understand why you're demeaning yourself with such manual labor."

Demeaning? Was she really demeaning herself? She might have once thought so, but after the week of baking, and even last night helping with the bread making, how could that be demeaning? Had she simply viewed herself too narrowly as she'd attempted to fit into the mold that most gentlewomen used to define themselves? What if she didn't fit that mold? What if she was meant to be different? What if they all were?

"People are also questioning your connection with the baker," the lieutenant continued. "He's a troublemaker and most certainly not the type of man with whom you should associate."

"I've only known him to be kind." In fact, he'd been generous and helpful and considerate, not only to her but also to everyone he met.

Lieutenant Drummond frowned. "He gained quite the reputation for his carousing and womanizing while up in the mining camps."

"Lieutenant," she quietly chastised, her cheeks flushing at his mention of a subject that was inappropriate for a lady's ears. Even though he didn't spell out what he meant by womanizing, she could easily guess.

"I apologize for my vulgarity." His expression smoothed into one of appropriate chagrin. "But I only want you to be thoroughly aware of the baker's base nature."

"He's given up his waywardness and turned his life around."

"Even if he has—which I highly doubt—people are still prone to gossip. In fact, I've already heard rumors regarding you and the baker."

She pressed a hand to her heart, which was suddenly racing erratically. With the other hand, she unfolded her fan and began to blow air against her overheated skin. "I hope you know such rumors are entirely unfounded."

Even as the words came out, they sounded hollow. She couldn't deny the attraction that flared to life between her and Pete on occasion. While she would never act on it and lead Pete on, she'd clearly done a poor job of masking it.

"Some are saying they've seen him in your apartment."

She'd suspected gossip, but she hadn't expected anything so sordid. Or true.

Shame pummeled her so that she scrambled to her feet without waiting for the lieutenant's assistance. She situated her broad-brimmed hat securely on her head and began to don her gloves. "Lieutenant Drummond, I did not take you for the sort of man who repeated gossip."

The lieutenant was on his feet in an instant, taking her elbow and steadying her. "I deeply regret causing you any distress, Arabella. But I feel it is my duty to help you understand the serious repercussions that could result from your current living situation."

She had the urge to yank her arm free and stalk toward the overland path that led through the stretch of woodland separating Esquimalt from Victoria.

"As much as I am enamored with you," he continued, "I'm afraid that if your reputation is soiled by the baker, neither I nor any other gentleman would be able to salvage it."

She couldn't hold back a small cry. "Please, Lieutenant, say no more! You must believe me when I declare my innocence." The few moments of passion she'd experienced with Pete meant nothing. She couldn't let her fleeting interactions with him ruin her chances at securing a good marriage and having a secure future here in this new land.

"I didn't move into the bakery because of Pete. I did it because of Haiel-Wat." The words poured out in a desperate attempt to redeem herself. "I found her by the garbage bins in the Marine Barracks. She was sick and weak and needed help. And Pete agreed to house her until she's better."

Something flickered in the lieutenant's eyes, warning Arabella that perhaps she'd said too much. But she couldn't stop. She had to make the lieutenant understand the rumors about her were entirely unfounded. "I wanted to take care of Haiel-Wat. She's such a little thing and was so weak and sick. Pete offered to let me stay with the girl in the apartment, and he willingly moved to the storage building with his assistants. He only comes in from time to time to visit with the little girl. That's all."

She grabbed her hat as the breeze tugged at it and threatened to wrestle it off her head. The coolness coming off the bay soothed her skin, but somehow it couldn't soothe the hot pressure that had built in her throat and at the backs of her eyes.

"I just wanted to help," she whispered. "And I am planning to return to the Marine Barracks as soon as Haiel-Wat is recovered."

The lieutenant's jaw flexed, and the fingers upon her elbow tightened. "I pray to God she doesn't have the smallpox."

Arabella shook her head. "No, she already bears the scars of the disease and instead suffers from dysentery—"

"Let us hope you've been exposed to nothing worse." He shook his head, frustration lining his forehead. "This is just like Peter Kelly's usual foolishness—not only exposing you but all of Victoria."

"We've been very careful and discreet—"

"He delivers bread all over the city, Arabella. Consider the numerous people who could be infected by now."

"Lord Colville assured us Haiel-Wat's condition wasn't contagious." But even as she spoke, doubts began to creep in, including the remembrance of Dodge's illness the previous night.

What if the lieutenant was right? What if in trying to care for the native girl, she'd started an outbreak of some other disease?

She closed her eyes and willed her growing panic to subside. As she dragged in a breath, the lieutenant startled her with a soft touch to her cheek. Her eyes flew open. "I didn't mean to cause so much trouble. Honestly, I didn't."

"Arabella," he said tenderly, caressing her cheek again, "we shall work this all out. I promise."

She swallowed the rush of emotion that threatened to undo her.

"You did the right thing in telling me." He began guiding her toward shore, where one of the rowboats had just been abandoned by another couple.

"What shall we do?"

"On the morrow I shall make arrangements to have the child quarantined. And then I shall have some of my men move you back to the Marine Barracks where your reputation will remain untarnished."

"But I cannot stay at the Marine Barracks much longer—"

"If I ask around, I shall eventually make other arrangements for you to live someplace more suitable."

Arabella nodded, knowing his plan was wise but unable to stop a tremble of trepidation. What would Pete say? He didn't like the lieutenant, but he would see the benefit of moving Haiel-Wat out of the bakery, wouldn't he? Whatever the arrangements, surely they could both continue to visit Haiel-Wat and take care of her.

"Will you allow me the opportunity to speak with Pete on my own?" she asked. "I think he'll take the news better if I can explain the rationale behind the decision."

Lieutenant Drummond hauled the bow of the boat farther onto the bank and then held out his hand to assist her inside. "I don't think that's a good idea."

"I need to do this." She placed her hand into his and gave him what she hoped was a beguiling smile. "Please, Lieutenant?"

He hesitated, the hardness in his eyes softening. "If you're certain."

"I am." She owed Pete an honest explanation. It was the least she could do after he'd been so kind to her.

Holding the lieutenant's hand, she hefted her skirt and climbed into the boat. It swayed, and she grabbed on to him with both hands to keep her balance. As she stood close to him, grasping his shirt and vest into fists, he bent and pressed a quick kiss against her cheek.

When he shifted back, she had the urge to wipe away the moist imprint left from his lips. She couldn't keep Pete's whispered words at bay: *"When I kiss you, you won't wipe my kiss away afterward. You'll be asking for more."*

No, she thought angrily. She wouldn't wipe the lieutenant's kiss away this time. She'd welcome it and embrace his attention.

She took a step into the boat and allowed the lieutenant to help her sit. From now on, she had to concentrate on letting her feelings for Lieutenant Drummond develop and grow. And that would be easier if she moved back to the Marine Barracks and cut Pete out of her life completely.

"I don't like this. Not at all." Hayward paused in folding and placing another one of Arabella's unmentionables into the trunks that lined her bedchamber of their London home—the only home Arabella had ever known. The maidservant cocked her head so that her loose gray bun slid to one side of her head. She fixed her stern gaze upon Arabella, her lips pressed tightly.

"I have no choice, Hayward," Arabella replied, laying a lacy shawl on top of the gowns already folded and stowed carefully in one of the largest of her trunks.

"No choice?" Hayward's voice rose a notch. "Pshaw. You always have a choice."

Arabella's heart had been heavy since she'd crept away from the study after eavesdropping on her father and Mr. Major. Yes, she was anxious about the prospect of getting married, and she couldn't set aside the deep, jarring sense that something wasn't right.

But more than her anxiety, a strange disappointment had weighed upon her—the disappointment that her father had so easily believed Mr. Major's claims about her fickleness.

She understood that Mr. Major's threats had given Father no choice but to proceed with the wedding. She didn't want Father to have to give up his employment on account of her. And she certainly didn't want to become the source of his downfall among their social circles.

Even if he couldn't change her fate, he could assure her he cared about her. But other than calling her into his office and telling her the wedding must continue as planned, he hadn't spoken another word to her.

"I've never felt right about these marriage plans." Hayward retrieved another stack of Arabella's unmentionables from her chest of drawers and placed them on the end of the bed next to Toby, who watched the exchange with perked ears, his curly white fur in need of a cut.

Arabella scratched the dog's small head and earned a lick to her hand. "Sometimes we're called upon to make hard sacrifices for the people we care about."

"That may be. But not with a man like Oriel Major. I'm afraid of what that man is capable of doing to you."

"Once we're married, I'm sure all will be as it should."

A knocking upon the bedchamber door brought their conversation to a halt. When a maidservant ushered Pym Nevins into the room, Arabella wanted to jump into one of the trunks and hide.

Mr. Major's stout butler had become a regular visitor, arriving nearly every day with some form of communication from Mr. Major. And with each visit, Arabella tried not to squirm under Pym's scrutiny. It was as if he'd been tasked with the job of reporting back to Mr. Major every detail of what he witnessed during his visits.

After delivering the invitation to dine with Mr. Majors that evening, Pym peered around the room at the trunks. "With the wedding only three days away, Mr. Major wanted to know how the packing was coming along and when your belongings will be ready to transport to your new home."

Arabella hadn't started packing until this morning since she'd been so sure that she'd have no need to move.

But now, as Pym strolled from trunk to trunk and glanced at the scant amount inside, disapproving lines creased his wide forehead. Reaching the last chest at the end of the bed, he halted and clucked his tongue. "Mr. Major won't be pleased with your progress, Miss Lawrence. I suggest you enlist additional staff to aid the packing efforts."

Toby chose that moment to jump up from his spot on the bed and start barking at Pym.

The butler swatted at the dog in an attempt to quiet him.

With a deep growl, Toby lunged and sank his teeth into the tender flesh between the man's thumb and forefinger, drawing blood and plenty of curses.

"Stupid dog." He slapped Toby on the nose, hard enough that the dog yelped and slunk backward. "You can be sure I'll be reporting this incident to Mr. Major. He won't take kindly to having a dog that bites."

"It was just a nip," Arabella said. "And he's usually a very sweet dog."

"He's a little monster." Pym held up his hand, now dripping with blood.

Arabella wanted to yank down her collar and ask Pym what he thought of his master biting her neck. But of course she'd behaved as any lady would by calling for servants to tend to his wound and making sure he was taken care of in the best possible way, and praying he wouldn't carry through on his threat to tell Mr. Major about the bite. She couldn't abide the thought of leaving Toby behind.

She tugged at her collar at the same time that she tugged herself out of her past. Lieutenant Drummond had brought the chaise to a halt in front of the bakehouse and was coming around to assist her down.

In the fading evening light, the windows of the shop were dark, as were the windows in the apartment above. Pete would likely still be asleep in the outbuilding—unless he was hiding in the shadows, awaiting her return, just as he had been the last time. Perhaps he'd even suggest another reading lesson.

As her feet connected with the dirt street, the lieutenant's hand lingered upon hers. "Are you sure I cannot stand by your side while you deliver the news?"

"I must do this myself," she insisted. "Pete deserves that much."

Beneath his cap, Lieutenant Drummond's expression was shadowed, but not enough to hide his wariness.

"You have no need to worry." She offered him a smile. "I shall do exactly as we've talked about."

He hesitated.

She pulled her hand free of his grasp and took a step away.

"Are you certain? The baker can be quite persuasive when he puts his mind to the task."

Pete could be persuasive, but surely he'd agree the bakehouse was no place for a child who might be ill with a contagious disease. With Dodge getting sick last night, they couldn't take any more chances and possibly expose the entire community to whatever was afflicting Haiel-Wat.

"He'll understand," she said, praying that was true.

After convincing the lieutenant not to accompany her any farther, she made her way around the bakehouse, fingering the cross in her pocket and praying for the courage to say what she needed to. All the while she held it, she couldn't keep from noticing the irony of using the cross Pete had given her for the courage to face him.

Rounding the corner, she waited for Pete to step out of the shadows with a cup of coffee in his hand, glance up at the sky with its glow of the setting sun, and remark on its beauty. But as she started up the stairs, his voice didn't stop her. Even when she slowed her steps and waited for him to say something— anything—he remained silent.

Finally, at the landing, she paused and searched the outbuilding and the yard. As far as she could tell, there was no sign of him. She wasn't sure whether to feel disappointed or relieved.

Quietly, she let herself into the apartment. All was silent as she crept through the main room to the bedroom door. "Mercy?" she whispered. But even as the young woman's name left Arabella's lips, her pulse slowed to a crawl.

Mercy wasn't there. And neither was Haiel-Wat.

As an autumn night breeze blew through the open crack of the window, Arabella shivered and drew her shawl around her shoulders. There had to be a reasonable explanation for why Haiel-Wat wasn't here.

She stepped further into the bedroom and searched, praying the girl was simply sprawled out on the floor with Jennie. But neither the dog nor child were anywhere in the apartment.

With her pulse picking up speed, Arabella backtracked until she was standing on the landing again, this time openly and frantically scanning the yard. Still without any signs of life, she descended and barged into the bakehouse only to find it was as deserted as the apartment above.

She made her way to the outbuilding, tentatively knocking on the door. When no one answered, she opened the door a crack. "Pete?" Without windows, the interior was too dark to make out anything except for several large bags of flour that had been tossed onto the floor.

"Miss Lawrence?" came Dodge's sleepy voice from somewhere inside, in addition to snoring that was loud enough to rival a rumbling steam engine.

"'Tis I." She tried to swallow her panic and behave as a lady and not a hooligan. "How are you faring? I do hope you're feeling better."

"Mercy took care of me, and I'll be up for work tonight right on time."

"Surely you'll need to rest another night."

"Not at all, miss."

She wanted to insist he stay abed—or at least stay away from handling the food—until they were certain he didn't have the same illness as Haiel-Wat. But she held herself back, deciding once she found Pete, she would convince him to give Dodge another night off, and she'd offer to take the boy's place again.

"I need to speak with Pete," she said. The yard, the shops, and even the street out front were too quiet.

"He's gone," Dodge replied through a yawn. "Been gone for hours looking for that Indian girl."

"For Haiel-Wat?" The chill moved straight to her heart.

"Yep."

"What happened?"

"Guess she got tired of staying here and left."

Arabella felt the blood drain from her face. Her worst fear had come true. Haiel-Wat had run away.

seventeen

$\mathcal{P}$ete glanced up at the apartment. The light was off, and the windows were black.

He needed to give Arabella the news, but it would have to wait for the morning. Besides, with the falling of darkness over an hour ago, he couldn't delay his work any longer. Dodge and Blind Billy would have already started mixing the dough without him, and Blind Billy would be as ornery as an old goat at having to do the bulk of the stirring.

Releasing a weary breath, he opened the bakehouse door and let Jennie enter first. He braced himself for Blind Billy's barrage of complaints, then stopped short at the sight that met him.

Mercy stood at the side of the trough, pouring flour. And Arabella, Dodge, and Blind Billy were up to their elbows in the sticky dough. His attention locked on Arabella, on her shirt-sleeves rolled as high as they could go, to the layer of dough and flour sticking to her arms, apron, and even to her nose and chin. Shifting wearily, she blew at the loose curls that dangled across her flushed face.

"Haiel-Wat?" Her eyes were hopeful.

He shook his head, the frustration of the past hours of searching swelling like a summer squall. "I didn't find her."

Arabella's thin shoulders slumped.

"But I have a lead." He offered her the only hope he'd been able to find after the hours of scouring Victoria and the surrounding area. "An old Salish guide who lives in the area recognized her name and said she's from a village several miles up the Strait of Georgia. He's willing to take me there tomorrow."

"Then you think she went back to where she's from?"

"It's possible." A dozen things were possible, many of which were too disturbing to mention.

Arabella focused on the dough again, blinking rapidly, clearly trying to keep her tears at bay.

Pete's chest tightened. He hadn't wanted to disappoint her, had prayed so fervently all the while he'd searched that God would help him find the little girl. Not just because he feared what might become of her, but because he'd known how much Arabella wanted to help Haiel-Wat, how hard she'd been trying to win her over with gentleness and kindness.

"We need to find her," Arabella said. "She's not fit to be out there trying to get by on her own again. She needs to be here."

"You know I'll do my best to track her down. But I have to wait for morning light before I can do anything more."

For a second, from the determined jut of her chin, he was afraid Arabella might run out and continue the search on her own right then and there. When she finally went back to stirring the dough, he allowed himself to take a full breath.

"What time do I need to be ready to go in the morning?" she asked.

"You can't go, Arabella. We'll be traveling by canoe."

"I promise I won't get in the way or slow you down." She didn't break the rhythm of her stirring. "I shall help."

When she glanced up, the challenge in her eyes dared him to let her help him, just as she was doing at that moment. As much as he wanted to pull her away from the trough and take her place doing the backbreaking work of mixing the dough, he could sense her need to finish what she'd started, even if it exhausted her to do so.

Not only would the ride through the straits be arduous, but there was no telling what kind of trouble they might encounter. And she had to know that even if the Salish guide took him to Haiel-Wat's village, he couldn't predict what they'd find or even if the girl would be there.

She paused. "Please, Pete?"

All along he'd wanted to show her she was capable of doing more than she allowed herself. This was another opportunity to let her step outside her carefully constructed world and try something new—even if it was dangerous. With her tender green eyes upon him, begging him, how could he say no?

He gave a nod. "That means you won't be able to do any cake baking tomorrow."

"This is more important." She let her sights drop back to the dough, but not before he caught a glimpse of something in her eyes he couldn't name. Was it guilt? Remorse?

"You gonna stand there all night," Blind Billy grumbled, "or are you plannin' to do some work?"

Pete grabbed his apron from the hook near the door. "Looks like you're doing well enough without me. I might just go to bed."

Blind Billy harrumphed.

Pete started to shed his shirt as he did every night, but paused with the garment halfway up his torso. The memories of last night flooded him, the way Arabella had looked at him with such fascination. The curiosity had been like a flint shooting sparks into his blood. And the desire that had flared within her eyes a moment later had fanned the sparks into a blaze.

He'd liked that she found him desirable. He'd liked it a lot—so much so that after she'd run out of the bakehouse, he'd had a difficult time turning his thoughts away from her. More than once, especially while resting and waiting for the bread to rise, he'd nearly gotten up and sought her out. He'd ached with the need to pull her into his arms and kiss her.

Each time he'd silently cried out to the Lord for help in resisting the temptation, knowing he was weak and that kissing her wasn't a good idea—especially not when he was filled with such need. He didn't want to take advantage of her and use her to sate his own desires. Instead, he wanted to do things right by her. Cherish her. Make her feel special. And put her well-being ahead of his own.

The problem was, after watching her ride away with Drummond earlier in the day, a quiet desperation had stolen over him. After all his confidence that he'd win her, a low warning had nagged him all day, the terrible gut feeling that he was losing her.

After the entire afternoon and evening of loathing the thought of her being with Drummond, he realized he had to change his strategy, had to do more, had to work harder. But he didn't know what else he could try that he wasn't already doing, except the one thing he knew he shouldn't . . . capitalize on the physical attraction. He could take full advantage of the desire that was fanning to life between them. He could kiss her senseless until she melted into his arms and even into his bed. He'd pleasure her so that she'd willingly become his. And once his, she was too proper to do anything but marry him.

The wild sinner he'd once been wouldn't have hesitated at the thought of carrying through with such a plan. Even the God-fearing man he was now couldn't keep from entertaining the notion of enticing her.

But Pastor Abe's wise words whispered within the nether regions of his soul—the wisdom of doing things God's way, according to the guidelines laid out in His Word. Even when his own plans seemed easier and more productive, Pete had already learned that taking matters into his own hands and living by his own rules led to heartache and frustration.

With another silent prayer for strength to do what was right, he tugged his shirt back down and headed toward the door, needing a dose of cool air to clear his mind.

The light of dawn brushed the horizon with a hazy pink. Pete had only just washed up from the hot hours of shoveling bread in and out of the ovens when Arabella stepped into the bakehouse.

The exhaustion lining her face caused his protective instincts to rise, and he encouraged her to go back to bed and rest for a few more hours. But when she insisted on coming with him, he was secretly glad he couldn't persuade her otherwise.

With a bundle of supplies, food, and canteens of water, they set out through the quiet streets to the secluded cove where he stored his canoe. As soon as they arrived, Tcoosma, the old native who'd agreed to help him, stepped out of the brush nearby and greeted them. An indispensable guide to the English, Tcoosma had been allowed to remain in Victoria when most of the other natives were expelled.

A short and unimposing man, he wore a leather breechcloth and leggings with his moccasins and had no shirt beneath his frayed English cape. His silvery-black hair was gathered into two braids, revealing large abalone shells piercing his earlobes and making them sag low. His dark eyes were half hidden under the brim of a bowler hat, keen eyes Pete hoped would help them in finding Haiel-Wat.

Pete had agreed to pay the man in blankets, and he gave Tcoosma half with the assurance he'd deliver the rest once they were safely returned to Victoria. Tcoosma argued with him for only a few moments about the arrangements, wanting more since Arabella was coming. But Pete held fast to their original agreement, and the old man finally nodded his assent.

Pete helped to situate Arabella at the center of the canoe.

Then he took up the stern to provide the power while Tcoosma sat in the front to guide them.

Arabella gripped the rim of Pete's dugout, a prized possession he'd purchased from the Nootkas, who were known for their craftsmanship in carving canoes from red cedar. Her fingers were rigid and her back stiff as they glided swiftly past Discovery Island and around Cadboro Bay. Although she didn't say so, he guessed this was her first time in a canoe.

With the sun rising over the distant mountain peaks on the mainland, the sky took on an ethereal glow that soothed Pete's soul and reminded him of God's goodness. He hadn't deserved saving, hadn't deserved a second chance at life, but God had given it to him anyway. And he vowed again, as he did almost every time he ventured outside Victoria into the beauty of the wilderness, that he'd make up for his past, that he'd do better this time, that he'd prove himself to be a worthy man like his dad.

For a while, they voyaged in silence, the early morning calls of the birds greeting them—the croaks and high-pitched bleats of the murres, the deep guttural grunts of the cormorants, and the wailing *kok-kok* of the loons.

The calm of the deep green waters revealed the sharp crags underneath that made the straits nearly impossible for large sailing vessels to maneuver safely. The lighter navy gunboats were better able to traverse the inland waterways, but not so well as the native canoes, which, when fully manned, could fly through the water.

As they rounded a bend in the bay, a black-tailed doe and her fawn stood on a nearby rocky shore, their reddish-brown coats gleaming in the early morning light. At the soft slap of paddles against the water, the pair raised their ears and noses, ever alert for danger.

He could tell when Arabella saw the deer by the soft intake of her breath. With wide eyes she watched the two until they bounded away into the heavy growth of flowering berry shrubs, ferns, and seedlings.

Her grip on the canoe was no longer one of fear but of anticipation. She glanced at him over her shoulder, her eyes wide, reflecting the lush green of the hemlocks lining the shore. "I've never seen anything so beautiful," she whispered.

"Just wait," he replied. "It only gets better."

They passed by small islands, each wooded to the water's edge with evergreens, their boughs outstretched as though reaching for the boulders thick with barnacles and stained with seaweed in shades of red and brown. He pointed out the various waterfowl perched upon the rocks and swimming near the shore. When Tcoosma spotted a family of river otters in a small estuary, Arabella pleaded with them to stop and watch. Pete used the opportunity to feast upon Arabella, upon the eagerness in her expression, the wonder in her eyes, and the gloriousness of her smile.

Pete could sense that Tcoosma was enjoying watching Arabella's delight just as much as he was, that she'd won his heart as easily as she'd won Pete's.

When they reached a cleared area of sandy beach that had once been a native village but was now nothing more than burned remains, Tcoosma motioned to a nearby narrow inlet marked by rugged rocky points. Entering into the narrow corridor, canyon walls rose up on either side, so close that Arabella reached out to touch the lichen and soft moss that grew on the rocks.

Farther in, an ancient trunk hung low with clumps of maiden hair dangling overhead. In several places, the passage narrowed so that the canoe was hardly able to pass through. As they glided out of the long, cold shadows into the sunshine, a glassy lake spread out before them with hills rising all around, reflected in the still waters in a portrait of perfection.

Arabella gasped and rose to her knees. "Oh, Pete. I've never in my life witnessed anything so exquisite."

He let his paddle grow idle and joined Arabella in taking in the scene—the endless hills of conifers that surrounded the lake. It was stunning.

"I could almost be persuaded to build a house here instead of the plot I've got picked out near Victoria."

"It would be a perfect place," she replied reverently.

"Except that it belongs to the Salish peoples, and I can't imagine that they'd be willing to sell it."

"If there is anyone left," Tcoosma said in broken English. "I see no smoke."

The absence of the usual hazy blue from campfires wasn't a good sign, especially in the autumn when the natives were always busy smoking salmon for the coming winter.

Tcoosma pointed to a distant clearing on the far shore. "The village is there."

Arabella followed his direction and sat up on her knees even further. "Do you think that's where Haiel-Wat is from?"

The old native shrugged. "If this is the child who begged at the Northerner's Camp, then she claims to have her home here on Lake Toquaht."

At the silence and stillness, Pete guessed that even if this had once been Haiel-Wat's home, like so many of the villages in the area, it had been decimated by the smallpox outbreak.

With rapid strokes, they crossed over until they reached the cluster of cedar-plank longhouses that sat back from the rocky beach. The punkwood fires were cold and black, the salmon racks barren, the scents of woodsmoke and curing fish completely absent. Half-woven grass baskets lay abandoned, and the frames used to make clothing out of tree bark were tipped over. Herring rakes, hooks, lines, harpoons, and other fishing equipment were scattered across the beach as if quickly thrown from departing canoes.

Tcoosma hopped into the shallow water and waded, pulling the dugout canoe onto shore. Only a lone totem greeted them.

The figures carved into the cedar were intricate and showed the expert handiwork and artistry of the natives. This particular totem had a raven at the top, prominent with a strong, straight beak. The other sacred symbols below the raven represented people, fish, plants, and animals Pete didn't recognize but guessed came from their legends.

He stepped warily onto the beach behind Tcoosma, his skin crawling with foreboding. He wanted to warn Arabella to stay in the canoe, at least until he and Tcoosma had the chance to explore the lodgings. But Arabella was already carefully making her way to the front of the canoe, her curious gaze taking in the deserted village.

He assisted her out, and when her feet touched ground, he wrapped his hand around hers. Her startled gaze flew to his, and she began to pull her hand loose. He held her fast. "If you don't want me to toss you back into the canoe, then you need to stay by my side."

She glanced around the beach and village again. "But we're alone."

"We have no idea who or what might be lurking in these buildings."

His words had the intended effect. She blanched, then nodded, making no further effort to separate from his hold. Instead, she sidled closer, her forehead creasing and her attention darting around as though expecting warring natives to charge out of the buildings at any second, whooping murderous threats.

Even though he'd made friends with Sque-is and had gotten to know the natives living in the Northerner's Encampment, Pete was under no illusion that all natives were friendly or that he'd never encounter any problems with them.

The presence of the Royal Navy had brought a measure of security to the colonists, but tension with the natives still simmered under the surface. Officers of the Crown believed an exhibition of force was required to uphold peace and English law, while those with Hudson's Bay Company and Governor Douglas exercised more caution and forbearance.

Whatever the method, Pete had learned early on that, like any people group, the natives weren't without their faults. While the sale of liquor was illegal to the natives, they readily obtained and became inflamed by the drink. In addition, the tribes were often warring with each other and took hostages to sell into slavery even though the English laws strictly forbade the practice.

Pete fingered the handle of his pistol at his belt. He didn't count himself a foe to the natives, but with Arabella at his side, he wasn't about to take any chances. Tcoosma approached the nearest lodge, his hand upon the sheathed knife at his waist. His slow, cautious steps said he wasn't taking any chances either.

At the open doorway, he paused and peered inside. "Gone," he said after a moment.

Pete let his hand rest easier on his pistol.

They moved from lodge to lodge, finding nothing but the scattered remains of a few old belongings and trinkets.

At the last empty house, Arabella's expression reflected disappointment. "She's not here."

Pete studied the surrounding woodland. Tcoosma was already heading down one of the paths that led away from the camp. He disappeared in the foliage but seconds later burst back into the clearing, his mouth and nose covered, his eyes watering.

"What is it?" Pete started toward the path, tugging Arabella with him.

"No. Do not go." Tcoosma's reply was muffled but clear enough.

"Is it Haiel-Wat?" Arabella asked.

Tcoosma shook his head. "A burial ground. Not all are buried."

At the mere thought of what the old native had encountered, Pete's stomach rolled. "The result of smallpox?"

"Hard to tell."

Pete guessed it was so. What other explanation could there be for the decaying bodies left to fester? He was just surprised they weren't lying around, rotting where they'd been left behind.

If this was Haiel-Wat's village, then his guess was that since she'd been infected with the disease, her tribe had left her behind to die with the others who were sick. When she hadn't perished, she'd had to find a way to survive on her own and had gone into Victoria for food.

Perhaps she'd hiked back to her home yesterday, hoping to find that her tribe had returned during her absence. Or perhaps she'd learned where the remnants of her tribe had gone and planned to join them.

Either way, the native child was nowhere in sight. And the truth was, no matter how hard they looked, they probably wouldn't find her, especially if she didn't want to be found.

eighteen

his is the spot," Pete said, stopping at the top of the knoll.

Winded from the climb, Arabella halted beside him, knowing she ought to tug her hand free from Pete's, but somehow she was unable to make herself do it. When he'd assisted her from the canoe at the bottom where they'd left Tcoosma, she could have insisted then. Instead, she'd convinced herself she needed his steadying presence during the short hike, just as she had when they'd explored the deserted Indian village.

Now without any excuses, she could do nothing but admit she liked the pressure of his fingers and the strength of his hold, especially because he made no move to let go.

"This is where I plan to build my house." His voice was hopeful and proud and determined.

As she followed his gaze over the knoll and the bay beyond, she dragged in a breath and let the late morning breeze cool her cheeks. The view wasn't as spectacular as Lake Toquaht, yet it was beautiful nonetheless. A mixture of conifers and deciduous trees dotted the hill, as well as shrubs and late-blooming wildflowers. In the distance across the bay, snowcapped mountains rose above the foothills.

"You must situate the house so that it faces those mountain peaks," she said. "With enormous windows so you can see the view from every room."

A slow grin spread across his scruffy countenance, bringing out the dimple in his chin and making him ruggedly handsome. "I like that idea. In fact, I like it a lot."

Pleasure wafted through her, filling her with a sense of satisfaction she couldn't begin to explain. "You must also build a large porch on the front, like some of the houses in town."

"Aye. I like that too." His fingers caressed hers, sending tingles up her arm. "Imagine sitting out here in the spring when the fruit trees are blossoming all over this hill."

"I imagine it will be the loveliest sight in all of Vancouver Island."

"Not quite." His voice was suddenly low, and his shoulder brushed hers. "You'll always be the prettiest sight."

She couldn't resist a sideways glance and found he was studying her profile, his eyes dark and serious.

Warmth pooled inside. "Peter Kelly, stop that."

"Stop what?" The rumble in his voice only stirred the warmth into an eddy.

"Stop flattering me."

"You know me well enough by now to know that the only person I flatter is myself."

She laughed, and her laughter drew the attention of Tcoosma, who waved at them impatiently from where he waited in the canoe.

The old native hadn't wanted to stop, but Pete had insisted on showing her the land he wanted to buy and where he planned to plant his orchards. While it was slightly out of their way, Pete had promised Tcoosma another blanket for the extra trouble.

"I love it here," she said even as Pete began to guide her back the way they'd come.

Their downhill momentum pushed them faster. Even so, he

slowed his steps to match hers until they reached the last half of the hill, which was covered mostly with tall grass.

"I'll race you," he said, pulling her to a stop.

"Ladies do not race."

"Why not?"

"'Tisn't proper."

"Who determines what's proper for a lady and what's not?"

Her mouth stalled, and she fumbled to find a suitable response. Her stepmother had always referred to popular etiquette books. But who decided what should go in the books?

"Exactly," Pete replied.

"Exactly what?"

"You have no idea who made up all the rules and why you follow them."

She couldn't argue with him.

"Mayhap it's time to let go of having to be such a proper lady and allow yourself to enjoy life." His eyes were warm and encouraging.

Was he right?

He released her hand. "Ready, set, go." Without waiting for her, he took off, bounding down the hill.

She hesitated only a moment before releasing herself from having to follow proper etiquette—at least at this moment. Letting her feet carry her forward, she ran with an abandon that made her heart light and her laughter spill out.

At the bottom, Pete spun and grinned at her, his wavy hair in disarray, a curly lock falling over his forehead. "I won!"

Somehow she felt as though she'd won as she plummeted the last few steps and he caught her. Their laughter mingled with the sunshine and beauty of the morning.

Breathing in the scent of the wild grass and the sea, she tilted her head back to allow the sun's rays access to her face, loving the warmth even if it took away from the pale complexion behooving a lady. With a cool breeze bathing her and the gentle waves lapping the rocky shore, she knew this was what Pete had meant about enjoying life. This was a moment she'd never forget.

His smile reached his eyes and turned them the color of the sky overhead. "You had no chance of beating me."

"Of course not. Not when you start ahead of me."

"Are you calling me a cheater?" His hands at her waist slid up to tickle her ribs.

She startled at his touch. But at the merriment in his expression and another tickle, she laughed again, which only made him tickle her until she was squirming and squealing. Finally, with her skirts in a tangle, she fell into him.

His arms slipped around her waist, steadying her.

For a moment, she held herself motionless and marveled at his closeness. Her chin brushed his shoulder, her cheek only inches from his, so close that if she turned, she could kiss him. As if coming to the same conclusion, he shifted, and the warmth of his breath hovered over her cheek.

She closed her eyes and waited for the press of his lips. Only yesterday, while picnicking, the lieutenant had kissed her cheek and she'd been tempted to wipe it away. Would she do the same if Pete kissed her? He'd warned her she wouldn't, that instead she'd ask him for more.

That night she should have told him they could never kiss, that they must keep the boundaries of friendship firmly in place and nothing more. On the hilltop moments ago, she shouldn't have allowed him to keep hold of her hand. And now standing in his arms, she most certainly needed to pull away.

But as with everything else regarding Pete, she couldn't seem to make herself do what she knew she ought to. Instead, she waited for the brush of his lips, her stomach flipping in anticipation.

Rather than kiss her, he splayed his hand at her lower back, his fingers caressing her in a move that left her knees weak. He let the tip of his nose touch her cheek before moving to the loose strands above her ear. Once there, he nestled into her hair. In the same motion, his mouth made contact with the outer rim of her ear, and his hand at her back tightened.

Heated pleasure spilled through her, and she gasped before she realized it. To keep from crumpling, she clutched him, digging her fingers into his shirt.

His nose burrowed deeper, and his breathing turned jagged, making her chest rise and fall in a sudden swell. She shifted her head just a little, wanting to give him access to her lips—in case he had the urge to shift too.

His hand at her back seared through the layers of her garments. As if her fingers had a will of their own, she tugged him closer, wanting—even needing—him in a way that was unfamiliar but that felt normal and right.

Yet he didn't shift to kiss her. He only seemed to bury his face deeper into her hair, his arms straining, his chest taut as though he was determined not to kiss her.

"Go home" came Tcoosma's voice behind them. "Then kiss her all you want."

At the crude suggestion, Arabella wrenched away from Pete.

He released her, but steadied her with a hold on her elbow while at the same moment grinning at the old native. "I like that plan."

"Oh my" was all Arabella could say as she fanned her face with her hand.

Tcoosma grunted and pointed at the canoe with his paddle.

She allowed Pete to guide her to the narrow vessel. When his fingers circled hers to help her inside, the touch sent sparks over her skin so that she almost gasped again.

"What do you think of Tcoosma's plan?" His whisper brushed her cheek as she stepped inside.

Was Pete serious? She couldn't keep from glancing at him.

His eyes met hers, a mixture of mirth and desire dancing

in the deep blue. "All you have to do is ask me and I'll gladly oblige."

"Ask you?"

"Aye. I won't kiss you until you're sure you want it."

Her breath came up short at the mere thought of where such asking could lead. She lifted her chin, needing to get a grasp on her emotions and the situation. "Peter Kelly, you're positively conceited."

With a widening grin, as though she'd paid him the highest possible compliment, he climbed into the canoe behind her.

As Tcoosma pushed away from the shore and they commenced the journey to Victoria, Arabella's body was strangely alive, every nerve aware of Pete's movements—the way he plunged the paddle deeply into the water and the effortlessness of his labor. She was attuned to the rhythm of his breathing and was somehow even keenly aware when he scrubbed a hand over his jaw.

With each stroke, the reality of her situation also ebbed against her. Whether she liked it or not, something was happening—had been happening—between her and Pete. The attraction was growing. But where could it possibly lead?

She might be able to temporarily bake cakes and live without servants and make do for herself. She might be able to stop worrying so much what other people thought about her. And she might even be able to let go of some of her properness and run down a hill like a girl. But she certainly couldn't cut the ties with her class permanently, could she?

It was one thing for a poor woman like Mercy to marry Lord Colville and gain more than she could ever want or need. But it was another thing altogether to lose one's class and status and comforts. Wasn't that what would happen if she pursued a future with Pete?

She hadn't run away and left her family in such terrible straits only to become a poor working-class woman. She wanted to make a good match, write home to her family, and prove that all the heartache she'd caused them hadn't been for naught. Maybe she'd even have the means to help them emigrate.

As Victoria's coastline came into view, she realized she didn't want to hurt Pete in any way. But she couldn't be with him, could she? She had to go through with the plans she'd made with the lieutenant yesterday to return to the Marine Barracks and guard her reputation more carefully.

She needed to somehow make Pete understand she appreciated all his efforts to help her with the baking and with caring for Haiel-Wat, but she had to consider the long term consequences of her behavior.

She had to tell him now while they had a modicum of privacy.

The problem was, the more time she spent with him, the less she wanted to leave.

"Thank you for letting me come along," Arabella said over her shoulder to Pete, trying to work up the courage to explain that she couldn't do anything like this with him again.

"After spending yesterday with the dandy, I figured you needed a day with a real man." He winked.

She turned her face away from him before he could see her smile. Even though their mission to find Haiel-Wat hadn't been successful, the ride up the coast had been beyond anything she could have imagined, a hundredfold more beautiful than her rowboat ride the previous day with Lieutenant Drummond. But she certainly couldn't tell Pete that.

"I see that smile," he said from behind her. "And I know exactly what it means."

She tried to smother her humor and make her expression stoic.

"It means you like being with me better than the dandy."

"That dandy is a gentleman."

A spray of water splashed against her back, and she sucked in her breath at the coldness as well as the surprise of it. She pivoted and glared at Pete. "You did that on purpose, didn't you?"

219

"Just wanted you to know I'm most definitely not a gentle-man."

"I am already well aware of that fact." She glanced at the clear water the canoe was slicing through. Before she could talk herself into behaving, she lowered her hand into the icy water and flicked the spray backward so that it blew into Pete's face.

He stopped paddling and spluttered, blinking away the water.

At the front of the canoe, Tcoosma paused mid-motion and craned his neck to watch Pete.

Arabella knew she should feel mortified. She was acting like an undisciplined child. But at the surprise rounding Pete's eyes, she couldn't keep from smiling with pretend innocence. "Oops. My hand slipped."

"Did it now?" He rested his paddle across his lap, regarding her through narrowed eyes that twisted her insides into knots of strange anticipation.

Sensing she needed to act before he did, that she had to take him by surprise again, she quickly dipped her hand into the water and sent another spray toward him as forcefully as she could.

As the deluge ran down his face and into his shirt, he didn't move except to narrow his eyes even more.

She couldn't contain a smile at having bested him . . . until another cold blast hit her back and side so that this time she spluttered.

Twisting in the canoe, she cupped her hands and started throwing water on him while he did the same to her, leaving Tcoosma to direct the canoe toward the secluded strip of beach they'd used when departing hours ago.

As the bottom scraped against the rocks, Tcoosma hopped out, shaking his head and muttering at the amount of water that now sat in the bottom of the canoe.

"Shall we call a truce?" she asked, flipping a piece of wet hair out of her face.

Pete climbed into the water and sloshed in the shallow waves, water dripping from his hair and shirt. "A truce? Where's the fun in that?"

Towing the canoe the rest of the way onto shore, his wet garments clung to his body, outlining his frame. The vision of his bare chest filled her head, and she quickly looked away, silently chastising herself for being so bold.

When the boat was finally out of the water, he assisted Arabella, letting his hands linger upon her waist. Something in his eyes told her that whatever was going on between them was definitely not over, that he'd never be satisfied with a truce.

She shivered, her need for him prickling her skin so that she wanted to be in his arms again.

"You're cold," he remarked, sweeping his gaze over her. His sights flickered upward and lingered for the briefest of moments before he tore his attention away and focused on Tcoosma, swallowing hard in the process.

When she glanced down, she gasped in mortification and crossed her arms over the thick folds of material molding to her womanly form.

Pete was already in the process of unfolding one of the blankets he'd given Tcoosma as payment. Averting his gaze, he held it out to her. She wrapped herself in the wool covering amidst Tcoosma's protests and Pete's assurance that he'd furnish another in replacement.

As they walked back within the city limits and made their way toward Humboldt Street, silence stretched between them. She could no longer keep at bay the impending move to the Marine Barracks, and she needed to divulge the news to Pete. Although she hadn't secured the hour of departure with the lieutenant, she suspected he'd send his men in the afternoon, so that he might give her as much time as possible to pack her belongings and ready herself.

What would the lieutenant say when he learned Haiel-Wat had run away? Would he be relieved he didn't have to deal with the illness and possible ramifications? And would he understand Arabella's concern that such a small helpless child was on her own and having to fend for herself again?

Halfway down the street, Tcoosma touched Pete's arm and ducked behind a nearby building. "Queen's men ahead. I wait for blankets here."

Before Arabella could make sense of Tcoosma's words, Pete was already sprinting forward. "Hey!" he yelled. "Stop!"

Arabella glanced ahead, only to see a marine step out of the bakehouse and toss baskets into the middle of the busy thoroughfare onto a growing pile of items from the bakery—an overturned dough trough, a bag of flour that had been slashed open in several places with flour spilling out, broken crocks, the long-handled peels, and more.

What was happening?

With dread thudding harder with each step, she picked up her wet skirt and ran. She had to help Pete stop these men from destroying his livelihood. She wasn't sure what she could do, but she had to at least try.

When she entered the bakehouse a moment later, two marines restrained Pete between them. A third swung a bludgeon into his chest. The thwack was followed by Pete's grunt.

The air squeezed out of Arabella's lungs. Before she could release a scream, the marine lifted the bludgeon and brought it down on Pete's shoulder. This time Pete couldn't stifle his pained cry.

Though muffled, Pete's agony tore at Arabella's heart and raced along the scars on her back. Her own wounds were still too fresh and too vivid for her to be able to watch another person take a beating.

As the marine swung the weapon toward Pete's stomach again, she screamed. It contained all the terror and despair and agony she hadn't been able to release, that she'd held in these many months. Now watching Pete, she couldn't keep it in any longer.

As the scream faded, she clamped a hand over her mouth. Tears stung the back of her eyes, and an ache pushed up into her throat.

Pete wrenched free from the marines and started toward Arabella, his brow furrowed above concerned eyes. Before he could reach her, the marine stepped into his path, the bludgeon once again poised for a blow.

"No!" Arabella shouted, tears trickling down her cheeks. As a lady, she'd never before even raised her voice, much less shouted. "Don't hit him again!"

Before the man could lower the bludgeon, the back door of the bakehouse swung open and banged against the wall. The lieutenant entered and crossed rapidly toward the marine. With a scowl, he grabbed the bat and tossed it to the floor. "What do you think you are doing?" he said. "I instructed you to refrain from aggression around Miss Lawrence."

The soldier shrank back and murmured his apologies.

Arabella sagged against the doorframe, and the lieutenant turned toward her, his eyes filled with concern. "I heard a scream. Are you harmed?"

She shook her head.

His eyes widened as he took in her bedraggled hair and the wet garments beneath the blanket. His gaze shot to Pete, taking in his soggy clothing before returning to Arabella. "Did he do this to you?"

She hesitated, unsure how to respond. She couldn't very well inform Lieutenant Drummond that during her canoe voyage with Pete they'd been teasing each other, that the splashing had all been in good fun. He wouldn't understand. Yet she couldn't lie either by insisting she'd fallen into the water.

"I don't understand the reason for this attack against Pete," she said instead. "And why are your men wrecking the bakehouse?"

nineteen

Why indeed? Pete waited for Drummond to find a way to explain his presence and the destruction of the bakehouse to Arabella without making himself look like the fool he was.

Already Pete's shoulder throbbed and his ribs ached. From the painful pinch in his side, he wouldn't be surprised to have a cracked rib or two.

"Pete hasn't done anything to deserve such destruction." Arabella's words came out wobbly, and she swiped tears from her cheeks.

Pete wasn't sure what had brought about her scream. The terror in it had frightened him, had warned him that her outburst had much more to do with something from her past than what was going on in the present.

"But what has happened to you?" the lieutenant persisted, taking her hand. "Did you nearly drown?"

"No, nothing so awful." She spoke uncertainly, as if she didn't quite know how much to reveal. "After Pete showed me the land he's planning to buy, I got wet. But 'tis only a little and nothing to worry about."

"I see." A throbbing vein in the lieutenant's temple stood

out. He released Arabella's hand and pivoted to face Pete. "So, Mr. Kelly is attempting to impress you with his lofty goals for the future with land he'll never be able to afford and a life he'll never be able to have."

"I'll have it," Pete insisted. "You might try to keep the working class to an inferior station, but there's no law against me buying land and having whatever life I choose."

Pete wasn't naïve about the objectives of many in the upper class, namely that they wanted to transfer long-established traditions, customs, and class distinctions to the new colony. Yet he'd lived long enough in this place to recognize that although the divisions were still strong, the opportunities here were boundless compared to anything in the Old World. Pete had every intention of capitalizing on those opportunities. And now that he'd turned his life around and was attempting to please the Lord, surely his life would go better—much better—than before.

Drummond took several steps closer. "The problem is that you think too highly of yourself, Mr. Kelly."

"Then I guess we're both suffering from the same problem."

Drummond paused, the muscles in his jaw and hands flexing as though he wanted to strike out at Pete. But with Arabella in the room, Pete knew he'd refrain from doing so. "I'm afraid not. In addition to exposing Miss Lawrence to all manner of misfortune this morning, including negligence in the water, you are also harboring an infected native."

"Harboring an infected native?" Pete said.

"Yes. Miss Lawrence spoke to me of the native child who's suffering from illness."

Arabella had confided in the lieutenant? Why had she done such a thing?

"You know that Indians are not allowed within the town limits, Mr. Kelly. And not only did you willingly bring a contagious savage into Victoria, but you also brought the child into your business—your bakehouse. Think of all the customers who are quite possibly infected even at this moment due to your poor decision."

"She was in the bakehouse only once in passing. Besides, her illness wasn't contagious. Lord Colville diagnosed her with dysentery."

"A sick savage doesn't belong here. I think we can all agree upon that." Drummond glanced at Arabella as though waiting for her to chime in.

She dropped her attention to her wet shoes, her hair hanging in a tangled mass. Her hands trembled even as she clutched the blanket around her body. Her lashes lifted in a quick peek Pete's direction, long enough to reveal guilt.

Aye, she'd told the lieutenant about Haiel-Wat. But what if she hadn't known Drummond's position on the natives or his role in evicting them in the spring at the start of the smallpox outbreak?

Should he finally expose Drummond's actions toward the natives over the past months? Doing so would incriminate the dandy and turn Arabella away from him once and for all. But even as the truth pushed for release, Pete held back as he had before. He didn't want to win Arabella by default—because she no longer wanted Drummond. He wanted to win her outright, fairly, and with honor.

He'd have to let her figure out Drummond's faults on her own.

"You need to hand the girl over, Mr. Kelly," Drummond continued. "You can no longer continue to harbor her here in your bakehouse."

"She's gone," Pete stated.

"Likely story. Your boy over there"—the lieutenant nodded at Dodge, who was curled up in the corner—"said the same thing, and we gave him a thrashing for lying."

Pete clenched his fists and lunged for Drummond. But two

of the marines grabbed him and wrestled his arms behind his back.

"Dodge?" Arabella's voice rose an octave, and she glared at Drummond with tear-filled eyes. "You thrashed Dodge?"

"He's a part of this too," Drummond responded with a dismissive wave of his hand.

"But he was telling the truth." This time her voice cracked with a sob. "Haiel-Wat ran away. We were looking for her this morning and cannot find her anywhere."

"You're certain she's not here?"

"She was gone when I returned from the picnic last evening."

The lieutenant turned to Pete again. "Either way, I'm taking you down to the lockup and letting you spend a couple of nights there."

"On what charge?" Pete asked.

"You're a rebel, Mr. Kelly. Not only do you make trouble in our peace-loving community on a regular basis, but you've proven you have no regard for the safety and welfare of the public."

Pete was tempted to laugh at the lieutenant's words when Arabella's voice cut into the argument. "Your accusation is unfair."

Her declaration echoed in the room, and he couldn't keep from thinking back to the night of Pioneer's wedding when the lieutenant had leveled nearly the same accusation and how she'd said nothing in his defense.

As if remembering the same, she glanced at him, her freckles standing out against the paleness of her complexion and making her appear more vulnerable.

"Miss Lawrence," the lieutenant responded smoothly, "please do not trouble yourself any longer over the matter."

Arabella clutched the blanket tighter. "If you should arrest anyone, let it be me. I'm the one who brought Haiel-Wat here. Pete wouldn't have involved himself in the matter if not for me."

"Arabella, please," the lieutenant continued as though speaking with a child. "You're new to the area and ignorant of the natives. But Mr. Kelly is well aware of the dangers they pose, especially with the smallpox outbreak. He should have known better than to bring a sick child into the community." Drummond nodded to his assistants, who began to shove Pete toward the door. He complied, knowing he'd only make matters worse and end up in jail longer if he resisted.

"Haven't you already done enough to punish Pete?" This time Arabella's question was louder, more demanding.

In the process of following his men, Drummond halted.

"You've hurt his assistant and ransacked his bakehouse," she continued, her voice gaining strength. "Isn't that enough?"

Drummond's brows lifted in surprise—perhaps even disapproval—of Arabella's boldness. "Surely you understand the need to clean out the bakehouse of everything that has been contaminated by the Indian child?"

"You and I both know this destruction has nothing to do with contamination," Pete cut in. It had everything to do with his meddling into the navy's involvement with the smallpox affair. And maybe now it also had to do with Arabella.

"Pete is innocent. Let him go." The trembling in Arabella's hands had ceased, and her eyes flashed with determination.

The lieutenant's gaze flickered to the small audience they'd gained from passersby watching from the street and doorway. He cleared his throat before speaking in lower tones. "I'm doing my duty, Miss Lawrence. That's all. Now, if you'll excuse us, my men and I shall return later to help you move your belongings to the Marine Barracks."

Arabella was leaving? Had the lieutenant somehow convinced her to go back? Mayhap that was the real reason the lieutenant wanted to find Haiel-Wat. So that Arabella would no longer have an excuse to stay in the apartment above the bakehouse.

The lieutenant bowed his head at Arabella as if the matter were settled. As he spun, she didn't respond except to purse her lips.

A shaft of disappointment speared Pete. Deep inside, he'd known Arabella wouldn't stay above the bakehouse forever, that the arrangement was only temporary. Even so, that hadn't kept him from hoping . . .

"Please do not trouble yourself in returning, Lieutenant Drummond." Arabella's voice followed them.

Drummond paused in the doorway. Before he could respond, Arabella continued, loud enough for everyone to hear. "I have the highest regard for Mr. Kelly. He's done nothing deserving of this treatment. But since you insist upon his arrest, you leave me no option but to remain during his absence and lend my aid in baking bread."

Pete strained to get a glimpse of Arabella over his shoulder. With her wet hair and gown hanging limply, she appeared delicate, almost childlike. But the set of her shoulders and the jut of her chin revealed an inner strength he'd glimpsed at times, but that was now showing itself in all its glory.

"Miss Lawrence," the lieutenant replied. "Please carefully weigh your decision as well as the ramifications."

"I am well aware of the ramifications. And I am quite prepared to accept whatever may come."

The taut exchange between the pair contained an unspoken message, likely something from a previous conversation. Inwardly, Pete smiled. If nothing else came of today, at least he could be assured his arrest and the destruction in his bakehouse hadn't been a complete waste. The circumstances had given Arabella the chance to push past her timidity and fears and learn to stand up for herself. Such a lesson was well worth his discomfort.

"You can place that last basket by the door," Arabella said to yet another of the helpers who'd rallied to carry items back inside.

After the lieutenant had taken Pete away, she'd stepped out of the bakehouse and had stared at the heap in the middle of the street for only a moment before crossing to the pile. The instant she'd picked up the first thing and started lugging it back, neighbors from all the surrounding businesses had come out and joined her.

"That oughta do it," someone said just outside the doorway. "Everything's off the street now."

"Thank you for your help." She combed a damp piece of hair back into her hastily fashioned twist and glanced around at all they'd salvaged. Though a few things couldn't be fixed, the majority simply needed to be cleaned and put away.

The man tipped the brim of his hat. "Pete's a good man, always cheerful and always helping everyone else. It's the least we can do for him."

Arabella nodded. "I know he'll appreciate it."

As the neighbor took his leave, Arabella hugged her cloak around her wet gown and tried to ward off a shudder. Her parting words to the lieutenant seemed to hang in the air and add to the chill. *I am well aware of the ramifications. And I am quite prepared to accept whatever may come.*

Her brave words from only a short while ago didn't seem so brave now. When she'd rebuffed the lieutenant's offer to help her move and had insisted on staying at the bakehouse, she had in all likelihood ruined her chances with him. He wouldn't want to court her any longer.

Her stomach twisted. Had she thrown away her chances of making a good match not only with him but with any other gentleman? If people were already gossiping about her association with Pete and his being in her apartment, then by remaining at the bakehouse she'd quite possibly ruined her reputation altogether.

Whatever the case, she needed to put the room in order. Already Dodge was at work in front of the kneading trough, adding a nail to stabilize it while Blind Billy ran his fingers along the legs, feeling for any other damage and grumbling under his breath.

A carriage rattled to a stop outside the bakehouse. The door flew open, and without waiting for assistance, Mrs. Moresby began to climb out. Her full hooped gown could hardly fit through the opening, but somehow she managed to descend— albeit ungracefully. As she started forward, she straightened her hat, a wide-brimmed creation covered in the biggest faux roses Arabella had ever seen.

"Miss Lawrence," the matron said, her voice and expression aghast, "I was riding to the government building when I saw the lieutenant and his men dragging Peter into the police headquarters . . ." She stopped short at the sight of Arabella's bedraggled state before her attention shifted to the disorderly room. "What on earth is going on here?"

Arabella gave the woman the short version of the happenings and then hung her head, again feeling the weight of her choice to stay. What must Mrs. Moresby think of her now?

The matron bustled past Arabella. "Well, what are you waiting for? Let's get to work."

"Get to work?"

"Yes, we need to get this place cleaned up and put in order before Peter returns." Mrs. Moresby shed her hat and discarded her gloves.

"You're not disappointed in my staying?"

"Of course not. Opening your own confectionary is a perfectly respectable opportunity for you. Don't let anyone tell you otherwise. And no one can condemn you for aiding a sick child, Indian or not."

Arabella lifted her shoulders and drew in a breath. "But what about Lieutenant Drummond? I've likely alienated myself from him and the other eligible gentlemen."

Mrs. Moresby tossed aside her cloak. "Does it really matter?"

Did it? "All along I've assumed I'd marry a gentleman of my class—"

"Character is much more important than class."

For a moment, Arabella had no response and could only watch as the matron surveyed the room, homed in on a broom in the far corner, and crossed toward it.

"Somewhere in Scripture," Mrs. Moresby said as she picked up the broom, "it says, 'Man looks on the outward appearance, but the Lord looks at the heart.'" She began to sweep up the powdery white film coating the floor. "I always figured if God thinks the condition of a person's heart matters more, then I should too."

Mrs. Moresby's words were reminiscent of the wisdom Hayward had always shared with her, advice that had long since been drowned out by her stepmother's. Maybe it was past time to ignore—maybe even cut out altogether—her stepmother's voice and let the wisdom of God's Word guide her instead.

Mrs. Moresby paused in her sweeping and pinned her gaze upon Arabella. "Even if Peter is a bit unconventional at times, you can't deny he's a man of character."

"No, I won't deny it. He's a good man." Arabella fumbled for the nearest item, one of the long wooden peels. Was her blossoming attraction toward Pete so evident that even Mrs. Moresby could see it? She brushed at the dust and dirt covering the peel.

"Peter Kelly is more than good. He's God-fearing, and that makes all the difference."

"You're quite right."

"Then don't be afraid to give him and your relationship a chance. It certainly won't hurt anyone to see where things go." Mrs. Moresby started sweeping again, this time more vigorously, raising a cloud of flour dust.

Arabella placed the peel down and stuck her hand in her pocket. Even though she wanted to take up the matron's challenge to give Pete and her relationship with him a chance, she wasn't sure she could so easily put aside her fears.

Her fingers surrounded the smooth silver cross. *Courage.* Silently, she lifted up a prayer for courage. And for the hope that Mrs. Moresby was right—that it wouldn't hurt anyone to see where things might go.

twenty

$\mathcal{P}$ete stepped through the front door of the bakehouse and was greeted by Jennie's wet nose. She wagged her tail ferociously and rubbed against him.

"I'm glad to see you too," he responded. Before he could bend to give her the attention she wanted, Pete stopped short at the sight that met him. The jarring movement sent pain through his middle, and he put a hand on his cracked ribs to ease the discomfort.

The low flame in the oil lantern above the worktable dispelled the darkness of night and reached the far corners of the room. When he was taken away hours ago, the place had been a disaster, but now he could only stare at the transformation.

The bakehouse had never been cleaner or more organized. The tables were back in position and scrubbed to a shine. The baking utensils were all hung from hooks in the wall. The few sparse shelves were lined with supplies and bowls and crocks in an orderly fashion. The dough troughs had been repaired and covered with towels. Even the floor was spotless.

"Everybody in the neighborhood pitched in." Dodge rose slowly from a flour sack. "Then Arabella organized it all. Even Mrs. Moresby lent a hand."

"Whoo-hee." Pete whistled under his breath. "They were busy. Mayhap I should get myself arrested every week."

Dodge offered him a grin but then grimaced and held his side.

"Got a few broken ribs too?"

"Reckon so."

"Sorry you had to take what was coming to me."

"Ain't nothin' that my dad didn't used to do."

Whenever Dodge talked about his dad, Pete was reminded again at what a faithful man of God his own dad had been and how foolish he'd been to spurn his dad's wisdom and love. If only he could know for certain his dad had received his letter and knew how deeply sorry he was for taking him for granted and not loving and respecting him.

Pete peeked under one of the towels covering the trough. "Didn't expect to be making bread tonight."

"Blind Billy got the sponge set right away, but it needs a mite longer before it'll be ready to turn into dough." Dodge gingerly lowered himself back to the sack of flour, which apparently someone had salvaged from the street. The twenty-stone bags from the miller weren't cheap. He'd have lost at least a day's profit, if not more, over one ruined bag. As it was, resetting the sponge was costly enough.

"Everyone abed?" Pete rotated his aching shoulder, the bruise there as sore as his ribs.

"Blind Billy's catching a few winks." Dodge leaned his head back against the wall and closed his eyes. "Heard the womenfolk talking about going to the cricket game to watch Lord Colville play."

Pete glanced to the darkness out the window. The hour wasn't late, but certainly with the onset of darkness the game was long over. "They back yet?"

Dodge started to shrug, then caught himself. "Ain't heard nothin'."

Pete wished he could plunge a fist into Drummond's arrogant face for beating the boy. "Go on and get yourself to bed—you deserve the night off."

Dodge cracked an eye open. "If you can handle a battering and going to jail, I figure I can put up with a mite of bruising."

Pete nodded his gratitude before exiting through the back door. He was surprised to see a faint glow in the apartment window. Mayhap the women were home after all. If Dodge had been asleep, he probably hadn't heard their return.

He doubted Arabella expected him home tonight. He hadn't expected it for himself. But fortunately, the constable on duty had let him go since Drummond hadn't been able to round up enough evidence to keep him locked away.

"I don't want to see you here again anytime soon," Officer Green had warned as he led Pete out of the corridor away from the cell.

"We both agree on that," Pete had assured the man. But the truth was, if he had to do it all over again, he would. He didn't regret helping Haiel-Wat and prayed the child had found her family and wouldn't have to survive on her own any longer.

Treading silently and skipping the squeaking steps, Pete made his way to the top. He paused at the door only an instant before opening it a crack. A peek inside showed that the room was empty. Mayhap he'd take the opportunity to go wash up and change before Arabella returned from wherever she'd gone. With the growing darkness, he suspected it wouldn't be long.

A soft sound from the bedroom stopped his retreat and propelled him into the room and to the interior door. A glance through the dark room revealed someone lying on the bed, legs and arms tangled in sheets. Long hair spilled over pillows. Long wavy hair.

His heart knocked against his chest. Arabella was home. And she was sleeping.

The need for her that he'd harbored all afternoon rose swiftly.

It wasn't a physical need so much as the need to be with her after all that had happened and to make sure she was okay. Her scream still ricocheted in his head and tore at his heart. Even if she'd shown courage to stand up to the lieutenant, he suspected it hadn't been easy, that the whole experience had taken its toll.

He took a step into the bedroom, then stopped. What was he doing walking into the middle of temptation like this? He needed to run away while he still had a shred of resistance left.

His gaze swept over her again. Enough light from the front room illuminated the bed for him to see her bare feet poking out from under the sheet. And her ankles. At the sight of the elegant curves, his mouth went dry.

Fisting his hands, he forced himself to move back. One step. Then two.

Her soft cry followed by thrashing stopped him. It lasted only a moment, tangling the sheets even further around her legs.

Was she having a nightmare?

Thoughts of his own needs and desires slipped away. He crossed to the side of the bed and reached out to comfort her. Dare he brush her hair back? He didn't want to awaken her, but the urge to ease her fears and pains—whatever those might be—overrode everything else.

He grazed the hair from her shoulder and was surprised when her bare skin met his touch. He didn't realize until too late that her nightgown was ajar, that with her hair out of the way, a stretch of her back lay exposed.

His shadow spread across her. Without thinking, he stepped aside and let the faint light illuminate her pale skin, giving him a better view of what he knew he shouldn't be looking at. Instead of the silky cream he'd been expecting, puckered scars and red welts crisscrossed her skin.

What in the name of all that was holy had happened to her?

His shock melted into a low burn of anger. The more important question was, who had done this to her? Pete trembled with a sudden need to go hunting for the culprit, to lay him out, and beat him until his back was in shreds. Even then, the beating wouldn't repay what he'd done to Arabella.

With the anger bubbling into hot rage, Pete closed his eyes and forced himself to take a deep breath. He'd waited long enough for Arabella to tell him about her past. He needed to know tonight. Now.

Lowering himself carefully to the edge of the bed, he touched her back again, this time tracing the path of one of the longer scars that disappeared behind her nightgown. At his caress, she shifted and released a soft sigh.

Under any other circumstances, sitting on the bed, seeing her bare shoulder and ankles, and hearing her sleepy sighs would have driven him into a frenzy of need. But the only thing he could think about was the pain she'd endured—an excruciating amount. The bite on her neck was bad enough, but this was worse. Much worse.

Tenderly, he traced her shoulder blade and combed the long silky strands that had pooled around her neck.

She drew in a breath and then lifted to her elbows and turned her head to take him in. "Pete."

"Aye. It's me."

The delight in her eyes and voice should have moved him, should have given him a taste of victory after how hard he'd been working to win her. But his heart was too heavy and his blood too hot.

She pushed herself all the way up until she was sitting. The sheet fell away, but she seemed heedless of that fact or of her flimsy nightgown, which continued to slip off her dainty shoulder. Instead, she rose to her knees and grasped his hands.

"I've been so worried," she whispered. "From what Dodge said, I didn't expect you to be out for a couple of days."

"They had no reason to keep me." At times, the navy tried to take the law into their hands, but there were still many justices, lawyers, and other government officials who prided themselves on having a fair and just legal system like that of England.

"How do you feel?" She gently touched his shoulder. "Are you hurt?"

"I've fared worse."

"I'm sorry, Pete," she rushed to say, even as she took both his hands in hers again. "This is all my fault. I regret I said anything to Lieutenant Drummond about Haiel-Wat. I never imagined he'd harm you or wreck the bakehouse the way he did."

"I know. And it's all right."

"Then you forgive me?"

"There's nothing to forgive."

She smiled, and once more the smile contained a joy that should have made his heart lighter. But he couldn't fathom smiling at a time like this. Instead he let himself linger over how stunning she looked even in the darkness, with her long hair cascading down her shoulders, framing her pale face and making her eyes more luminous.

As though sensing his volatile mood, her smile dimmed. "Did he threaten you again?"

"No. He can't do anything to me, and he knows it."

"Then what's wrong?" A note of worry crept into her tone.

He wasn't sure how to broach the topic with her, didn't want to frighten her so that she refused to tell him anything. Rather than speaking, he freed one hand from her grasp and swept her long hair to her back, letting his thumb brush her shoulder.

She expelled a soft gasp, and her fingers tightened against the one hand she still held, reminding him of earlier in the day when they'd strolled through his land and she'd let him hold her hand. He'd loved describing his plans to her and could envision her sitting next to him on the front porch of their home sharing the beauty of the view together.

In fact, the more time he spent with her, the more he couldn't imagine life without her. Aye, he could admit that at first he'd been infatuated with her beauty. But after getting to know her more every day, his feelings went much deeper. He'd never been in love before, but he suspected these deep and entangled emotions came close.

"Arabella," he whispered, wondering if he should simply blurt his feelings. He wasn't the kind of man who held back. And yet something inside warned him that she wasn't ready to hear his true feelings, not yet.

He drew his finger along a scar that touched her shoulder. "Who did this to you?"

She stiffened and then jerked away from his touch, releasing his hand and drawing her nightgown up over her body, hiding the damage.

Ignoring the desire to reach for her, he rested his hands on his thighs. "Please tell me what happened, Arabella."

She tugged at the sheet, trying to untangle it, her hands shaking.

Gently, he helped to ease the linen out from the confines of her body, freeing it and drawing it up to her chin.

"You know I only long to bear this burden with you," he said. "I'd take the scars from you if I could."

Her eyes were wide, revealing the pain she'd buried there. She started to shake her head, and he was afraid she would refuse to tell him. Then she spoke in a harsh whisper, one that contained all her heartache. "I attempted to cancel my wedding."

Pym Nevins ushered Arabella into the sitting room of Mr. Major's London townhouse. She'd been to his home only once before, several years ago when she'd accompanied her father and stepmother to a Christmas party that Mr. Major had hosted for his employees.

At the time, he was married to a pretty young woman who had played the role of hostess to perfection. The decorations, the food, and the entertainment for the evening had been dazzling. Arabella had been awed by the extravagance of it all, as well as the lovely home. But she remembered feeling sorry for Mrs. Major, who seemed unable to relax. A quiet urgency had surrounded the woman, as though her life depended upon the success of the party.

"You may wait for Mr. Major here," Pym said as he straightened his red bow tie, revealing the bandage that covered the dog bite on his hand from earlier. "Dinner shall be served shortly."

Arabella crossed to a lovely porcelain vase on a pedestal table, the rainbow of colors shimmering in the light of the glittering crystals that dangled from the sconces.

"You should know," Pym added, pausing in the doorway, "Mr. Major has agreed with me that having a dog in the house—especially one that bites—just won't do."

Without allowing her the chance to reply, Pym exited the room. She stared after him, her heart throbbing with an unexpected lurch of pain. Toby had been like a child to her over the past years. How could she leave him behind? Who would take care of the sweet creature?

Certainly not her father or brother. They only tolerated Toby. Her stepmother would just as soon sell the dog to a black-market butcher than have it around the house. And her sister Florence wouldn't want to keep the pet, not with a babe taking up so much of her attention.

And yet if Mr. Major forbade her from bringing the dog, what choice did she have?

Hayward's words from earlier came back to her: "*You always have a choice.*"

Arabella gripped her reticule and fan, wanting to flee from Mr. Major's house. As the clock on the mantel slowly ticked away the seconds and minutes, Arabella attempted to reassure herself that everything would turn out for the best, that she'd eventually adjust to living with Mr. Major, that hopefully she'd soon be busy with her own babies.

But with every passing second, she could only think about having to give Toby away, losing her closest companion and living in this house with a man whose presence she'd begun to dread. How could she do it? How could she possibly make herself go through with the wedding? And yet how could she avoid it?

Her father's efforts to cancel the wedding hadn't amounted to anything. Maybe if she spoke plainly to Mr. Major about her concerns . . .

Of course, gentlewomen weren't supposed to speak plainly. Softness of voice, agreeableness, and impeccable manners were more important than making one's demands known.

However, in this case, if she didn't speak to Mr. Major about her true feelings regarding the upcoming nuptials, she'd quite possibly lose her last chance to put off the undesirable match. Surely, if presented in a kind and humble way, he'd understand and refrain from punishing her father.

"Good evening, Arabella." Mr. Major's voice from the doorway startled her, and she spun to face him. His thin silver hair was smoothed down but couldn't cover the growing baldness, even though he clearly tried, and his long bristly sideburns were trimmed. He smiled at her pleasantly as he straightened his evening coat hemmed with black velvet. "Forgive me for making you wait. I had a long day at the office."

She inclined her head graciously. "'Tis no trouble at all."

He reached into his coat pocket, retrieved a small box, and held it out to her. "I hope this will make up for my delay."

Another gift? She fingered the diamond bracelet he'd given her earlier in the week. She couldn't accept anything else, not when she needed to call off the wedding. "There's no need, sir. You've already been more than generous—"

"I like bestowing gifts upon you." He didn't make a move to cross to her. Rather, he waited with the box extended, as though he expected her to approach him first.

Her pulse sputtered forward in starts and stops. She didn't want the gift. Didn't want him. But did she dare tell him?

"Come now," he said more insistently. "Don't be modest."

"I cannot." The words rushed out before she could halt them.

His brows rose, along with the bumpy moles that dotted his forehead. "You can't accept my gift?"

"I cannot accept your gift or the offer to marry you." Once the declaration was out, she unfolded her fan and pumped air against her rapidly heating face. "I've realized this week that I am not suitable for you. Though you think I might make you happy, I fear we shall only be miserable. 'Tis best we part ways now before we make a regrettable mistake."

Mr. Major tucked the box back into his pocket. His expression had lost all softness, leaving a cold rigidness in its place.

She tried not to shudder. "I'm confident there is another woman who will make you happier than I will."

"You're confident?" His tone had turned ominous.

She swung the fan faster, wishing she could slip past him and out the door. "Surely another woman will be more to your liking."

"It appears you presume to know more about my needs than I myself do."

"No, I'd only hoped you'd reconsider our wedding arrangement."

Mr. Major stepped into the hallway and snapped his fingers. A moment later, Pym Nevins was at his side. "Please escort Miss Lawrence to the billiard room. She's asked me to reconsider our wedding arrangement, and I shall give her my answer there."

Pym bowed his head in deference.

Then without another glance, Mr. Major strode away, his footsteps echoing loudly against the marble foyer floor.

"Come, Miss Lawrence," Pym said, motioning her out of the room. "This way."

"I wanted to leave his house," Arabella said as Pete's thumb skimmed her cheek, wiping away a tear she hadn't known had escaped as she shared the miserable details leading up to that fateful night. "Everything within me cautioned against following Pym to the billiard room. But I believed I could yet convince Mr. Major to change his mind and so prevent my father any problems."

"Men like that are beasts of the worst kind." Pete's voice was taut.

Arabella nodded and forced the last of her story out. "You have discovered for yourself Mr. Major's answer to my request."

Pete squeezed her hand tenderly, letting her know that no more words were necessary.

She was relieved he didn't press her for the details of the beating. Besides, Pete could deduce that to make such scars, her back had been laid bare. Pym Nevins had held her down while Mr. Major stripped her down to her shift.

Not only had Mr. Major used a billiard stick to beat her, but he'd taken the gift out of his pocket, opened it, and revealed another bracelet—this one of stunning emeralds. Then he'd proceeded to lash it across her tender flesh, the jewels tearing her skin open. She'd been in such agony, she finally passed into blessed unconsciousness.

When she'd awakened hours later, she found herself fully dressed and in the carriage, on her way home with Pym Nevins escorting her. At the front door, he'd pressed the emerald bracelet into her gloved hand. "Mr. Major wanted me to make sure you had his gift and to let you know he'd like you to wear it for the wedding."

Even though someone had wiped the bracelet clean of her flesh and blood, at the sight of it she'd bent over and retched. The scrape of her clothing against the wounds on her back nearly made her pass out again.

"So rather than marrying that beast, you joined the bride ship?" Pete concluded.

"When Hayward realized what Mr. Major had done, she suggested the possibility, along with killing Mr. Major."

"She's my kind of woman." In spite of the humor in his tone, the glow of the lantern light coming from the front room revealed the harsh lines on Pete's face.

"Even though Hayward secretively gathered details regarding the bride ship, I wasn't inclined to leave."

"You weren't?"

She shook her head. "After experiencing Mr. Major's cruelty, I feared even more what he'd do to my family if I didn't marry him."

"But surely your father understood the need once you told him about the beating."

"I didn't tell him—couldn't tell him, not with Pym by my side every second during the three days before the wedding."

"The beast was afraid you'd run away, so he sent his pet monkey to make sure you didn't escape?"

"Something like that."

"Now I understand the fear that I heard in your scream today when Drummond's man was roughing me up." Pete lifted her hands and pressed a kiss to one set of knuckles before kissing the other.

The warmth and softness took her attention away from the horrors of her past, a past she didn't want to think about but that she wasn't sure she'd ever be able to forget. As he released the pressure of the kiss, her fingers brushed against the stubble on his chin. It was scratchy and masculine and strangely appealing.

She let her fingers explore his jaw further. The move was bold, but in telling him what had happened, she somehow felt free. It was the same feeling she'd had when racing him down the hill, as though she were cutting herself loose from the constraints that had always held her in place, unraveling her life into something simpler yet nonetheless beautiful.

This openness with Pete, this baring of her soul, was scary. But it was also thrilling.

"Thank you for telling me what happened," Pete whispered.

"Thank you for pushing me to do so." She continued to trace his contours, relishing the light layer of hair coating his chin and jaw and cheek.

"I was serious about wanting to kill him." Pete made no move to back away from her exploration.

"I'm safe here." At least she prayed she was.

"That monster sounds like the kind of man who'd go to any lengths to show he's in control, even come halfway around the world to claim what he thinks is his."

Her hand stilled upon his cheek. "Sometimes I imagine I see Pym Nevins in a crowd staring at me, waiting to corner me alone so he can lock me up and take me back to England and Mr. Major."

Pete didn't react with the scoffing she'd expected. "Describe the monkey. If he does come looking, then I'll be ready."

At his easy assumption that Mr. Major might indeed send Pym to search for her, a chill raced up her backbone. She let her fingers fall away from his cheek.

He caught her hand and laced his fingers through hers. "I promise, I'll keep you safe, Arabella. I vow it, upon my life."

Something warm and sweet welled up to replace the fear—that same something she'd felt when she'd awoken and realized he was sitting on the edge of her bed—out of prison and safe.

He rested their intertwined hands upon his thigh. And suddenly she was aware of their proximity, that he was still on the bed with her and that they were alone in the apartment. The nearness of his presence was not only comforting but it also made her insides quaver with wanting—a wanting for more of him.

She could no longer push aside the attraction she held toward Pete, could no longer hide behind the possibility of courting the lieutenant. She liked Pete too much, and Mrs. Moresby's words from earlier reassured her that there was nothing wrong with allowing her feelings for a good man like him to develop.

Surely a kiss—just a small one—would confirm her feelings.

He'd told her that he wouldn't kiss her until she asked him. But he had to know a lady would never ask for a kiss. Such behavior was unseemly. A man ought to be the one to initiate it, not a woman.

Maybe if she gave him the slightest encouragement, he'd kiss her first.

Her sights dropped to his mouth—to those warm but strong lips that had pressed against her knuckles. And that same wanting from a moment ago swelled so that she rose up onto her knees, bringing herself to his level and spanning the distance until he was only inches away.

He didn't blink, didn't lean in, didn't seem the least affected by her nearness . . . except for the tightening of his fingers that were laced with hers.

She made a point of studying his lips once more. His attention shifted to her mouth, and he swallowed hard before tearing his gaze away.

"Tell me how you got away from Pym," he said, exhaling slowly.

"Later," she whispered. Was he trying to distract himself?

His sights landed upon her shoulder. Her nightgown had slipped down again, revealing her collarbone and the freckles there. He tugged the fabric back up and in the process let his thumb graze her skin.

The touch was exquisite, and she couldn't prevent the hop in her breath that brought his gaze back up to hers. She wasn't sure what he saw there—likely her desire was as plain as daylight. Whatever it was, he took it as permission to continue the caress, this time letting his fingers skim up her neck.

At the feathery stroke, she almost swayed in to him, wishing he'd pull her into his arms, wanting more than a few stolen touches. When his fingers slid into her hair, she couldn't hold in her gasp. His hand went deep, combing her strands and arching her head back in one motion, leaving her mouth in a very kissable spot.

All he needed to do was bend down. She wouldn't resist. He had to know she'd welcome him.

But even as she waited breathlessly for him to close the distance, he dug deeper into her hair, this time bringing a fistful to his mouth and nose and breathing it in. From the tautness of his hold, she knew he was every bit affected by her nearness as she was to his.

And yet, as much as he clearly desired her, he was keeping his word and wouldn't kiss her until she gave him permission.

Could she? Was she ready? What would a kiss with Pete mean?

He dragged in a deep breath, his hands twining into her hair.

Suddenly he stiffened. For a second, she was confused. Then, before she could figure out what was happening, he released her and was on his feet with a pistol out and pointed at the door.

twenty-one

*A*n intruder was in the other room.

Inwardly, Pete cursed himself for not paying better attention. If he hadn't been so consumed by wanting Arabella, he might have heard the impostor enter and cross the apartment sooner.

"Show yourself," he commanded.

"It is I." A man's voice spoke in halting English.

Pete's pulse quickened in recognition. "Sque-is?"

The man moved out of the shadows so Pete could see him more clearly. The young face was hard and unemotional and the body rigid as though ready to fight. But Pete was accustomed to Sque-is's fierce mannerisms, knowing that underneath the strength the native was one of the kindest men he'd ever met, compassionate enough to save a worthless drunk hanging upside down in a ravine.

"My friend." Pete stuffed the pistol into his belt. "It's good to see you."

After the months of not hearing from Sque-is and not knowing if he'd survived the smallpox outbreak, emotion welled within Pete, clogging his throat.

Though they hadn't seen each other often since Pete moved

251

to Victoria and took over the bakehouse, they'd spent months together after Sque-is had rescued him. The young native had taught Pete a wealth of information about hunting, fishing, and the wildlife and land of British Columbia. Sque-is had been a patient teacher, treating him like a brother.

"You have wife." Sque-is nodded in the direction of the bed.

"Not yet." Pete glanced at Arabella, who'd pressed as far back against the headboard as possible, the sheet pulled up tightly to her chin as if somehow that would save her from an attack if Sque-is made one.

"This is Sque-is," he said gently. "He's the friend I told you about."

She nodded but didn't take her rounded eyes from Sque-is.

The native watched Pete's expression carefully. "You tell me you wait to share bed with woman until she is your wife."

"I am waiting."

"This"—Sque-is waved a hand at the bed—"is not waiting."

Sque-is had been present during Pete's long talks with Pastor Abe about the dangers of giving in to the lust of the flesh, when Pete had argued that choosing celibacy until marriage was unrealistic and antiquated. In his kind but convicting way, Pastor Abe had challenged Pete to trust God's standards as not only trustworthy but also relevant.

"The holding back of intimacy develops self-control," Pastor Abe had said as they'd shivered together in his drafty cabin in Yale. "And if you can develop self-control over temptation before marriage, imagine how much stronger you'll be when faced with sexual temptations later."

Pete had eventually accepted Pastor Abe's reasoning—that developing self-control, patience, self-discipline, and other godly traits during the courtship process would help shape him into a man of integrity in his marriage.

Sque-is had heard Pete's sincere prayers for forgiveness and his commitment to trust God's plan even when he didn't always like it. And now Sque-is had caught him on the bed with Arabella—almost kissing her.

Almost.

It had nearly killed him to hold himself back. He'd barely done it. And he had the feeling that if Sque-is hadn't shown up, he might have given in.

From now on, he had to do a better job of protecting himself and Arabella from temptation. Even more, he had to persuade her to marry him soon.

"I'm planning to marry Arabella just as soon as she'll let me," Pete said, trying to lighten the moment.

"She wants you," Sque-is said. "Get married tomorrow."

Arabella's quick embarrassed intake brought a grin to Pete's face.

"I like that idea." Pete shifted his attention to Arabella. "What do you say? Since you want me so badly, how does tomorrow morning sound?"

Surrounded by long lashes, her wide eyes were beautiful enough to stop his heart. He genuinely wished she'd put him out of his misery and say yes. But his teasing grin earned him a glare. "I do not want you. And it's ridiculous for you to say so."

"Just repeating what Sque-is observed."

"Observations can be deceiving," Arabella retorted. "Besides, it's too dark in here for him to see much of anything."

"I see enough to know you must marry soon." Sque-is's tone was matter-of-fact.

"My friend Sque-is is a wise one," Pete added. "I always listen to him."

Sque-is managed a slight smile. "Listen well and you will become as wise."

"There." Pete made a grand wave. "There you see. Now I really must marry you tomorrow, because then I'll be as wise as Sque-is."

Finally, Arabella cracked a smile.

"We talk now." Sque-is jerked his head toward the other room. "I must go away before bluejackets and queen's men are out."

Pete followed his friend into the front room and wasn't surprised when Sque-is extinguished the lantern so that no one passing by, not even at the back of the bakehouse, would be able to see him.

Sque-is was attired in English clothing—trousers, shirt, and a straw hat. Pete suspected he'd donned the garments to blend in while inside the city, which meant he was well aware of the unfriendly atmosphere that still existed around the Victoria area.

"I've been searching for you all these months," Pete said, reverting to Chinook, all humor now gone. "I didn't know if you were dead or alive."

Sque-is peeked out the window before hiding in the shadows near the wall and speaking quietly in Chinook in return. "I took my family, my people, to the mainland, up into the mountains so they would be far away from the sickness."

Pete nodded at the wisdom of Sque-is's plan. He dreaded to think what might have become of Sque-is and his tribe if they'd gone to their home on the northern end of the island. He only had to picture Haiel-Wat's deserted village to guess his friend would have suffered the same fate.

"Have you decided to return?" Pete asked.

"No. It is still too dangerous. The sickness spreads everywhere. It has come inland. And I am *hiyou quash*."

Very afraid. Sque-is's words were drenched with fear. Pete's heart would have been filled with terror if he'd been in his friend's position, with a wife he loved more than life and a babe on the way. What if their roles had been reversed and Pete was the one trying to keep Arabella and their unborn child safe?

"There is no place left where we can escape to," Sque-is continued. "The sickness follows us like a ravenous wolf pack."

"What can I do to help?" Pete asked. "Tell me what I can do—anything—and I'll do it."

The darkness of the room was broken only by the soft glow of moonlight, which revealed Sque-is's strong outline but not his expression. Even so, Pete knew his friend's face was stony with pride. Sque-is didn't want to ask him for a favor. He wanted to take care of his family in his own way and by his own means. But he'd grown desperate enough to seek Pete out.

"We are brothers?" Pete asked.

"Yes. Brothers."

"You saved my life. Let me repay my debt."

Silence settled over the room so that he could hear Arabella's rustling. No doubt she was getting dressed.

Pastor Abe's love and kindness to Sque-is had brought the native to a place of turning to God and accepting the gospel's saving grace. At the time, Sque-is had been trading fish among the mining camps, was wounded in a brawl, and was fortunate to come under the loving care of Pastor Abe, who had just arrived in the mountains.

Once Sque-is recovered, he'd stayed to act as a guide and interpreter for Pastor Abe, who'd been sent by the Church of England to shepherd the souls of the colonists. The young reverend's zeal and passion for the Lord had changed Sque-is, which eventually had led him to Pete.

Aye, he owed Sque-is and Pastor Abe an enormous debt for helping lead him out of darkness and into the light.

"I must take the medicine back to my people," Sque-is said quietly.

"The vaccine?"

Sque-is gave a quick nod.

Pete silently scrambled to find a solution to the request. He could go to Victoria's doctors, but would they have enough of the vaccine left? Even if they did, they'd probe into why Pete needed it, forcing him to explain Sque-is's presence.

Mayhap he'd fare better by going to Mr. Garrett at the Northerner's Encampment and asking for the vaccine there. If the reverend had enough to spare, he wouldn't ask any questions. He'd give whatever he could to Sque-is and show him how to administer it.

"I'll start looking tomorrow at the Northerner's Encampment."

"Then I'll meet you there." Sque-is moved to the door.

"No, stay hidden for now."

Sque-is nodded curtly and started to leave.

"Do you have food? A place to stay?" He wasn't ready to say good-bye to his friend yet. He wanted time to find out how he was doing, how he was liking married life, and what more his friend might need, especially as winter approached.

"Two others came with me. We camp where no one sees us."

Pete understood what Sque-is was insinuating—that not only were they afraid of being evicted again, but they were also afraid of catching the disease. His people, including his wife and unborn child, were relying on him for survival. He had to make it back to them.

"Take whatever I have," Pete offered. He'd do anything he could to help his friend, even if he had to sacrifice himself in the process.

⚓

The following morning, Pete made his way up the beach after stowing his canoe. The low gray clouds had begun to spit upon the sea and stir up its anger, making the last miles of his travel more strenuous. His body still ached from yesterday's beating, and his head pounded from his need for sleep. But he was relieved he'd made progress in locating a supply of the smallpox vaccine for Sque-is.

Mr. Garrett had promised to gather what he could. The Northerner's Encampment was nearly out, yet the reverend seemed confident he'd be able to find enough for Sque-is to take back to his people.

"I just investigated another report that you're harboring more natives, Mr. Kelly."

The voice came from the waterfront. The sharp commanding voice of Drummond.

Pete's steps faltered, and he turned to see the lieutenant standing on the wharf next to a longboat, where several other marines were seated with oars in hand. The lieutenant stood with his back straight and head high, as regal as a king in spotless white trousers and blue naval coat, the gold buttons shining as bright as the yellow stripes on the sleeves.

"Miss Lawrence insisted there were no other natives present," Drummond continued.

Pete's neck prickled. What had the dandy done to Arabella? "She's not a part of our disagreement, Lieutenant. Leave her out of this."

"She'll learn soon enough she's making a mistake in defending and associating with a scoundrel like you."

"I guess she picked the lesser of two evils."

"Miss Lawrence will see the error of her ways eventually," Drummond said. "And when she does, she'll plead with me to restore her into the good graces of Victoria's fine citizens."

"The only thing she'll plead with you to do is stay far away."

The lieutenant took a step down the wharf toward Pete but then glanced behind him at his men, who were watching the interaction. He drew in a breath as though drawing in renewed strength and willpower. Then he pulled a slip of paper out of his inner coat pocket. "She might be enticed by the knowledge that I became a landowner today."

Something looped in Pete's stomach and stretched into a knot. Landowner? Since when did a naval officer decide to purchase land?

"I bought myself an especially beautiful stretch of country just east of town. Acreage adjacent to the Bowker farm on McNeil Bay, a lovely knoll that overlooks Mount Olympus."

The knot in Pete's gut cinched painfully. Drummond had purchased his land. After Pete's show of determination to rise above his station, he should have figured the man would do anything to stop him—even if he had to purchase a piece of property he didn't want and would probably never settle.

"The surveyor's clerk said something about the site being set aside for someone else, but of course he couldn't turn down my generous offer of immediate cash." Waves slapped with growing fierceness against the wharf, but the lieutenant didn't sway.

Pete couldn't find a suitable comeback and probably wouldn't be able to speak past the constriction in his airway even if he'd thought of something witty.

The dandy's lips lifted into a smirk, no doubt seeing Pete's dismay, even though he was attempting to hide it.

"Good day, Mr. Kelly." The lieutenant tucked the paper—likely the deed to the land—back into his pocket and then turned to the waiting longboat. He stepped down inside with the agility of a man accustomed to the sea. Before he took his seat, he tipped his cap up to reveal his dangerously dark eyes. "You should have taken my advice earlier in the year, Mr. Kelly. Stick to your bread making and stop aspiring after things that don't belong to you."

Pete suspected Drummond was referring to Arabella more than he was to the land. "She doesn't belong to anyone." After the welcome she'd given him last evening in the bedroom, he knew something had shifted in their relationship. He didn't know what exactly, only that it had. Even so, Arabella wasn't a possession for any man to own.

"We'll see about that, won't we?" With a final half smile, the lieutenant ordered his men to push off.

"Aye, you'll see alright," Pete muttered as he continued up the shore, his feet suddenly too heavy to carry the keen disappointment on his shoulders. He'd lost his land. The land he'd been dreaming about for months. The land he'd mapped out and planned for. The land that had represented freedom from the baker's life that he'd never wanted.

He'd been so sure that new possibilities awaited him here, that if he worked hard enough and saved his money, he'd be able to make his dreams come true, and that God would bless his efforts to live an upright life.

Had he been wrong?

Mayhap he could find a different place eventually, somewhere he'd still be able to plant orchards and call home. But even as he attempted to console himself, a new fear settled inside him. If the lieutenant could so easily steal his land, what would stop him from doing the same with Arabella?

twenty-two

Sitting on the bottom apartment step, Arabella dug her fingers into Jennie's soft coat. "If he's arrested again, 'twill be my fault, girl. All my fault."

Heavy raindrops splattered in a slow sprinkle around her, but Arabella couldn't make herself ascend to the apartment, not without first knowing what had become of Pete.

Jennie stretched her head around and licked Arabella's hand as if to reassure her. But nothing could calm Arabella's tempestuous mood. Nothing had for the past hours since Lieutenant Drummond's visit. Not even baking two jam cakes that had brought eager customers to the door and earned her the best day yet. In fact, she should have been ecstatic that the owner of a nearby hotel had stopped in and asked if she would consider taking cake orders.

Thankfully, the lieutenant and his men hadn't done the same damage today as they had yesterday as they searched the bakehouse and apartment. But they'd been careless and had still left a mess to be cleaned up, both upstairs and down.

Arabella had just started her cake making when the lieutenant had arrived. He'd treated her as cordially as he always had, so much so that Arabella almost believed the lieutenant had given up his grudge against Pete and had perhaps come over to set things right.

After finishing the small talk, he'd then inquired whether he could persuade Arabella to change her mind about moving back to the Marine Barracks. When she informed him she wanted to stay, at least until Mercy got married and moved out, the lieutenant's expression hardened.

Only then did Arabella realize her answer was the factor determining the outcome of the lieutenant's visit and whether or not he'd continue to hassle Pete. Only then did the lieutenant order the search of the premises with the claim that someone had seen a native man visiting last evening. Only then did he question her and badger Dodge and Blind Billy.

Of course, she'd told the lieutenant she hadn't seen anyone—which was partly true. The darkness had mostly obscured Sque-is from her view. And she told the lieutenant she hadn't heard anything—which, again, was mostly true since Pete and Sque-is had conversed in Chinook for most of the visit.

Through all the probing, she tried to understand why the lieutenant was so opposed to Pete helping the natives. And she'd come to the conclusion that the lieutenant saw the local natives as undesirable just as so many others did. "Don't they deserve our charity, Lieutenant," she'd asked, "rather than our scorn?"

"Many have attempted to be charitable to the natives," he'd remarked, "and it only leads to their slothfulness and dependence upon charity. A firm hand of discipline, like a father with a child, is required now."

Jennie licked Arabella again. "If not for me saying something about Haiel-Wat being here, the lieutenant wouldn't be harassing Pete." She moved to stroke Jennie's head when the dog stood and perked her ears.

A second later, the squeal of the side gate opening signaled a visitor. Arabella rose, praying Pete was finally returning and that the lieutenant hadn't located him and thrown him in jail again.

She worried only an instant longer before Jennie's thumping tail told her the newcomer was a friend and not a foe. As Pete came into view, her heartbeat sped at the sight of his strong frame, broad shoulders, and cocky swagger. The same desire she'd experienced last night and yesterday—and every time she was with him now—pulsed through her veins so that she wanted to rush to him, wrap her arms around him, and hold him.

He patted Jennie on her head at the same moment his gaze connected with hers. He tossed her a lighthearted grin. "Couldn't wait to see me?"

"Of course I could," she insisted, heat infusing her cheeks. "I was just sitting outside with Jennie and enjoying the beautiful afternoon."

He glanced to the overcast sky and then to the sprinkles that had dampened the wood steps. "Aye, mighty beautiful day it is. Mayhap I'll sit outside and enjoy getting rained on with you."

She held out a hand to catch a raindrop. She'd been too preoccupied with thoughts of him to move inside, but she couldn't tell him that and risk it going to his head.

"Lieutenant Drummond was here earlier today." She hoped that would suffice as explanation for her presence there.

Pete's expression turned sober. "I saw him as I was coming ashore. He didn't do anything to hurt you, did he?"

"Of course not."

"Good. Then I guess I don't have to chase after him and beat him up." Humor returned to his eyes and softened his words.

"This is serious, Pete." She lowered her voice to a whisper. "Someone must have seen Sque-is come or go last night and reported it to the lieutenant."

Pete moved so that they were less than a hand's width apart. "Mayhap he has a spy watching me."

"Do you think so?" Her gaze darted to the building next door, to the darkened upper windows overlooking the back of the bakehouse.

His hands circled her waist and drew her close. The slight brush of their bodies and the spread of his fingers at her hips made her stomach tumble with the same warm pleasure she'd had last night when he touched her hair.

"Mayhap we should give the spy something to report back to the lieutenant," Pete whispered. "Something that'll make that dandy really angry."

"And what would make the lieutenant really angry?" she asked, wanting to close her eyes and simply bask in the feel of Pete's hands upon her.

"This." Pete tugged her again. This time she tumbled against him fully, so that their bodies were pressed together, giving her no choice but to melt into him. His arms slid around her back, encompassing her and somehow assuring her that as long as they were together, everything would be all right.

"There is one other thing that would make the dandy jealous," Pete whispered, his voice husky near her ear.

"What's that?"

"You finally deciding you want to kiss me."

Visions of the previous night flooded her, bringing more heat—the way Pete had held her on the bed, the low desire in his voice, the barely restrained passion. The same question that had taunted her last night taunted her now. What would a kiss with Pete mean?

"Thought I warned you," came a grumpy voice from the direction of the outbuilding. "No hanky-panky."

Arabella jumped and backed away from Pete. Thankfully, Blind Billy was blind enough that he couldn't see her face, which was no doubt as red as the changing maple leaves.

"Aren't you supposed to be asleep right about now?" Pete called to the stoop-shouldered man.

Blind Billy waited in the half-open doorway of the supply house, his thick white hair standing on end and his shirt askew. "It's a good thing I'm not, since you obviously need a chaperone."

"We have a chaperone," Pete said with a quick grin. "The spy Lieutenant Drummond has watching the place."

Blind Billy snorted. "That man can go drown himself in the straits."

"I hope he didn't ruin the sponge again today."

"I'd-a ruined his face if he'd touched it."

"That would have been a pleasure to watch."

The sprinkles against Arabella's cheeks helped to cool her overheated skin. The growing patter was the nudge she needed to go upstairs. Even though she wanted to stay with Pete a little longer—maybe even a great deal longer—he needed to sleep, especially after being absent for most of the day.

She moved to the bottom step, but not before Pete caught her hand. The thrill of his touch shot through her arms straight to her belly. His eyes locked with hers, the desire there informing her he didn't want her to go, that he wanted to be with her too.

"Got a couple packages today," Blind Billy was saying. "I expect you'll want to take a look at 'em right away."

"I'll do it later," Pete said, lacing his fingers with Arabella's.

"And I expect you'll want to catch a few winks now too." Blind Billy's tone turned obstinate.

"I might in a little bit." Pete's cocked smile at Arabella said he'd much rather continue their conversation from a few minutes ago.

Her insides fluttered. "You need to sleep. Blind Billy is right."

"Of course I'm right," the older man groused.

Pete caressed her hand in his. "You know you can't put it off forever," he whispered.

"Put what off?" she asked, even though she knew what.

"The packages can't wait any longer," Blind Billy said, his

expression suddenly urgent and his voice dropping to a near whisper.

Pete finally turned his attention fully upon his old assistant, apparently seeing something in the man's face that made him release her hand.

Shaking his head, Blind Billy shuffled into the supply building. Pete strode after him, and Arabella rushed to follow, not willing to be left behind.

"Close the door," Blind Billy said in a loud whisper as he crossed the windowless shed.

"How am I supposed to see the packages in the dark?" Pete asked.

Arabella pulled the door shut as she stepped inside the damp room that reeked of the sourness of hops. Blind Billy was already fumbling to light a lantern, doing so by touch alone. As the flame flickered to life, she took in the crowded interior. The walls were lined with barrels and crates, as well as the big bags of flour.

Blind Billy's pallet was spread out on the dirt floor, a worn blanket shoved aside. She saw no sign of a bed or other furniture, nothing that would make the shed a warm and inviting place in which to live.

Pete had given up his apartment to sleep here? He was too kind. And she was too thoughtless. How could she have taken over his place with no consideration of what the sacrifice had cost him?

"We need to hurry," Blind Billy said. "Otherwise that spy might get suspicious."

"This new barrel?" Pete asked while fumbling with the lid of the large barrel closest to the door.

"Careful now!" Blind Billy shouted.

As Pete started to lift the plank, Arabella's anticipation mounted. When he tossed the covering aside, she wasn't surprised to see a child inside.

"Haiel-Wat!" She sidled past Pete, heart racing with excitement. But she stopped short at the sight of two dark heads and two pairs of eyes staring up at them.

Pete spoke to Haiel-Wat and at the same time gently lifted her from the barrel. When she was standing, she spoke in a whisper while glancing around as though afraid someone might jump out of the shadows and snatch her.

"Her sister," Pete explained as he shifted back to the barrel. The girl inside was as scrawny as Haiel-Wat. From the sunken cheeks and hollow eyes, she appeared just as sickly as Haiel-Wat, if not more so.

Pete bent to pick her up, but she cowered against the staves and raised skeletal arms above her head as if she expected a blow. Pete spoke in tender tones and Haiel-Wat said something as well. Then, after a moment, the girl allowed Pete to lift her out.

Once she was firmly on her feet, she stood taller than Haiel-Wat by a couple of inches. Haiel-Wat had told Pete she was eight years old, which meant her sister was probably a year or two older.

"Her name is Kwa-nis," Pete said.

Haiel-Wat nodded and reached for her sister's hand. "Kwa-nis."

"It means *lily*."

Kwa-nis had a few smallpox scars on her arms and face but not nearly the amount as Haiel-Wat. It was clear they'd both suffered from the disease and had somehow survived.

Haiel-Wat again spoke to Pete, even as Kwa-nis leaned against the younger girl.

Pete met Arabella's gaze, his expression grave. "When their family rowed away from the village early in the summer, they left the girls behind for dead. Haiel-Wat eventually found an abandoned hut closer to Victoria, where they've been living. It sounds like Kwa-nis has been very weak and that Haiel-Wat has been the one scrounging for their food."

Their family had left them behind? Even though that shouldn't have surprised Arabella after all Pete had already told her about the outbreak, horror still welled up to choke Arabella. How could anyone do such a thing? Even if the tribe had been trying to save those who were alive and unaffected by the disease, how could they abandon two small children and leave them to fend for themselves?

"She must have gone back to Kwa-nis and carried her here," Pete explained, "hoping we would be able to help her sister the way we helped her."

"I heard them behind the building when I came out a while ago," Blind Billy said. "Figured I needed to get 'em inside without anyone seeing, so had 'em climb into the barrel."

Haiel-Wat didn't look at Arabella. She waited stiffly, her chin lifted as if she expected Arabella to rebuke her.

Arabella's heart ached for the child, for the rejection she'd faced, the suffering she'd experienced, and the responsibility she'd shouldered. Arabella's eyes pricked with tears, and she dropped to her knees, wanting somehow to assure Haiel-Wat that she understood in her own small way the burdens the girl had carried.

She grasped Haiel-Wat's hand.

The girl flinched but thankfully didn't pull away.

Arabella lifted the girl's fingers to her shoulder, to the place where Haiel-Wat had touched her scars, hoping the child would understand that Arabella could relate to the suffering, that they shared the burden.

At the contact with Arabella's shoulder, Haiel-Wat cautiously lifted her gaze. Arabella offered her a smile. "You did the right thing bringing Kwa-nis here."

Haiel-Wat stared, her dark eyes unreadable.

Arabella moved the girl's hand to her hair, which was bound in a thick knot. Then Arabella touched Haiel-Wat's hair before gently grazing Kwa-nis's braid. "Brush?"

Haiel-Wat nodded.

Arabella longed to draw the girls into an embrace, but she held herself back, knowing she'd only frighten the children if she displayed such enthusiasm. She could only pray that some-day they'd learn to trust her.

"We need to bring them up into the apartment," she said, standing and facing Pete and Blind Billy.

After Lieutenant Drummond's searches over the past two days, Arabella waited for the men to protest. Keeping the sick girls anywhere on the premises was risky, especially since the lieutenant obviously had tasked one of the neighbors with moni-toring their comings and goings.

But what else could they do? The girls would fare best and recover the fastest if they were somewhere warm, dry, and well fed. There was no better place than the apartment under Ara-bella's care, along with the help that Mercy and Lord Colville provided.

"I'll carry them up to the apartment in the barrel," Pete sug-gested.

Blind Billy harrumphed. "Anyone looking on is gonna sus-pect something since you never take barrels upstairs."

"You have a better idea?" Pete asked.

"'Course I do." Blind Billy scowled. "Take 'em inside the bakehouse in flour bags. Once they're inside, lift 'em up through the hatch."

Pete's face lit. "Perfect."

"Hatch?" Arabella asked, trying to picture any such con-traption.

"The builder left a covered hatch," Pete explained, "a place where inside stairs could later be added to reach the second floor. I haven't wanted to add them since it would take up too much valuable work space."

Arabella watched as the two men proceeded to argue over how to remove the hatch without leaving any noticeable marks the lieutenant or his men might notice on their next visit. Gratefulness surged into her heart that neither one had stopped for a second to consider the danger the endeavor might cause to them and the bakehouse. They cared more about the welfare of others than their own.

Even if she appreciated how willing they were to help and sacrifice for these two girls, she didn't want them to get in trouble. "What if Lieutenant Drummond returns for another search?" she asked, cutting into their debate.

They fell silent.

Haiel-Wat lowered her sister to the ground and carefully situated her against a crate. The older girl closed her eyes, weary and weak and desperately in need of help.

"I don't want you to get arrested again," she said to Pete.

"I don't care if I do." His jaw flexed as he watched Kwa-nis's head loll to the side and Haiel-Wat shake the girl to keep her awake.

"Can't do anyone much good behind bars," Blind Billy grumbled.

"They can't lock me away for good, not when all I'm trying to do is help."

"Hire 'em," Blind Billy said. "Every one of those rich families hires Indians and Chinese to work as servants. Why can't you?"

"Don't need servants."

"What if I hire them?" Arabella asked, thinking quickly and trying to formulate a plan that would keep everyone safe. "I shall hire them to help me in my business. They could assist with mixing the batter or washing dishes."

"Aye, and if you have the help, you'll be able to bake more."

With the growing interest in her cakes, she truly could use additional employees. But at the same time, they were only children, young girls, and she certainly didn't want to take advantage of them.

As if sensing her hesitancy, Pete touched her arm. "If anyone wonders why they're here, then we have a way to explain it. That doesn't mean they'll stay."

Arabella's racing pulse slowed. He was right. For all their plans, Haiel-Wat and Kwa-nis would probably only remain until they were well. For now, though, if someone happened to question the girls' presence, they had an excuse. One that would keep Pete safe. At least Arabella prayed it would.

twenty-three

"Where are you going so early?" Arabella whispered from the landing, closing the door softly behind her. In the middle of crossing the backyard, Pete halted. "Miss me so much that you're keeping track of my coming and going?" Through the darkness she couldn't see his smile, but his voice contained it nonetheless.

"Of course not," she replied, even as she fought back a wave of embarrassment. "I do not trouble myself with your schedule. Not in the least."

That wasn't entirely true. During the time she'd lived in the apartment, she'd grown quite familiar with his timetable and habits, enough to realize that this morning he'd left the bakehouse too early and that Dodge and Blind Billy were still working, likely getting the delivery baskets filled with rolls and bread.

"I was simply wide awake early this morn and heard you come out of the shop. 'Tis all."

"'Tis all?" Again his voice hinted at the smile that surely lit his handsome face.

She considered telling him the bed was crowded, yet she certainly didn't want to imply she was thinking about the bed,

273

especially when they'd sat there together and he'd tangled his fingers in her hair.

Over the past three nights with Haiel-Wat and Kwa-nis both in the bed, Arabella hadn't been able to sleep well, too uncomfortable in the cramped quarters. Mercy had graciously offered to give up the sofa, declaring she could bed down on the floor since that was where she'd slept for most of her life anyway. The kind offer had only made Arabella realize all the more just how spoiled and pampered she was.

If only she could learn to be as humble and kindhearted as Mercy. She'd once believed she could teach the poor woman so many things. But it was becoming clearer every day that Mercy was doing the teaching and Arabella was the one with much to learn.

Arabella tugged her shawl around her shoulders to ward off the predawn chill of October. She ducked her head and silently chided herself for having rushed outside at the sight of Pete leaving the bakehouse. But she hadn't been able to stop the worry from surfacing, the worry that Lieutenant Drummond had discovered they were harboring the native children. Though he and his men hadn't returned, the threat still hung in the air.

Pete ambled toward the steps. "I've missed seeing you."

"You have?"

"Aye."

He'd been gone off and on over the past few days looking for the smallpox vaccine. She knew he was anxious to gather enough of the medicine so Sque-is could return to his wife and people. However, in the process of his searching, she'd seen very little of him.

"Admit you've missed me too," he said softly.

"Very well. I admit I've missed your assistance with the cakes." She'd taken over most aspects of her cake business, including purchasing the necessary supplies. With word spreading about her delectable creations, the demand continued to grow every day, assuring her the business was wanted in the community and in time could even become quite successful.

"Do I need to come up there and make you admit you missed *me* and not just my assistance?" His voice turned playful so that her nerves zinged with sudden energy. He certainly wouldn't have to work hard to gain her admission. He'd likely see it written all over her face.

"If I admit to such a thing, you'll never allow me to forget it."

"True." He moved to the bottom step, then glanced at the stars as though gauging the time. "Regretfully, I'll need to force your admission later. I must be on my way . . . for a little whale watching and fishing."

"A little whale watching and fishing?"

"Aye. That's right."

She knew he'd never leave the bakehouse early for whale watching and fishing. He was too compassionate to abandon his assistants while he sought pleasure. But she suspected he'd said so for the benefit of anyone who might be listening and reporting back to the lieutenant. He was most definitely doing something else, and she wanted to discover what it was.

"I shall accompany you."

He was silent a moment and then started to shake his head.

"I have wanted to see whales," she continued. "I promise not to be a bother."

"We won't have a chaperone."

Normally he wouldn't care. Was he offering this as an excuse because he didn't want her to go along? Her curiosity only piqued further and strengthened her resolve. "'Tis no concern. If we're in a canoe on the water, we have all of nature to act as our chaperone."

"Still don't think it's a good idea, Arabella."

Was he attempting to tell her that whatever he was doing might be dangerous? In that case, maybe he'd need her help. "Please, Pete. I want to go."

275

He ran his fingers through his hair and stared straight ahead before finally dropping his hand. "All right. You can come with, but you have to promise you'll do everything I say."

"I promise."

She rushed back inside and donned her cloak and boots as quietly as she could.

"Is something wrong, miss?" Mercy's sleepy voice came from the sofa.

"No, Mercy. Nothing's wrong. I'm accompanying Pete on a whale-watching trip and shall be back before the girls wake up."

Mercy sat up. "You're a-going with Pete alone, miss?"

Arabella squirmed at the question as she finished tying her cloak. When a proper lady spent time with a gentleman, she needed to have a chaperone at all times. Arabella understood and agreed with the rule. But one by one she'd been cutting away the tangle of propriety so that with each thread she cut loose, she was slowly finding the freedom to be herself and not someone else's version of who she ought to be.

"I shall be fine, Mercy," Arabella reassured the young woman as she tried to quell the quiver of excitement at the adventure ahead with Pete. Surely a ride in a canoe was harmless.

In fact, minutes later, as she walked along with Pete, she realized that very few people in Victoria were yet awake to witness her indiscretion—if one could call it that. At the predawn hour, the town was deserted. Even the taverns were dark and quiet.

When they reached the waterfront, Pete assisted her into the front of the canoe and handed her a paddle. "You may as well learn how to navigate this beauty." He hunkered down in the rear and shoved away from the shore with the tip of his paddle.

For some time he patiently instructed her on how to maneuver the blade to steer the canoe, turning the shaft first one way and then another to increase or decrease the water flow. Eventually they were rowing in tandem, although she was sure Pete was doing the majority of the work.

The canoe glided through the calm water, the low tide pushing them along into the Strait of Georgia. As the sky began to lighten with the first glow of morning, she recognized some of the landmarks from the trip she'd made not too long ago to Haiel-Wat's village.

Though the shadows still obscured most of the beauty, the peace of the wilderness settled around Arabella and gave her a sense of awe the same way it had the previous trip. They seemed to be the only two people alive in the early minutes of daybreak.

As they passed by a bay and a grassy knoll, she strained to see it. "Is that your land? It looks like the place we visited, but I cannot be sure."

He was quiet a moment. "Aye, it *was* my land. But it's been sold." His voice was soft and raw.

"Oh, Pete, I'm sorry. I know how much you loved it."

"Thankfully, it's not the only piece of land for sale around here."

But it had been the place he most wanted. She only had to visit with him one time to see the excitement in his eyes and hear the thrill in his voice as he'd shared all he hoped to accomplish— the clearing of the land, building a home, planting orchards, and more.

"It was bound to sell before I saved up enough for it," he said. "I'll find something else eventually."

The resignation in his tone told her that he was trying to put the painful matter behind him, that to speak further of his loss would only stir up a longing he needed to put to rest.

She changed the subject. "Will you tell me what you're really doing this morning?"

He kept paddling, digging the blade deep for several strokes before switching sides. "I think I've finally got enough smallpox vaccine for Sque-is, and I arranged to meet him at dawn to give it to him."

She wasn't surprised this trip had something to do with the

277

tall native friend. "Do you think he'll be able to administer it to his people in time?"

"I hope so. His wife is expecting their first child, and he'll do anything to save her."

She shifted and dipped her paddle into the water. "I don't understand why the Indians weren't vaccinated at the first signs of the outbreak."

"Many of us tried to make that happen," Pete explained. "Unfortunately, there were those who pushed hard for their removal. Editorials began to appear in the newspaper criticizing the natives and calling their camps outside the city 'ulcers festering at Victoria's door.'"

"'Tis a bit harsh, isn't it?"

"Aye. Finally, a naval gunboat headed up to the Northerner's Encampment and ordered the natives to leave. The guns pointed at their camp gave them no choice but to cooperate."

A sick lump formed in Arabella's stomach.

"All the natives within Victoria who didn't live with whites were warned to leave too. Marines and police were stationed at the bridge and other main town entrances to make sure Indians left and none entered."

"How horrible."

"Only the sick and infected remained at the Northerner's Encampment, in a makeshift hospital run by Mr. Garrett. Most of the rest of the camp was burned to the ground, supposedly in an effort to stop the infection."

"But it didn't." She rested the paddle across her lap, too distressed to continue.

"Aye. The natives thought they left the disease behind, but there were many already infected who had no symptoms. It didn't take long for them to spread the illness everywhere they went up and down the coast."

"So making the natives leave Victoria was the worst suggestion anyone could have given?"

"Depends who you talk to. From the military's standpoint, the disease happened to be a very easy way to get rid of the native threat that had been building to the north."

"You don't think they sent the natives away to purposefully wipe them out, do you?"

Pete didn't respond, which was answer enough. She sensed Pete's grief, and it weighed heavily upon her as well.

They paddled quietly for a while with the lap of the waves against the canoe and the occasional morning birdsong the only sounds.

Pete finally drew the canoe onto a small stretch of shore on a rocky island. "Il-la-hie," he said as he stepped through the canoe past her and hopped out onto land. "This little island is Il-la-hie. The perfect place to see orcas."

"So we shall watch the whales after all?" She gripped the sides of the canoe as he hefted it farther inland, rocks scraping the bottom until he settled it on a level place.

"Aye, we might." He extended a hand to assist her out. "A large pod makes their home near here."

"You've been here before, then?" The faint light of morning illuminated the rocky coast of the island and the conifers that rose up in a thick covering. She should have been frightened by the wilderness and the creatures it likely contained, but with Pete and his knowledge of the area, she sensed she was safe.

"There's a tide rip here with an endless supply of salmon," he said. "Makes a good fishing spot for both orcas and man."

As he released her hand and finished hauling the canoe onto the beach, the breeze blowing from the west pierced the layers of her clothing and made her shudder with a chill. She half expected Sque-is to appear from out of the forest and approach them as stealthily as when he'd come to the apartment.

But at the silence and the stillness, she suspected they'd arrived well ahead of the native. From the way Pete scanned the darkened straits and other waterways, she wondered if he was checking whether they'd been followed. He'd probably arranged to arrive here early for that very reason—so he could ensure there were no threats to his friend.

"We have a few minutes." He grasped her hand. "I'll show you one of my favorite fishing spots."

As he led her over rocks up an incline, her blood began to warm from the exertion. By the time they reached a large smooth-topped stone along a high ridge, she was breathing hard but no longer cold.

Pete sat and tugged her down next to him. As she situated herself, he didn't release his hold but instead situated their hands together more intimately, twining his fingers through hers in that languid way that made her wish he was caressing more than just her hand.

"There." He peered at a spot almost directly below them. "Look carefully and you'll be able to see three, mayhap four orcas."

She leaned forward and studied the gently lapping waves. In the growing light she could make out what she thought were fins.

"They're talking to each other," he said.

She listened, hearing short clicks above the sound of the water slapping the rocks. "What are they talking about?"

"Mayhap they're wondering who the pretty lady is."

She smiled.

"The pretty lady with the hair of fire," he added.

He'd apparently heard Haiel-Wat and Kwa-nis talking about her hair. Each night the girls took turns helping her with the one hundred strokes. The wide-eyed awe on their faces as they brushed always made her smile.

"I think Haiel-Wat is finally accepting me," she said, thinking of the way the girl followed her around the apartment asking about the English names for different things.

"They both like you because they sense you truly care. It's

why Haiel-Wat decided to come back with her sister. She knew she could trust you."

Trust. It wasn't an easy thing to give, Arabella knew that well enough. But she was slowly learning to do so just like Haiel-Wat had. Whenever Haiel-Wat brushed her hair, she gently fingered Arabella's scars. Perhaps the girl was thinking of her own wounds and taking comfort in that she wasn't suffering alone. Whatever the case, Arabella had never imagined that her beating and her scars would be worth anything except a reminder of pain and all that had gone wrong with her life. But perhaps God could use personal pain as a bridge to reach others who were suffering.

"They like you more," Arabella said. "In fact, I think they worship the ground you walk upon."

"Naturally."

She bumped her shoulder against his.

He laughed and nudged her back.

"I oughtn't to compliment you ever," she said. "Except I've learned that under all the bluster, you're one of the humblest and kindest men I've ever met."

She waited for a comeback, for another witty remark. But he was quiet. Finally he cleared his throat. "Thank you. After how hard I've worked to turn my life around and become like my dad, your words mean more than you know."

"If he could see you now, he'd be proud."

"I hope so." The wistfulness in Pete's tone reminded Arabella he was still waiting for a letter from his family, and that when it arrived he longed to be able to read it for himself. She needed to schedule another reading lesson with him.

She wanted to reassure him his father sounded like the kind of man who'd never stop loving him no matter what he'd done. But the truth was, their running away had caused both of their families a great deal of trouble, possibly misfortune. There very well might always be rifts that wouldn't ever heal.

"Even if he's not, I'm proud of you." She squeezed his hand. In fact, she was more than proud of him. If she was completely honest with herself, she knew she'd come to adore him—probably even more so than Haiel-Wat and Kwa-nis did.

He shifted to face her, his shoulder brushing hers. In the glow of dawn, his features were ruggedly handsome, the unshaven stubble, unruly hair, and wrinkled brow beckoning her to touch him. Before she could talk herself out of being forward, she lifted her hand to his cheek and caressed his jawline.

The hard muscles there flexed beneath her fingers—his only reaction to her touch.

The affection, the desire, the admiration for this man swelled within her so that the pressure brought an ache to her chest. Maybe she'd once believed he was inferior to her, that he could never be the kind of man a woman like her would consider.

But now, at that moment, she couldn't foresee a future without him in it. He was everything she'd ever needed but hadn't known until now. He treated her fairly, without the condescension that many men used with women. He gave her opportunities to try new things, challenged her to do more than she believed she could, expected her to admit her mistakes, and allowed her to be herself without pretense.

"Pete, I . . ." She didn't know what she wanted to say, didn't know how to begin to tell him everything she felt.

His gaze flickered to her lips before returning to the orcas.

Maybe she didn't have to speak. Maybe a kiss would explain it all—that she trusted and wanted him.

She leaned closer, her heart racing faster and her lungs constricting. Could she really do this? "Pete . . ." she breathed again, studying the curve of his lips, the smooth contours, the crevices that smiled so easily. "I'd like to—I want to—"

Releasing him, heat infused her face, and she turned to look at the sea.

He expelled a short breath. Was he disappointed she hadn't asked him?

She had to do this, had to move past her fears and anxieties and everything else that held her bondage, and she had to show him she accepted him—accepted them. She'd already thrown off the constraints in other areas of her life. If she didn't do this now, when would she ever gather the courage?

Before she could find any other excuses, she swiveled, leaned in, and pressed her lips to his cheek. The scruff, the scratch, the warmth of it was as delicious against her lips as it had been against her fingertips.

But somehow his cheek wasn't enough. And she sensed he wouldn't be satisfied with a kiss to the cheek either, that he'd been waiting for more. But how did she do more? Dare she ask him?

Even as she debated, she brushed her lips toward his, tasting the stubble. When her nose touched his, she sucked in a breath. She was so close.

"Kiss me," she whispered, her lips grazing his.

"You sure?" He grazed her lips in return.

"Yes."

Her one word was captured by his mouth. His lips descended with a power and possession that curled through her.

She didn't know how to kiss. But somehow her lack of experience didn't seem to matter. Her body reacted with a need to meet him, to press against him, to fuse her soul to his. And she found herself fervently kissing him back with all the desire that had been growing over the past weeks.

His hands slipped around her, drawing her closer as if he felt the need too. And she could do nothing less than cling to him, helplessly lost in the kiss, in the melding of their mouths and the sweet tangle of their lips.

twenty-four

Pete couldn't get enough of her. He'd dreamed of this moment, had wanted it for so long. And now that it was happening, he was desperate to satiate his hunger for her, desperate to pull her nearer, desperate to finally throw aside all the barriers that had kept them apart.

His hands had somehow moved to her back and made a trail up her spine to her neck, to her cheeks, to her shoulders. He reached down for her waist, ready to lift her onto his lap, needing to feel more of her.

But as his fingers spread out along her hips, he could hear Pastor Abe's voice of wisdom in his head, reminding him to use self-control. He was a new man in Christ, and he wanted to do things the right way, especially with a special woman like Arabella.

God, help me, he silently pleaded as he broke their kiss.

She gasped in a breath, and the soft sound only fueled his blood.

Before he could bend in and feast upon her lips again, he tugged her into a hug, one that hid her face in his chest. He pressed a kiss against her temple, unaware that his hands were trembling until that moment.

Never before had he desired a woman the way he did her. Was that why he was trembling? With his need for her? Or was he trembling from fear? Fear that he'd end up doing something wrong and hurting her?

God, I love her. The silent prayer reverberated through him with such power he wondered if she could somehow hear it. He loved her. He supposed he had from almost the start, but for all his confidence mayhap he'd still been worried he'd lose her to a better man.

But she'd kissed him. She'd wanted it. Wanted him. He'd felt it in every soft movement of her lips against his, the pressure, the longing. Just thinking about it made his pulse spurt faster with fresh desire.

He closed his eyes and placed another kiss to her temple. He had to cool off and keep himself under control.

"Pete," she whispered, her breath tickling his neck.

"Hmmm," he said, not daring to move lest he find himself unable to resist taking another taste of her.

"I would not stop you"—her voice was low and thick—"if you should decide . . . you'd like to . . . kiss me once more."

He gulped and squeezed his eyes tighter. He wanted nothing more than to kiss her again, but *once more* would never be enough. "Didn't I warn you that you wouldn't want to wipe away my kisses?" he said, trying to lighten the moment.

"You were right." Her admission was muffled against his shirt.

"Does this mean you're asking me for another kiss?" he teased.

She playfully slapped his chest. "Peter Kelly. You're terrible."

He laughed, trying to release the tautness in his body that was urging him to kiss her again.

She started to wiggle out of his grasp. "With such an arrogant attitude, perhaps I shall wait to kiss you again until you are the one asking me."

He held her fast, unwilling and unready to let her go yet. "You wouldn't have to wait long."

At his admission she ceased any struggle to move away.

His arms slid around her more fully. "I would beg you at this very moment. But since we're alone and I'm a weak man, I don't know if I'd have the willpower to stop kissing you if I started again."

She snuggled deeper into him, his answer seeming to content her.

"Next time I kiss you had better be our wedding day." The words were meant as a tease, but once they were out, he had the overwhelming need to solidify their relationship, to ask her to marry him for real, and to set a date for the wedding.

He wanted to spend his life with her, so why put it off? Especially when there were so many other men who might attempt to steal her away if given half a chance? He'd left enough hints with her that he had marriage on his mind—like the night Sque-is had shown up and urged them to get married as soon as possible.

And yet, just because she'd allowed him to kiss her didn't mean she was ready for him to propose marriage.

For long moments, he held her, his thoughts warring with uncertainty. The impulsive man he'd always been wouldn't have hesitated to ask her to marry him. But Mrs. Moresby had warned him to use his head and not just his heart with a gentlewoman like Arabella.

What ought he to do?

Before he could make sense of his inner turmoil, the outline of a canoe emerged from the dark pine boughs that overhung the rocky coast. As the canoe glided closer, he distinguished three people inside it—Sque-is at the front.

"They're here." He released Arabella and climbed to his feet. As he assisted her back to the stretch of shoreline where they'd left his canoe, she seemed quieter, more contemplative.

He hoped her silence meant she was thinking about what their kiss meant and opening her heart to the possibility of loving him.

When the canoe reached the shore, Sque-is bounded out with the grace of a bobcat and approached Pete.

Pete quickly shed his coat and his shirt so that he could remove the pouch he'd strapped underneath. The morning air slapped his bare skin but woke him to the reminder that he was on a dangerous mission. Mr. Garrett had secured enough of the vaccine from various sources but had warned Pete not to let anyone know he had the medicine. And if he was caught with it, he couldn't say where he got it, or he'd jeopardize the reverend's good work among the natives.

He lifted away the leather bag and caught Arabella watching him with the same curiosity and interest he'd seen on her face the night she'd taken Dodge's place in the bakery. Although he wanted to tease her about her fascination, now wasn't the time.

"We must hurry," Sque-is said with a glance over his shoulder. "No-good navy men lie in wait."

"Lie in wait?" Pete followed Sque-is's gaze, his nerves tensing. Had someone followed them out of Victoria?

"They have been hunting us like a fox hunts a hare." Sque-is reached for the pouch, and Pete relinquished it to his friend. "But we are too quick for them."

"They have no right to harass you out here. These waterways and islands belong to everyone."

Sque-is shrugged and opened the pouch.

"Mr. Garrett instructed me on how to administer a dose," Pete said. "I'll give you the shot to show you how it's done."

"No." Sque-is shook his head so that his loose black hair whipped sharply. "I will give to my people first and make sure there is enough."

"You have to protect yourself," Pete countered, "or you might not make it back alive to help them."

Sque-is was silent as Pete put back on his shirt and cloak. "If you won't let me vaccinate you, then I'll need to show you on one of the others." Pete nodded toward the two young warriors waiting in the canoe.

Again, Sque-is shook his head curtly. "I will do it."

Pete was thankful the sun had begun its ascent and afforded him more light. While he'd watched Mr. Garrett give the vaccination to other natives in the Northerner's Encampment, he'd never done it himself. And now the fate of his friend, and possibly a whole tribe, depended upon how well he instructed Sque-is.

After pouring a miniscule amount of the vaccine from one of the tubes into the syringe vaccinator, he scored Sque-is's upper arm with the narrow-bladed lancet. Sque-is didn't flinch at the cut or the blood that began to flow from it. Pete proceeded to place the sharp tip of the syringe into the cut, squeezed the medicine out, and then prayed he'd gotten it deep enough.

Once the deed was done, Pete showed Sque-is how to clean both the lancet and syringe.

Sque-is peered inside the leather pouch. "This is not much."

"Only a small amount is needed. If you don't waste any, you should have enough for everyone. I made sure of it."

His friend cinched the drawstring on the leather pouch, wound the strap over his head, and settled the bag against his chest. As he drew his English coat back on, he met Pete's gaze. "You are my brother. I will never forget what you have done."

At a shout from one of the young natives in the canoe, Sque-is had his double-edged dagger out and was clasping the whalebone handle before Pete could figure out what was happening.

"Navy men come to make trouble," Sque-is said as he strode toward the canoe.

From the shadows of the island coastline came the outline of a small pinnace. Under full sail, it was moving rapidly toward them. Sque-is and his companions would have a difficult time out-paddling the vessel.

As if realizing the same, Sque-is sprinted the remaining distance, calling instructions to his friends. The two pushed the canoe off the beach and hunkered low inside, an oar in one hand and a musket in the other. Pete wasn't sure where or how they'd gained their weapons, but he suspected Sque-is was so desperate to get back to his people that he'd fight anyone who tried to hinder him.

Pete unstrapped his pistol and had it out in a heartbeat. He motioned to Arabella, who'd grown pale while watching him administer the vaccine. "Stay behind me."

Thankfully, she did as he bid without question, moving behind him and leaning in.

As the pinnace drew nearer, a quick count showed half a dozen marines, and they were bearing rifles.

Sque-is leapt into the already moving canoe, and his companions plunged the oars deeper in an attempt to get away before the sailing vessel could intercept them. In an instant, Sque-is was kneeling in the center, adding his power to the rowing so that the canoe began to glide away at a pace that would make for a difficult chase.

Pete offered a silent petition that his friend would escape without any confrontation. Sque-is might not be able to outrun the military boat, but with all the many inlets and islands, hopefully he'd find a place to hide and eventually slip away.

The marines in the pinnace shouted to the natives in the canoe, but they didn't slow their pace. A moment later, a crack of a rifle echoed in the early morning air, followed quickly by another crack.

Smoke rising from the pinnace told Pete the marines were firing upon Sque-is. His finger tightened around the hammer and trigger of his pistol. He wanted to shoot and distract the marines, but he couldn't chance having the marines fire back at him, not with Arabella anywhere nearby.

The distance between the canoe and pinnace was closing.

A tall marine at the bow stood with one foot propped on the hull, sighting down the barrel of his rifle. A shorter marine with a thick bushy beard and rounded belly clung to the mast and yelled at Sque-is and his men again.

"Why are they trying to stop Sque-is?" Arabella said, peeking around him. Her hand upon his arm shook, and he realized he should have gone with his gut instinct and made her stay at the bakehouse. While he knew his mission would be fraught with peril, he hadn't been able to refuse her, had wanted to allow her the freedom to explore and discover the world.

He just should have waited for another morning.

The tall marine fired again. Pete held his breath, praying the bullet wouldn't hit Sque-is or his friends. The marines were surely only attempting to frighten the natives and had no intention of harming them. The British policies with the natives required the use of peaceful methods first before resorting to a show of aggression.

Yet, in spite of the official governmental stance, Pete wasn't naïve. He knew shore patrols sometimes took matters into their own hands. Before the smallpox outbreak, it was no secret that sailors—especially when filled with drink—stopped at villages along the coast and created a nuisance of themselves, often molesting native women.

A shot resounded again, this one coming from the canoe. One of Sque-is's companions had apparently fired back.

The shorter marine with the overgrown beard cried out, lost his grip on the mast, and toppled overboard with a splash. Shouts from the other marines filled the air, and they scrambled to lower the sails to slow the pinnace.

Flailing in the water, the overboard marine cried out in distress. He slapped the slight waves and fought to keep his head above the surface. Like many sailors, he clearly didn't know how to swim.

Pete tensed and gauged the distance between the shore and

the marine. Should he swim out and help the man? While he wasn't a terrific swimmer, at least Sque-is had taught him the basics. Even though the sailors were making quick work of lowering the sails and turning the vessel, he feared they wouldn't reach their companion in time.

"Here," he said, thrusting the pistol into Arabella's hand. "Hold this and stay well away from the shore."

She took the gun as if it were a dirty piece of laundry. "Where are you going?"

He was already shedding his coat. "The marine won't make it without help."

"You're going out there?" Her voice contained a note of panic.

"I can't stand by and watch a man drown." He tossed off his shoes and, heedless of the rocks against his tender soles, ran into the water and dove under. Kicking his legs, he propelled himself toward the drowning marine. Once his breath stung in his lungs, he surfaced and used both arms and legs to push himself forward.

With strong strokes he reached the marine and grabbed his shirt to keep him from going under. For several long seconds, the man struggled against Pete, but finally Pete's commands seemed to penetrate his panic.

Pete beat his feet to keep them both afloat and started to swim toward the pinnace. The sailors were manning the oars now and bringing the boat slowly closer.

"Hold tight!" Pete called as he towed the marine behind him.

The man choked against all the water he'd swallowed, and his eyes bulged with wild fear.

"Almost there." Pete tried to keep his voice filled with assurance even as the tide pulled at them and threatened to drag them away from the pinnace. He pushed harder even though his arms, legs, and lungs had begun to burn with the effort. When the boat finally pulled close and hands reached for the marine, only then did Pete notice blood cascading with the water down the man's arm.

Strong hands gripped Pete. "I gotcha," said a kindly voice. Within seconds, Pete found himself being hauled over the leeward side of the vessel. Once safely inside, he flopped against the hull, trying to catch his breath.

The rescued marine was sprawled out next to him, clutching his shoulder and moaning. Blood and water oozed through his fingers. Had the Indian bullet hit him?

The marine with the kindly voice who'd pulled Pete from the water was an older man with a deeply puckered scar that ran from his temple to his chin. "Reckon you saved Hollis's life."

Pete gulped in a breath and then pushed himself up so that he could catch his bearings and make sure Arabella was safe. The rising sun was high enough to send its rays over the craggy rocks and towering pines behind her so that sunlight touched her head and brought out all the gleaming red of her hair.

"That your woman?" the older marine asked with a nod in Arabella's direction.

"Aye," Pete said, unable to take his eyes from her.

"She's a beauty."

"Aye, that she is."

"Once we put you ashore," the marine said, dropping his voice, "I suggest getting out of here and pretending you didn't see anything."

Pete nodded. Sque-is and his friends would be gone by now. They had the supply of vaccinations and would be safe enough. He wasn't sure what this patrol had wanted from Sque-is, but he suspected the old man was giving him the chance to get away before anyone decided to question why he was out at this time of the morning interacting with the natives.

As the crew rowed him to his canoe, he hopped out when the water level became shallow. When they called out their thanks, he waved them off and then raced to Arabella. Her hands were trembling when she returned his pistol. With the marines pre-occupied with their wounded man and raising the sails, Pete quickly helped Arabella into the canoe and then pushed away from the shore.

They rowed silently, the morning birdcalls accompanying their journey. Arabella remained pale and clearly shaken by all she'd witnessed. And Pete was too intent on putting as much distance as possible between himself and the marines to try to carry on a conversation. Only when Victoria's shoreline came into sight did Pete allow himself to breathe normally again.

twenty-five

Arabella held the paring knife against the apple and attempted to peel it the way Dodge had shown her earlier. But somehow, no matter what she did, she couldn't get the peeling to cooperate.

Haiel-Wat had taken a seat at the small table across from her, having just come from the bedroom where she'd fed Kwa-nis a rich chicken broth that was helping her regain strength.

Like most days, Mercy was helping Lord Colville at the hospital with the many patients he was caring for there. Although the doctor had offered to come and check on Kwa-nis and Haiel-Wat, they'd all agreed to wait, knowing the doctor's visit would likely raise the lieutenant's suspicions and draw him to the bakehouse for another unwanted search.

Though Kwa-nis was still weak and abed, she was a sweet and undemanding girl. It was clear Haiel-Wat was the more dominant of the two and prided herself on taking care of her older sister.

Haiel-Wat held out her hand to Arabella and said something in her native language. Arabella was eager to learn Chinook, yet Haiel-Wat was more insistent upon having Arabella teach her English.

"Try?" It was a question the girl was voicing more every day.

Arabella glanced at the basket of apples she'd purchased earlier in the morning when she'd gone out to get the fresh supplies she needed for the day's baking. When she'd discovered the locally grown apples at the general store, she'd been excited about the prospect of using the fresh apples in place of currants in her recipe for a fruit cake. She'd even considered making an apple butter or jam that she could substitute in the buns instead of the raspberry jam she'd previously used.

But after working for nigh to an hour with only a few apples peeled, she was beginning to question the wisdom of her plan.

Haiel-Wat beckoned toward the half-peeled apple. "Try?" she said again, taking in Arabella's pathetic attempts.

Arabella relinquished the apple and paring knife. "Be careful. 'Tis sharp." She pointed to the blade, knowing her warning was foolish, that Haiel-Wat was likely very aware that knives were sharp. Nevertheless, Arabella's protective instincts continued to surface around the girls, making her long even more for the day when she'd have a houseful of babies and children surrounding her.

Of course, she'd need a husband before she could have babies. Ever since embarking on the bride-ship journey, she'd expected to find someone of her class—a respectable and proper gentleman who would court her and then eventually give her the life of privilege and wealth she'd always known.

But with every passing day, her expectation was fading and a new one was taking its place—a vastly different picture of a vastly different kind of man. This man was one who accepted and learned from the mistakes of his past but who moved on to live with integrity and honor in the present. A man who opened his home, shared all he had, and did so with no care for the cost to himself. A man who helped not only his friends but who also had compassion—even a willingness to risk his life—for those he might consider a foe. A man who could see past disappointments and lost dreams in order to still find hope and joy in living.

The face that took shape in her mind whenever she thought of that man was Peter Kelly, especially every time she remembered the kiss they'd shared yesterday morning when they'd been whale watching.

Just the merest thought of the kiss sent flutters through her stomach and made her want to close her eyes and relive the moment—which she already had a dozen times or more. His kiss had been so powerful that she'd embarrassed herself afterward by doing the very thing he'd warned her she'd do. Instead of wiping his touch from her lips, she'd wanted more of him so desperately that she'd betrayed her good breeding by asking him to kiss her again.

Even now, her face flushed just thinking about her brazenness. She was most certainly infatuated with Pete. But was he really the man for her? She might be able to get by without servants now. And she might like making cakes for the time being. But could she do so indefinitely? Could she live in a reduced station for the rest of her life? More important, could she see herself marrying a man without any status?

For truly, what was the point in kissing him if she had no intention of being with him long term? The intimacy would only bring them closer and make parting ways all the harder when the time came.

Haiel-Wat slipped the paring knife along the apple's peel and it slid off as easily as silk stockings. She rounded the apple and then held it up for Arabella to see.

"Excellent." Arabella smiled her encouragement.

The girl nodded back and returned her attention to the apple.

At the sudden stomp of footsteps clamoring up the apartment stairway, Arabella pushed away from the table and stood. Haiel-Wat froze, staring up at Arabella, her eyes round with worry. The girl might not realize the danger she'd brought to

Pete and the bakehouse, but she understood enough to know she and her sister weren't wanted in town.

A moment later, the pounding of a fist against the door propelled Haiel-Wat into action. She jumped up from the table and raced into the other room. Meanwhile, Arabella scrambled to erase any trace of the girl's presence from the front room. Then, trying to calm her rapidly beating heart, she crossed to the door and opened it.

"Miss Lawrence." Red-faced and breathing hard, Dodge stood on the landing.

She expelled a breath and released the tautness in her shoulders. "Oh my, you startled me."

"Sorry, miss." His hat was gone, and his straw-colored hair was sticking on end. "I 'spected you'd want to know right away."

"Know what?"

"It's Pete."

Arabella nodded, having watched from the front window when Pete had departed a couple of hours ago to help with the bread deliveries.

"He's been arrested."

Her breath caught. "What? Why?"

"They're saying he had a part in murdering a marine."

She could only stare at Dodge, at his panicked expression and wild eyes. "I don't understand."

"Sque-is and two other Indians were caught and hauled in. Guess they shot and killed a marine yesterday. And Pete was with 'em when it happened, so they threw him in the lockup too."

Sque-is and his friends had been caught? She thought they'd gotten away. And Pete was in jail? How had all this happened?

"I went with Pete," she said, certain Dodge already knew. "And no one was killed. The natives injured one of the marines, and he fell overboard. But Pete swam out and saved the man."

"You gotta go tell them officers what really happened," Dodge said. "If you say so, they'll listen to you, a real gentlewoman and all."

She pressed her hand against her heart, which had begun to thud a dreadful rhythm. "Which officers, Dodge? Do you know who was involved in Pete's arrest?"

"It were Drummond, miss. Pete was on his way back here when they got him and took him to the lockup."

She wasn't surprised Lieutenant Drummond was involved. But she was surprised he could invent a charge of murder when the marine had only sustained a wound to the shoulder.

"You want me to take you over to Esquimalt?" Dodge asked. "I'll row you over in Pete's canoe."

"The lieutenant is already gone?"

Dodge nodded and moved down a step, clearly ready to be on his way.

Everything within her urged her to storm out to Esquimalt, corner the lieutenant, and confront him about his terrible discrimination not only toward the Indians but also toward Pete. And yet a warning rose within her, like the Union Jack rising up a flagpole.

If she went to the officers' headquarters in Esquimalt and met with Lieutenant Drummond or anyone else, she'd have to admit she was with Pete yesterday and that they'd been without a chaperone. If she'd thought her reputation was at stake before, such an admission would most certainly ruin her.

She'd finally have to sever the final threads binding her to the upper class. The other bride-ship ladies might have tolerated her break with tradition thus far, but they and the rest of Victoria's gentry would completely shun her if they discovered her romantic inclinations toward Pete.

Even if she cut herself off from the upper class, ignored the rumors, and pushed onward in a new life of supporting herself through her confectionary, a ruined reputation would certainly

299

harm her new business. What if people decided not to support her? What if they shunned Pete too?

Was that what she wanted?

"Let's go," Dodge insisted. "I'll take you over to the base straightaway."

"I'm not quite ready." She backed into the apartment and glanced at the table where she'd left the apple parings. "Perhaps I shall hire someone from Bowman's Stable to drive me over." The livery delivered mail to Esquimalt and had a hack service as well. She could easily ride there later.

"We gotta go now, miss." Dodge moved down another step. "You're the only one who can get Pete freed."

He was right. Pete—and Sque-is and his friends—needed her help. She was a credible witness to what had happened. She'd be able to straighten things out in no time.

She shuddered against the gray morning that was laden with a damp chill. Pete needed her. How could she do anything less than defend him? After all he'd done for her, all he did for others, she had to do whatever she could to help him now. Even if she had to put her future and well-being at risk to do so.

"Very well," she said before she could talk herself out of going. "Give me a minute and I shall be ready."

"I'll tell Blind Billy where we're going and meet you out front." Dodge trotted down the stairs as noisily as he'd come.

Arabella pushed the door closed to block out the coldness, but it had crept inside with her, surrounded her, and made her shiver. She pulled her shawl tighter, then slipped her hand into her pocket. Her fingers caressed the smooth beams of the silver cross. Knowing what she did now about Pete's estranged relationship with his father, she understood the sacrifice he'd made in giving her the cross—the last connection he'd had with his father. Though it meant everything to him, he'd handed it over to her, a complete stranger, because he'd had compassion.

His kindness had given her the courage to move on when

she'd been paralyzed with insecurity and fear. And over the past weeks, the cross had been a reminder that God would continue to supply His courage for all the situations she was facing here in this new land, even this challenge of defending Pete and Sque-is.

"Courage," she whispered, clutching the cross against her palm. She had to have courage. If Pete had been able to make such a sacrifice for her, surely she could do this for him.

"Lieutenant Drummond will see you now," the warrant officer said as he approached the chair Arabella had been given in the hallway when she arrived at the officers' building a short time ago. Attired in his naval uniform, the officer held himself stiffly, his manner formal and brusque.

She rose, smoothed the embroidered muslin of her best skirt, the three flounces falling in an overlapping display, each plaited with green ribbon. She'd wanted to look her best so that she could appear the part of a lady as much as possible, even as she had to admit her shortcomings to the lieutenant.

As the warrant officer led her, their footsteps echoed against the wood floor and limewashed walls. Other than a distant door opening and closing, along with the sound of footsteps overhead, the place felt deserted.

"Here you are, Miss Lawrence." The warrant officer waved a hand toward an open doorway.

She stepped into a plainly furnished parlor that contained a few mismatched worn chairs, a writing table where the lieutenant sat, and a bookshelf with an assortment of papers and official-looking tablets and books.

While the day was cloudy with lingering fog, the room was bright with the parlor window overlooking Esquimalt Lagoon, which at low tide revealed several small gravel bars covered with gulls making the most of the shellfish left behind.

At the sight of her, the lieutenant rose, his manners impeccable as he offered her a chair adjacent to his at the table. If he knew why she'd come, he didn't let on.

For a short time, they engaged in polite conversation regarding the weather, the latest naval ship that had arrived from England, as well as an upcoming ball being held at the government building in Victoria. Although their refined exchange was like a thousand others she'd had in her life, somehow she couldn't keep from viewing the visit through different eyes, seeing it for what it was—shallow and superficial. After being able to drop pretenses and be herself with Pete and Mercy and Dodge and Blind Billy, and even with Haiel-Wat and Kwa-nis, she could see all the more clearly how empty her old life had been.

She'd been satisfied with eating crumbs in her relationships when there were feasts that awaited if she just had enough courage to partake.

Holding the small cross in her gloved hand, she tightened her grip on it and took a deep breath, knowing she needed to speak before she lost the opportunity.

"Lieutenant Drummond, you must be able to guess why I've come to visit you today."

He sat back in his chair, his hands clasped casually on the writing table, his expression unwaveringly pleasant. "I suspect it has to do with your landlord, Mr. Kelly."

"Yes. His assistant informed me he was arrested, and I've come to speak on his behalf."

"As kind as that is of you, I'm afraid your efforts are for naught."

"I'm told he's accused of being party to a murder," she continued. "But I am confident he is innocent."

The lieutenant smiled indulgently. "You are much too gracious, Miss Lawrence, always seeing the best in people. I appreciate your sensitive nature and your willingness to defend those beneath yourself."

Was that how the lieutenant saw Pete—as beneath them? She was ashamed to admit she'd once viewed him the same way. She swallowed the anxiety pushing into her throat, threatening to silence her and keep her from speaking her mind. "I have solid evidence of Mr. Kelly's innocence."

"And we have solid evidence of his guilt in conspiring with the natives to attack a marine patrol."

Her body was beginning to overheat. Rather than dig through her reticule for her fan, she loosened the cloak string at her throat and let the heavy garment fall from her shoulders.

She'd harbored hope she might be able to persuade the lieutenant without sharing the details of her involvement. But he would clearly not be moved by anything other than the full truth. She must come out with her confession. "Lieutenant, the reason I know of Pete's innocence is because I was with him and saw everything that happened." She stared at her clasped hands, unable to meet his gaze and see the shock and disappointment that would surely show upon his countenance.

"Miss Lawrence," he said smoothly, "the marines I spoke with indicated you were quite some distance away on the shore."

Her gaze shot to his. For the first time since sitting down with him, his eyes took on a hard glimmer that told her he already knew she'd been present at the scene of the skirmish. "I would like to share my account of what occurred."

"I already have plenty of witnesses and do not need one more, especially a woman. Everyone knows women are unreliable witnesses, generally allowing their emotions to cloud their judgment."

The whirlwind inside her chest increased its tempo. This wasn't going at all the way she'd planned.

"Besides," the lieutenant went on, glancing at the open door and lowering his voice, "I assumed you'd thank me for keeping your indiscretion as private as possible."

She darted a glance at the door too, suspecting the junior

officer was standing just outside and could hear every part of their conversation, which meant she would have to be even more careful about what she said.

"I wasn't so far away that I couldn't see what happened," she said, attempting to keep her tone civil. "The marines fired upon the natives first. When the natives returned fire, one of the marines was hit and fell overboard. Pete swam out and rescued the injured man from drowning."

"My marines are adamant he swam out to finish the man off but that they rescued him before Mr. Kelly could do so."

"That is absolutely not true. Why would he risk his own life in such a manner?"

"To allow his accomplices time to escape."

"The marines had already ceased their chase of the natives and were turning around to retrieve their friend by the time Pete swam out. He rescued the man and then dragged him to the boat. When they pulled him out of the water, he was alive. Though his wound was bleeding, it wasn't life-threatening."

"He died of a heart attack a short while later."

"There, you see, no one murdered him."

"Would you contradict the findings of the naval surgeon, who concluded that the combined trauma of the gunshot wound and near drowning caused the heart attack? If the natives had submitted to the patrol's routine questioning, none of this would have happened. As it is, now the natives and Mr. Kelly are responsible for a marine's death, and as result they are all being charged with murder."

Arabella didn't realize she'd slid forward to the edge of her chair and placed her hands upon the writing table until he reached out and covered her hands with his. The tender hold and ensuing squeeze surprised her, and although she wanted to jerk her hands away, she held them motionless. Already her defense of Pete was weak; she couldn't make the matter worse by offending the lieutenant.

"Arabella," he whispered gently, "I have no wish to involve you in this matter as I want to protect your reputation more than anything."

"I understand and I thank you for your concern," she whispered in return. "But I am prepared to sacrifice my own well-being if necessary in order to defend the innocent."

"That is very noble of you. Still, you stand to lose what little credibility you have left if word spreads that you were alone with the baker at the early morning hour."

The truth of his statement pierced her already burdened heart. Very few would listen to the testimony of a woman, much less a woman of ill-repute. The storm in her chest pushed up into her throat, tightening it and bringing the sting of hot tears to the back of her eyes. Was there nothing, then, that she could do to defend Pete or the natives?

She drew her hands from the lieutenant's and searched in her reticule for a handkerchief. As she dabbed the corners of her eyes and fought back the tears, she tried to find her voice. "I was there, Lieutenant. Please believe me when I tell you Pete is innocent of all wrongdoing."

He was quiet for a moment, rubbing his mustache. "I want to believe you," he finally said, "but how can I know for certain you're not simply defending him because you have a slight infatuation with him?"

Slight infatuation? Was that what the lieutenant believed about her relationship with Pete? Earlier, when peeling apples, she'd wondered how to describe her relationship with the handsome baker. She might not understand everything happening between them, but she knew with confidence that what they shared was more—much more—than a slight infatuation.

The things she felt for Pete went beyond anything she'd ever known or believed possible. She could almost believe that maybe what she felt was akin to love. But did she dare admit such a thing even to herself? It was almost too frightening to dwell on.

Before she could find a suitable response, the lieutenant continued, "If you prove to me you're not defending Mr. Kelly out of some farfetched romantic notion, then I—along with others—will be more likely to take your version of what happened more seriously."

Even though the lieutenant's expression remained placid, his mustache twitched and his eyes glimmered with something she couldn't name except that she felt a sickening twist in her stomach. It was same trapped sensation she'd had when she overheard Mr. Major threaten her father regarding losing his employment.

The lieutenant was cajoling her into doing as he pleased. She doubted he would recognize his behavior as manipulation and likely believed he was making a great concession to give her lowly testimony greater credence.

Nevertheless, she understood clearly enough that to gain the lieutenant's help with Pete, she would need to do as he asked—whatever that might be.

Silence stretched so that the mournful calls of the gulls in the lagoon wafted into the room. At the opening of a door nearby and subsequent footsteps in the hallway, she forced herself to continue the conversation. "How might I prove myself?"

His answering smile told her she'd asked the question he'd been waiting for. "To begin with, you need to cut off all communication and interaction with Peter Kelly and his bakehouse."

She should have expected such a demand. Could she really cut herself off from Pete?

"That means returning to live at the Marine Barracks and behaving as a gentlewoman in all manner of activities. If you seek employment, do so appropriately with the right people."

"But his assistants will need help with the bread making during his absence," she countered. "I have become familiar with their routine and can be of aid."

"They will have to hire someone else or learn to get along

without the baker," the lieutenant replied. "It's possible I could use my influence to prevent him from being hanged with the natives. But he will likely be shipped back to a prison in England."

Hanging? Prison? Dread settled deep into her bones. How could that be possible? Neither the natives nor Pete had done anything to warrant such drastic measures. Could they really be charged as guilty on the testimony of the marines alone? Surely some of the men would confirm her version of what had happened. Unless they were angry that one of their own had died and desired the retribution—no matter how unfair it was.

"Will you not give them a fair trial and allow a jury to decide their fate?"

"Whitehall and the Colonial Office have given Governor Douglas and the navy the leeway to develop policies and respond to problems with our own authority. They realize that in this wilderness, we will often need to employ quick action and on-the-spot policies, especially in the face of Indian threats. If we don't react decisively, the savages will interpret our lack of action as a sign of weakness, and soon we will have threats of violence erupting all around us."

"But the natives you arrested pose no threat," she insisted. "Pete was giving them the smallpox vaccine to take back to their tribe."

"The natives should seek out the missionaries in their area who are administering the vaccine," the lieutenant replied. "It's unrealistic and even wasteful to consider giving every tribe their own supply. Many are superstitious and may end up wasting the valuable medicine or selling it for liquor."

She understood his position, but couldn't he make an exception for some of the natives, especially in this case since Sque-is was a personal friend of Pete?

The lieutenant shifted a paper on the writing table before looking at the mantel clock. Arabella sensed she was running out of time. As far as she could tell, the only recourse left was to accept the bargain the lieutenant was offering. If she had any hope of saving Pete, she had to cut off her friendship with him.

Again she fingered the cross she was still clutching tightly. "So if I prove myself to be above reproach, then you will give considerable weight to my testimony?"

"Yes," he said, shifting another stack of papers. "As I said, I can only consider testimony from reputable sources."

She cared about Pete too much to allow anything to happen to him, not even a prison sentence. With a glance again toward the door, she lowered her voice. "What must I do to ensure Pete's complete freedom?"

The lieutenant stopped fiddling with the papers and studied her face. What was he trying to read there? Was he attempting to determine to what lengths she'd go and how much he could require of her?

She braced herself. She'd do anything for Pete. Anything at all.

"Well, Miss Lawrence," the lieutenant said slowly, "it may help your cause if you are engaged to be married to a gentleman of the highest caliber. Such an alignment will show everyone you are trustworthy and reliable."

A gentleman of the highest caliber—was he implying himself?

The sick feeling in her stomach pushed into her throat. She didn't want to be trapped into another engagement, but what other choice did she have?

She rose from her chair, nearly dropping her reticule and the cross. At her rising, the lieutenant stood and circled the table toward her. His expression was earnest and filled with longing.

"Arabella," he said gently, starting to reach for her hands but then letting his arms fall to his sides. "I cannot deny I would be honored to be that man. I have been smitten with you from the first moment I saw you on the ship, and I have harbored the hope you might return my affection."

She swallowed hard, pushing down the nausea. She didn't want to compare the lieutenant to Mr. Major. The lieutenant had been nothing but soft-spoken and respectful toward her. While she didn't approve of his negative view toward the natives and those beneath his status, he wasn't uncommon in his attitude. Many of the upper class felt the same.

"If I can help you in this way," he continued earnestly, "all you need do is say the word and I would gladly marry you."

He could offer her the life she was accustomed to and always assumed she'd have. If she married him, she'd be easily accepted by Victoria's wealthy gentry, and her days would be filled with teas, parties, picnics, dances, and much more. Her children would never want for anything. And if the lieutenant returned to England, her life there was sure to be just as comfortable, if not more so.

The problem was, she didn't love the lieutenant. Of course, love had never entered her thoughts—not when she'd agreed to marry Mr. Major, not even when she'd joined the bride-ship venture. Yes, she might have hoped for some affection in the long term, yet she'd never expected to love someone or be loved.

Until she met Pete . . .

Although he'd never spoken of love, his affection for her was obvious. And somehow, somewhere, sometime, she'd come to care about him. Deeply. Not only did she respect and admire him, but she loved spending time with him, talking and teasing and learning and growing. And of late, she'd only longed to be with him more.

In addition, she was attracted to him in a way she couldn't explain. His merest touch made her skin sing and her blood hum. Just the way he looked or smiled at her could turn her belly into warm mush. Thinking about him in the dark hours of the night made her body quiver with the need to hold him and be with him.

Could she really give all that up? Now that she'd gotten a

taste of the fullness of such a relationship and what it might truly become, could she go back to anything less?

"Yes." She breathed out the word before she could stop herself. She could—and would—do whatever she had to in order to save Pete from prison and gain his freedom.

"Yes?" The lieutenant's brows rose above surprised eyes.

"Yes, I shall marry you."

twenty-six

As the lockup door squealed open, Pete blinked against the yellow shaft of light that pierced the cell, telling him the sun was shining at its fullest. Which meant he'd been jailed for over twenty-four hours.

From the first moment he was shoved behind bars and had seen Sque-is and his two tribe mates lying bloody and bruised on the floor, he'd been surprised that they were there. Apparently, another gunboat farther up the coast had heard the shots and then taken over the search, lying in wait for the natives to come out of hiding before chasing them down.

Since hearing the tale, Pete hadn't been able to shake the terrible feeling that this time there wouldn't be an easy way out, especially when he'd learned that Hollis, the marine he'd rescued from drowning, had suffered a heart attack and died. The navy wanted to pin the blame for the man's death on someone, so why not them?

Officer Green made his way down the passageway toward the cell, and Pete was disappointed to see that no one was with him.

"Were you able to send word to Pastor Abe?" Pete stood, his limbs stiff from the cold.

"I tried," the stocky man answered, "but no one over in New

311

Westminster has seen him recently, which means he's probably back up in Yale."

Pete grabbed on to the iron bars to hold himself steady. Hunger gnawed at his insides, making him weak. More than that, the news was a blow since he was counting on getting in touch with Pastor Abe. The reverend was the only one who'd be willing to defend not only him but Sque-is too.

"I need to find him." Pete's voice radiated with desperation. "I'll send a message with someone traveling up the Fraser River. Can you find anyone leaving today?"

"Already done," said the bluejacket. "I sent word with Mr. Roberts."

"Thank you," Pete replied. But deep inside, he guessed the effort would be too little, too late. By the time Mr. Roberts, another reverend in the Fraser River Valley, relayed the news that he and Sque-is were in trouble, the three natives would likely be dead. Pete might be too, though he doubted the navy would carry out a death sentence against him, even if they persisted with the murder charge. Too many people would protest the lack of trial by jury. If only they'd protest the same for the natives.

Officer Green thrust a wrapped bundle between the bars into Pete's hands. "Your assistant came by with food."

"Dodge?"

"Yep, the boy." The officer strained to see behind Pete. Sque-is stood at the far end, having paced the length of the cell for most of the night and day. His companions sat against the wall, having finally picked themselves off the floor.

Thankfully, somehow during the confrontation with the marines, Sque-is had managed to slip the pouch with the vaccination in a rocky crag. Without it, the navy couldn't trump up additional false charges against the natives. Pete had no doubt they'd accuse the Indians of stealing if they could. As it was, the murder accusation was severe enough.

"No other visitors?" Pete asked, his fingers tracing the outline of the rolls and apples and other food items within the package.

"Only Lieutenant Drummond."

"What did Drummond have to say this time?" Pete was surprised the lieutenant hadn't come back to the lockup to gloat over Pete landing in enough trouble to put him away for good.

"He said to let you know he may have found a credible witness regarding your part in the murder. If the witness cooperates, the lieutenant believes he may have evidence that could work to your advantage."

"Who's the witness?"

The officer shrugged. "He said you'd know who."

Was it Arabella? Had she gone to the lieutenant?

"Oh, and he told me to let you know he's engaged," Officer Green said.

Pete froze. There was only one reason Drummond would want Pete to know about his engagement . . . because it had to do with Arabella.

The officer started back down the hallway away from the cell.

Pete pressed against the bars, as if by doing so he could challenge the bluejacket and stop the news from being true. "Did he say who he's marrying?"

"That pretty redhead from the bride ship," the man called over his shoulder. "Said they're getting married in a couple of days."

"No." The word echoed against the windowless walls and pierced Pete's chest.

"It's true," Officer Green countered as he reached the far doorway. "He said they're having the ceremony at Christ Church Cathedral and to let you know you're invited if things go well for you and you get out of jail in time."

As the door closed, leaving utter darkness behind, Pete slid down until he sank to his knees. With his head resting against the bars, he couldn't move. The only thought pounding through his head was that he'd lost.

He'd lost.

The slamming against his temples was hard and heavy. He'd lost. He'd lost. He'd lost.

Behind him, Sque-is said something, but Pete couldn't distinguish what it was, not with his thoughts clanging so loudly. Arabella had agreed to marry Drummond. Just like the last time he'd landed in the lockup, had she assumed the worst about him? Even if she hadn't, apparently she'd decided a man like him wasn't worthy. Why would she want someone who was always ending up in jail for one thing or another? She'd probably concluded that their association had gone too far, that his tarnished reputation would damage her own if she continued their partnership.

Now that he was being accused of murder, perhaps she'd been desperate to put as much distance as possible between them. Had she decided that an engagement to Drummond would salvage her standing in Victoria?

Whatever the case, he supposed he didn't blame her. Mayhap she was better off without him.

The pain in his head seeped into his chest and lungs. *God, he silently cried out, I repented of going my own way. Turned my life around. And have been trying hard to live a righteous and godly life. Wanted to do things right this time, to be an upstanding man of integrity just like my dad. Thought that kind of life would please you and that things would go better for me.*

He tried to take a breath, but the air only snagged.

But nothing has gone the way I planned. Seems like everything I want is jerked right out of my hands. First my dream land. And now the woman I want to marry. Why can't I have at least one of them? Is that too much to ask?

He was pressing his forehead into the iron bars so forcefully he could feel the imprint. He'd believed that when he left his sinful ways behind, he'd finally be free from all those things that had enslaved him—the drinking and gambling and carousing. He thought he'd be done with trouble.

Why then was he still finding himself on the wrong side of the law? Even when he hadn't committed a crime, when he'd only been trying to help?

God, why is everything still falling apart? Why isn't my righteous living bringing about the kind of life that bears fruit?

He tried to listen for God's response, to feel a sense of peace, to regain his confidence. But instead of the calm assurance that usually came, a swirling angry voice rose from within and demanded to know why God was treating him this way. Especially after all he'd done to put aside his old life and become a new man in Christ.

After trying so hard to please God, was this how God showed that He cared? Why work so hard to be a good man if it made no difference?

twenty-seven

*A*rabella stepped into the front hallway of the Marine Barracks, following the men who were carrying her trunks. As she quietly closed the door behind her, the marines paused and looked to her for further instructions.

"You may put my belongings upstairs in the first room to the left." She pointed to the stairs beyond the coat tree. At least she assumed she could return to her old room and bunk bed for the few days that remained before her wedding.

At the thought of the impending ceremony, anxiety reached out to clutch at her arms and legs, immobilizing her. What had she gotten herself into?

The four marines who'd arrived at the bakehouse after she returned home from the Sunday service at Christ Church Cathedral had cleared out her trunks and loaded them in a waiting wagon. Thankfully, they'd waited outside as she walked through the apartment to make sure she'd gathered all her belongings. Of course, she'd used the few moments to call Haiel-Wat and Kwan-is out from underneath the bed so she could say her good-byes.

Even though she'd already attempted to warn Haiel-Wat that she was leaving and getting married, the little girl hadn't wanted

317

to hear it, had turned away from Arabella, her expression hard and her eyes angry. Arabella had tried to reassure Haiel-Wat that Mercy would take care of her and Kwa-nis, but the words only seemed to make Haiel-Wat more agitated.

Arabella supposed the child realized Mercy would be getting married to Lord Colville soon and would leave them as well. Perhaps she felt as though everyone she trusted eventually left her—first her family and tribe, and now her and Pete.

"Pete will be home before too long," she'd said, wishing she could explain that her marriage to the lieutenant would hasten Pete's return. But how could she make them understand her complex situation when she could hardly make sense of it herself? All she knew for certain was that Pete's life was in danger and she'd do anything to save him, even if she had to marry a man she didn't love.

As the men clomped up the stairs of the Marine Barracks with her trunks, she reminded herself again as she had a dozen times since she'd left the bakehouse that she was giving up Pete in order to protect him. She had to sacrifice her desire for him so he could live. In the short term, she would miss him and their friendship. But hopefully they would both be able to move on and make new lives for themselves.

"Miss Lawrence?" Mrs. Moresby stepped out of the front parlor into the hallway, holding an embroidery sampler. In hooped petticoats and bell-shaped sleeves that made her appear twice her girth, the large woman stared first at the marines and then at Arabella, surprise and concern written on her face. "What on earth are you doing here? Are you moving back in?"

"Good afternoon, Mrs. Moresby. Indeed, I am returning—if I have your permission to do so. And only until Wednesday."

The older woman was without her usual garish hat and instead wore a scarf that looked as if it were made out of ostrich feathers. "You're always welcome here, Miss Lawrence. Since we last spoke, I assumed you and the baker were getting on so fabulously . . ."

Arabella swallowed the swift lump that rose in her throat. "I'm not sure if you've heard, but I have agreed to marry Lieutenant Drummond. We've set the wedding date for Wednesday."

Mrs. Moresby's eyes widened, pushing her eyebrows high. Her scarf slipped from around her neck and would have fallen, except at the last moment she snagged it and flung it back over her shoulders. "I assumed you'd marry Peter Kelly. With the way that man cares about you, I figured he'd have proposed a dozen times by now."

A dozen times? Pete had joked about marriage, but he'd never officially asked her to marry him. Maybe they would have eventually talked more seriously about it—if he hadn't been arrested.

But not anymore. She had to put her past behind her and move on with the lieutenant, especially if she had any hope of finding peace with her decision. If she continued to cling to her feelings for Pete, that certainly wouldn't be fair to the lieutenant.

"I am marrying Lieutenant Drummond," Arabella said with more conviction. "He's the perfect gentleman."

One of Mrs. Moresby's eyebrows rose even higher. "If you ask me, Peter Kelly might not have been the perfect gentleman, but he was perfect for you."

A tiny sob slipped out before Arabella could stop it. At the noise, she cupped her gloved hand over her mouth, horrified with the display of emotion.

Mrs. Moresby studied Arabella's face, her brow drawing together in concern. "Seems as though you have some more explaining to do, Miss Lawrence. You go ahead and wait for me in the kitchen while I put an end to the embroidery social this afternoon."

Arabella nodded and moved to obey. Even though she didn't

want to embarrass herself any further, Mrs. Moresby wasn't the type of woman anyone could easily contradict.

After last instructions and gratitude for the marines unloading her belongings, Arabella made her way to the kitchen. A few minutes later, Mrs. Moresby bustled into the room, closed the door behind her, and crossed her arms over her ample bosom. "Now, I think it's time you tell me what's going on."

Arabella had already discarded her cloak, hat, and gloves, and set about tidying up the worktable, which was in disarray with dirty dishes and utensils. She needed to busy herself or she was afraid that this time she'd release more than just a sob.

"I'm marrying Lieutenant Drummond," she repeated, trying to keep her voice from wobbling. "Long term, such a union would work out the best for everyone involved."

"I highly doubt that," Mrs. Moresby replied in her no-nonsense way. "I'm guessing this union somehow works in favor of Lieutenant Drummond."

Arabella wiped at a sticky spot on the table. "He believes we'll be allowed to move into a house on the base soon. Eventually, he wants to retire from the navy and live here on a piece of land he recently purchased."

Mrs. Moresby didn't respond, almost as if to say that Arabella's answer confirmed her suspicion. However, the opposite was true. Arabella was the one gaining an advantage from the union—she was gaining Pete's life and freedom.

"It is rather strange that your engagement follows Peter's imprisonment," Mrs. Moresby remarked calmly. "One might almost conclude that the lieutenant made promises to free Peter from jail if you agreed to marry him."

At Mrs. Moresby's blunt statement, Arabella fumbled, bumped into a pan, and sent it toppling to the floor with a crash. She hurriedly bent to retrieve it even as the older woman's conclusion rattled in her head, growing louder by the second.

"Of course, I've been wondering if the navy has any right to hold Peter at all," Mrs. Moresby continued. "They're saying he was trying to drown a marine who fell overboard. But those of us who know Peter Kelly can vouch for his character; he wouldn't purposefully drown any man, not even his worst enemy."

"He didn't try to drown him." The words were out before Arabella could think of the repercussions. "He told me the marine wouldn't make it without help and that he couldn't stand by and watch a man drown."

Mrs. Moresby's eyes narrowed. "So you were there?"

Arabella grabbed the rag and began to scrub the table again.

"You were there with him." This time, Mrs. Moresby's voice held no question. One look into her serious eyes told Arabella the woman knew the truth and warned Arabella not to deny it.

Arabella stopped wiping, nodded, then hung her head. What must the woman think of her now? Was she shocked? Disappointed?

"Good."

Arabella's head shot up. "Good?"

"It's a good thing you were with him," she said matter-of-factly. "That means you can tell everyone what really happened instead of relying solely upon the story of the marines who were on patrol, marines who will likely say whatever the lieutenant tells them to."

"You don't think Lieutenant Drummond influenced their version of what happened, do you?"

Mrs. Moresby huffed. "It's no secret the lieutenant and Peter have been at odds since the smallpox outbreak. The animosity just got worse after you arrived and they both set their sights on you."

Unease sifted through Arabella. "At odds since the smallpox outbreak?"

"I don't know all the details. But from what I understand,

the lieutenant was part of the group of officers who enforced the eviction of the natives. And Peter was among a vocal group of citizens who opposed the forced relocation."

Pete had told her some of what had happened, but he'd never mentioned Lieutenant Drummond's role. Why had he kept that information from her? He easily could have besmeared and defamed the lieutenant to his advantage.

"The lieutenant has been looking for a way to lock Pete up again," Arabella mused, thinking of the searches at the bakehouse, the spying, and the hostility. If the lieutenant had already disliked Pete, then her moving into Pete's apartment and doing business with him had only made matters worse.

"All we need to do," Mrs. Moresby said, pulling herself up and situating her ostrich-feather scarf, "is have you tell your side of the story before the naval board—"

"I cannot," Arabella cut in.

"You must." Mrs. Moresby spun toward the door.

"No one will believe me."

The matron stopped with her hand on the knob. "We have to at least try to sway the officers."

Arabella hesitated before responding. Part of her wanted to do as Mrs. Moresby suggested and try. But what if she couldn't persuade the officers to see her version of what happened? After all, she would be one woman against the other marines who'd been present. If she failed to convince the naval board, she'd lose her chance to save Pete.

She shook her head sadly. "I am sorry, Mrs. Moresby. Speaking the truth is too much of a gamble. If the board doesn't believe me, then I shall have ruined my only chance to save Pete. And I cannot do it."

Mrs. Moresby pursed her lips.

For a moment, Arabella feared the older woman would insist. Or at the very least attempt to talk her out of marriage to the lieutenant. But Arabella lifted her shoulders and chin, determined to do whatever she could, even if that meant marrying a man she didn't love in order to save the man she did love.

She loved Pete. At the realization, her heart thudded against her chest painfully. She loved him and she could no longer deny it. And not just because of how handsome and funny and charming he was. He was all those things and so much more—so very much more.

Mrs. Moresby smiled. "I've got it!"

"Got what?"

"I have a better plan." She swung the door open. "It will take me some time and hassling, but I think I may have a way to make the lieutenant change his mind about Pete."

"How will you do that?" Arabella asked cautiously.

"I plan to check into the Indian eviction." She bustled into the hallway, her heavy steps directing her to the coat tree and her cloak.

Arabella followed after her. "How will that help?"

"I'm not sure that it will, but in the meantime, you must keep up the pretense that you're still planning to marry the lieutenant so he doesn't grow suspicious."

"Suspicious of what?"

"Suspicious of my investigation."

"Please be careful," Arabella urged. "We cannot ruin a sure way of saving Pete on the off chance something else might work."

"I have good connections," Mrs. Moresby replied. "Let's just pray we can find what we need in time."

Arabella could only watch helplessly as the woman donned her outerwear, including a hat covered with the same bright blue ostrich feathers as her scarf. She was out the door and gone in a flurry that left several feathers floating in the chilled breeze that now filled the hallway.

Arabella crossed her arms and hugged herself—not sure if she was cold or merely frightened. One thing she did know. Her wedding plans to the lieutenant weren't a *pretense*. She had every intention of walking down the aisle and marrying him on Wednesday morning. Even if Mrs. Moresby found another way to free Pete, marrying the lieutenant was the surest way to keep Pete safe from any further danger, not only now but also in the future.

Arabella just needed to persuade herself that marriage to the lieutenant was exactly what she wanted and that his offer was more than she'd ever expected for a spinster like herself. It was also a much better situation than she'd had with Mr. Major. In fact, several months ago she would have been honored and thrilled at the prospect of marrying the lieutenant.

But ever since meeting Pete, everything had changed. She had changed. She'd learned how to truly live. And truly love. Now that she'd experienced both, she saw the world around her in a new way. It was almost as if she'd been nearly blind like Blind Billy, but now someone had given her spectacles so she could finally see.

Expelling a sigh, she leaned against the hallway wall. This was all Pete's fault. If she'd never met him on the *Tynemouth* that first day after arriving. If he'd never come to the Marine Barracks to deliver bread. If she'd told him from the start she wasn't interested in him. Then none of this would have happened. She'd still be blissfully blind and unaware of the beauty of life she'd been missing.

"Peter Kelly, why did you do this to me?" she whispered as an ache tightened her throat. "If you'd just left me alone, then I would have been completely happy with marrying the lieutenant."

Is that what she wished for? To go back to the way things were before? To go back to being blind?

With a cry of frustration, she slapped the wall and then was startled by her completely unladylike outburst. She closed her eyes and willed herself to remain calm. She was still a gentlewoman and would behave as such. If she moved forward with her plans with the lieutenant, she didn't have to go back to being blind. She could still discover meaning and passion and beauty in the world around her, couldn't she? She'd just need to do so with the lieutenant instead of with Pete.

If she worked at their relationship, eventually she'd develop a love and a friendship with the lieutenant. They'd find things they enjoyed doing together. They'd make a good life with each other here in Victoria.

All she had to do was convince herself that things were never meant to be with Pete. And put him out of her mind. Forever.

twenty-eight

*L*et me out!" Pete's voice was hoarse from all the shouting, but he hadn't been able to stop. The desperation pulsing through every vein in his body wouldn't let him rest.

He shook the bars again, wishing he could tear them from the ceiling and floor. But they didn't budge. All he'd done was bruise his hands and arms.

Keeping track of the days had become difficult in the dark cell, yet he knew today was Wednesday. And he knew that Arabella was marrying Drummond at ten o'clock at Christ Church Cathedral.

The dandy had stopped by the police headquarters an hour ago and had sent one of the bluejackets back to the lockup to inform Pete of the imminent nuptials, along with the assurance that he was still in the process of reviewing evidence regarding Pete's part in the murder and might have found a testimony that could aid Pete's release but that he wouldn't know for sure until tomorrow.

Pete had understood the message loud and clear. If Arabella went through with the wedding today, Pete would soon find himself a free man. The problem was, Pete would gladly give up his freedom to keep Arabella from marrying Drummond.

If only he could talk to her just once . . .

Even if he was released, this latest stint in jail and the accusation of murder would hurt his business. No doubt he'd lose customers. Maybe he'd be better off doing something new—like building roads in the mountains. It was dirty and dangerous work, but the Royal Engineers would hire him even with his jail record.

No matter the bleakness of his future, he didn't want a bleak future for Arabella. She might not want him, but she didn't have to settle for a man like Drummond.

"Let me out!" he shouted again. "If you let me out for an hour, I promise I'll come back! I give you my word."

All he had to do was find Arabella and tell her the bakehouse was hers, that he was giving it to her. She could hire someone else to help Blind Billy and Dodge with the bread, and then she'd be able to bake cakes during the day. Already the confectionary was proving to be a profitable venture. She'd make enough to live comfortably.

Surely she wouldn't marry Drummond if she knew she had a way to provide for herself.

He pounded his fists against the bars and kicked them, releasing a yell of frustration. Time was slipping away. How long did he have until she married the lieutenant? Minutes?

At the *clink* of chains behind him and then a firm hand on his shoulder, Pete bowed his head.

"We have tried our plans and not succeeded." Sque-is's voice was full of regret. He and his friends had attempted an escape two days ago and had failed miserably. Pete had warned them, but Sque-is had acted anyway.

They hadn't gotten far before being beaten back into the cell. In spite of Pete's pleas, the bluejackets hadn't shown any mercy. They'd battered and bludgeoned the natives until they could hardly move before binding their hands and feet with chains.

Only today had Sque-is finally stirred from his spot on the floor. And only now had he spoken since the beating.

"Pastor Abe is not coming this time." Sque-is stated what Pete had already concluded. "But if he was here, he would tell us we have been foolish to rely upon the plans of man."

Pete leaned against the bars. He'd been wrestling with God for the past three days. Mostly he'd been lobbing angry questions at God and crying out his frustration. Even now his anger simmered at the injustice of their situation.

"I am a warrior," Sque-is continued. "I have been trained to fight in my own strength. But Pastor Abe says God fights our battles for us, that we must wait upon Him, that our help comes from the Lord, the Maker of heaven and earth."

Pete wanted to shout out again and tell Sque-is that he was done waiting on God. No matter how much he'd tried to turn his life around, God didn't seem to care, at least that Pete could see. If He did care, why had He allowed so many bad things to happen?

His dad's voice came from the past to answer the question: *"For it is better, if the will of God be so, that ye suffer for well doing, than for evil doing."* His dad had quoted the Scripture verse whenever bad things had come his way, even those times during the last years together when he'd suffered loss of income for refusing to cheat his customers as so many other bakers were doing.

It was better to suffer for doing right than for doing evil. Pete let the thought settle over him. He supposed in some ways he hadn't expected to suffer at all once he'd turned his life around. He'd thought God would bless him, that things would go better, and that his troubles would diminish.

But if he looked at his dad as well as people in Scripture— like Job or the Apostle Paul—Pete didn't see ease and comfort, rather loss and problems. Just like him, Job lost everything he loved—his land, his livelihood, and his family. Just like him,

Paul ended up in prison on numerous occasions for doing what was right.

If God allowed those men to face trials and tribulations, what made Pete think his life would be any different?

His dad had claimed trials and difficulties would produce deeper character and genuine faith. At the time, Pete had scoffed at such an idea. But now, in the midst of his own tribulation, he saw the wisdom in it. And suddenly he realized he was at a crossroads. He could continue to wallow in anger at God and push Him away whenever things didn't go smoothly. Or he could trust that God wasn't as concerned about giving him a happy life as He was about developing a holy heart.

Sque-is squeezed Pete's shoulder. "We will pray to the God, the Maker of heaven and earth, together."

"Aye," Pete replied, even as he started to slip to his knees. He'd pray for the will to trust God's plans along with the strength to continue to live rightly even if he was persecuted for doing so. And he'd pray to accept the lot given to him, even if that meant he'd lost everything, including Arabella.

Arabella folded her gloved hands in her lap against her silk wedding gown and peered out the carriage window to the passing businesses.

The lieutenant had arranged for her to be picked up from the Marine Barracks in a carriage from one of Victoria's many liveries. He'd wanted her to be transported in style to Christ Church Cathedral, where he and a number of important guests would be waiting for the wedding ceremony to begin, including all the remaining bride-ship women living in the Marine Barracks.

Though she'd appreciated the lieutenant's kind gesture to make the morning special, she hadn't been able to squelch the rise of disappointment when the coachman had come to the door in his blue uniform with all its polished brass buttons. As he'd helped her inside the carriage and situated her amidst the folds upon folds of creamy silk with puffings edged with more silk, she'd glanced around, hoping to see Mrs. Moresby running toward her, shouting at her to stop, that she'd found what she was looking for and that Pete had been freed.

Unfortunately, with each roll and tumble of the wheels, Arabella saw no sign of the matron, and the sadness only pushed higher into her chest and throat. And she saw no sign of Mercy either. The sweet friend had visited her at the Marine Barracks and encouraged her to find a different way to save Pete besides marrying the lieutenant. But Arabella hadn't been able to think of anything else.

Now it was too late. Arabella was on her way to the church. She'd be married to the lieutenant within the hour. And then hopefully by the morrow, Pete would finally be allowed to leave the jail.

Of course, Mrs. Moresby had stopped by the Marine Barracks yesterday and pulled Arabella aside to inform her the lawyer she'd hired to do the investigating was making progress but would likely need several more days. Mrs. Moresby had urged her to find a way to postpone the wedding. But when Arabella had asked the lieutenant, he'd insisted on keeping to his original plan, indicating he couldn't guarantee the safety of the prisoners if they delayed the wedding.

She'd nodded her understanding and resigned herself again to getting married this morning. Or at least she thought she'd resigned herself . . .

She twisted the silver cross between her fingers. She'd hardly let go of the cross over the past few days. And even now she prayed for the courage to go through with her nuptials. How could she back out now?

The carriage turned down Humboldt Street, and as it drove past the bakehouse, she leaned against the window and peered out, hoping for a glimpse of Haiel-Wat and Kwa-nis even though they were supposed to be hiding. Mercy had updated her on the girls during the recent visit. Apparently, they were still in the apartment but missed Arabella.

Watching it now, silent and still for the day, she couldn't stifle her deep longings—not only for Pete but for the two native girls who needed her, the cake making she'd grown to love, and the independence she'd enjoyed. She even missed grouchy old Blind Billy.

When the bakehouse passed from her view, a bubble of panic burst inside her. What was she doing? The crunch and bump of each wheel rotation settled the question deeper until all she could think about was the ride to the church on the day of her wedding to Mr. Major.

Hayward had accompanied her. Pym Nevins had been in the carriage too. Although Arabella had sent most of her trunks of belongings to her new home the previous day, she'd finished stowing the last of her clothing and toiletries only that morning.

Pym had insisted the final trunks and bags be loaded onto the carriage, informing Arabella that Mr. Major wanted her to feel completely at home after the wedding. Arabella had guessed he simply didn't want her to have any excuses to return to her father's house.

"You're not wearing the bracelet Mr. Major gave you earlier in the week," Pym had said, examining Arabella's wrist.

"I suppose I've forgotten it," Arabella lied. When she was getting ready for the wedding in her boudoir and looked at the glistening emeralds on her dressing table, all she'd been able to think about was the jewels tearing into the tender skin on her back. A fresh wave of fire had rippled over her flesh, and such nausea had welled in her throat at the prospect of donning it that she'd nearly been sick.

"Mr. Major insisted you have it on for the wedding." Pym's

fleshy forehead wrinkled above his worried eyes. "We'll need to go back for it."

"I'm sure it won't matter." Arabella sat gingerly on the seat, careful not to recline and so aggravate her wounds. As with his first attack when he'd bitten her neck, she felt as though somehow she was to blame, that if she'd only been more compliant as a gentlewoman ought to be, she wouldn't have brought such harsh retribution upon herself.

Pym yanked the pull cord urgently. A moment later, the carriage came to a jerking halt that would have caused Arabella to fall back against the seat if Hayward hadn't steadied her.

The portly servant opened the door and called out instructions for the coachman to return to the Lawrence home. When he returned to his seat, he straightened first his bowler hat and then his red bow tie. "I should think you've learned by now that you cannot disregard anything Mr. Major requires of you."

While she had indeed learned this, still she couldn't wear the bracelet. "Will he not be angry if we're late in arriving at the church?"

"Fortunately I made sure we left early, so we have a few extra minutes to spare."

Arabella scrambled for an excuse—anything that might get her out of having to wear the bracelet. To some degree, she realized her abhorrence was misplaced, that it wasn't the bracelet so much as Mr. Major she despised. But since she couldn't avoid him, she needed something she could.

When they arrived in front of the townhouse, Hayward offered to go inside and retrieve the item. After waiting for several long minutes, Pym began fuming about their being late. Cursing under his breath, the short man finally hopped out of the carriage to search for both Hayward and the missing bracelet.

Mr. Major's butler had been gone for only seconds when Hayward appeared outside the carriage. She spoke urgently to the coachman and then climbed inside, closing the door behind her.

As the carriage began to roll away at top speed, Arabella reached for the pull cord. "Wait. We've left Mr. Nevins behind."

"No." Hayward directed Arabella's hand away from the cord back down to her lap. "Mr. Nevins is right where we want him to be—stuck at your house without a conveyance."

Arabella could only stare at her faithful maidservant.

With her family already having gone ahead to the church, Pym would indeed be stuck. "Mr. Major will be very angry when I arrive without Mr. Nevins."

"You're not going to the church." Hayward patted the tiny straw hat she wore over her loose bun. "You're going to Dartmouth."

"Dartmouth?"

"You're leaving England." Hayward pressed her lips together. "I knew that man would return to the house for the bracelet. All I had to do was wait in the shadows of the servants' entrance for him to go inside."

For long seconds, Arabella was speechless.

"Since the first moment your father engaged you to Mr. Major, I've been checking into ways I could free you from him. And the only thing I found that wouldn't require you to put forward a great deal of money and draw suspicion from your father or Mr. Major was the Columbia Mission Society's upcoming endeavor to help women emigrate to British Columbia."

"British Columbia?" Arabella sucked in a breath. "I couldn't possibly!"

"You can and you will," Hayward replied firmly. "The cost of the travels is fully funded by the Columbia Mission Society. And I've already taken care of all the arrangements, the application, the letters of reference, a note from your physician regarding your good health, and the travel details."

Arabella's mind spun wildly. Was it possible for her to escape?

"You must go. If you don't, you'll be dead in a year or two. That man hasn't had a wife who's lasted more than two years."

Arabella shrank back, horrified at the revelation. But as her spine touched the leather seat, the pain pushed her forward again.

"But what about my father? What about Mr. Major's threats—"

"What kind of father sells his daughter's soul for his own comfort?" Hayward's voice dripped with disdain. "No, I won't let him do it. You're going somewhere better where you can make a good life for yourself and where you have a chance at finding a loving husband."

"I'm an old spinster. If no one wants me here except for old men like Mr. Major, who would want me there?"

"Pshaw. You're not old. You're young and beautiful and have so much of life yet ahead of you." Hayward reached for her hand and squeezed it, tears forming in her eyes. "I won't let you throw it away here when there are so many possibilities for you there."

A thrill of excitement whispered through Arabella. "If I go, what will I do when I get there? Where will I live? How will I survive?"

"They say there are many more men than women in the colony and that the men have requested good Christian brides be sent from the motherland."

More men than women? Men who were requesting brides? The possibility seemed too good to be true.

"I have no doubt you'll be one of the first women to be snatched up by some young man who loves you more than life itself," Hayward said through her tearful smile.

A man who loves you more than life itself.

Did Lieutenant Drummond love her more than life itself?

Arabella sat forward on her seat as the carriage turned onto another of Victoria's wide streets. Hayward had wanted her to find a man who loved her more than life. The parting words from the dear servant reverberated through Arabella's mind.

The man who loved her more than life was sitting in jail. Although Pete hadn't spoken of love, she had no doubt of it because he'd shown his love to her in a hundred different ways. And deep inside, she knew Pete wouldn't want her to go forward with marrying the lieutenant, not even to save him. He'd want her to live with courage and boldness.

She pressed the silver cross. *Courage.*

For so long she'd lived the way everyone else had wanted her to—not only the way polite society dictated but also at the beckon of her father, stepmother, Mr. Major, Pym Nevins, the chaperones on the ship, and now the lieutenant.

Was it time to finally stop living according to the expectations of everyone else and instead find her direction from God alone?

twenty-nine

Kneeling in the filthy straw that covered the floor, Pete lifted his petition to the Lord. Next to him, Squeis's whispered prayers rose in the cell along with Pete's, and he sensed a new peace had replaced the anger and frustration that had weighed him down the past few days. Gratefulness swelled in his chest, and he thanked God for the gift of peace, the friendship of a brother in the Lord, and even for the forgiveness that he could extend toward the lieutenant.

He never would have believed the charge of murder, which had been intended to ruin his life, could bless him. Was that how God worked? In unexpected and often ironic ways?

At the squeal of the far door and the beam of light that broke into the darkness, Pete raised his head and shielded his eyes. The despair that would have prodded him to his feet only moments ago was gone now. No, he didn't want Arabella to marry Drummond, and he'd continue to plead with the Lord to prevent the wedding. But in the meantime, Pete had to commit his ways to the Maker of heaven and earth.

"Heavens above, I can't see and I can't breathe" came a woman's voice from the doorway. "How can anyone possibly stay here? This place isn't fit for barn animals."

Officer Green mumbled something Pete couldn't hear, and then the woman spoke again. "What? You can't possibly mean to tell me you allow the prisoners to sit in their own filth day after day?"

Another mumbled response was interrupted by the woman's impatient tone. "Bring them out here, Constable. Immediately."

"The savages are too dangerous." This time the constable's voice was clear. "They need to remain chained."

Pete rolled his eyes. When would the prejudices end?

"Then bring out Mr. Kelly. You cannot expect me to meet with him under such conditions. And I shall speak with my husband about your treatment of the prisoners. Perhaps I'll even go to the newspaper to report what I've witnessed here." The brusque voice sounded familiar. Even so, it took a moment to place it as Mrs. Moresby's.

What was Mrs. Moresby doing at the police headquarters demanding to see him?

Several bluejackets strode down to the cell to unlock it and hold back the natives from trying to escape again. "Hurry it up, Pete," said Officer Green. "If the lady's here to help get you out, don't make her wait."

Mrs. Moresby was here to help get him out? Hope flared inside Pete.

As he started down the corridor, he glanced back at Sque-is, who was still kneeling on the cell floor. With the light breaking through the darkness, Pete caught a glimpse of the dried blood that caked Sque-is's face, the swollen and bruised eyes, broken lip, and the chains that shackled his hands and feet.

Anger slipped back into Pete's chest—anger that his friend had been so mistreated. "I'll find a way to save you," Pete called to his friend.

Sque-is nodded. "Go to the woman you love. Save her first."

Pete hurried out of the lockup and into the front room, squinting at the brightness that greeted him. The constables who remained at the headquarters on guard duty stood with Mrs. Moresby, along with a short gentleman Pete didn't recognize.

Mrs. Moresby had an embroidered handkerchief over her nose and mouth. And as Pete drew nearer, she pressed the handkerchief more thoroughly.

"Peter Kelly," she said in a nasally voice from behind the delicate linen, "you need a bath and a change of clothing immediately. But unfortunately we don't have the time for such niceties, not if you're going to stop Miss Lawrence from making the biggest mistake of her life."

"The wedding to Drummond?"

"It's at ten this morning," she replied with a glance at the wall clock. To Pete's dismay, the minute hand was almost upon the hour. He had no time to delay.

He glanced at the door. Dare he make a run for it?

"Pete, this is a friend of the family, Mr. Bigbee," Mrs. Moresby continued from behind the handkerchief.

Pete shifted his attention to the gentleman. He was short and stout, and a fleshy chin seemed to take the place of his neck, leaving very little room for his bow tie. Mr. Bigbee wrinkled his nose—no doubt to combat Pete's stench—yet he nodded politely, his eyes kind but tired-looking.

"Mr. Bigbee is a lawyer, and I've been paying him to uncover what really happened this spring at the start of the smallpox outbreak. Like you, I've always been curious as to why the natives were sent away rather than quarantined and vaccinated."

At another look at the clock, Pete's muscles tightened with the need to be on his way. Aye, he was still frustrated that such unwise decisions had been made and that no one had been held accountable for them. But right now wasn't the time to discuss the matter, was it?

As though sensing his impatience, Mrs. Moresby got straight to the point. "After working all through the night, Mr. Bigbee finished uncovering the evidence he needed, and we just presented it to the naval board this morning. They decided that rather than have a scandal that could undermine the safety and integrity of the military presence here in the colony, they would prefer to keep the findings private and will immediately dismiss the officers involved and send them back to England."

Pete stared from Mrs. Moresby to Mr. Bigbee and back again, the words finally registering in his mind.

Mr. Bigbee cleared his throat and continued the explanation. "Lieutenant Drummond's signature is upon the order calling for the removal of the tribes around Victoria. In fact, I found several correspondences indicating that he and the other officers involved perpetrated the dispersal as biological warfare."

"Biological warfare?" Pete asked.

"It was their explicit intention to use the smallpox outbreak as a way to reduce the native population and so diminish the growing threat of war."

"I'd already suspected such a tactic but had no way to prove it."

Mrs. Moresby waved her hand impatiently. "The important thing is that the marines who were on patrol the morning of the shooting are changing their story. Now that the lieutenant is being sent back to England and no longer has the authority to threaten them, Mr. Bigbee was able to elicit separate testimonies from each man regarding the true nature of what happened. You have been cleared entirely of murder charges."

Relief poured over Pete with such force he almost dropped to his knees. Inwardly, he offered up another prayer—this one of gratitude that God had brought about justice in His time and in His way.

"You are free to go, Mr. Kelly," Mr. Bigbee stated.

"Yes," Mrs. Moresby added from behind the handkerchief. "Again I'd advise a thorough bath, but I'm afraid there's no time. You must be on your way and stop a sweet young woman from marrying the wrong man."

"Aye." That was what he'd wanted—what he'd been begging for all morning.

"Hurry now," Mrs. Moresby urged. "You haven't a second to waste."

He started across the room, half expecting one of the constables to grab him and stop him. But no one made a move. When he reached the door, he paused. "I can't go."

Mrs. Moresby had finally dropped the handkerchief, and Mr. Bigbee had resumed a conversation with the chief of police. At his words, they fell silent.

Pete released the door handle. Although his blood was pumping hard with the need to make it to the church on time to stop Arabella, he couldn't leave—not yet.

"Mrs. Moresby and Mr. Bigbee," he said, "thank you for what you've done to bring about my release. I'm indebted to you both. But I can't leave my friends behind to sit in jail. They're no more guilty than I am of any crime."

Mrs. Moresby paused in opening her reticule. "Don't worry about them. We've gained permission for their release as well. We're simply waiting for the marine forces to arrive to escort them out of town."

Pete bristled at the unfairness of the situation—that he'd been set free in a moment's time while Sque-is would have to wait and then be kicked out of town as if he were no better than a pesky dog. Pete was tempted to go back inside the cell and update his friends on what had happened and say goodbye.

But he knew Sque-is wanted him to go to Arabella. His friend understood that Pete loved Arabella the same way he loved his wife, that he'd do anything, go anywhere, and even sacrifice his life for her if necessary.

With a nod, Pete opened the door.

"I advise you to marry her soon," Mrs. Moresby called after him, "so that she doesn't slip away again."

"Are you suggesting I push the dandy out of the way and take his place this morning?"

Mrs. Moresby smiled. "I always knew you were a smart boy."

Pete grinned in response and then stepped out of the police headquarters. He hoped he never had to see the inside of the jail again, but he also knew he'd keep on doing what was right even if he had to suffer for it.

Then, praying he wasn't too late, he sprinted down the street.

"Stop!" Pete yelled as he threw open the double doors of Christ Church Cathedral. "Stop the wedding!" He stumbled inside, breathless, his lungs burning and his side aching.

Heads turned, mouths gaping.

"Arabella!" he shouted. "Don't marry Drummond! You need to marry me instead!"

The nave was dimly lit by sconces on the walls, as well as candelabras on the altar, and Pete had to blink several times to see the front clearly.

"Arabella!" he called again, stalking down the aisle, quite aware he was bringing the stench of the prison with him, especially when wedding guests began to wave fans and cover their noses and mouths in his wake.

Halfway down, he realized only one person was standing at the altar rail—Lieutenant Drummond, attired in his naval uniform. The bishop was in his seat to the side of the transept, holding the *Book of Common Prayer*, but Arabella was nowhere to be seen.

His pulse jumped with the realization that she hadn't yet arrived and that he wasn't too late to stop the wedding.

"Mr. Kelly," Drummond said, his brows rising above genuinely surprised eyes. "What are you doing here? How did you manage to get out of jail?"

Only then did Pete realize that Mrs. Moresby and Mr. Bigbee had likely come straight from their meeting on Esquimalt. If the lieutenant hadn't gone to his office yet this morning, he probably hadn't heard the verdict regarding the release of the prisoners. And more important, he hadn't learned of his own fate.

Pete had the sudden vindictive urge to spill it all, to embarrass the lieutenant in front of Victoria's most elite families who'd gathered for the wedding. He could tell them everything—from the lieutenant's role in using smallpox as a weapon against the natives to his disgrace in being sent back to England to the false murder charges against Pete, Sque-is, and the other natives.

But the quiet peace Pete had experienced when he'd been kneeling and praying next to Sque-is settled inside him once more. He'd come to marry Arabella, not to judge the lieutenant and shame him publicly. His superiors would do that soon enough.

"Arrest Mr. Kelly!" the lieutenant commanded several marines standing in the far aisle. "He's an escaped murderer and must be taken back to jail at once."

The marines exchanged glances among themselves.

"Go on!" Drummond barked. "Get him."

The men moved to obey their commander, circling Pete with the intention of trapping him.

"You can't touch me this time," Pete said, seeing the lieutenant had left him little choice but to share the recent verdict. "You've been dismissed from your position and you're being sent back to England. You no longer have any authority here in the colony."

A flurry of gasps and whispers filled the nave, and the marines stopped to stare at the lieutenant.

Drummond remained stiff and unmoving. "You're lying."

"Mr. Bigbee has been investigating matters that happened in the spring with orders made regarding the smallpox outbreak. He presented his findings to the naval board just this morning."

"There are no findings." Drummond glanced around nervously as though realizing for the first time he'd just opened up a very sensitive topic in front of Victoria's highest-ranking families. No doubt he'd given them fodder for gossip.

"You're done for," Pete replied. "That's why the patrol unit finally gave the real version of what happened, because they aren't afraid of you any longer."

"They already gave the real version. If they've spoken otherwise, then they've undermined their own credibility."

Pete wanted to say more but held himself back. The marines had stopped advancing upon him and were now looking to Drummond for further instructions. Yet Drummond seemed to have forgotten about them.

The whispers and conversations of the guests rose to a low hum.

Drummond pulled himself up, straightening his shoulders and lifting his chin. In his pristine white naval trousers, blue coat, gold braids and stripes, he cut a dashing figure. For a moment, Pete could only see himself as everyone else did, with filthy clothing, disheveled hair, and unshaven face, along with the grit of several days of jail coating him.

Was he truly worthy of Arabella? She certainly deserved someone better than Drummond. But did she also deserve someone better than him, a sinner-turned-baker who someday hoped to become more but maybe never would? Did she deserve someone who wouldn't end up in prison every other week for helping the helpless?

He caught a whiff of his own stench and resolved to stay only long enough to warn Arabella against marrying Drummond. He certainly couldn't marry her himself. Could he?

The bishop rose from his chair and methodically crossed to the center of the aisle, taking his place in front of Drummond, clearly ready to begin the ceremony. The lieutenant stared at the open doors as though expecting Arabella to enter at any second.

Pete braced his feet apart, unwilling to let Arabella walk down the aisle once she entered.

"Eh-hem," the bishop said, clearing his throat and brushing a hand down his long white robe and the dangling red chimere that fell to his knees. "Are we yet waiting for the bride's arrival?"

The congregation grew silent, swiveling and facing forward, their attention focused on the bishop.

"No," Pete replied quickly.

"Yes," Drummond said at the same time.

The bishop glanced between Pete and Drummond, his eyes widening.

"If there's to be any wedding, it'll be mine," Pete said, "not the lieutenant's."

"Might I remind you," Drummond said, "that Miss Lawrence agreed to marry me, not you."

"Do you seriously think she'll want to marry you now?" Pete prayed she wouldn't.

"Please," the bishop said. "Since this is the Lord's house and a place of peace, I suggest we take this discussion outside the church doors."

All the better as far as Pete was concerned. He didn't want Arabella getting anywhere near the altar with Drummond.

As Pete made his way back outside the church onto the street, he searched both ways for any sign of Arabella but didn't glimpse her beautiful red hair anywhere.

Drummond exited not long after him. Now in the full light of the morning sunshine, Drummond surveyed Pete from his head to his toes, a derisive smile slowly spreading. "You're a real catch, aren't you, Mr. Kelly? Thanks to you, Miss Lawrence will take one look at you—and one sniff—and run right into my arms."

"It's a good thing Arabella isn't as shallow as you. She can recognize a treasure even when it doesn't look—or smell—like one at first glance." Pete's cocky words wiped the smile from the lieutenant's face. But even as his witty remark hit its target, he hoped he was right—that Arabella would still care about him even after all that had happened.

thirty

Arabella lurched forward on the seat and grabbed the pull cord. The carriage rolled to a stop. She didn't exactly know what to do or where to go. But one thing was certain—she couldn't marry Lieutenant Drummond. In fact, she had to run away to a place where he wouldn't think to look for her, a place where she could delay everything so that she could think and pray and hopefully come up with a new plan to free Pete.

She needed to have the courage to love Pete for as long as they had left together. If that meant she had to go public with her testimony regarding what had happened that fateful morning, then so be it. If that meant she ruined her reputation forever, then she'd learn to adjust. And if that meant the lieutenant wouldn't be able to help her free Pete, then she'd have to push for another way.

"Can you drive me to the eastern cove?" she called to the coachman. Mrs. Moresby had asked her to delay the wedding, and now she'd found a way. "As fast as you can, please."

She held on tightly as the coachman drove wildly through town. When he finally drew the carriage to a halt, she immediately spotted Pete's canoe among the tall reeds. She wouldn't be able to navigate the vessel herself. She'd have to hire someone to help her.

As the coachman helped her down, she scanned the waterfront, which was busy with fishermen unloading boats of their early morning catches, marine patrols, and other vessels passing by.

"Tcoosma?" she called to the nearest group of men. "I'm looking for an older native named Tcoosma?"

At her question, she suddenly found a dozen pairs of eyes upon her, and immediately she regretted drawing attention to herself. In her elegant gown with its lovely beaded bodice and full skirt with a short train, she was hardly inconspicuous. If she hoped to run away without leaving a trail for the lieutenant to follow, she'd certainly made it easy for him.

The advantage, she quickly realized, was that the men were eager to help her, and before long someone had found Tcoosma for her. She didn't know where he'd come from or even where he lived, but apparently he'd received word that his services were needed.

As he approached, wearing the leather breechcloth, leggings, and moccasins, his keen eyes took her in, recognition softening his features. He wore the same bowler hat, coat, and shells in his ear as the last time she'd seen him, only this time he'd donned a shirt—albeit a very dirty one.

"Can you assist me?" She pointed to Pete's canoe.

He looked at her attire, the canoe, and then shook his head.

"I shall pay you," she said, reaching for the cloak she'd discarded as she waited in the morning sunshine. She held out the fine garment.

He took it cautiously, studying it and turning it over in his hands. Finally, he gave her a nod. "We wait for Pete."

"No, he's in jail." She glanced around, her insides growing more jumpy with every passing moment. She had to get away before the lieutenant came looking for her and tried to persuade her to accompany him to the church. "I need to go now."

Tcoosma frowned. "Pete not happy if I go without him."

"Please." She reached for an earlobe and unclasped one of the dangling jewels. "I shall give you my earrings too."

She haggled with him for several more long moments before he gave in, took her earrings along with the cloak, and helped her onto the bench in the front of the canoe. The crinoline and satin folds of her dress rose up around her almost as if to drown her. Nevertheless, she found a way to manage the paddle to aid Tcoosma in her getaway.

When the shoreline began to fade, she allowed herself a deep breath. The same sense of relief filled her that she'd had the day she'd ridden out of London and away from Mr. Major. She might have hurt her family in the leaving, but she could no longer take the guilt of their welfare upon herself.

Although she would have sacrificed much for her family, even going with them to the workhouse if need be, she saw now that no woman should be expected to give up her dignity and endure an abusive relationship in order to protect those she loved. Hayward had tried to tell her as much, but she'd been too bound by being a proper gentlewoman to listen to her faithful servant's wisdom.

Her voyage to the colony had been the first step in breaking free. Yet each day since then, she'd slowly cut away all the constraints. And now, today, she'd severed the final cord. She'd made the choice to free herself from living under someone else's demands and plans so she could at last be free to be herself.

As the breeze teased the loose wisps of hair she'd curled around her forehead and temple especially for the wedding, she closed her eyes and let the sunshine bathe her face. Let it darken her skin and give her freckles. She didn't care. In fact, she might as well get used to changes, because she'd likely face many of them when she returned to Victoria and went to the police headquarters with her testimony.

Outside the church, as the minutes passed with no sign of Arabella, Pete's heart began to thud with a new anxiety. Arabella had already run away from one wedding. Aye, the circumstances had been completely different since she'd been trying to get away from a monster. But if she'd done it once, what was to prevent her from doing it again?

By the time the church bell rang at eleven o'clock, most of the guests had trickled out and left. Drummond issued orders for his men to secure a carriage from the closest livery so that he could search for Arabella.

As Drummond rode away, the urgency inside Pete only swelled. He had to find Arabella first. He had to get to her and tell her everything Mr. Bigbee had discovered. Once she knew all that Drummond had done, she'd likely reject him.

But even as Pete sprinted through town, he realized with a sinking heart that he couldn't be the one to tell her about Drummond's faults. As before, Pete didn't want Arabella to choose him as a backup because things didn't work out with Drummond. He wanted to be her first choice, the one she picked because she loved him.

He searched the bakehouse and apartment for her, but no one had seen her. As he threw open the door and stepped out onto the street, he found himself bumping chests with a tall man with fair blond hair and concerned blue eyes.

"Pastor Abe?" Pete had to hold himself back from launching against his friend and embracing him.

"It's me and none other." Pastor Abe was disheveled too—his face unshaven, his wool trousers and flannel shirt wrinkled and dusty from travel. He didn't hesitate before drawing Pete into a hug, regardless of Pete's appearance or his odor.

The pastor's genuine warmth and kindness always reminded Pete of his dad, this time no less. Even so, Pete pulled away quickly, unwilling to subject his friend to his stench for long. "I know I smell like a bed of newly bloomed flowers, but try not to be too jealous."

Pastor Abe smiled. "I see I've come too late. You've already managed to charm your way free."

"Aye. It's my charm and pretty smile that work miracles every time."

"I came as soon as I got word," Pastor Abe said more soberly. "How is Sque-is?"

"He and his companions will be set free too—once the escort arrives to usher them out of town."

"I'll go put in a good word for Sque-is. Maybe they'll let them go without an escort."

"Not likely. Not after Sque-is and his friends attempted an escape. Every constable at the headquarters is afraid of them."

A carriage rattled past, and Pete couldn't keep from peering into the window for Arabella and then up and down the street. Where was she?

"Who are you looking for?" Pastor Abe asked.

A quick, witty comment formed on Pete's lips, but somehow a serious, almost choked answer came out instead. "The woman I love."

"Is this the same woman you told me about the last time I was in town, the one you claimed was about to drag you to the altar?"

"Aye. Except she ran away on her way to the wedding."

Pastor Abe gave a low whistle.

"Not to our wedding," Pete hastily explained. "She was getting married to someone else."

His friend's mouth stalled around his response.

Pete shook his head. The explanation was only making him look like a fool. Mayhap he was. Even so, he wasn't giving up his search for her. "I've gotta find her," he admitted, his voice raw with emotion.

"A runaway bride?" Pastor Abe asked, scraping his hand over his chin. "When I was landing just a short while ago, I saw a woman paddling away in a canoe. She was wearing a fancy gown—one that looked like it very well could have been for a wedding."

Pete's pulse spurted. "The color of her hair, did you see it?"

"Reddish-brown."

"Aye, that was her!" Pete glanced around at the few men loitering outside the bathhouse and attempted to rein in his excitement. If Drummond was still looking for Arabella, Pete didn't want the dandy learning any of this information. "Which direction was she going?"

"She was heading east with Tcoosma," Pastor Abe answered. "The sight of her in a canoe in such an elegant gown was strange, but I was in too much of a hurry to get to you and Sque-is to think much on it."

If Arabella was heading east with Tcoosma, Pete guessed she was likely returning to one of the spots he'd taken her. There weren't many places, and he trusted Tcoosma to keep her safe. Even so, he couldn't take any chances. If Pastor Abe had seen Arabella, then others had too, which meant if the lieutenant poked around on the waterfront, he'd discover everything Pete just had.

Pete couldn't delay another minute. He had to get to her before Drummond did.

thirty-one

Arabella pointed to a gently rolling hill. "There. Let's stop there."

"Not Pete's land anymore," Tcoosma retorted as he maneuvered the canoe around the bay.

"I realize that." Arabella dipped her paddle into the water, first on one side and then the other. "But I shall always think of it as his, even though it's not."

"That lieutenant is a bad man," Tcoosma said. "He tricked Tcoosma into showing him Pete's land. Then he returned to town and bought it for himself."

Arabella's heartbeat stalled. "Which lieutenant?"

"The dandy," Tcoosma replied, using Pete's nickname for Lieutenant Drummond. "He is no good, that one."

Arabella closed her eyes and fought off a wave of dizziness. She'd been the one to mention visiting the place Pete intended to buy. The ensuing argument had probably fueled the lieutenant's desire to purchase the land to spite Pete and show him who was more powerful.

As the bottom of the canoe scraped against the rocky shore, Arabella blinked back the dizzying feeling. Was this the land the lieutenant was referring to when he'd spoken of building them a home? Did he think her so pliable that she'd actually agree to live on land he'd all but stolen from someone else?

Heedless of her dainty slipper-like shoes, she climbed out of the canoe without waiting for Tcoosma's help. She soaked her shoes and silk stockings along with the lower portion of her gown. But she was too frustrated to care.

What else had the lieutenant done to spite Pete? Had he trumped up the charges of murder? Was he the reason Pete and Sque-is had ended up in jail?

Her thoughts racing, Arabella climbed up the knoll. At the top, she slowed her pace, trying to catch her breath, but she didn't halt until she'd reached the spot where Pete had told her he planned to build his house. She stood in the center of the level area and turned slowly, taking in the view on all sides— wooded land to the north and west of the hill, with the sea and distant mountain peaks to the southeast.

It was as breathtaking this time as it had been the first time she'd seen it. Only now a painful thud radiated in her chest.

Was there any way she could restore this land to Pete? What could she say to the lieutenant to convince him to sell it?

Maybe she wouldn't be able to regain the land for Pete. She didn't even know if she or Mrs. Moresby would find a way to keep him from being sent away to prison. But she had to carry on with the responsibilities God had given her—responsibilities she'd never expected but that she couldn't relinquish simply because her situation had become difficult.

She had to go back to the bakehouse, to Haiel-Wat and Kwa-nis. They needed her loving care. She'd help Blind Billy and Dodge with making bread. And she'd attempt to sell her cakes to whomever would have them. Through it all, she'd trust that God would continue to untangle the future just as He had her past.

She breathed in the woodsy scent of damp leaves and moss that a gentle north breeze brought her way. Lowering herself to the ground, she stripped off her wet slippers and stockings.

Though the sunshine was warm, the long grass felt cool and unfamiliar beneath her feet. She'd never bared her feet outside of her bedroom.

Against the lush green, her toes were pale and delicate. She dug them in and relished the softness tickling the arch of her foot. She marveled at the brazenness of her bare feet, the sight of her ankles, and the fact that she'd defied convention and canoed out into the wilderness with only an Indian guide.

She lay back and closed her eyes. For a while she simply let the sun bathe her face and relished the quiet freedom of the hill. Eventually, however, her thoughts strayed to Pete, and her heart ached to see him.

When she returned to Victoria, she knew the first place she had to go was to the jail, and she'd plead with the officers to allow her to visit him. She wasn't letting the lieutenant's displeasure, the ladies' gossip, or even worry about the future keep her away. She'd waited long enough, and now she wanted him to know she planned to support him no matter what he faced in his future.

At a sudden shadow falling across her face, her eyes flew open. Pete stood above her with the sun behind him outlining his overlong hair, his broad shoulders, and his thick arms.

She blinked to clear her vision. Was she dreaming?

"Arabella," he said, breathing hard as if he'd run up the hill. The one word was filled with both longing and relief.

For a moment, she could only stare up at him, taking in the rugged lines of his face, the dark stubble, the handsome cut of his jaw and cheeks, the dazzling blue of his eyes. His hair was damp, as if he'd recently bathed, and his garments were clean.

"You're free?" she asked, her throat clogging with emotion.

"Aye."

"Sque-is?"

"Aye, Sque-is too. He and his friends were given their canoe and are even now being escorted out to the strait."

Her eyes stung with the elation that was building in her heart and spreading throughout her body. Mrs. Moresby had apparently unearthed everything necessary to aid in the release.

"Are you free?" he asked, glancing at her left hand.

"Aye," she said with a smile, mimicking his answer from a moment ago. She was free in more ways than she could explain.

"Then you're not marrying Drummond?" He looked around as though expecting the lieutenant to come charging out of the woods.

She started to scramble up, but he reached for her hand, lifting her easily to her feet. "I only agreed to it because he said that then the officials would listen to my testimony, which would help gain your freedom."

"I wouldn't have wanted you to make such a sacrifice, Arabella. Never." His voice was more somber than she'd ever heard it.

"I know that now. But I couldn't abide the thought of you being sent away and suffering in prison."

His hand tightened around hers. "I didn't want to be sent away either. But I'm starting to realize that when we stand up against injustice, we'll likely suffer for doing the right thing."

The thought made her quiver, and deep in her soul she suspected God had much more to teach her about courage in the days to come. But for now she only wanted to relish this moment with Pete.

"Drummond's searching for you." Pete glanced around again. "And I was afraid he'd find you first."

"Even if he had, I still wouldn't have married him. I know now I couldn't, not when I so desperately want to marry someone else." She spoke the words bravely before she could find excuses for why she shouldn't.

Pete's labored breathing came to an abrupt halt.

Suddenly embarrassed by her confession, she threw herself against Pete's chest and buried her face there.

His arms came around her almost fiercely, and he held her as though he couldn't get enough of her.

Her body sagged into him, the despair and worry and frustration of the past few days falling away. A sob of relief rose up. Pete was safe. He was here. And she never wanted to let go of him again.

"It's my fault you lost your land," she whispered. "If I hadn't mentioned it, the lieutenant wouldn't have known—"

"Shhh," he whispered, his lips warm against her temple, his kiss firm and possessive. "It doesn't matter. Nothing else matters but you. I love you more than anything else."

She reveled in his declaration, his embrace, the power of his love that emanated from his body.

"I love you too," she whispered into his neck.

―――――⊶⊷―――――

Pete breathed her in. His heart still hadn't stopped racing from his frantic paddling from Victoria. Even with Pastor Abe in the front of the canoe helping him, he hadn't been able to get here fast enough.

When he'd arrived to the sight of just one canoe—his—he'd grown weak with relief. Even so, he'd sprinted up the hill as fast as he could, leaving Tcoosma and Pastor Abe behind.

Had Arabella not only told him she loved him but also insinuated that she wanted to marry him? His pulse picked up pace again just thinking about it.

He pressed another kiss into her hair. In the same instance, her lips connected with his neck. At the warmth of her breath and the silk of her lips, he closed his eyes, and as she made a trail of kisses to his jaw, he held himself motionless.

When her mouth drew near his, he couldn't keep himself in check any longer. He released a moan and found her lips, capturing her softness, melding together, and needing her in a way that set his blood on fire.

She wanted him. She'd run away from her wedding because she'd realized she wanted him. The thought drove through him, making him want her all the more in return. His kiss delved deeper as he claimed her, and she willingly let him.

"It's a good thing I dragged you to the bathhouse before we left" came Pastor Abe's mirthful voice behind him. "I see we are in sore need of a wedding, and soon."

With a gasp, Arabella broke away from Pete, and he suspected she would have pulled away altogether if he hadn't chased after her mouth, claiming her lips again, this time more languidly and gently.

Even though he could sense her hesitancy, she clearly craved his kisses enough that she was paying no heed to the properness of their situation, and that thought pleased him and only fueled his desire for her.

"Maybe a wedding is in order right now?" Pastor Abe said with a chuckle.

Pete grinned, breaking away from Arabella's lips but unwilling to release her from his hold. "I'm definitely not opposed to that."

Arabella's cheeks were flushed a rosy pink, and her eyes were bright, the adoration in her expression everything he'd dreamed of and more. "Yes," she whispered with a shy smile. "Let's get married. Today. Now. Here."

"You're sure?"

"I'm ready. I even shed my shoes." She poked her foot out from underneath the hem of her wedding gown. He was surprised at the sight of her bare foot.

"Does this mean your runaway bride days are behind you?"

"No more running," she assured him with a smile.

He brought her hand up to his lips and kissed her knuckles gently. "Unless you're running into my arms. Which I guarantee you'll be doing quite often."

"You guarantee it?" Her focus dropped to his lips.

"Aye."

"Do you promise I shall be asking you for it?"

His grin quirked higher. "Over and over."

"Then I am yours." She lifted her lips for another kiss. "Forever."

He kissed her then, knowing that if anyone would be doing the asking, it would be him. Forever.

thirty-two

*A*rabella flipped the page of the book on the kitchen table, pointing to the words on the page and sounding them out for Pete.

His fingers glided up her arm to her neck and into the hair he'd already loosened.

She tried to keep her voice steady, but it wavered at his touch.

As his hand slid deeper into her hair and combed the long strands away from her neck, the words on the page faded in anticipation of his kiss.

A second later, his lips grazed the spot below her ear, this time filling her whole body with need.

"I thought you wanted another reading lesson," she whispered.

"I thought I did too." His breath was hot against her skin, and she closed her eyes at the pleasure his smallest touch brought her.

"You will never learn to read at this rate."

He lifted her off her chair and dragged her onto his lap. She didn't resist but came to him willingly, eagerly. She slipped her arms around his neck and lifted her lips to receive his kiss. But instead of giving her what she desired, he teased her, letting his mouth hover just out of reach, brushing his lips across hers so that she couldn't keep from arching in to him.

"Must I ask again, Mr. Kelly?" she asked.

"Aye, Mrs. Kelly," he said just as breathlessly.

"Kiss me. Kiss me now before I perish with need."

His smiling lips moved against hers more firmly, answering her need with his own insatiable desire.

Bright daylight filled the apartment, and Arabella knew she needed to head downstairs soon to begin her cake-making preparations. With opposite work schedules, they had so little time alone. But with the growing income she was bringing in from the confectionary, she hoped they would be able to afford to buy land sooner than they'd planned.

Tcoosma had been the one to come to Pete on the day Lieutenant Drummond left Victoria in disgrace to sail back to England. The old Indian guide had arrived with the news that the lieutenant had sold the property back to the Surveyor's Office and that Pete's land was once again his.

Of course, Tcoosma hadn't understood that Pete didn't have the means to purchase it yet. But Pete had gone over to the surveyor and given him a down payment—all the money Arabella had made thus far with her cake making.

Their opposite schedules and hard work would soon allow them to make another payment on the land, drawing them closer to the realization of having their own place. Pete had already contacted an orchard for fruit trees and hoped to begin the planting in the spring, just as soon as the land was theirs. And he'd begun drawing up designs for the new house he intended to build on the hill.

The apartment was no longer big enough—or private enough for their family. Even though Mercy and Dr. Colville had finally gotten married, Haiel-Wat and Kwa-nis had stayed and seemed to have no intention of leaving. Now that the girls were fully recovered and gaining strength, they'd become much more active and inquisitive with both the bread and cake making. Arabella had started giving them easy tasks that they were both quick to learn.

Pastor Abe had made sure to let the city officials know that the girls were employed at the bakehouse and confectionary so no one would question their presence—although with the lieutenant and other officers like him gone, the attitude toward the natives had thankfully begun to shift.

"Let's just pray next time I come, it's not to get you out of jail," Pastor Abe had said after he'd performed their wedding ceremony on the hilltop of Pete's land.

When they'd parted ways, Pete asked Pastor Abe to send him word if he learned whether Sque-is had made it back to his tribe in time to save them from the smallpox. In the month since the wedding, Pete hadn't heard anything. Not from Pastor Abe or Sque-is.

Arabella had finally written to both her father and Hayward, letting them know where she was and that she was happily married. She realized a month was much too soon for a response. After all, Pete had sent his letter over a year ago and still hadn't received word.

But even if she never heard back from them, at least she'd brought a sense of completion to her past. She'd also come to learn that the man she'd mistaken for Pym Nevins was actually Mr. Bigbee. With the lawyer's stout build and bright bow ties, his physical appearance was always a jarring reminder of Mr. Major's butler. Fortunately, that was as far as the resemblance went, as Mr. Bigbee was the kind of man who pursued justice rather than avoided it.

Arabella's chest rose and fell rapidly against Pete's, his kiss taking her breath away just as it always did. "I need to go start the cakes," she managed as his lips made a trail down her neck to her collar.

"Kwa-nis is able to start them," he whispered between kisses.

Arabella couldn't make her voice work to protest even though she knew she should go.

A creak of the door was followed by a gust of cold November air entering the apartment. At the sight of Haiel-Wat standing in the doorway, Arabella tried to wiggle away from Pete. But he kept hold of her waist and continued to plant kisses on her neck.

Haiel-Wat smiled, her eyes bearing testimony to her happiness. Though her face still bore the scars of her hardship, the same way Arabella's body still did, she was moving on, stronger than ever.

The girl spoke something in Chinook to Pete. He responded and then bent in to kiss Arabella on the lips several times in quick succession, making Haiel-Wat roll her eyes.

Arabella was gradually learning the language and realized with embarrassment that the girl had told Pete he kissed his wife too much and that Pete had responded he didn't kiss her enough.

"You must see your visitor," Haiel-Wat said, this time in broken English.

"Tell them I'm busy," Pete replied, tossing the girl a grin, "and to go away."

"He says he is father."

Pete froze, his hand in Arabella's hair, his mouth poised for another kiss. Slowly, he released Arabella and turned his full attention on Haiel-Wat. "Father? As in *my* father?"

Haiel-Wat nodded, although from the girl's confused expression, Arabella guessed she didn't understand Pete's question.

Pete's body had turned rigid. As he finally met Arabella's gaze, his eyes brimmed with both anxiety and excitement.

"Go see," she gently urged, sliding off his lap onto her feet.

"What if it's not him?"

"Even if not, the visitor may have news from your father. Perhaps the letter you've been waiting for."

Pete rose and reached for Arabella's hand. "Come with me."

"Of course."

She wrapped a shawl around her shoulders and followed Pete down the outside stairway and through the back door of the bakehouse. As they stepped inside to the warmth of the ovens and the heavy scent of the fermenting sponge, Pete stopped short at the sight of the couple waiting just inside the front doorway.

An older man stood with his arm around a petite woman. When they saw Pete, their eyes rounded, a mixture of love and longing etched into both of their faces. Their features were sallow and thin, telling a tale of hardship. The bags at their feet were ragged, their clothing dirty and threadbare, their shoes worn and patched.

Though haggard, the man's face was familiar, with hints of the handsome man he'd once been, the blue eyes still keen and very much like Pete's.

"Peter," the man said softly. "I don't know if I'm welcome here, but after your letter . . ."

Pete released Arabella and swiftly crossed the room. Without a word he fell to his knees before his father, grabbed the man's hand, and pressed it to his tear-streaked cheek.

Pete's father's eyes welled with his own tears as he exchanged a tentative glance with his wife. The woman's lips trembled, and she nodded at her husband. He raised a shaking hand above Pete's head and then lowered it until it rested on Pete's tousled hair.

"I have no right to ask for your forgiveness," Pete said brokenly, his head and shoulders bent. "But I long for it every day."

"Oh, son," his father said, his voice cracking, "I have already forgiven you, seventy times seven, and I've never stopped loving you."

Arabella swiped at her own tears. Pete's father had forgiven him long ago, even when Pete hadn't asked for it. Could she do

365

the same for her father? For the way he'd failed to defend her? Could she even forgive Mr. Major?

Their callousness and abuse had been wrong. They'd hurt her and left scars—both on the inside and out—that she'd live with forever. But would forgiving them release the past and, more important, release her so that she could give herself and her love to Pete completely without anything holding her back?

She slipped her hand into her pocket and felt for the cross there. Perhaps forgiveness took the greatest courage of all.

Pete lifted his head then, tears still streaking his face. "And I have never stopped loving you. I only pray that someday I'll be a godly man just like you and finally be worthy of your love."

"You already are worthy, son. You always have been." His father pulled Pete to his feet, held out his arms, and drew him into an embrace. Pete didn't hesitate to return the hug. He held fast to his father for a long moment before finally releasing the man.

Wiping his cheeks, he turned to his mother. "I covet your forgiveness too, Mum. I know I hurt you—"

Before he could finish his apology, the petite woman gathered him close, her muffled sobs filling the room.

Pete held his mother gently until she quieted, pulled back, and gave him a wobbly smile. "We didn't know if we'd find you, but we prayed every day that God would lead us back to each other."

"Are you here to stay?" Pete asked, looking hopefully from one to the other.

"Aye," Pete's father said. "When you said bakers were needed here in the colony and that a man could earn an honest living, I knew that was God opening a new door for us. I sold the equipment I had left and had just enough to purchase two steerage tickets."

"I could use the help. Business is booming."

"I was hoping you'd have work for me," his father admitted, "at least until I can save up enough to branch out."

"Aye, soon enough my bakehouse will be in need of a new baker. And it'll be yours." Pete shared a smile with Arabella. If his father eventually took over the bakehouse, Pete would have more time to spend on his orchards and in building their new house. If his father was willing, they couldn't ask for a better arrangement.

Pete's father and mother followed Pete's gaze toward her, seeing her for the first time.

Pete held out his hand to her, encouraging her to come forward. She hesitantly made her way to her husband's side and took his hand.

"Mum, Dad," he said, gazing down at Arabella with all the love and adoration she'd come to expect. "This is my beautiful bride, Arabella."

Arabella fumbled in her pocket, retrieved the silver cross, and held it out to Pete's dad. "You gave this to Pete, and he gave it to me. It has blessed us both and has taught us to seek after the One who can truly give strength and courage in our greatest hour of need. Now I return it to you. May God give you courage in the days to come."

As his father took the cross, he nodded his thanks, too overcome to speak.

Pete's warm smile told her he approved of what she'd done.

She never would have believed that first day in Victoria, when the men came aboard the bride ship, that she'd end up marrying Peter Kelly. But now she couldn't imagine her life without him. She intertwined her fingers with his and silently thanked God for bringing her exactly what she needed, in His way and in His timing.

author's note

*W*hen I first heard of the concept of bride ships, I was both horrified and fascinated by the idea that women would willingly board ships, leave everything they'd ever known behind, and sail to a strange land, all for the purpose of marrying complete strangers. I couldn't help but ask myself, What kind of woman would do such a thing, and why?

In the 1860s, several bride ships left England's shores with the destination of Victoria on Vancouver Island, which at the time was still a colony of England and not yet part of Canada. As I researched these ships and the women who took the voyages, I searched frantically for the answer to my questions, namely: What sort of desperation did these women face that would drive them to take part in one of the bride ships?

In this second book in THE BRIDE SHIPS series, my hope is to show the perspective of one of the wealthier brides who sailed halfway around the world in search of a better life. While we can reasonably understand why the poor women joined such an endeavor, it's more difficult to understand why a wealthy woman would want (or need) to do so.

A valuable resource I used in writing this series was *Voyages of Hope: The Saga of the Bride-Ships* by Peter Johnson. He gives some background into the social climate of England at the time, including the fact that in the decades before the bride ships, thousands upon thousands of young men had left England because of a depression. By the early 1860s, the Columbia Mission Society stated that there were 600,000 more women than men living in England.

Essentially, young marriageable women, even among the wealthy middle class, had a very small pool of eligible men from which to choose. Many were destined for a life of spinsterhood, because most of these wealthy women didn't work outside the home. Employment opportunities weren't available to them—even to educated women, and so they had very few options outside of marriage.

With so few choices for employment and marriage, the possibility of traveling to one of England's colonies must have held some appeal to many gentlewomen who'd already passed the ideal marriageable age. When an 1861 census of Vancouver Island and British Columbia revealed that females comprised only 11 percent of the total population, which meant that men outnumbered women approximately 10 to 1, it seemed only reasonable to begin sending England's surplus of marriageable women to the colonies to provide wives for the many men who wanted them.

While the poorer bride-ship women came to take roles as domestics and laborers until they could find husbands, the wealthier women aboard the *Tynemouth* expected to find positions as governesses, music teachers, and seamstresses, as well as other work suitable to their station.

In studying the lives of some of the real middle-class women, I learned that most of them eventually married into their class and became a part of Victoria's gentry. There were a few, however, who ventured beyond the rigidness of their class and took advantage of the opportunities in the colony to shape a new destiny. One woman by the name of Florence Wilson opened a stationery and fancy goods shop. Eventually she founded a library and professional theater.

Thus, in creating Arabella Lawrence's character, I wanted to portray the journey of a wealthy woman, including her perspective and aspirations. I hoped to show the conflicting opinions regarding the duties and goals of a proper lady and how some women were beginning to break free of their constrictions in small steps. Arabella's hesitations and concerns, while foreign to the modern woman, would have been very real and valid at the time.

Finally, in developing Peter Kelly as a baker, I was inspired by a true story of a baker in Victoria who used his daily rounds to customers and his charm to win over one of the bride-ship women. Through Peter Kelly I also hoped to give a glimpse into the smallpox epidemic that ravaged the area natives in 1862. While no one has proven that the epidemic of 1862 was part of a biological-warfare plot, there are speculations that sending the natives away from Victoria, instead of vaccinating and quarantining them, was a way to control what was perceived then as a growing native threat.

I hope you've enjoyed taking this bride-ship journey with Arabella as she learned to break free from the world's expectations and find courage to embrace God's expectations and plans for her. I pray that as you search for God's purposes and plans for you, you'll find strength in His courage. Don't forget that He's walking with you and has promised to never fail or forsake you!

Jody Hedlund is the bestselling author of over twenty historical novels for both adults and teens and is the winner of numerous awards, including the Christy, Carol, and Christian Book Awards. Jody lives in Michigan with her husband, five busy teens, and five spoiled cats. Visit her at jodyhedlund.com.

Sign Up for Jody's Newsletter!

Keep up to date with Jody's news on book releases and events by signing up for her email list at jodyhedlund.com.

More from Jody Hedlund

After facing desperate heartache and loss, Mercy agrees to escape a bleak future in London and join a bride ship. Wealthy and titled, Joseph leaves home and takes to the sea as the ship's surgeon to escape the pain of losing his family. He has no intention of settling down, but when Mercy becomes his assistant, they must fight against a forbidden love.

A Reluctant Bride
THE BRIDE SHIPS #1

You May Also Like . . .

Determined to keep his family together, Quinten travels to Canada to find his siblings and track down his employer's niece, who ran off with a Canadian soldier. When Quinten rescues her from a bad situation, Julia is compelled to repay him by helping him find his sister—but soon after, she receives devastating news that changes everything.

The Brightest of Dreams by Susan Anne Mason
CANADIAN CROSSINGS #3
susanannemason.net

As Chicago's Great Fire steals away their bookshop, Meg and Sylvie Townsend make a harrowing escape from the flames with the help of reporter Nate Pierce. But the trouble doesn't end there—their father is committed to an asylum after being accused of murder, and they must prove his innocence before the asylum truly drives him mad.

Veiled in Smoke by Jocelyn Green
THE WINDY CITY SAGA #1
jocelyngreen.com

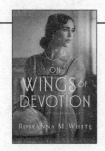

All of England thinks Phillip Camden a monster for the deaths of his squadron. As Nurse Arabelle Denler watches him every day, though, she sees something far different: a hurting man desperate for mercy. But when an old acquaintance shows up and seems set on using him in a plot that has the codebreakers of Room 40 in a frenzy, new affections are put to the test.

On Wings of Devotion by Roseanna M. White
THE CODEBREAKERS #2
roseannamwhite.com

◊BETHANYHOUSE